The Last Train
to Brackley Central

An Inspector Vignoles Mystery

Stephen Done

British Library Cataloguing in Publication Data:
A catalogue record for this book is available from the British Library
ISBN 978-1-904109-23-5

Published 2012

The Hastings Press
hastings.press@gmail.com
www.hastingspress.co.uk

Set in Garamond
Cover design by Bill Citrine
Printed and Bound in Great Britain
by TJ International Ltd, Padstow, Cornwall

THE LAST TRAIN

An Inspector Vignoles Mystery

~ ACKNOWLEDGEMENTS ~

I would like to thank all those who have encouraged and helped along the way, especially my family, both close and extended. Sincere thanks go to Bill for another splendid cover design and to Helena of the Hastings Press for her work in preparing the text.

I am grateful to the Sefton-Smith family for the photographs taken in the desert campaign in Egypt, and especially to Mrs Ivy Clarke for the wonderful photograph of herself near Staverton Viaduct as a J39 Class locomotive passed, taken in 1949 by the late Harry Clarke.

A number of books have helped provide background, in particular the outstanding *Austerity Britain 1945–51* by David Kynaston (Bloomsbury, 2007); *The Great Central: Then and Now* by Mac Hawkins (David & Charles, 1991); the glorious photographic books by Colin Walker, of which *Great Central Twilight* (Pendyke Publications, 1986) and *Mainline Lament: The Final Years of the Great Central Route to London* (OPC, 1973) proved useful. *Steaming into Northamptonshire* by Richard Coleman and Joe Rajczonek was invaluable.

The excerpt from *A Dream in the Desert* by Eliot Crawshay-Williams is used with special thanks to Miss Sylvia Crawshay.

Stephen Done

~ Author's Note ~

The Great Central Railway ran between London Marylebone, Leicester Central, Nottingham Victoria and onwards to Hull, Manchester and Birkenhead. Tragically, Britain's newest main line (it was completed in 1899) was closed by 1966–7, a victim of a short-sighted move to save money (it would have saved building the HS2).

Two sections of the GCR have since been reopened by enthusiasts and are run as preserved lines. One runs from Ruddington to Loughborough; the other from Loughborough to Leicester. They remain Britain's only mainline, double-tracked heritage railways, and will one day be reconnected. I can thoroughly recommend a ride on either section and a visit to Buckinghamshire Railway Centre at Quainton Road, which holds a huge collection of stock. Books in this Inspector Vignoles series, when purchased from the GCR, will help support its operations. Find out more at www.bucksrailcentre.org and www.gcrailway.co.uk

There was never a railway detective department, and considerable liberties have been taken with reality to create this work of fiction. Any similarity to persons living or dead is unintentional.

About the author

Stephen Done was born on 3rd August 1960. On his eighth birthday, Stephen declared he wanted to become the driver of a steam engine. On 6th August that same summer, the very last steam locomotives ran in revenue service on British Railways. Unfortunate timing, so he took up writing about them instead.

A museum curator, he has worked at Bristol Industrial Museum, Cyfarthfa Castle Museum in Merthyr Tydfil, and, since 1997, has set up and run the Liverpool Football Club Museum and photographic archive at Anfield. A railway modeller, birdwatcher, avid book reader and collector, he also enjoys a pint of real English ale. Stephen can be contacted via his website www.inspectorvignoles.ukwriters.net

This is the fifth novel in Stephen Done's Inspector Vignoles series. Details about the first four can be found at end of this book or on the publisher's website www.hastingspress.co.uk

For Adrian and Rosemary

> *It is all a dream,*
> *A dream in the desert,*
> *A jewel fashioned*
> *From barren sand,*
> *From toil and strife*
> *And the heat o' the sun;*
> *A dream in the desert,*
> *All a dream.*

Eliot Crawshay-Williams
Egypt, August 1916

CHAPTER ONE
Egypt
July 1882

The line of camels plodded slowly but sure-footedly through the white sand, the sky sapphire blue and broken only by a line of palm trees shimmering on the horizon, marking the place where the single-track railway crossed their path. A dark locomotive smoked sootily below the palms at the head of a short line of cream-coloured coaches swimming in the heat haze whilst it took on water at the pretty little station at El Alamein.

The heat seemed to soak up sound like a dry sponge takes on water, rendering the scene almost a silent mirage, and those travelling with the caravan could hear only the small and intimate sounds of their own progress: the heavy plod of the seven camels on the undulating ground, the creak of saddles and the straps and stays of the many packs slung across their flanks, the occasional snort or grunt from the beasts and the gentle clink of bridle metal. The brightest sound was the tinkle made by the jewellery of Anoukh El Ali as she swayed, rhythmically, to the steady tread of her camel.

She was dressed in all the finery of a Nubian woman of considerable wealth and status, wearing a closely-fitting tunic of white cloth relieved by two emerald green and scarlet stripes, the deep cuffs of which were woven with designs in the same scarlet and green but also shot through with yellow. Her pantaloon trousers revealed thick ankle-bands of gold above bare feet, whilst her long and voluminous headdress hung in great, pale billows about her body and flowed elegantly down the back of the camel's hump. Anoukh's upper arms were gripped by chunky bracelets and half moons of gold swung from her ear lobes, whilst about her neck hung many necklaces made of finely-cast bronze discs and squares of gold which clinked gently against her chest, sending darts of light into the eyes of Mustafa, her manservant, whenever he looked back to see if she needed water.

His lady was troubled. Her face an impassive mask that resembled the gigantic statues of long-dead ancestors, carved in black stone and standing in the temples beside the Nile, destined to stare into unblinking infinity. Her almond-shaped eyes had wide, black pupils, like polished beads, her young skin a flawlessly-smooth cocoa brown and her generous lips elegantly sculpted as if from obsidian. She looked far ahead with an enigmatic expression that betrayed little emotion, masking her inner turmoil and sense of loss. Mustafa turned away and made a clucking sound with his tongue to urge the haughty camel forwards, concentrating on maintaining a perfect straight line to the caravan.

Anoukh sighed, silently, but no less long and deep, seeking a release from the great press of sadness swelling inside. She had left in such a hurry, with hardly time to even think of what she was doing, but there was now time enough to appreciate the dreadful reality slowly unfolding before her. She had been dragged away, tears streaming down her face and forbidden to even see the body of her husband; just bundled onto the waiting camel and told to adorn herself as if it were her wedding day, with her most precious jewellery, and what she could not wear, she must keep close to hand, for it was time to flee with everything of value that it was possible to take.

A shell fired from a British naval gun had killed her husband instantly. It was impossible to see his mutilated body, she had been told, impossible to kiss his cold lips one last time and say goodbye.

The bombardment of Alexandria had been sudden and terrible; a terrifying day filled by great detonations that rocked the ground and sent shockwaves of heat rolling along the streets that physically pushed people aside like a stubborn camel will sometimes body-charge its keeper. Fires had raged unstoppably and the acrid smoke and stench had been held low upon the houses by the immense heat of the day, rendering it almost impossible to breathe, making everyone choke on the poisonous fumes. Confusion and panic had spread faster than the flames as the warships pounded the fortified walls of the ancient city, and soon the hysterical talk was of an imminent invasion, and of the terrible, unspeakable things that these imperial marauders would do to the Egyptian women.

Her servants had begged and pleaded with her. She must escape the city, for a few weeks at least, until things calmed down and order was restored. And so it had been but a matter of hours before they trudged out of the burning city and headed west. They had taken tents and clothes and just some of the smaller and more valuable of her possessions.

Anoukh cast her eyes down to a small pouch slung over the pommel of the saddle and slipped a long-fingered hand inside, removing a small square box of dark wood decorated with patterns of inlaid ivory and brass. She opened the lid and carefully lifted the ring from the velvet lining.

It was an object of rare beauty. A simple gold band supporting a large solitaire diamond. Holding the ring between thumb and forefinger, she lifted it until the late afternoon sunlight pierced the stone. Even an untrained eye could tell this was no ordinary gem.

The light flashed and burned inside, appearing to move with an almost fluid quality, or perhaps even smouldering like the embers of a fire, and whilst the outer edges of this intense light were of the purest white, deep in the heart of the stone it appeared tinged with yellow or shot through with green.

'Almost pure white and completely free of occlusion, of any imperfections, all except for one tiny and surprising detail. There is a stain of yellow, no more than a pinhead of colour, and the jeweller has used this imperfection to his advantage, placing it at the heart of the stone, where all the light collects and reflects in a masterstroke of his art. The effect is like looking into a cobra's eye!' Her husband had spoken these words on presenting the diamond to her, his face alight with an almost fanatical excitement. 'Look, Nushka, it transfixes you, just as a cobra does with his eyes when poised ready to strike!'

Although thrilled by the obvious quality and beauty of the ring, she had been less enthusiastic about the analogy. An angry cobra was something to fear, not to love, and as the days and weeks had passed and she had repeatedly gazed into the depths of this truly remarkable diamond, she could not quite shake off the feeling that it held nothing less than a drop of deadly venom that rolled and pooled deep inside the heart of the stone. It was a ridiculous notion, and she had tactfully remained silent on the matter, but his insistence that henceforward the diamond be known as the *Cobra's Eye* had done nothing to quell her unsettled feelings. He had written the name on a slip of paper in his elegant, cursive script and pasted it to the base of the box, although she was insistent that she would never forget. The truth was, she preferred not to be constantly reminded of this strange name.

As Anoukh now turned the ring and felt the brief darts of blinding refracted light prick her eyes, she was filled with a mixture of profound sadness and creeping fear. Since Muhammad had bought the Cobra's Eye, nothing had gone right for them. Her husband had paid a considerable sum for it, of that she was sure, but soon afterwards his thriving trade in antiquities had unexpectedly taken a painful loss when a once-loyal customer swindled him cruelly. Their finances had been put under a terrible strain as a consequence. They had also started to bicker and argue in a way they had never done before in the two years since their marriage, and Anoukh's mood was not improved when her beloved pet dog was struck down by a heavy cart in the street and died in agony. And now Muhammad himself was dead. Blown to pieces amidst the ruins of his shop in a stroke of unpleasant irony, by a shell from a British warship. The valuable stock he had traded with wealthy British tourists doing the Grand Tour was now probably burned, mangled or looted. Anoukh was not sure if a ring could carry bad luck, but it certainly felt that way now.

Was it coincidence that she had forgotten to wear it the very morning the shelling had commenced? Had this curious oversight somehow spared her life? It was an unsettling idea, but there was no denying that she and her loyal servants were now safe in the desert, and if she sold this ring, could raise more than enough money to live comfortably for a very long time. When things quietened down, she would travel to Cairo and rid herself of the bad influence she was increasingly sure this odd stone had brought into her life.

She closed her eyes for a few moments, holding back tears. But this was the last thing her dead Muhammad had given her, and his hand had written the little label pasted to the base. Could she really part with it?

Anoukh placed the ring back in its box and closed the lid, lifting her eyes to the horizon. She watched as the train pulled away from the station with little black puffs of smoke that hung in the sky like the explosions from the warships off Alexandria, the sound of the chuffing finally reaching her ears, delayed by the distance and out of synchronisation with the appearance of each cloud from the chimney. As she watched the departure, she felt for the opening of the pouch and let the little box slip inside, her mind now made up to sell the diamond at the earliest opportunity.

But she made a mistake. Her fingers had not found the opening of the pouch but instead had slipped between it and the soft blanket thrown over the saddle, fooling her into thinking the box would drop safely to join the other pieces of antique jewellery and a clutch of gold coins that lay there. Instead, it tumbled silently to the ground, unseen and unheard, to be immediately pressed into the sand by the hind leg of her camel.

CHAPTER TWO
Egypt
4th July 1942

'Bugger me, I'm parched!' Private Raymond Coulson of the 7th Armoured Division spoke aloud and to no one in particular as he threw his dusty bedroll onto the ground and dropped his pack beside it. Unscrewing the top of his water bottle, he drank heartily to clear the cloying dust from his throat, enjoying the sound of the water glug-glugging from the constricted opening. At that moment, it tasted better than a pint of the elderflowery Hopcroft & Norris IPA in the Red Lion.

Driving a Humber Mk II armoured car across a scorching desert was hot and dusty work. His clothes were damp and in places stained white with sweated salt; his neck and forearms burned pink from the sun and his eyes dry from staring into the heat haze. They were peeled raw from trying to detect Rommel's Afrika Korps, whom they knew was lying dangerously close, coiled like so many angry cobras in the sand and ready to spring and bite in their desire to halt the allied push west towards distant Tobruk.

Coulson and his crewmates had just finished lashing up a makeshift canopy of sun-bleached canvas to one side of their vehicle and were now selecting a billet spot for the night. The others had chosen to bed down beneath the awning in what would be a crowded huddle, but Coulson needed more room.

Squeezed into the pint-sized vehicle all day, smelling the sweat and fear of the crew, their arms and legs continually pressed close to each other's with no room to stretch or change position, he now needed space to breathe freely. He wanted to lie on his back and stare at the stars during the bitterly-cold desert night, and to feel his body cool after roasting in that Tommy-cooker of a Humber and gratefully drink in the fresh air, seeking to eradicate the constant stink of exhaust fumes, cordite, sweat and motor oil.

Loosening his blouson jacket, he flopped onto the bedroll to remove his boots. Stuffing his noxious socks into the boot openings to prevent scorpions from climbing inside, he wriggled his toes and already felt more comfortable. He pulled a packet of Camel cigarettes from his top pocket, extracted one and rested it on his cracked lips. Catching the eye of 'Bounder' Baker leaning against a stack of water cans, he raised the packet in a gesture of silent invitation. Bounder grinned and Coulson expertly flipped the cigarette across the divide in a spinning, catherine-wheel flight.

He lit his own cigarette and lay down, preparing for a few minutes of luxury with his legs stretched out fully for the first time that day. He wriggled his back, trying to get comfortable, but then sat up, patting the bedroll and feeling for the lump jabbing into his spine. Stones were always the impediment to a good night's sleep when off the deeper and softer dunes. The land near El Alamein was relatively flat, and the sand only partially masked the rocky terrain below. This made it easier for their vehicles to traverse, but was a right pain in the backside when bedding down. He noted the many stones on either side of his bedroll and decided against trying another spot; instead, he knelt down and peeled the top corner back to reach underneath and explore with his fingers.

He was surprised at the neat and regular shape he encountered and the sharply-defined corner standing proud of the sand. Clearly, this was not a stone. Peering around the bedroll he saw a small ornamental box poking out of the sand at an acute angle. He immediately felt a tingle of anticipation. Palming it in one of his big hands, he made a play of throwing some distance away the two flat stones in between which the box had been trapped, and then patted his mattress flat.

After checking that no one had noticed his discovery he lay down again, but this time on his side and with his back to the Humber and his crewmates. He placed the little box close to his body and opened the lid. He dragged heavily on his cigarette to mask the involuntary inhalation of breath he was forced to take. The Cobra's Eye sprang alive as the evening sun filled it with light for the first time since Anoukh El Ali had inadvertently dropped it over half a century ago. Coulson stared in wonderment at the yellow fire inside the perfectly-cut diamond, marvelling at how it appeared almost alive as he slowly turned the ring in his fingers, making the stone glint and sparkle. He knew nothing of gemstones, but he knew quality and beauty when he saw it. This was special. It was almost bewitching.

This was a ring any woman would love to wear, and now he, Private Ray Coulson, a garage mechanic from a small market town in Northamptonshire, was going to be the man who gave this to his darling Betty Boo. It would make a perfect engagement ring, and he felt a rush of excitement course through his veins as he imagined Betty's face when she saw it. If he could just get through this next campaign and ship home on leave... Somehow, they had to avoid those deadly long-range 88mm guns all the Tommies feared. He closed his eyes and offered a silent prayer.

He swiftly kissed the cold stone, thanking the Lord for this extraordinary piece of good fortune then closed his fist, hiding it from view. Hauling his pack towards him with his free hand and puffing on the fag wedged between his cracked lips, he stuffed the empty box into the bottom and rummaged about until he located his emergency sewing kit.

As the red ball of the sun slipped towards the distant sea and sent impossibly long shadows reaching across the undulating desert, burnishing the outline of a wrecked locomotive and a line of damaged railway wagons in a siding beside the distant station, Coulson carefully sewed the precious ring into the bottom of one of the pocket liners of his shorts, answering the curious enquiry from Bounder that he was 'just mending a hole'. It would be safe from loss or detection, and yet would remain with him at all times. If the Humber took a hit and they had to bale out, his pack might be lost or burnt, and they often shed their jackets and undershirts in the terrible heat of the day, tying them onto the outside of the turret, but assuming he could stay alive, he would always be in his trusty, if rather voluminous, army-issue shorts.

CHAPTER THREE
Helmdon
20th September 1942

It was hot, and the air was standing Sunday-still above the land with just a trace of breeze to rustle the long grasses and set bobbing the many wild flowers on the lush embankment. The sun beat down upon the broad vale, and Helmdon village, glimpsed between the arches of the Great Central Railway viaduct, was shimmering in the haze as it straggled up the valley side in a succession of picturesque cottages built from a pale limestone and topped by thatched or stone-slabbed roofs.

A tank engine and two grubby coaches looked like a toy in the sleepy little station. Built by the long-forgotten Northampton and Banbury Junction Railway, the buildings cowered, as though overawed and humbled, below the dominating presence of the newer grand trunk line that spanned the valley on a giant construction of blue brick carrying the twin tracks of the main line to London.

A skylark climbed, its trilling, burbling song tumbling towards the land like the sound of tiny bells, the complex melody counterpointed by a flock of noisy crows wheeling and cawing about a stand of beeches, in the shade of which clustered cows contentedly chewed the cud.

Betty Askew was seated on a tartan blanket, her legs stretched out before her, glad she had chosen to wear cycling shorts so the sun could warm her legs to just above the knees. She was leaning back upon her elbows, head tilted upwards to soak in the delicious warmth of the day and helping her feel relaxed and at ease, despite being completely alone with Ray for what was really the first time. She had been feeling nervous and self-conscious as they had taken the short train journey north from Brackley Central to Helmdon.

Until today she had always met Ray in the company of others, apart from when she allowed him to accompany her on the short, late-evening walk along the broad main street back to her parents' house, where they enjoyed a few stolen moments in the moonlight at the gate, during which his arms encircled her waist as he tentatively sought a goodnight kiss. He had looked so eager when he'd invited her to Helmdon, his eyes like that of a sad dog, that she just could not refuse. And besides, she'd not wanted to turn him down.

'What a day! It's a real Indian summer.' She closed her eyes for a moment, seeing red as the light passed through her eyelids. 'Gosh, but never mind India, is it hot like this in North Africa?'

'Far hotter than you could ever believe. At midday we couldn't even be outside.' Ray grinned at Betty, enjoying the look of incredulity on her face as she tried to imagine the desert sun and its terrible heat.

He was lying on his side, propped up on one arm, with a long blade of grass in the corner of his mouth, enjoying the bitter green taste as he chewed the end whilst making the seed heads flick like a pony's tail at the other. He had just used another precious frame of film in his Box Brownie camera to capture the image of Betty in the sun with the viaduct behind her, and now he gently rubbed the side of his thigh, massaging the ache he still felt from the deep shrapnel wound that had sent him home to recuperate.

'Goodness, I don't think I could stomach that.' Betty brushed a damp lock of hair back from her forehead and felt a drop of perspiration trickle between her shoulder blades, hoping she did not look an overheated mess in the photograph when it came back from Boots the Chemist. 'How do you manage inside your armoured car? It must be stifling.'

'It's terrible at times, what with the sun beating down, and then there's the engine and exhaust right next to you. You almost can't breathe and the metal is so hot it burns your hands to touch. But at least we're under cover; you would fry like a piece of bacon in the sun.'

Betty gave him another look of disbelief.

'The lads joke that if we rubbed lard on our skin we'd make a perfect Sunday roast by the end of the day!'

They both laughed, as so many did these days when trying to make light of something deadly serious; seeking to ease the burden of the dangerous and frightening reality that continually preyed on their minds and haunted their dreams; looking to find a twist of black humour in a war that could kill either of them in a moment.

'You're still as brown as a gypsy boy.' Betty gave an admiring glance at his wiry frame covered by his open-necked shirt and light flannel trousers.

He inspected his forearms, bared by rolled-up shirtsleeves. 'It's faded since I've been home. I was browner than a cobnut at one time.' He looked up, his face now serious. 'But it must be just as hard for you on those steam engines in this weather.'

'Not *that* bad.' Betty gave him a gentle smile, 'Though it can get jolly hot when I'm crawling between the motion whilst the firebox is roaring and the boiler is making steam above my head. Oh, Ray, we must look such a frightful mess! What with the grease and the oil and coal smudges all over my face, and then there's the lovely perfume of the engine shed in my clothes that's just *so* hard to wash out. I've got through more packs of Frisky soap powder than you can imagine.' She wrinkled her nose and grinned cheekily. 'I do hope my hair doesn't still smell of that darned shed.'

'Not a bit of it, Betty. But you lot are not so different from us "Desert Rats". He smiled sympathetically and they both laughed. 'That's what Jerry calls us. We're the "Tobruk Rats" — supposedly meant an insult — but we liked the name and have adopted the title proudly. It's become a sort of badge of honour, being a Desert Rat.'

'I know what you mean.' She paused, trying to decide whether to carry on. 'We call ourselves the "Dirty Girls Brigade". It's a bit of a scandalous title, but that's Mary Barrett for you. She's our boss — more like our ringleader — and quite a character with it. The name was her idea, of course.'

Ray Coulson raised an eyebrow but grinned encouragingly.

'We're such a sight, what with our uniform of blue overalls, bright headscarves and heavy boots, and we like to sing all the time when we're cleaning the locomotives, to keep our spirits up.'

'I can believe you'd need something to help. It must be a rotten old job...'

'Oh no! I love it. Most of the time, anyway.' She paused and wrinkled her nose. 'Ok, in the winter it can be jolly hard, especially at 5a.m. when the alarm wakes me...' Her voice brightened as she continued, 'but it makes one feel like one's doing something important. Helping to make a difference. Releasing a man to go into the forces.'

As if to illustrate her point, their attention was drawn to the sound of yet another train approaching; one of a seemingly never-ending succession that had passed in both directions across the viaduct since they had laid their rug on the grassy slope. She shaded her eyes with a hand and ran an expert eye over the filthy black engine with prominent dribbles of white staining the boiler barrel like spilt distemper, and an ugly scar of livid orange burnt into the base of the smokebox door at the front.

'A V2. They're really good engines, Ray. They'll go forever and can take a heck of a beating.' She spoke with the confidence of someone who knew about locomotives.

'Yeah?' He squinted at the unprepossessing beast as it slowly huffed and panted towards them, hauling an immensely long train of box vans that rattled and clattered past for what felt like an age. He looked unimpressed. 'Let's just hope this blessed war is soon over and you can do something more suitable.'

'What do you mean, "more suitable"?'

'It's no job for a woman, is it? Cleaning engines. I mean, it's all right as an emergency measure, I suppose, but...'

Betty flashed her eyes at him in mild rebuke and drew herself up into a seated position, with legs crossed. 'Well, I love it', she replied, defensively, 'it makes me feel completely alive and happy, in a funny sort of way. I'd hate to be stuck in a boring office, filing papers all day, or to be some mousey shop girl.' Her voice took on a contemptuous tone. 'In fact, Raymond Coulson, I'm really not so very different from you!' She gave him a defiant look, with a glint in her eye. 'I like to get my hands dirty and mend things. I enjoy getting everything running sweet. You know what? Sometimes, when they're short handed, I'm even allowed to help a fitter fixing up an engine. Only simple tasks, I know, but still, it's satisfying to help get them up and running again.'

Ray grinned at her. 'Well? What's so funny?' she continued, 'you love your cars and lorries and mending engines and gearboxes and whatnot, and in the same way I love these wonderful iron horses.' She looked across at the brakevan bringing up the rear of the goods train and the smoky trail left by the engine that was now dipping behind a stand of Scots pines, her eyes taking on a wistful look. 'I just wish I could drive them. The Soviet women do, you know.' She gave him a look that defied him to argue against this fact.

He laughed out loud, but looked at her with admiration, eyes twinkling. The truth was, he liked her tomboy qualities, even if some men might consider her unladylike. She certainly looked woman enough to him, with those thick, auburn curls caressing her shoulders, a flatteringly-thin, close-fitted summer shirt and shorts that revealed a tantalising hint of soft thigh.

She was right about him as well: he was a mechanic at heart — the son of a garage owner — and could imagine no other life. Not for him a life of books or numbers or whatever it was people did in offices, nor the relentless toil of the factory floor, working like automatons and just praying for the hooter to signal the end of shift. He liked nothing better than tinkering with a car in the garage, trying to solve a ticklish mechanical problem, or even puzzling how to effect an emergency repair to their armoured car in the middle of a barren, burning desert. Yes, a woman like Betty would suit him very well, and he felt they understood each other. Perhaps they shared similar dreams. He could imagine she would approve of his wish to carry on his father's motor-garage business when the time came.

Another train rumbled over the viaduct, this time hauled by two heavy freight locomotives in tandem, each working hard to pull a line of olive-green painted flat wagons bearing a load tightly wrapped in brown tarpaulins bearing the initials 'WD' in white lettering; strong chains securing the secret loads on wagons constructed from immense pieces of riveted steel. Although the War Department cargo was concealed, it was obvious this was war equipment and, judging by the distinctive shape and bulk of the wrapped packages, was probably a line of tanks.

They watched in mute silence as the monstrous train rumbled on its way, the engines barking and throwing dirty clouds of smoke into the sky as they dug into the incline. This unavoidable reminder of the war jolted them both back into harsh reality and the effect of the soothing sunshine and the cheerful skylark were forgotten.

'When do you return? Have you heard?' Betty Askew bit the inside of her lip, not trusting herself to speak more without betraying emotion.

'I have.' He blurted it out. 'I—I didn't have the heart to say until now.' He gave a nervous cough, and could feel the official letter folded tightly into his rear trouser pocket, pressed close to the little wooden box. 'I leave for the coast tomorrow.' His voice sounded clipped and dry, and he tried to soften the sound by swallowing saliva to ease a sudden dryness that was constricting his throat. 'My leg is mended and will strengthen on the voyage over. I'll be fully fit by the time I reach Alex. Good as new!' He tried to sound thrilled at the prospect.

They looked at each other in silence for a few moments, the laboured panting of the two engines echoing across the vale was like their own gulped breaths and pounding heartbeats. When Betty eventually spoke, her gaze fell onto the tartan pattern of the rug.

'Tomorrow?' The word held so much meaning, rendered more heart wrenching for the slight break in her voice. 'So sudden.'

'That's why I begged you to come here today. I was desperate to have an hour or so with you away from everyone. Just the two of us, alone.' He felt a grip of nerves in his chest and a pounding in his ears.

Betty threw him a glance, but hurriedly looked away, using the shrill whistle of the tank locomotive in the valley floor as an excuse to do so, her vision suddenly blurred by a stinging in her eyes, and the little train swam past as though it were under water. She unconsciously touched the metal cap badge she had been wearing as a brooch since Ray had returned to Brackley as war wounded.

'I wanted to... be with you, like this. Because I—er...'

He stopped. He'd rehearsed this speech a hundred times during the last few weeks, endlessly practising the lines in his head, trying to imagine how Cary Grant or Spencer Tracy might handle it, but now it came to the moment he found his tongue felt too big for his mouth and the words failed him, just as his nerve had repeatedly failed the whole time he had been back in England. He had not once managed to pluck up the courage to broach the subject that filled almost his every waking hour since that fateful discovery near El Alamein. Well, this was it. It was now or never.

Betty managed to surreptitiously wipe the moisture from her eyes and force a smile, suddenly pushing all scruples aside and reaching out to lightly touch the back of his hand with her finger tips, by way of encouragement. She could not trust herself to speak, but knew her gesture would stand in for any number of foolish and fumbled words.

Ray placed his free hand upon hers and gave it a squeeze. 'I leave at seven tomorrow. I don't know exactly when I shall return. Perhaps I won't...'

'Don't say that!'

'But it's true. We both know that's how it is. But the one thing I do know for certain is that I need a reason to return. I need something, some*one*, to keep me hoping and praying as I drive that blessed tin cooking pot on wheels towards the boche, and that reason is you. My darling Betty Boo.' He could see her eyes fill with tears and felt her nails dig into his hand.

He gently released her grip to allow him to sit upright and delve into his back pocket. Now facing her, he brought his balled fist around into the space between them and slowly opened his fingers.

'W—what is this?' Betty allowed tears to run freely down her cheeks as she felt her heart miss a beat. Such a small and beautiful box could surely hold only one thing...

'Open it!'

'I—I can't... my hands are shaking too much!' She was not fibbing. Her hands trembled as she tried to open the ornately-decorated lid. 'Gosh, but is this really what I think it is? Oh, my giddy aunt!'

Ray grinned and nodded, 'Look inside. It's yours if...' He tailed off and watched with anxious anticipation.

'Oh, dear Lord!' She took a deep intake of air. 'I just can't believe it. It's so beautiful, so... I can't find the words...' Her eyes were wide and her face glowed with excitement as she gazed at the single diamond glinting with its potent inner fire in the velvet-lined box. 'Oh, Ray! Does this mean that we—' She bit her lip.

'—are engaged? Of course!' His eyes flashed. 'Now, come on: I want to see it on your finger...if you agree, that is.'

She nodded quickly, her lower lip held gently between her teeth and she watched as he took her left hand and slipped the ring onto her finger. It fitted perfectly, as if made for her.

'With this ring I ask you to marry me.' He rushed the words out before he lost his nerve. 'When the war is over, when we've both made it to the other side, we will marry.'

Betty held her hands over her heart for a moment, her breasts rising and falling as his words sunk in. 'We're engaged? Such a surprise, a bit of a shock.... oh, what I mean is, of course, yes! Yes!' She leant forward and kissed him once, twice, then pulled back and, with one hand on his shoulder she held her left hand between them, twisting and turning her wrist to allow the sunlight to strike into the heart of the stone.

'My goodness, Ray, this is simply the most beautiful thing I have ever seen. The colours are incredible. Nobody would ever think it's not a real diamond. And I just love it so very, very much.'

'But it *is*, silly! This is not paste. It's real.'

'W—what? How? I mean...it's impossible, on army pay.'

He gave a boyish grin, he felt relaxed now he had heard her accept his proposal. After relating how he had found the box he explained, 'It wasn't stealing, Betty; it really was lost. Heaven knows who lost it or how long ago, but it was just buried in the sand right in the middle of nowhere. It was meant to be. It's a gift from above, just for us.'

'My goodness, what a story. And you immediately thought of me?' Betty blushed.

'Of course! See here—' he flipped the little box over to reveal a paper label pasted to the base, '—I got one of the wogs in camp to translate what it says, and it's called the Cobra's Eye, would you believe?'

'Ooh! How thrilling!'

'I didn't let on about the ring, just told him I'd found the box, but he was intrigued, I could tell, and offered to buy the empty box!' He suddenly looked serious. 'When I was shipped home, soon as I could get around on my crutches, I had the ring looked over in London. The jeweller described it as being of the very highest quality.' They exchanged excited looks. 'And he stated that it is extremely valuable.'

She swallowed and sat in silence for a moment, trying to take everything in. 'And you would give this to me?'

'If you agree to marry me.'

'Oh, I do, I do, I do!'

They kissed again and she allowed herself to be gently laid back onto the warm blanket. She felt his arms enfold her and hold her tight as they both admired the stone against the cobalt blue of the cloudless sky, its strange yellow fire mesmerising them. Betty stretched her fingers straight, making the sunlight flash in their eyes in pulses as she repeatedly altered the angle of the diamond.

'Like a signal lamp,' Ray observed. 'We sign to each other across the desert with handlamps. They wink like eyes in the night.' His burning desire to caress his best girl as she lay in his arms, her body now trembling with excitement and her usual reserve apparently diminishing as she pressed herself close to him was quelled in a moment as if he'd been plunged into an icy pool. He felt a sudden cold flush run through his veins, chilling him to the marrow as he recalled being at the Front. Now he felt only a need to hold her close and press her hair to his face and breathe in the scent of her hot skin, whilst images of the vast desert night sky scored by incandescent rocket-tails, searing burning traces made by high velocity bullets and the great thunder flashes of explosions crowded into his mind.

She sensed the change, and also lay still, her mind a turmoil of acute excitement and a deadening weight of sadness that pressed onto her like a sack of potatoes, making her insides ache. She gripped one of his arms as she silently stared, firstly into the sky and then into the indestructible solitaire diamond that she once again held aloft on her outstretched hand, praying that their love, now declared and sealed by this ring, would prove as enduring.

A solitary Spitfire droned overheard. It was flying slow and low and the pilot had left the canopy open, perhaps also to enjoy the day. Betty could clearly see the brown leather flying helmet and sheepskin-collared jacket of the figure inside. The pilot appeared to be in a happy and unhurried mood, for the aircraft described a gentle arc across the sky to allow a clear view of the couple embracing on the rectangle of tartan blanket below. The green-and-brown plane with the big red-and-blue roundel on the side, having completing a wide circle, was now even closer to the ground as it passed over them again in a throaty roar. Suddenly, Betty spotted that the pilot was a woman — part of the Air Auxiliary delivering a new or repaired plane — and the aviatrix, at that very same moment, raised a gloved hand above the cockpit side and waved. Betty smiled and returned the gesture, almost as if showing off her engagement ring. The plane waggled its wings before rapidly accelerating away, the Merlin engine throbbing and crackling as it gained both height and speed, until it looked as small as one of the many crows gliding and swooping over the Northamptonshire hills.

CHAPTER FOUR
Woodford Halse
23rd September 1942

The massive buildings of Woodford Halse Locomotive Depot completely dominated the northern end of what was really no more than a large village. It was an unexpected and perhaps even shocking sight to a visitor not forewarned of its sprawling and brooding presence in the midst of one of the remotest parts of rural Northamptonshire.

There it lay, forever smouldering and never completely at rest. Even in the darkest dogwatch of the coldest morning there was at least one sooty figure slinking between the dark flanks of the great metal beasts stabled in tidy ranks; moving between icy engines with a shovel of oily wadding and broken kindling ready to set a fire; or quietly turning a valve or shutting a damper on one or other of the slowly dripping, creaking, ticking machines that still held a fire within its belly; nursing them through until clocking-on time, when the fifty or more engines were stoked and prodded, watered and fed back into roaring life. And then this railway metropolis hooted and clanked and rumbled, punctuated by frequent bursts of noise like short landslides from the tall, 'Cenotaph' coaling tower, whilst acrid smoke rolled across the gently-dipping fields and verdant copses, animated only by the occasional chattering jay and rattle of pheasant, the sough of wind in the leaves, the bark of a farmyard dog or the clink of a horse harness at the furrow.

The running shed of the 'loco' was large, spanning six parallel tracks and topped by a forest of ventilation chimneys that attempted to remove the thick smoke belching from the stabled engines within, although when the day was as windless and hot as it was now, with little draught to draw it upwards and out, the interior soon became blue-grey with a pungent, eye-stinging haze that made those working inside hack with dry, tickly coughs. When the sun shone it forced its way through filthy side-windows to create bright, delineated diagonals of light that scythed through the viscous, smoggy gloom, vividly highlighting the crowded engines that were all so filthy that they looked monochromatic in their subtle hues of greys, dusty fawns and oily purple-browns, each engine standing over a black inspection pit and worked on by figures slowly turning just as devilishly dark with the all-pervading filth.

But today, as the bells of St Mary's sounded, the strong midday sun was doing its best to bring some cheer, illuminating a welcome splash of brilliant scarlet on the front buffer-beam of an ungainly freight engine that Betty Askew and some of her fellow 'Dirty Girls' had been attending to that morning.

Betty had scrubbed the front end almost clean, appreciating that the red warning colour might alert a railway worker to the engine's approach and so help save his life. She now sat upon the front of the footplate of the O2 class freight engine, one steel toe-capped boot on the massive coupling hook, the other swinging free past the big, gold-blocked number 3839 painted on the buffer beam. Her hair was wrapped inside a turban of orange cloth with a silvery metal regimental badge pinned to one side, which glinted as her head bobbed in and out of the dust-laden sunbeam. Her colleagues were gathered about in a loose semicircle, all gripped with eager suspense.

Like Betty, most of them were wearing boiler suits long faded to varying shades of pale blue and coated in differing levels of grime and oil, and heavy work-boots or rough clogs Leather belts cinched at their waists helped improve the fit of these shapeless garments. They had further enlivened this rather dour uniform with coloured scarves tied at their throats and turbans or headscarves that offered glimpses of surprisingly glossy and perfectly arranged curls or rolls of hair, whilst bright lipstick completed the look. It was considered a woman's duty to keep her spirits up and to demonstrate through these little details that she was not beaten or cowed by Hitler, despite the acute wartime restrictions. However, despite their brave attempts at femininity, they were all grey and grubby, and as they urged Betty to 'get on with it and put us out of our misery', some of them removed an odd assortment of thick gloves or leather gauntlets, and these, once cast off, retained much of their shape due to being impregnated by gunge and grease, making them appear like so many severed hands lying on the locomotive footplate.

'You can't keep us in suspense a moment longer!' Rosalind Dale looked almost in pain with the anticipation, her pencil-thin eyebrows forming two narrow lines of copper red against her freckly skin.

'Don't go coy on us, we need to see that blummin' ring. Whip it out, girl!' Rosie McMahon was one of the wilder members of the gang, seen as more 'forward' and outspoken than the others.

As she spoke she lit a cigarette perched on her bright scarlet lips and winked in an exaggerated manner.

'Patience is a virtue.' Betty Askew grinned, her expression a mixture of glowing pride and embarrassment. 'I won't wear it on my finger at work for fear of damaging it, so I've decided to keep it on this...' She worked her fingers beneath an orange-and-white scarf at her neck and pulled at a thin silver chain, carefully easing it free of her blouse to bring the ring into view.

'Ray won't mind; he'll be wanting a peek down there all the time!' Mary Bennett rolled her eyes suggestively whilst accepting a Lucky Strike from the packet being proffered by Rosie. 'Good excuse! Might have to try that trick myself. Haha!'

'He'll love getting his hands down there!' Pearl Cooper laughed like a drain whilst somehow managing to keep a cigarette stuck to her lower lip, expelling puffs of blue smoke in rhythm with her laughter. The others joined in. She gave Betty a friendly nudge in the ribs: 'Good excuse for a fondle, eh?'

'Oh, stop it!' Betty looked a little shocked, but still smiled. 'This is just whilst I'm at work.' Her eyes gleamed with excitement as she held the ring between thumb and forefinger for all to see.

'Oh my, just you look at that diamond!' Susan Gibson clapped her hands together like a seal. 'It's quite unbelievable.'

The appearance of the ring caused their jokes to cease instantly, to be replaced by sighs and coos of admiration, turning into a breathless and hushed wonderment as Betty rotated the ring in the light. Rosie pulled on her cigarette thoughtfully; Pearl just held her unlit cigarette still, frozen in the act of lighting it, as if caught in a snapshot. The loudspeaker hanging in the roof space crackled into life as someone switched the radio on for *Workers' Playtime*, and the words of Al Bowlly singing 'That's A Plenty' seemed to strike an appropriate chord.

'Dear God, I've never seen anything so perfect.' Mary spoke in little above a whisper.

'It must be worth a king's ransom!' Ros Dale was shaking her head in disbelief.

'I think it might be, actually.' Betty clapped her free hand over her mouth and opened her eyes wide. 'I don't exactly know, of course. It doesn't matter. It's not ever, ever going on sale.'

'Of course not,' Susan Gibson nodded solemnly. 'Doesn't matter what the price tag is.' She was the only woman not wearing overalls, just a flimsy, short-sleeved floral print shirt over a thin, green vest, both damp with perspiration, beneath a pair of dungarees with the bib folded down and the braces tied around her slim waist. A small, enamelled, v-shaped brooch in red, white and blue was pinned to her shirt collar. She was still breathing hard from having rushed across at the appointed hour from the neighbouring wagon repair works where she was a rivet-hotter, assisting in the sweltering task of heating steel rivets on a forge until red hot, then holding them in place with tongs whilst the riveter turned the ends over with blows from an immensely heavy hammer. And so, through this relentlessly backbreaking work, they held the massive components together on the wagons they repaired. She considered it not unlike assembling an oversized Meccano construction kit.

Susan Gibson caressed her own gold wedding band, as if reassuring herself it was still there. She then mopped her glistening brow with the back of a hand, making a grey smudge of ash on the centre of her forehead, as though she had just returned from the altar rail on Ash Wednesday. 'There's nothing more precious. Especially at a time like this', she added, wistfully.

'When did he propose?' Mary's eyes were wide with excitement. 'You kept that little secret quiet, you minx.'

'It's not a secret, Mary. It's just that...' Betty gave a thoughtful half-smile. 'Oh, you'll think me a silly goose, but it came as a bit of a shock. A nice one, but I still needed time to take it in; time to adjust to the idea that I am going to be Mrs Raymond Coulson.' She laughed, 'Gosh, it sounds awfully funny saying it out loud.'

'Better start getting used to it, my duck.' Rosie leant forward to get a closer look at the diamond.

'I'm sure I will. Assuming Ray will... you know, be OK.' Her smile faded. 'Anyway, he left straight afterwards. Shipped out again, to the Front. Gone at the crack of dawn the next morning.'

'Woke you up, did he?' Pearl gave Betty a lecherous wink and elbowed her knee suggestively.

'No, he did *not*, Pearl Cooper!' She carefully stressed the name in the same way her own mother used to do when she was being admonished. Betty's eyes flashed with indignant outrage, but she still laughed along with the others, hinting that Pearl was not too wide of the mark. 'My feelings have taken a bit of a shake-up,' she continued, her eyes suddenly turning glassy and her voice cracking as she hurriedly ended the sentence.

Susan Gibson, who had joined Betty on the front of the footplate, put a consoling, if slightly damp, arm around her shoulders. 'That's normal, Betty. We all know how you feel. You've just won yourself a wonderfully generous, kind man and you want to start dreaming of your future together. But now he's off overseas again, back to that beastly war.'

Betty nodded quickly. 'I know I mustn't be glum. That'll never win the war.' She took a sharp intake of breath. 'It's just that, well, I don't know how to say it right, but since Ray gave me this ring, since everything became so serious between us, I just can't shake off the most awful feeling of dread. There's a sort of black cloud hanging over me and I can't stop worrying. I've not felt like celebrating, or even talking about it.' They fell silent, allowing the sounds of the engine shed to encroach. The soft hiss of steam, the rhythmic clang of a hammer on metal, a distant telephone started to ring and an engine 'peeped' its whistle somewhere outside the shed.

'Ray will be back before you know it, just you see!' Margi Dickinson, a later arrival at the gathering, gave Betty a friendly pat on the hand.

'Course he will! Back in no time,' Rosie tried to sound bullish.

Ros dropped her gaze to the oily concrete floor and looked thoughtful. 'It will be little consolation, of course, but every night I cry myself to sleep praying my Derek will return home safe. When our bombers are buzzing overhead my heart leaps and I look up and wonder if he is on board and if perhaps he's looking down to earth to see me looking back, giving me the thumbs up that all's well. Until I get his telephone call from the base, I'm in such a state of nervous suspense. I can't know what ops he's flying, nor even when he's in the air, so I just survive each of the long nights, hoping and praying, and I'm only ever released from the burden during those few precious hours following his call. Then it starts all over again.'

Betty tone became sad. 'It must be so hard. And here I am acting like I'm the only girl in the world with a man in the war. I'm sorry, Ros. I must buck myself up. He's on the ship to Africa, so I really shouldn't be worrying, not just yet, anyway.'

'That's the spirit!' Mary smiled.

'And it *is* the biggest rock, ever!' Pearl grinned, eager to dispel the sense of gloom circling about them like unsettled ravens and threatening to pitch them all into a slough of depression. 'Hell's bells, Betty,' she adopted something approximating an American accent, 'whatever happens, you just got yourself set up for life with this little baby!' She slapped her thigh and gave an extravagant stage wink.

They all laughed. As Betty looked up, her attention was drawn along the line of locomotives and the rows of cast iron roof supports, to the open front of the shed and towards a solitary plump magpie hopping confidently amidst the ash and clinker near an engine resting in the noonday heat. She wiped her eyes dry and tried in vain to catch sight of its mate.

One for sorrow...

CHAPTER FIVE
Brackley
1st September 1950

'Hoy, over here, Digger!' Adrian Turvey called and whistled to his dog, who merely wagged his tail in acknowledgement but kept his eager nose to the ground whilst he weaved from side to side, moving quickly from a clump of grass to one small bush and then to another, as if he were vacuuming around them. Digger's alert, amber-coloured eyes furtively monitored Turvey's progress along the narrow path beside the Great Ouse until he judged it was time to bound across to his master, brush past his legs, then surge forward to buy himself some more quality sniffing time.

Turvey was walking in steady treads along the narrow path beside the meandering river, away from the pretty village of Turweston. He would soon cross the river on a rickety wooden bridge and pass Brackley Mill, the roof of which he could see nestling below the railway viaduct amidst a clump of trees. He would then cut up past St Peter's and climb up Church Lane before having a couple of jars of the local brew whilst soaking in the last rays of sun on the bench outside The Greyhound.

It was a perfect evening, the day still firmly clinging to summer. The air was warm, though a trace of coolness was creeping in after the intense heat of earlier, releasing a damp smell of loam and an aromatic perfume from the cow parsley florets that swished against him as he walked. A waft of scented, blue wood smoke hung in the air, curling lazily in circles and bleaching white when caught in the sunlight, whilst clouds of tiny insects danced above the path, back-lit against the tea brown of the sluggish water. A metallic dragonfly darted above the river in a flash of jewelled green. The bricks of the enormous viaduct were darkening almost to the colour of the ripening blackberries as the sun slipped behind the tree-topped hill to the right, leaving just the upper courses and coping stones to be set aflame by the fiery orange light. The massive edifice appeared almost insubstantial, softened around the edges by the haze lifting from the valley floor.

As they neared the base of the viaduct pillars, the path became noticeably less clogged by the verdant vegetation. Turvey looked up at the steep and regular slope of close-cropped, sun-bleached, grassy railway embankment studded with dandelion clocks and daisies in a riotous profusion of colour against the cloudless sky above. A few dense bushes huddled at the base of one of the massive supporting walls of the viaduct that sank into the slopes like the ramparts of a castle.

Digger bounded up the nearest bank without noticing the incline, his energy apparently limitless, happily nosing around a few straggly hawthorns. His master stopped and rested on his stick as he watched a smart, blue express locomotive trundle across the viaduct. He narrowed his eyes and could just discern the name 'Victor Wild' on the brass nameplate. It was hauling a long train of teak-built coaches that were every hue from golden brown to that of tea without milk and even a sad, lifeless grey, although he observed that one boasted a fresh coat of creamy-white and bloody-red that sparkled in the sunlight. Turvey recalled reading in the paper that this was to be the new livery for passenger coaches and wondered how long it would take them to repaint the many thousands across the system. It sounded like it would be an awfully long process, and quite a tedious one, and felt glad he was not a carriage painter.

He could just hear the brakes squealing as the train slowed to a halt at Brackley Central, a sound not unlike that made by the many swifts swooping and racing under the viaduct arches before describing a spectacular u-turn and hurtling back, flying low with deft twists and turns that made Turvey's head spin if he tried to follow one on its flight. As the clock of St Peter's chimed seven he decided it was time for that pint, and so he walked below the towering vault spanning river and path, relishing the echo of his footsteps as he did so, before stopping abruptly as his dog clattered down the embankment and almost knocked him over.

'Steady boy! Now, what you got there, then?'

Digger wagged his tail furiously.

'Come on, give!' Turvey carefully took a little bone from his dog's mouth. Digger sat on his haunches and looked up expectantly. 'What've you found, eh?' He turned the delicate, pale bone in his fingers and puzzled over it for a moment. 'Where'd you find this? Show me.'

His hound needed no further encouragement. Bounding back up the bank, eager to show how clever he was, he recommenced sniffing around the base of a thick bush with gusto. Turvey stayed where he was and tilted his head back to watch. After a few moments,

Digger pushed his brown-and-cream snout into the tall grass below the bush and then lifted his head, proudly holding something in his mouth, his tail working even more frantically. Without waiting to be called, Digger dashed headlong back down the slope and skidded to a halt, just inches from the riverbank.

'Another?' Turvey held the two slim bones in his palm, the most recent still glistening with saliva. Both were picked clean but in otherwise perfect condition. 'They don't look like sheep bones. No, Digger, they're no use to you. Too sharp.' Digger looked crestfallen for a few seconds, then lost interest in this emotion and trotted off, cocking his leg against a suitable fence post.

Turvey was about to toss the bones into the river when he paused. Was it the many swifts whirling close by? Or a trick in the way sound carried from the distant station? Whatever the reason, he could have sworn a sad, almost inaudible, feminine voice had just whispered in his ear.

Find me. Nothing more. It was a tiny sound borne on a breeze, little more than a breathy sensation deep inside his ear, almost as though someone had placed a speaking tube there and whispered down it as softly as she could.

Find me.

He looked around, but was alone. Was it the voice of a child playing somewhere? Had he imagined it? Either way it startled him and he felt an odd sensation of discomfort crawl over his skin, making the hairs stand up on his forearms and instantly robbing him of the comfortable sensation of ease he had been savouring just moments before. As he watched the wheeling swifts, his lovable old dog fussing around beneath a bush and the sunlight on the sluggish river he started to feel calmer, and made an effort to brush this odd experience aside.

He took another look at the little bones and chewed the inside of his mouth in a contemplative manner. What animal were these from? A badger? He was not convinced; he looked back up the embankment and thought it an unlikely location for an animal corpse.

Turvey stood, lost in thought, for a moment longer then shrugged his shoulders and slipped the bones into the top pocket of his threadbare jacket. He decided to ask his friend Geoffrey what he made of them. Geoffrey Austin was the town's chief librarian, but he fancied himself as an amateur naturalist and archaeologist, and was generally reckoned to be 'good on bones', having famously once discovered and identified part of a Roman skeleton in a local dig before the start of the Great War.

Whistling his faithful old dog to heel, he walked into the town, his thoughts already turning towards that well-deserved pint of Brackley Bitter.

CHAPTER SIX
Woodford Halse
3rd September 1950

'Nearly done!' Violet Trinder was holding a pair of long wooden tongs that hinged using a strip of curved metal at one end. She was using these to prod the steaming mass of white nappies inside the zinc tub on top of the stove, swirling the hot, soapy water and lifting and turning those on the bottom to the top, releasing a pungent, chemical smell in a cloud of steam as she did so. Once satisfied, she clamped the lid back on and rested the tongs on top, cut off the gas flame and turned to Anna Vignoles, who was seated on the far side of the big wooden kitchen table, idly reading the back of a brightly-coloured soap box.

'I'll let them stew a few minutes longer whilst we finish our tea. I can rinse and wring out later.'

'I'll help you, it'll take half the time, and if Robbie wakes you can look after him.'

'Oh, thanks, Anna. It's the mangle that takes up all the time when you're on your own.' Violet looked out into the sun-drenched yard as she was speaking.

'The sooner we get them on the line in this lovely weather, the quicker they'll dry. Gosh, I love laundry dried in the sun and fresh air, don't you?'Anna smiled. 'Do you find this Omo is any good?'

'Yes, I think it does a splendid job. One of those pesky door-to-door salesmen got me onto it. I normally have nothing to do with them, of course, but he offered me a free sample and I've rather stuck with it since. I always used Oxydol or Reckitt's Blue before.' She pulled the lid off a circular tin bearing the images of the present king and queen. 'Now *do* have a flapjack, they're made with local honey. Sorry, they're a little overdone on the sides.'

'I like them like that,' Anna deliberately chose one with a darkened edge. 'Crunchy on the edges and soft on the inside!' She raised her finely-plucked eyebrows and took a bite.

'You're too kind. I left them in too long because Robbie needed me at just the wrong moment.' Violet looked across at the shiny, cream-and-black pram with its four large wheels and upswept pushing handle, and at the tiny, pink-faced bundle lying inside, breathing softly beneath a white crocheted blanket. 'He's having a nap. If he could just stay asleep until we get the nappies on the line, that would be perfect.'

Little Robert Trinder was just three months old. His father, Detective Sergeant John Trinder of the British Railways Detective Department, worked directly under Anna's husband, Detective Inspector Charles Vignoles. The department was based at Leicester Central; however, for the past year, Trinder had taken over a tiny cubbyhole of an office at Woodford Halse station two days a week in an arrangement that allowed the department better cover along the lower reaches of the Eastern Region's run into Marylebone. It also meant that he could cover the many circuitous cross-country lines that intersected at Woodford Halse.

Apart from the operational advantages, it meant that Violet and he could continue to live in the rooms above her shop, which could hardly be closer to the railway. The rented shop was at the end of a terrace that sat almost in the shadow of the great embankment and bridge that carried the railway striding across the village of Woodford Halse. It was right at the bottom of Station Road, which formed the main street. Although little more than a long row of typically-Victorian, red-brick, two-storeyed shops with sun-bleached awnings sagging above the windows, it was the centre of village life, away from the dominating presence of the railway and its vast, clanking marshalling yards and smoking locomotive depot.

The two women had become close friends, and both had long since become accustomed to the stresses and strains, odd hours and unpredictable happenings their husbands encountered in their work, and had even become embroiled in some startling incidents themselves. Violet had first met her future husband during one especially unpleasant incident involving her grown-up daughter, Jenny (born out of wedlock following a single night of ill-advised passion, when Violet was just seventeen). A gang of desperate men on the run had kidnapped Jenny, and it had turned into a dangerous and dramatic chase to liberate her. Violet and Anna had taken to each other immediately in the aftermath of this incident, and a close bond soon developed, a friendship also fuelled by a mutual love of fashion and nice fabrics.

In Violet's case, this was also a professional interest, as she ran her own dressmaking business, in her maiden name of McIntyre. Anna, although of English birth, was of Italian parentage, and had apparently inherited the Italian women's innate love of stylish clothes, aided by a figure and looks that turned heads. Indeed, she had famously stopped DI Vignoles in his tracks whilst he was walking along the platform at Leicester Central station one day in 1942, and the poor man had been rendered unable to think of much else other than her wavy, chestnut-coloured hair and dark brown eyes until they were married in an austere service the following year. Whilst their wedding was much affected by wartime restrictions, Anna had worn a simple but perfectly fitted dress that served to perfectly accentuate her natural beauty through its unfussiness. Years later, when Violet saw the wedding photographs for the first time, she immediately spotted Anna's potential as a living mannequin and encouraged her friend to wear some of her own creations or else skilful adaptations of life-expired garments. Anna's reputation for stylish dressing was the perfect advertisement to persuade others to commission or buy more of Violet's creations.

Their conversation that morning had already touched on the latest dress patterns, and they had agreed the design for an elegant evening gown for Anna. With a long, billowing skirt and a tightly-fitted bodice, it required a zip down the back, and both women had become quite excited about the delivery Violet had just taken of a consignment of fifty brand new zip fasteners — the first of these precious items since 1941. Until now, Violet had to be satisfied with re-using salvaged (and often malfunctioning) examples.

'I shall ration these carefully as I can't be sure of getting any more. The demand is going to be crazy. But don't worry: one of them is reserved for you. I can't wait to get started. You'll look an absolute dream, Anna.'

'I hope so. Or at least I hope Charles thinks so, as he's paying, bless him. It should be perfect for the autumn season.'

'You couldn't ask for a better birthday present: a gorgeous dress you'll love to wear and which he'll love you wearing!' They both laughed.

'Talking of perfect presents, I've not had time to show you before, but he also bought me something else...' Anna reached for her handbag and extracted a small, bottle-green, leather-bound book with gold lettering blocked onto the spine and an embossed design on the front. A narrow red ribbon dangled from between the pages. 'I was saying to Charles only a while ago how I wanted to learn more about the legends and folk stories of the area, and he managed to find this.'

'Gosh, what a lovely book.' Violet admired the leather cover and the marbled endpapers that swirled in complex fluid shapes of blues and greens. *The History and Antiquities of Charnwood Forest*, she read aloud. 'Looks interesting, is it very old?'

'1842.'

'But it looks almost as good as new.'

'It's a remarkable survivor and in almost perfect condition. I really love the woodcuts and the engravings inside.'

Violet turned the pages as Anna was speaking, noticing their eggshell smoothness and the rich, creamy colour supporting highly detailed engravings on full-page plates protected by sheets of translucent tissue paper, and the elegant woodcuts used on the chapter headings. 'I like this one of the fox running through the fields. It just seems to capture the landscape around here so well and, I don't know, it evokes something romantic inside me about England.'

'Doesn't it just?' They both admired a large plate showing a loose formation of ducks flying low above a river thick with bulrushes and reeds. The plate was entitled 'The Seven Whistlers'.

'I've only read a few chapters, but it reminds me how very old this country is. It reveals the layers of tradition and beliefs that lurk almost everywhere you look. There seems to be a mystery around every turn and some are even embedded in the very names of the villages, wells and woods. But I'm especially taken with the chapter on the supernatural.' Anna widened her eyes as she looked at Violet.

'Ooh, really? I *do* love a tale of the supernatural, although preferably in company and on a sunny day.' The warm, soapy smell in the air overlaying the scent of a Woolton Pie baking in the oven was suitably comforting and helped banish any fears of unwelcome hauntings.

'It's merely superstition and old wives' tales, of course, but I really can't resist them, and I suppose I do quite like the thrill. Part of me wants them to be true.'

'I'm never quite sure what to make of ghosts. I wonder if there's not a grain of truth behind the stories.' Violet shrugged her shoulders 'I've not actually seen one myself — but there's always a first time.'

'According to this book, we could get a chance to do so closer to home than I dared imagine.'

'What do you mean?' Violet sat upright, her voice slightly less confident, her blue eyes widening.

'Let me find it, if I may?' Anna took the book and flipped it open at the place marked by the ribbon. 'It's about the so-called shag-dog of Birstall. She rolled her eyes melodramatically. 'A huge, black, shaggy, dog-like creature with a chain around its neck that it drags along the ground and eyes that burn like coals. Woo-ooh... But guess what? This beast prowls a lane between Belgrave and Birstall, just yards from our house!'

'Oh, my goodness. Don't say that, I'll be petrified to visit you, especially now with Robbie.' Violet instinctively placed her fingers around the handle of the perambulator and gave it a gentle rock.

'Ah, but according to the legend it protects vulnerable people, especially women, and I'm sure small babies would be included, so we have nothing to fear.' Anna had by then found the relevant place in the book. 'Apparently an elderly woman told the author that—' and she began to read aloud '—*there is a shag-dog that lives in shag-dog pit. Sometimes I've heard him rattling his chain when I've been along the lane. They say he goes down to the Soar to drink.*' Anna glanced up at Violet, who now looked the very picture of alarm, one hand fiddling with strand of her light brown hair.

'She then tells of a young woman called Katie who was being followed one night down the lane by a drunken man whom she feared had sinister intentions, when *Suddenly she heard a deep, strange bark. The dog came bounding down the slope from the shag-dog pit, huge and black and wild, his open jaws luminous, like dying coals, his eyes wide and staring and glowing with unearthly light, padding silently behind young Katie.* The man was chased off by this beast, leaving Katie to continue home quite safely. The man was found drowned in the river the next morning.'

'What a strange tale. It could just be a mastiff or some such dog, and the girl elaborated it into something more, to make a good story.'

'I would imagine so. The funny thing is, Vi, there really is an old lady living in Belgrave who reckons the shag-dog helped her once, just like in the tale. Charles met her one time and she was so eager to tell him all about it, saying it was better than having a bobby walking the lane at night to keep her safe.'

'I'd be scared out of my wits if that great, slavering thing was behind me. Give me a detective sergeant anytime!' Violet laughed.

Anna nodded in agreement. 'Charles thinks the shag-dog pit was landscaped into a bunker when they made the golf course, so the beast might have moved on by now.'

'That's a relief!' Violet looked thoughtful. 'You know, it's funny you've brought this up, because John came home the other evening with a strange tale. He'd been down to Brackley Central on a small matter, something trivial that makes no odds, and he was taking a cup of tea whilst waiting for his train home that evening when a couple of the men working there got talking about some odd goings on. He told me they were really jumpy — 'spooked' was the word he used. All on edge about strange apparitions seen around the station.'

Anna bit her lower lip in mock alarm. 'What sort of thing?'

'They talked of omens — warnings of some kind. Something about haunting, whistling sounds in the night sky.'

'Not a very convincing argument on a railway station, as they are full of engines and guards whistling all the time', Anna smiled.

'I know, and you can imagine what John thought of *that* idea!' Violet laughed. 'But what it all boiled down to was, a few odd birds flying overhead and a so-called "woman in white" who had been spotted on the line on a number of occasions, pointing as if indicating something beside the track. As though she were alerting them to something. But, despite the signalman raising the alarm and some of the men racing down the tracks to remove her from the line, she vanished without a trace. Not a sight nor sound of her anywhere, and they found nothing by the line, either.'

'Of course this could easily be explained away...'

'Exactly what John told them. She was obviously a local who knew a short cut — a dangerous one perhaps — and no doubt she just melted into the fields and copses during the cover of darkness before the men could see where she'd gone. But he said the men were not convinced.'

'And that was it?'

'No; she has been seen at least once more. One of the men was returning from trimming the wick on the lamp of a distant signal, when he saw this "woman in white" standing on the line. He called to her, and she turned towards him for a moment. She raised her arms as if in alarm, but as soon as he hailed her she just slipped down the embankment and disappeared. The thing is', Violet leant closer, 'he reckoned that she had no hands...'

'Get away!'

'It was dark and a bit misty and he said she had a long coat on and that might have been too long for her arms. John told him he was letting his imagination run riot.'

Anna took a sharp intake of breath, her eyes sparkling with excitement. 'Well I never! A variation on the classic tale of the headless woman. They are nearly always dressed in white, according to this book.' She tapped it with her manicured nails.

'Gosh, well there you go. The men are convinced that a woman in white — with or without hands — is a ghost and is stalking the line near Brackley Viaduct.'

CHAPTER SEVEN
Marylebone station, London
3rd September 1950

'Your ticket please, sir.'

'Oh, yes. I have it here...somewhere.' Richard Irons put down his small, brown leather suitcase and fumbled inside his baggy, corduroy trousers, checking first one pocket, then the next, a look of consternation developing on his face as he withdrew a grubby handkerchief and a couple of coins, but no ticket. 'I only bought it a few minutes ago. Where on earth did I put it?' He patted his jacket wildly, an action that was unlikely to help find a tiny rectangle of printed cardboard.

The ticket collector took a deep breath, but looked at Irons indulgently, amused rather than irritated by the young man's actions. It was late, and there were only a few passengers beneath the echoing roofs of Marylebone station, so he was far from being rushed. He also had a fresh brew of tea steaming in a blue enamel mug on the wooden shelf of his little booth at the barrier, whilst the warmth of the glorious Indian summer day that London had just enjoyed still lingered, so he was content to watch this young man's growing sense of alarm.

'Ahem!' Someone cleared his throat.

'I really *do* have it.' Irons was flustered, not helped by the mockingly raised eyebrow on the railwayman's face.

'Oy! This wot yer lookin' for, mate? You left it on top of yer blummin' trunk!' It was the voice of a young porter who had approached the barrier hauling a flat-bedded, four-wheeled trolley laden with a couple of mailbags, a few interesting-looking parcels wrapped in brown paper and tied with string, and an old leather trunk with a label boldly declaring:

Richard Irons Esq.
Magdalen College Grammar School,
Brackley.

'How silly of me! Thanks awfully.' Irons gratefully took the ticket from the porter, who winked and laughed. The ticket collector now barely glanced at the ticket before waving him through, accompanied by a slight shake of the head, despairing of the 'young men of today'.

'I presume that's my train?' Irons nodded towards a short line of four coaches. Coupled to the front was a smooth-flanked tank engine which hissed quietly to itself in the otherwise deserted station.

'That's correct, sir. The last train to Brackley Central. Stops there and comes straight back, so if you happen to fall asleep, you won't miss your stop, as they'll shake you awake and turn you out.' The collector winked at Irons, judging from the young man's slightly dishevelled appearance and sallow complexion, coupled with the redness around his eyes, he'd probably enjoyed a riotous weekend and was feeling the effects.

Irons had indeed caroused long into the night. If that were not enough, he'd then been waylaid by two of his more riotous chums and encouraged just a few hours ago to have 'a hair of the dog' in the Marylebone station bar. The weekend had cost him deep in the pocket and left him somewhat the worse for wear, and, to top it all, he'd managed to miss the train he'd planned to take earlier that evening. Thank goodness for this late one. He really needed the journey to sober up and make himself presentable before he arrived at Brackley.

But he had no regrets, mainly because he had something to celebrate. He was heading out of London to start a new job; in fact, — summer holiday work and teaching practice excepted — this was his very first job: teaching mathematics to fourteen and fifteen-year-olds at a grammar school 'in the sticks'. Heaven knows what it was going to be like. He was more than a little apprehensive about the days ahead, but he had been impressed by the surprisingly ancient and authentically 'collegiate' look of the place, and the headmaster, Mr Stonehouse, whilst probably a bit of a tyrant and a dusty old cove dressed in his black gown, seemed straightforward and decent enough at the interview.

Another incentive, and one that was appearing ever more attractive at this moment, was that the school had overnight boarders, and he was to get his own (rather small and Spartan) room on site, with meals included, at a modest cost stopped out of his salary. This was going to prove a lifesaver, as he'd already mentally calculated the cost of his weekend celebrations. Money was to be strictly rationed until he repaired the deficit, and it was not as if his salary was going to be generous.

He walked along the platform towards the waiting train, the young porter on his heels, the rumble of the metal trolley wheels and the lad's jaunty whistling of an infectiously catchy tune the only accompaniment. Irons suddenly felt very weary. He mumbled a few words of thanks as the porter hefted his trunk into the guard's compartment, whilst he stepped through an already-opened door into the coach vestibule. Irons knew he should have tipped the lad, but he was low on coins, just one half crown and a measly farthing sat in his trouser pocket. To give a farthing seemed more insulting than no tip at all, but he was in no position to part with the half crown.

He flopped onto the creaky moquette of a bench seat in an empty compartment, in what sounded like an equally empty coach, and rested his now-throbbing head against the cool glass of the window. He closed his eyes. Almost immediately he felt himself drift into a semi-conscious state, comforted by the familiar sounds of the engine's hissing and panting, of a drowsy fly buzzing and bumping along the window ledge, the slam of a door, the porter's softly-whistled melody that he now recognised as being from *The Third Man*, a Film Noir that had gripped cinema-goers for many months. There was an echoing call across a far platform and the short blast of the guard's whistle close by, followed by the jolt and clatter of the starting train.

It was warm in the compartment and he was lulled into a deep sleep, rocked and rolled by the rhythm of the train clickity-clacking across the rail joints. The neatly compact L1 tank engine settled down into a faintly asthmatic huff-huff-huff as it trundled north through long tunnels and beneath bridges, threading its apologetic way between the salubrious north-west London suburbs, concealed in cuttings and hunched behind retaining walls as if embarrassed to disturb the middle-managers and aspirational office-wallahs during their evening radio show or quiet smoke in their handkerchief-sized yards. The train marked its progress with little iridescent clouds that tumbled and disintegrated on fences clothed in sweet-scented honeysuckle, or broke like waves on sturdy, brick back walls.

He was not sure for how long he had slept, but the sound of someone entering the compartment awakened him. He parted the fingers on the hand covering his face and, peering blearily though sandy eyes that refused to focus, was startled to see a young woman sitting diagonally opposite, close to the sliding door leading to the corridor.

It struck him as surprising that she had chosen a compartment occupied by a lone man. He closed his eyes again, not wishing to startle or unnerve her, but was intrigued by this turn of events, and his mind started whirring.

The woman must have observed he was asleep and, if she were travelling only to the next stop, perhaps thought there was little risk in sharing the compartment. Yes, that explained it. Or had the train suddenly filled up, leaving this the sole compartment with empty seats? No; he would have been disturbed by the sound of many voices, the clumping of feet in the corridor and the sliding and slamming of doors. As it was, he had been awakened by the faintest of sounds as she had crept, like a church mouse, into his compartment.

Well, it was she who had made the decision to join him. He needed to adjust his aching neck and sit upright. He did so slowly, not wanting to startle her, whilst glancing across to take a better look.

'Hullo!' He feigned surprise at seeing her there.

'Sorry, I did not mean to wake you.' Her voice was low, almost a whisper, like someone speaking in a library.

'Oh, I was just dozing.' Irons looked at the floor, staring stupidly into space, the alcohol and the short nap dulling his mind like a strong head-cold. He felt self-conscious, aware that his hair was probably a dreadful mess and that he must look dishevelled. He wiped a hand over his face, then blinked a few times to try and buck himself up. He risked another look in her direction and offered a pathetic smile. 'It was quite a long weekend. A few late nights...'

'You're tired. Please don't mind me.' It was a gentle voice, and yet one filled with sadness. 'World-weary' was how Irons was later to describe it.

'I am a little. But nothing that a cup of tea followed by a good night's sleep won't fix!' Whilst Irons was speaking, he was struck by her appearance. Her eyes were like pools of greeny-blue water glazed by a cold, silvery light, though this was probably just the effect of the pitifully weak bulb in the compartment ceiling that appeared to be dimming even lower.

She was gazing at the empty seat opposite, but he was sure she saw little of her surroundings, appearing preoccupied by something troubling her. Her skin was pale; so much so, he thought it almost without colour. She sat upright, looking the very picture of dejection, and virtually immobile save for an anxious movement of her hands. 'Excuse me, but are you all right?' Irons asked. 'Sorry, I don't mean to be nosy, but you seem rather blue...' He tailed off, aware that he was indeed being intrusive.

'Fine, thank you.' She hesitated. 'I also need rest. I'm weary of this endless travelling.' She twisted the fingers of her right hand around the ring finger of her left, in an anxious, nervous motion that was the only spark of animation about her. Her uneasy demeanour did not suggest she was about to be successful in achieving her desire for rest.

'I know the feeling: weekends are never long enough, are they?' He tried a touch of levity, but her unhappy countenance made him look away. He found it oddly disturbing in someone so young. She was about eighteen or so, although her sallow skin, and the dark rings beneath her doe-like eyes that were watery as if on the verge of tears, put some years on her.

'I can never rest. Sleep evades me,' she added.

'Sorry to hear that. It can be jolly miserable not sleeping well. I was like that in the days leading up to my interview: I just couldn't get a wink, and as I lay there in the night, it preyed on my mind that I would be too tired to make a good impression. Although I must confess, it's an affliction I rarely suffer from; normally I can sleep just about anywhere, just like on this train — I went out like a light...' He stopped himself short and winced. What an unfeeling ass he was. He was not accustomed to this sort of conversation with a young woman, and was babbling on like an idiot.

'You are lucky. A deep, untroubled sleep is something to crave.'

'I suppose I am.' Irons was puzzled by the strange turn the conversation had taken. How on earth was he discussing sleep, and all the implications of the bedroom this brought to mind, with this young woman? He felt safer adopting a more serious tone. 'Can a doctor not help? With a sleeping pill, perhaps? The National Health Service is jolly good, I'm sure they could do something.'

She looked momentarily puzzled, a slight frown appearing as if she had not understood, her fingers still worrying away at her ring finger. 'I have nothing to do with doctors. I don't trust them.' She narrowed her eyes. 'They're dangerous men, wielding power as they see fit.' For the first time, she became animated.

'Oh. I see.' Irons did not, but ploughed on regardless. 'I can't profess to have much experience of doctors, not unless you count the rather brutal army medic who decided that I had fallen arches and declared that I couldn't do National Service. I cannot truthfully say that I was mortified, haha! Got out of two years of yard bashing. Could have hugged the man! But seriously, they aren't all bad.'

'It pays to be very wary of men who have the power of life and death over us.' Her voice carried a note of anger, though it was still barely a whisper.

Irons was unsure how to respond. Her vehement reaction had momentarily floored him. He wanted to ask her why she held such a strong opinion, but realised that if she were speaking from experience, then he would be straying again into dangerously personal territory, and so opted to tactfully withdraw. He offered instead a lame nod of the head and a smile he hoped would appear sympathetic. She fell silent and returned to contemplating the seat opposite. He took this opportunity to take a good look at his curious companion.

If she did her hair in a more modern style and got into the sunshine to relieve the pastiness of her skin, ate a few slap-up meals and an extra ration of bacon and butter for a few weeks to feed her up a little, she would look a whole lot better. She was slim and trim, perhaps underfed, but then who was not these days? And whilst perhaps no magazine pin-up, she had a face he was sure someone could easily enjoy waking up to each morning. He noticed that the light summer dress she was wearing was made from a fabric that clung close to her body and hinted at what lay beneath.

He turned away from fixating upon her small, pointed breasts and stared out of the window into the impenetrable night and at the faint reflection of the girl, now rendered insubstantial in the grubby glass, a little surprised by his carnal thoughts. He could not deny that such close proximity to a young woman was thrilling. He had rarely been alone with one and never in such an intimate setting. He also felt a tender stab of sympathy towards her, wishing he could gallantly do something to relieve her obvious sadness.

Pure foolishness on his part, of course. Her boyfriend was probably the cause of her upset, and in no time at all they would make up and she would smile and laugh again. They'd probably just had a lovers' tiff over the weekend and she was now regretting not resolving this before parting. It was none of his business, and she didn't need his interference.

He felt a strong shiver and realised the compartment had turned surprisingly cold. The train heating was off and the little window wide open, but until now he had been thankful for the cool air it allowed into what had felt like a hot and muggy compartment, but now there was an icy draught. Perhaps it was the effect of the drink wearing off.

'Brrr. Are you cold? I think the night has cooled quite noticeably.'

'I don't feel it. But please, do as you wish.' She gave him a strange look, her eyes almost making him melt.

Irons stood and closed the window before slipping on his brown corduroy jacket and sitting back down. He was now shivering repeatedly and he shrugged his shoulders as icy fingers ran down his spine, a surprising reaction that had started the moment she held his gaze.

He extracted a slim book from his small case on the seat beside him, and idly flipped it open. He was not in the mood to swat up the algebra questions he might set his new students, and the dreadful lighting (that appeared to be on the verge of failing) made it virtually impossible to read anyway, but he knew the book would offer a refuge for his wandering eyes. He was becoming increasingly captivated, almost aroused, by this woman and knew he must restrain himself from openly staring at her. There really was something oddly compelling, and perhaps even just a little unsettling, about her. If only she would not look so darned unhappy.

'That looks serious.'

'It is rather dry, I suppose, but I need to think about the week ahead and what to give my new charges. I'm a teacher, you see. I start my new job tomorrow.'

She gave him a slight smile in response. 'Where is the school?'

'Brackley. Magdalen College Grammar for Boys. Do you know of it?'

'Yes.' She gave a slight start, as if hearing the name had surprised her. 'I know the place well. I was born in Brackley. I lived there until—'

'—I say, what a small world!' Irons interrupted her in his excitement. 'So you're travelling there? What a coincidence.'

'It's been a long time now.' Her answer was ambiguous. She took a deep breath, as if steadying herself, then gave him a look that for the first time held a spark of animation. 'It's a good school. You'll be happy there.'

Irons felt another wave of powerful shivers course through his body and wondered if he were catching a chill. That was all he needed: to be laid up in bed at the start of his first week. He closed his eyes and rested his head against the cushions as he answered. 'I'm glad to hear that. Please forgive me closing my eyes... awfully rude of me...' His voice was slow and heavy, the book abandoned on his lap. 'I fear I might be going down with something. I just need to... to rest my eyes for a moment...'

He desperately wanted to prolong the conversation, but was powerless to prevent the waves of intense drowsiness that now washed over him, and despite the coldness of the compartment he drifted in and out of sleep, always aware that she was there — although she made not a sound — but equally unable to open his eyes and talk with her.

After he knew not how long, he was jolted awake by a particularly noisy and aggressive application of the brakes, which interrupted a vivid dream about an exotically beautiful Egyptian girl with big, brown eyes leading a camel into the guard's van whilst another woman he could not see sobbed relentlessly and called his name, but he sensed that she had been standing there for some time, looking down and studying him whilst he slept. The instant he looked at her, however, she turned to leave the compartment. She glanced back for just a moment and he heard her say, 'Brackley Central. This is your station', before slipping down the corridor and out of sight.

He rubbed his eyes. The train was shuddering gently as it slowed, and he heard another compartment door slide open further along the coach and someone shuffling his feet on the floor as he gathered his things together. He was now hot, almost sweaty, and very uncomfortable. It was dreadfully stuffy in the compartment and far too warm. Why on earth had he felt the need to close the window and turn the carriage heating full on?

He stood up and loosened his tie. Looking briefly into the small, oval mirror on the compartment wall, he grimaced at his reflection and swiftly ran clammy fingers through his limp hair in an attempt to put it back in place, then wedged his hat on top of the untidy result. He returned his book to the small, brown, rectangular, leather case that had served his civil-engineer father as a briefcase for many years, and was ready to alight from the train the moment it came to a stand. He felt eager to say goodbye to the girl and expected to see her emerge from the door at the end of the corridor.

He stepped onto the platform, took a deep draught of cool air and immediately felt more awake than he had during the whole journey. The guard was standing on the platform, overseeing a porter who was unloading his trunk, along with a bicycle and two baskets of cooing pigeons. Irons nodded to the porter and pointed to the trunk to indicate that he was its owner, then took in his surroundings.

The station was small, but the island platform was long and quite wide with an open and airy feel about it, although it was now so dark he gained only a sense of vast remoteness all about, almost as though the station were a little ship becalmed on a black sea. He remembered from his previous visit for his job interview that Brackley Central was set right on the northern edge of the little market town, nestling in the lee of a hill topped by Scots pines, with both hill and trees serving to mask any sense of habitation close by, and this now added to the atmosphere of quiet isolation.

An elderly woman with a stick was plodding towards the stairwell that would take her up to the short bridge spanning one of the railway tracks and so to the tiny booking hall that commanded an elevated position on the crest of the hill. A thin man wearing a bushy moustache, herringbone pattern tweeds and a matching deerstalker was hefting onto his shoulder what appeared to be hunting guns in canvas bags, whilst two young lads in blazers — possibly Magdalen pupils — were sharing a joke as they hurried towards the exit. But of the sad young girl, there was nothing to be seen.

Irons presumed she must have moved along the train and, the instant it stopped, stepped out directly opposite the exit stairs to make a swift departure. He could not blame her for wanting to hurry home, but still felt a pang of disappointment. It was as if she'd deliberately made the decision to leave the train quickly so as to avoid him. That was a slap in the face. He was sure he'd not acted in a manner that could be considered 'fresh'. Indeed he'd fallen asleep and ignored her for much of the journey. Women really were the most perplexing of creatures he concluded, ruefully.

He watched his trunk being expertly propelled along the platform on a small, two-wheel trolley, the handles of which reached to the porter's shoulders, leaving only the lad's face and cap peeking over the top in a rather comical manner. Irons also started to walk towards the exit, and, as he did so, suddenly hit upon a perfectly rational — and less personally hurtful — reason for the girl's swift disappearance.

Her father would be meeting her. Walking though the ticket barrier accompanied by a strange man would place her in the embarrassing situation of having to explain who he was and why she was with him. As they didn't even know each other's names, it would be impossible as well as unnecessary and awkward. When he considered this explanation he realised that she had displayed a delicate touch of sensitivity that was quite appealing.

Well, she was a Brackley gal, she'd said as much, and it was a small town, so he would doubtless have other opportunities to meet her. It was time now to push such thoughts aside and concentrate on more pressing matters. He arranged for his trunk to be held at the station overnight and forwarded on to the school early the following morning on Bob Phillips's brand new 'Mechanical Horse', a vehicle that, he was advised (with much barely-concealed excitement by the head porter) was 'speshly reserved for such duties.'

Irons nipped into the gents' and splashed cold water on his face, rubbed fresh Brylcreem into his hair and combed it into place, neatened up his shirt and re-knotted his crocheted woollen tie, then shrugged on his jacket. He used his handkerchief to give his shoes a quick shine before making a readjustment to his hat. Not brilliant, but it was late, and dark, and he would not make too ghastly an impression when he rolled up at the school.

Suddenly feeling decidedly chipper through a mixture of nervous excitement about his new life ahead and the hope of meeting the girl again, he whistled the infectiously melodic *Third Man* theme music that the Marylebone porter had imprinted in his brain whilst he strolled down the long and wide, tree-lined avenue that formed the spine of the town. He walked past a little park filled with big, dark trees and the towering majesty of Winchester House Public School that looked like something King Charles might have lived in, and as he did so he imagined himself to be like Joseph Cotten arriving in Vienna for the first time, soon to encounter the beautiful, if beautifully sad and tearful, Alida Valli.

CHAPTER EIGHT
Leicester Central
5th September 1950

PC467, (christened Simon Howerth) was seated on one side of a large wooden desk in the main office of the British Railways Detective Department in Leicester Central station. The desk was one of a pair, dating from the opening of the line in 1899 and was rubbed smooth in places from countless uniform sleeves polishing and burnishing it to a deeply smooth patina. The chair on which he was perched was equally old and creaked alarmingly as he tipped it backwards on its rear legs in the way youths find irresistible. Indeed, the majority of the office fittings had not changed much since the end of the nineteenth century. The walls had been distempered a year or two ago and there were now electric bulbs in enamelled shades hanging from the ceiling in place of the original gas mantles, but apart from the telephones on the desks and a copying machine that only the WPCs seemed to know how to use, and which exuded a noxious smell of solvent, there were few concessions to modernity. In truth, it was a dour, grubby place, crammed with old filing cabinets, heaps of case-files bound together with red string, loose papers in untidy mounds on the desks, an assortment of ill-matching chairs and a lethal-looking electric fire on the end of a brown cord that was ominously frayed in a number of places. But, compared with the conditions Simon had previously known in the locomotive sheds, it was sheer luxury, made all the more so in that he had a big enamelled cup of tea close to hand and even a Garibaldi biscuit, courtesy of Mrs Green, the detective inspector's slightly fearsome secretary.

He was leaning as far back as he dared in his chair with his nose in a magazine, whilst PC Blencowe, seated opposite, was hammering out a report on the massive iron typewriter that occupied the greater part of his side of the desk, hunched over the machine with a look of intense concentration on his face. He was no typist, even after many years of practice, and used just his stubby forefingers to strike the keys. He had been belting away at what was only a short document for some considerable time. If he ever made it up the ladder to inspector rank he would be able to palm off all his typing chores to a secretary. The thought made him smile.

Blencowe slammed the typewriter carriage across for the final time, making the little bell ting, and wound the sheets of paper and the blue carbon out of the machine. He eased his not inconsiderable bulk back in the chair and stretched his arms above his head, groaning a little as he eased his shoulders. He then took a sip of his tea, wiped his unfashionable beard with the back of his hand and stood up to stretch his legs.

'Working hard eh, lad?' He gave the young constable the benefit of a raised eyebrow. 'So what's so interesting in that rag of yours?' Blencowe walked to the end of the desk, the better to deflect some of the warmth from the little fire onto the back of his legs.

'Sorry.' Simon hurriedly tried to pretend he had not been reading, although it was obviously a futile action. 'It's actually about police work…'

'Haha, I bet. *True Crime Magazine?*' Blencowe spoke the words with a mocking tone. 'Complete rubbish, I'm sure. Come on then, let's have a gander.'

He took the magazine from Simon. It was printed on thin paper, the ink smelling strongly and instantly smudging under his fingers with a lurid cover painting depicting a glamorous blonde with an impressively-curvaceous body squeezed into a revealing, red evening dress, all long legs and cleavage. She was lifting one arm in self defence, her full red lips opened in a cry of distress as the dark figure of a man in a long, black coat and fedora hat approached her up a flight of steps with a gun in his hand, his face screwed into an expression of pure malice, the scene illuminated by a strong side light that threw dramatic shadows. Blencowe studied the cover for a few moments and smiled.

'Hmm…I can see what the attraction was. Most instructive.' He gave Simon a stern look, his bushy eyebrows exaggerating his expression. 'Let's hope what's inside is more mature.'

'Some of the articles are jolly interesting. Real life cases where they explain exactly how the villains were caught.'

'Hoping to pick up some tips?'

'It can't do any harm. There's an awful lot I need to know about this job and anything that helps has to be a good thing.'

'You're not wrong there, at least.' Blencowe paused and pulled a puzzled face at a page for a moment, then continued skimming through. 'Proper detective work is built around hard graft and paying attention to the correct procedures, in chasing up every tiny little point of detail, not in rescuing scantily-clad damsels.'

'The cover is misleading. Though do you remember when Eddie and me were in a van spinning about on that frozen reservoir? And then there was that man found buried in the coal...'

'True.' Blencowe had to concede the point. There was no denying that Simon and his best friend Eddie Earnshaw had over the last four years somehow managed to worm themselves into more than their fair share of extraordinary scrapes and had even helped crack some of the most dramatic and dangerous cases which the department had been called upon to investigate. Hard though it was to believe, two young lads from sleepy little Woodford Halse, working their way slowly up the ladder to be loco crew, had been slap bang in the middle of some serious and challenging crimes.

It was this meddling in things they really shouldn't that had resulted in Simon Howerth now working for the detective department. A strange turn of events in the eyes of some, but DI Vignoles had seen in him a restless desire to solve problems, and whilst still rather too impetuous and ill-disciplined in his approach at times, the freckly, carrot-topped young man had an apparently innate ability to sniff out when something was not quite right. He had, according to Vignoles, 'a detective's nose for a crime'.

Simon's nose had certainly got him dangerously involved in an especially nasty situation the year before, but then he had made a creditable effort to extricate himself and see justice done — at no little risk. True, he had broken the law along the way and the railway authorities had no choice but to dismiss him from his job as a trainee fireman, but Vignoles had taken a punt. He'd stuck his neck out and brought the lad into the fold, 'Where I can keep an eye on him.' Initially, Blencowe had been sceptical, but was cautiously starting to think that his inspector was correct in his belief that the young PC one day just might make a detective.

'*The Startling Case of the Lady in Red*...What tommyrot! The rubbish they write...' Blencowe flipped more pages, shaking his head.

'Look at the article on unsolved crimes near the back. That's what's got me hooked.' Simon was trying to recover some kudos. 'The writing is more serious and they look at all sorts of crimes still puzzling the police, including two on the railways.'

'On the railways, eh? Righty-o. Let's see what they say.' The older man read for a few moments, occasionally sipping from a cup of tea. He nodded once or twice as if agreeing with what he read. 'I remember that one. The mail theft in '38, up Sheffield Darnell way. They've still not got the vicious bugger who shot the guard. How can anyone even think to kill a man for a few piddling postal orders, it beggars belief.'

'I said it was good reading.'

'Now, that's odd. I don't recall that.' Blencowe was the department's 'Mr Detail,' a man with a memory almost photographic and a penchant for lists, charts, maps and teasing out scraps of information from almost any source. Whilst not the quickest thinker, and certainly not the best at handling interviews, he was a highly prized asset to the team.

'What's that?'

'They call it *The Broad Street Trunk Mystery*. Yuck.' Blencowe looked disgusted. 'That's horrible. Now, why have I not come across this before?'

'Shocking, isn't it?' Simon looked more excited than horrified. 'You have to wonder how they never found out who left it there. It's really got me thinking about how to track down the killer. There just has to be a way!'

'Oh yes? Reckon you can crack the mystery, do you?'

'No...well...maybe. Seeing as it was a railway crime or, at least, the trunk was found in a station luggage office, so that makes it as good as a railway crime, I thought perhaps...'

'Now listen up, you young pup. You do exactly what the sergeant tells you to do, and nothing else. Right? You don't decide what gets investigated and you'd do well to not forget that! Keep your nose out of stuff that's none of your affair.'

'Of course.' Simon looked contrite.

'I'm still a bit miffed we never heard of this, though.' Blencowe was shaking his head slightly. 'May 1945 they made the discovery. I suppose we were too busy thinking about VE day. It was quite a time, mind, painting the town red and then of course there were the drunk and disorderly everywhere plus our own hangovers to nurse.' He still looked puzzled. 'I might have a word with some of the chaps down that neck of the woods.'

'So we are looking into it?' Simon instantly cheered up.

'No, we are not. I'm just curious. Now, PC467, get this

report onto the guvnor's desk, then take the post into town. When you're back I want these files putting away.'

Yes, sir; of course, sir; three bags full, sir! Simon remained silent however and, despite railing at being put in his place, he smiled to himself as he saw Blencowe sit behind his side of the desk still staring intently at the magazine page and slowly stroking his beard with one hand.

CHAPTER NINE
Brackley & London
17th September 1950

Irons was kept busy over the following two weeks trying to settle into his new job and to establish a rapport with both the other masters and the boys. He worked hard just to remember the names of his pupils, let alone understand their many foibles and tricks or begin to implant any serious mathematical understanding into their young minds.

Teaching was proving to be somewhat harder in reality than during his training practice, when he'd had the safety net of an experienced and seasoned practitioner looking over his shoulder, and he often sat up deep into the night planning and re-planning lessons in the hope that these would run more satisfactorily than he had managed so far.

With it being the start of both a new term and a new school year, the whole place felt like a tremendous shapeless muddle and confusion; what Timmy Bunyan, the Latin master, called 'the annual organised chaos', and to Irons it was a ceaseless series of misunderstandings caused by a succession of bewildered young lads looking for classrooms and frazzled teachers searching for books, pencils and other equipment that had mysteriously vanished over the summer hols, followed by lessons that never seemed to settle down until they were already halfway through their allotted time and ended with a mutual feeling of dissatisfaction.

Irons also had to learn to adjust to the relentless life of the school, extending into taking his share of dorm duty, a task that fell upon any teacher who chose to live-in. It involved being on call throughout the night in case any boarder felt ill, suffered homesickness or caused trouble through high spirits and japes. He soon discovered that, as the newest and youngest of the live-in staff, his turn on nights came around frequently. The lack of sleep it invariably caused did nothing to help his teaching.

All this meant that he had little time to explore the town or have a decent opportunity to chance upon the intriguing girl on the train, although he still harboured the hankering and, in odd quiet moments, imagined what he might say when they met on the street, or perhaps in the Oak Cottage Cafe on the edge of the market square.

However, his first thirteen days had largely been circumscribed by his room, the refectory (a chilly, noisy place), walking each morning to assembly in the school's twelfth-century chapel (that was the size of a small parish church), then skirting the pocket-sized quad with its square of grass edged by pungent box hedges to his classroom, housed inside the venerable main building.

He liked his classroom, however, and was starting to enjoy trying to stamp his personality upon it. There was a large and dusty blackboard with a shallow shelf of coloured chalks (their dust soon coated his clothes) and a heavy desk with a mechanical pencil sharpener screwed to one edge, a bottle-green Anglepoise lamp, a tall cupboard built into the wall which smelt of musty paper and was filled with life-expired books, erasers and rubber bands. The ancient windows with leaded glass looked onto the market square. Below them, a robust, Victorian-era iron radiator would be most welcome in winter. At odd times, when the boys were bent silently to a task in their workbooks, he allowed his eyes to stray out of the window in the vain hope he might catch a passing glimpse of the girl. So far he had not once seen her. He felt a nagging twinge of sadness that this were so.

Occasionally, he was required to walk along the edge of the Waynefleet playing fields at the back of the school to one of the more obscure classrooms located in a large (and supposedly temporary) shed that had been erected for Civil Defence use in 1939. The draughty wooden construction smelt pleasantly of pine impregnated by pungent malt and hops from the Hopcroft and Norris brewery that backed on to the school. Walking there of an afternoon gave Irons time to take in the sight of boys playing cricket in the fields that stepped down in broad terraces, the colours of this agreeable scene pleasing to his eye, with cricket whites against the green of the close-mown grass offset by the almost Golden Syrup coloured walls of the buildings; for both school and chapel were constructed from the same local ironstone that defined much of the town's architecture, and were of considerable antiquity. Indeed, parts of the building were survivors of the original Hospital of St James and St John, built in 1150 by the Earl of Leicester. The newer additions dated from 1548, when it was converted to a school, and so the walls were typically thick and pierced by heavily-mullioned windows and oaken doors worn smooth with the rub of many hands over hundreds of years. The roofs were formed of stone slabs and punctuated by tall, elegant chimneys. The ensemble clearly betraying a close allegiance to the great Oxford college with which it shared both name and origins.

One day, whilst he was attempting to explain long division to his youthful charges, he fancied he caught a glimpse of a slim girl in a green sundress carrying a pale mackintosh across one arm. She was walking down the steep 'barrel run' railway siding that lay to one side of the wooden classroom, down which short, heavy trains of wagons filled with firkins of freshly-brewed ale backed cautiously with considerable noise from the little tank engine tasked with this Herculean job as they dropped towards the Midland Region's Brackley Town station. Known as the 'bottom' station, it lay on the sleepy branch line that ran between Banbury and the lonely outpost of Verney Junction and the regular beer trains were one of the few moments of intense activity between the occasional arrival and departure of the virtually-empty passenger services.

Irons did not get a good view of the girl because the verdant hedgerow and many trunks of the trees that lined the barrel run incline repeatedly concealed her, but his heart still leaped as he was sure she was the one from the train, and wearing what must be the same dress.

He caused considerable surprise (and much sniggering) by dashing out of the classroom and sprinting the short distance to a gap in the hedge used as a shortcut into the playing fields. But he had been mistaken: the steep incline with track buried deep in fine, pale limestone gravel with the odd yellow-flowering weed was completely empty and he was forced to invent a story about catching sight of a rare bird to try pacify the incredulous boys.

This one moment was a rare thrill, but his walks to and from the wooden classroom were usually moments of relative calm amidst the constant chatter and clamour of the boys, the tentative and carefully-weighted conversations with senior staff, and the need for Irons to remain constantly vigilant for the unwelcome appearance by the ascetically severe headmaster. He was in the habit of prowling the school in his mortar board and black gown like a giant, malevolent raven, and was prone to walking unannounced into a lesson and commencing to prod and poke at the blackboard or flip open a book on a desk with the end of his thin cane, whilst rapidly firing questions about what was being taught, or challenging a terrified boy into dividing 203 by 7, or some other puzzle designed to fluster and humiliate the startled lad.

Irons found this most wearying. He knew that given time he would probably become accustomed to this way of life, but as his first Sunday completely free of any duty approached, he needed respite.

Having been practically confined to school since the night he arrived, he had spent little of his meagre salary, which was a positive bonus, and so had been able to justify the expense of a return ticket to London, travelling up on an early train out of Brackley Central to meet with one of his friends in the city, though with no intention of 'pushing the boat out' this time.

The weather had remained glorious and he had enjoyed strolling around Euston Road with Algie Meredith, window-shopping for goods neither could afford (even if it had not all been destined for export) followed by a cheap lunch comprising a bottle of stout and a bag of greasy fish and chips consumed while seated on a bench. They took a walk through Regent's Park, weaving their way between the endless ranks of allotments that now replaced the acres of grass that had grown there before the war. They marvelled at the profusion of vegetables, countless ramshackle sheds, the wooden wheelbarrows and lines of bean canes, laden fruit bushes and plump, late lettuces of all hues of green, and the diligent Londoners picking, pruning, hoeing or barrowing in the constant drive to feed their families. When they tired of all this eager market gardening, they stopped to lean over a cast-iron footbridge, soaking up the sun on their backs and watching the narrowboats quietly passing below on Regent's Canal.

Irons bade Algie farewell at 4p.m. and made his way to the station. He could have been back in Brackley by early evening, with time to run his eye over the lessons for the following day and for an early night; and yet, flying against all logic and reason, and in an action hidden from Algie, he did not.

Instead, he loitered at Marylebone station, seated firstly on one bench, then on another inside the cavernous hall. He took from his pocket a paperback of *Scenes from Provincial Life* that he had splashed out on when he first learnt he'd secured the post at Magdalen. The book was open in his hand, but he hardly read a page. Instead, in an act of unsubtle espionage, he peered across the top of his book and observed people coming and going. When he wearied of this he stood idly browsing the lines of emaciated magazines on WH Smith's bookstall until the proprietor ceased throwing him suspicious looks and insisted that Irons 'stop reading it all for free and bugger off!'

Suitably chastened, he moved across to the colourful and deliciously-scented flower stall just inside the stone-arched entrance, examining each zinc bucket filled with freshly cut flowers, debating at length whether to be reckless and buy a bunch. He resisted doing so as they were prohibitively expensive and it was a foolish notion to even consider that a bouquet of flowers would be well received, or that the opportunity would even arise to offer it.

He constantly checked the hands on the broad-faced station clock as they inched their way around the dial, creeping sluggishly towards the departure time of first one, and then a second train that could have carried him back to his new home. Why was he doing this? He knew the answer, but even formulating the equation in his head was faintly embarrassing. He was waiting to see if that same girl would board a train so he could engineer a second meeting.

Irons was of the opinion that, on the day they'd met, she had joined the train further along the line, but without knowing which stop all he could do was survey the crowds milling about at the starting point for every train north, whilst nurturing the hope that she might appear. In a profoundly illogical piece of thinking, he was actually marking time until the departure of the very last train to Brackley Central, intending to recreate the same journey on the same day of the week, in the pathetic hope that she might be doing likewise.

Was he going nuts? Or was he just a single man tired of the unrelenting company of men and boys, hoping that, as he had nothing pressing to do that evening, and having spent a refreshing day with his best friend, he was now in the mood to fraternise with a member of the fair sex, and perhaps tentatively explore the outer margins of the idea that they might strike up an acquaintance. There was little to lose, and he need not confess to anyone that he had spent the greater part of Sunday evening mooching about in a booming London terminus.

Of course, he knew that she would be back with her beau by now and he had almost convinced himself that, once clear on that point, this little adventure could be laid to rest in his mind. He was prepared for that eventuality and would take it on the chin like a man. He just needed to see that she had cheered up, that was all. Or was it? He suspected that a small part of him was secretly hoping that she and the boyfriend had broken it off. He would offer his shoulder to cry on.

Over the past thirteen days, the moment he ceased concentrating on his school duties, her face had a habit of appearing in his mind and he could easily recall her soft, sad voice. These were just foolish daydreams, but at times the images were surprisingly vivid and he had almost convinced himself that she was calling to him like the Lorelei sitting, half naked, on the rocks in the Rhine as they combed their long hair. And sometimes he found himself recalling her thinly-veiled body and imagined her, similarly unclothed, beside a river on a warm summer day... No, this was not helping.

As he sat on yet another hard wooden bench with the carved letters 'GCR' impressing themselves into his back, he forced himself to consider a less highly-charged scenario, that of sitting on the more comfortable seats of the train and her waking him from a pleasant snooze to announce that they had arrived at their stop. But this time, he would immediately follow her out of the compartment and to whichever door she alighted from, and not waste time staring in the mirror and flattening his hair and letting her disappear. Maybe this time they could exchange names and then she could introduce him to her father. That would move things forward to his satisfaction.

He drained the last cold dregs of a cup of tea in an impatient gesture, suddenly annoyed with this foolishness that was making him act like an imbecile. After returning the heavy china cup and saucer to the waitress behind her mobile tea trolley he strode purposefully towards the ticket barrier. As he proffered his ticket he realised that the collector was the same one as before.

'You're in good time.'

'Yes... Um, I didn't want to risk missing my train.'

'Gor blimey, not 'arf! But you've still missed at least two since I noticed you 'ere.' He gave Irons a questioning look.

Irons reddened and, irrationally, felt he owed the man some explanation. 'I—er, I like stations... the atmosphere, um, the trains.' He shrugged and gave an innocent smile.

'Most people stand at the platform end to collect the numbers, sir.' He nodded in the direction of three youths seated on a trolley part way up one of the empty platforms, a tall bottle of fizzy pop to hand, little notebooks on their laps, each sucking or biting the ends of their pencils whilst flipping through small reference books to compare their 'cops'. 'You get a better view of the engines from the platforms, rather than the concourse. But each to his own, eh?' The collector winked, but his eyes lacked the sparkle of mirth. 'Just as long as you're not loitering with intent to cause trouble.'

Irons was not really listening; he was watching a short train reverse into the platform from out of the indigo light of the dying day, stirring a chattering flock of starlings into looping about the lofty train-shed like dog-fighting aircraft. He was already feeling curiously excited that everything was almost an exact rerun of his previous journey.

He strode along the empty platform and, once the train had come to a halt, walked the length of the four coaches as far as the big tank engine at the front. It gleamed in its sparkling coat of glossy black paint, adorned by a painted stylized lion balancing precariously on what looked like a wheel, and big cream numerals declaring it to be number 69800. He paused for a moment, finding the sequence of numbers appealing to his eye, momentarily tempted to see what his mathematical brain could make of this as a mental puzzle, but realised that this was a needless distraction and so turned his back on the locomotive.

Having already checked that each coach was empty as he'd walked the platform he now stepped aboard and worked his way back, making a second sweep to be doubly sure she was not already aboard, then settled himself in the same compartment as before. This time, he was determined to stay alert. He sat upright, pensively looking across the compartment and the narrow corridor and out onto the platform. Nobody could pass by, or board the train, without his seeing.

He heard the guard talking outside the luggage compartment and watched as a handful of people walked past. None bore the faintest resemblance to the girl. He recognised the old lady with the stick making her slow progress along the platform; a red-faced vicar in a dog collar shuffled towards his compartment holding a pencil and notebook opened at a page covered with lines of locomotive numbers. The clergyman hesitated momentarily at the door as though about to enter, but Irons looked away and tried to give off unwelcoming and decidedly un-Christian thought waves, which perhaps proved successful, for the Man of God moved on. A few others boarded the train, but the sad girl was not amongst them.

Once the train was in motion, it again began to dull his senses, lulling him with its gentle rattles and squeaks, the rhythmic beat of the sturdy engine and the hypnotic rhythm on the tracks combined with the equally regular looping of the telegraph wires like Arabic calligraphy in the sky, all serving to make his eyelids grow heavy. He could feel the pleasant effect of having been in the sun all day, weariness from the walking and the beer. Oh, it was so hard to resist closing his eyes...

He suddenly awoke and instantly sat bolt upright, cursing under his breath at himself for dozing off. The train was accelerating smartly. Staring outside he saw a station running-in board sailing past the window in the gloom of the night and just had time to read 'Amersham'. Damn! How many stations had he already missed? Irons stared angrily at the indistinct moving silhouettes of trees and house roofs etched against the final, thin stain of pale light below a starry sky and wondered how he had managed to fall asleep at the most critical moment of his hair-brained plan.

His frustration was short lived, however. Moments later he saw the blurred and slightly fuzzy image of a slim woman reflected in the dirty window glass. He froze and held his breath, an action accompanied by an odd thrill: that now-familiar sensation of icy fingers running down his body that made him involuntarily shiver. It was the same girl, and she was entering his compartment.

Irons dared not move. He watched her reflection eagerly. To his amazement, she chose to sit on the middle of the three seats opposite, her legs almost touching his. He allowed himself to breathe and silently reminded himself to take it easy and not say or do anything daft.

'Hello again.' Her voice was just as soft, and just as sad.

He turned and smiled. 'Hullo! What a pleasant surprise.'

She offered a hesitant smile. 'I wondered if you might be on this train.'

His heart leapt. 'Me too.' He tried hard to conceal his eagerness and sound casual. 'As we both travel to Brackley I wondered if we might bump into each other again. And so we have!'

'You travel this line often?'

'Yes. Well, no. That's to say I want to try and visit London quite frequently — to see friends. I shall take this train whenever I return to Brackley,' he added pointedly. Even as he was speaking, Irons was mentally reviewing the cost of a return ticket and recklessly convincing himself that he could afford to repeat the journey the moment he had another evening free. 'But only when I can get time away from my school duties, of course. You may recall that I have just started at Magdalen College?'

She nodded. 'I also find it necessary to make this journey frequently.'

'Do you work in Amersham?' He nodded his head towards the window. 'I noticed the station nameboard.'

She frowned, and her eyes seemed to become glassier, the odd cold glint in them more intense. She stared at the floor for a moment, her hands starting the same nervous, wringing motion as before, worrying away at her empty ring finger. 'I am compelled to go there.'

Irons thought this an odd turn of phrase, but his attention was immediately distracted by a train passing on the opposite track, thundering close to the window with a sudden slam and a whoosh of exhaust followed by the noisy chattering and booming of empty, metal-bodied wagons, the sound making them start. 'Always gets me when they do that!' He wafted some smoke away with his hand, aware that a faint haze of locomotive exhaust now filled the compartment and rendered his view of her blurred and indistinct, despite their proximity. Even through the hazy gloom, it was obvious she was unhappy. Perhaps she had not repaired relations with her boyfriend? However, the little glow of encouragement this offered was offset by the fact that he was also starting to feel decidedly chilly once again, and cursed the rotten old carriage which, clearly, suffered terribly from draughts. He was trying to resist rubbing his hands together to warm them as he felt the first tremble of a shiver.

'I take it you're not exactly enjoying your work? It can be a rotten bore having to do something you don't like and commuting, on top,' Irons tried to keep his voice light and to prevent his teeth chattering.

'You are right,' she replied. 'But there's little point in complaining.'

'Indeed! Look, I say, we really ought to get the introductions out of the way.' He extended a hand. 'Richard, Richard Irons, fledgling junior mathematics master!'

She declined to unclasp her hands to accept the handshake, but did lift her head and look him in the eye. 'Elizabeth Askew. But everyone calls me Betty. Locomotive cleaner.' She managed a smile that appeased Irons, who now slowly withdrew his hand and consoled himself with the thought that she was of a more reserved disposition than he had initially imagined, although this seemed strangely out of kilter with her decision to take a seat so close to himself, in an act that suggested a desire for intimacy. Indeed, it was she who had opened the exchange by greeting him. Gosh, she really was a puzzle, though a delightfully intriguing one.

'A locomotive cleaner? I thought that was a man's job these days.'

She gave him a puzzled look. 'Not a bit of it! There's a whole gang of us girls. They'd never manage without us.'

Irons winced. 'I wasn't trying to suggest that you didn't work hard and do a decent job, only...'

Betty sighed. 'We are *still* working hard.' She frowned and added, *sotto voce*, as though to herself and not Irons, 'At least they were the last time I was at Woodford.' She looked down at her hands clasped together in her lap.

'Oh cripes, I didn't mean it to come out that way. Forgive me, Miss Askew, I don't know the first thing about railways and clearly have my facts completely wrong.' He smiled. 'I'd like to hear about what you do.'

Rather to his surprise, she talked about the engine shed and caused Irons to smile at her charmingly out-of-date notion that she should 'not give away exactly where it was, as one cannot be sure who might be listening.' She'd confided this whilst tapping her nose conspiratorially: 'Mum's the word.'

She must have picked up these wartime sayings from her parents, or older colleagues, and thought it cute to weave them into her conversation. Either way, she had let slip the name 'Woodford', and if she meant Woodford Halse, then, as this was nowhere near Amersham, travelling this part of the line was not connected with her job. This was a little confusing and on top of that, there was something about her story that did not seem to quite add up. He could not think how to challenge her, or to press her to clarify anything without coming across as intrusive, demanding or pushy. These thoughts were soon brushed aside, because he was more than content to just look at her, and to listen whilst she talked of the Dirty Girls Brigade.

'The engines steam and sigh like stabled beasts in the smoky shed', she continued, 'just like racehorses back from the gallops and in their stalls. I swear they are alive! As alive as any beast in the fields.' She became more animated as she got into her stride, telling of how she and the other girls would 'clamber over these magnificent machines like proper tomboys', scraping at layers of caked muck and grease, washing and scrubbing or raking clinker and barrowing away the contents of the ash pans and smoke boxes.

'In winter the engines without fires in them for a night or more turn so bone-chillingly cold your fingers stick to the metal because the frost is like strong glue. It can hurt you really badly. They look quite magical, though, rimed white all over, the hoar frost touching each rivet head, the wheel spokes and motion, everything picked out in white as if by an artist's brush. It is like those photographs you see in the paper that are too dark and they've painted in the highlights with white.'

Irons was captivated by her poetic turn of phrase. Her air of sadness seem to evaporate as she lost herself in recounting tales of the jokes, songs and the laughter the girls shared during their work. Her eyes regained some of their sparkle, and he could see they were blue as a summer sky. And then, just once, she laughed heartily with a light trilling sound free of constraint. It was like music to his ears, and yet she seemed to surprise herself by so doing, and this broke the spell. She stopped abruptly, frowned and withdrew into herself, as if annoyed for allowing any uncontrolled expression of pleasure.

An uncomfortable silence fell, the easy communion between them lost just as quickly as it had started, like a soap bubble that expands into a large and glorious shape described by swirling vibrant colours, only for it to suddenly burst in a tiny flurry of tears. As the uncomfortable silence extended, the guard sauntered along the corridor and glanced in at their compartment without slowing his pace, his gaze briefly meeting that of Irons for an instant until he passed out of sight.

Irons bit the inside of his lip, wondering at the curious contradictions of Miss Askew. He was sure she had explained earlier that she disliked her work and yet she was definitely excited when in full flow about life in the loco shed. It was very curious, and compounded his theory that women were delightfully perplexing.

However, there was a more important question that had been nagging away at him since their first meeting, and he decided to chance his arm and risk asking it, knowing that he must hear her answer even if it was not to his liking.

'I can't help noticing that you are always holding your ring finger, as if perhaps you —' He faltered, then plunged in, '— you once wore a ring and are missing it?'

She darted a look towards him, then dropped her gaze to her hands that were indeed twisting and turning again around the finger in question, caressing the place where a wedding or engagement ring would lie. 'I do? Yes, I suppose I must, now you mention it.' She shook her head, sadly. 'I do miss it — more than I can say. And yet I sometimes wonder if it is for the best that it's gone. It brought me no luck.'

'I am hazarding a guess that you were once married.' Irons held his breath. This was dangerous ground.

She nodded. Hands now still. Her chest heaved as she took a deep breath, 'Well, engaged to be. We had such dreams and hopes for the future, for when the war...' She fell silent, as if the effort of completing the sentence was too much.

'I'm sorry.' Irons considered this revelation for a moment, struck by the realisation that she must be older than her appearance suggested if she had become engaged during wartime, for peace had come five years before. That would make her at least twenty-one... which was possible...and yet... He then mentally slapped himself on the forehead for being so slow. She obviously meant the Korean War, which had started but a matter of weeks ago. Crikey, then no wonder she was feeling so blue. Her fiancé must have died very recently. Perhaps she had just received the news the first time they had met? It made complete sense. Hell's bells, he'd better show some sensitivity.

'Can I take it that he didn't return? Sorry, that sounds so beastly. I'm sorry, but I can't think how else to put the question.'

'Beastly, but true.' She gave a rueful shake of the head. 'I saw the letter they sent his parents. It stated that Ray had been *lost in action while engaged with an enemy aircraft on the front line.* It was a lie: he was not lost. They knew perfectly well where he was. He was killed. Killed in his armoured car near — well, it does not matter where. Of course, it was a successful push for our boys, so I suppose it was not in vain. I should feel proud of what he did. I am proud, of course I am. But all the same...' She let the sentence hang unfinished and briefly stopped wringing her right hand around the fingers of her left in order to touch, perhaps unconsciously, a regimental cap badge she was wearing in her lapel that occasionally caught some of the sickly light in the compartment.

'I truly am most dreadfully sorry.' He sat upright and leant towards her, one hand on his knee in dangerously close proximity to hers, trying desperately to resist the temptation to give her leg a friendly squeeze.

She looked up in response to the movement and gave a quick smile. 'Thank you. You are kind. I think you are a good man.'

'I don't know about that! But I would have to be made of stone not be touched by your story.' He felt a flush of guilt for harbouring private thoughts that were rather less honourable than she imagined, although he did feel genuine concern for her.

'Miss Askew, you're still so young... and as time passes the pain will fade and eventually you will start to look towards the future again. There's still so much life ahead for you.'

She looked perplexed, just as she had done once before, as though something he said made no sense to her. 'There is nothing ahead for me. Nothing at all.'

'Oh goodness, you mustn't talk like that. Life feels bleak now, but...'

Her eyes filled with tears.

'Oh dear, now I've upset you. I really am a blundering, insensitive clod.'

She shook her head and dabbed her eyes with a small handkerchief. 'No. You haven't — truly. Don't feel bad. It's nothing you've said.'

'Are you in some kind of trouble? Aside from your dreadful loss, that is? Perhaps I can help in some way.'

She looked at him through liquid eyes and he felt his heart melt. He wanted to hold her, comfort her, dry her tears and protect and cherish her forever. She dropped her gaze and gave a little nod of her head. 'There *is* something: I need help to right a dreadful wrong. I must lay something to rest and can only do so by seeking a form of...redress. But I fear it will not be easy.'

'Say it, and I'll do it! Whatever it is, I will do it — and gladly.'

'Don't be too hasty. It will not be easy.'

'Just tell me how I can help!' Irons felt a surge of excitement.

'It's my engagement ring. I no longer have it, but it meant so much. I want someone to help me... Oh, gosh!' She suddenly looked agitated, urgently turning her head to peer at the blackness beyond the window, her demeanour now one of extreme anxiety. 'We're nearly at Brackley. We'll soon cross the viaduct!'

'We will? I say, you must know this line awfully well, as I can't see a darned thing out there!' Irons cupped his hands around his eyes and peered out of the window into the night, but all he could see was a poor reflection of his own dark eyes and a few indeterminate shapes of trees moving against an almost equally darkened sky.

'I must go. We shall talk more another time.'

'But you've not told me how I can help.'

She began to stand up and so he did the same. They found themselves standing close together within the narrow well between the facing bench seats, both swaying to the rhythm of the train. Irons was shivering, desperately fighting to control the strong physical tremors gripping him and chilling him to the core; it was in complete contrast to the delicious frisson he felt looking at this young and lithe woman just inches away.

'Please don't be so downhearted, things will get better, I promise.' She looked up at him, dewy-eyed and appealing. She seemed to be willing him to kiss her. He tilted his head and moved it slowly forward in order to reach her lips with his, but her eyes suddenly widened and she pulled back as if stung, trying to avoid his touch. Did she scream? Or was it a long, sustained pull on the train whistle that wailed through the night and which reverberated inside his head and bounced around the small compartment?

What happened next was a blur. He saw her rush out of the open compartment door in a flash of summer dress and bundle of pale coat, hair tumbling onto her neck. He heard her call 'Next time!' to him over her shoulder, then suddenly the momentum of the braking train must have caused him to lose his balance because he lurched forward and fell face-first onto the seats.

He now leant on his hands, which were sunken into the soft cushions, feeling the old springs groaning beneath the horsehair stuffing, his nose pressed hard into the faded jazzy plush that smelt of old books and soot, and feeling thoroughly foolish.

That was a dumb move. He'd pushed things too quickly. He screwed his eyes closed for a moment, praying that he'd not ruined everything. But as he hauled himself upright, patted his clothes back into line and adjusted his hat, he was also shaking his head, not in self-rebuke, but puzzlement.

He had reached out just a couple of inches towards her, and in those brief moments had drunk in the sight of her light brown hair and the smooth, porcelain paleness of her skin, seeing it all with the startling clarity such intimacy offered, and yet, somehow, he had fallen over without even so much as glancing against her or feeling her clothes touch his. He had reached for her, but felt nothing; there was no contact when he'd tried to kiss her, and the shock and surprise of this failure to connect had tipped him beyond the point of recovery. In a kind of wild desperation he'd flung his arms around her, intending to steady them both. But he had missed her completely! How the heck had he managed *that*?

There had been a most peculiar sensation of falling *through* her, as though she were nothing but a mirage, as insubstantial as a cloud of steam. It was almost as though she were a... No, no; this was the way to madness. Quite impossible. Irrational. Maths teachers did not dabble with the irrational.

'Idiot, idiot, idiot!' Irons cursed aloud. He stopped, his attention now drawn to a tiny, but carefully-folded piece of paper lying on the seat. It was pale and very distinct against the mellow greens of the seat fabric and he was sure it had not been there before. Betty Askew must have dropped it as she left in such a hurry.

There was no time to think about what it contained now, so he stuffed it into one of his trouser pockets whilst hurriedly alighting from the compartment, eager that she not leave the station without his apologising for his appalling behaviour. He wiped his face with one hand, again feeling hot and flushed and no longer in the least shivery, and stepped out onto the platform. Betty Askew was nowhere to be seen. He stared along the gas-lit platform at a country gentleman hefting what looked like a fishing tackle bag onto his shoulder, and at the elderly lady with the stick being assisted by a porter, and wondered where the girl could possibly have gone. No more than a few seconds had passed before he had raced onto the platform, nothing like long enough for her to have crossed the platform and climbed enough stairs to be out of sight. She must still be on the train.

The guard was walking alongside the four carriages checking that each was empty and closing any open doors and windows. Irons followed behind him, painfully aware that this was turning into a nightmarish rerun of his previous experience. When they both reached the back end of the train the guard turned to face him.

'Can I help you, sir?' he asked, slightly suspicious of being followed. Irons turned sideways so that he could keep watch down the length of the train and the virtually-deserted platform as he replied.

'I'm looking for a young lady, she is wearing a pale green sundress and carrying a pale mac — did you see her?'

'She's meeting you?'

'No, she was on this train. You remember: you saw her in the compartment with me. Did you see where she went when she got off?'

'Nobody of that description was on this train, sir. She did not get on, she wasn't on board when I walked through, and she didn't get off.' Despite having three chances, the guard didn't notice her. Clearly he was outstandingly unobservant, and so she could easily still be on board.

'Then she's still inside', asserted Irons. He turned the handle of the nearest carriage door and opened it part-way, but the guard took a couple of steps forward and slammed it closed.

'Not so fast, sir. We terminate the train here, so you mustn't reboard, as we shall draw the empty carriages forward out of the station in a few minutes before reversing into the opposite side of this platform for the return journey. So, about this young lady. Did you have a tiff, or do something to upset her?' He gave Irons a steady look that challenged him to reply.

'No, everything is fine.'

The guard was not convinced and held his look, forcing Irons to continue.

'All right. We had a—a minor misunderstanding. It was nothing,' Irons added. 'She left the compartment just as we came to a stop and now I can't find her.' Irons gave an insincere grin but one he hoped would appease the guard.

'I see. Well, this is what I'll do, lad.' He spoke slowly and ponderously as if carefully weighing each word in a manner that was intensely irritating to Irons. 'As I walk to the other end again, I shall take another look inside the train to try and find this poor young lady whom you appear to have so recklessly misplaced, and meanwhile I suggest you wait along there by the exit steps in case she tries to make a run for it.' It sounded like a joke but the guard was not smiling, and neither of them laughed. 'I should warn you, young man, I take a very hard line on any funny business on my train — is that understood?'

'Funny business? Look here, that's a darned cheek!' But Irons lacked conviction, aware that he'd tried to kiss Miss Askew, quite possibly prompting her to run away, so rather than argue the point, he just turned on his heel and walked towards the stairs, peering anxiously into each carriage window as he did so.

The guard walked the length of the train a third time, humouring Irons by making a great show of looking through the windows into all the compartments once again. Reaching his brake compartment at the very rear, he stepped in and leaned out of the window. With a quick flick of his wrist he flashed a green-shaded light with his paraffin hand-lamp as a starting signal to the fireman standing waiting in the cab of the hissing tank engine. The train left the platform.

The stationmaster in his long-tailed coat and glossy top hat had overheard and observed the foregoing with professional curiosity. 'Is there anything amiss, sir?' He reminded Irons of the headmaster and this immediately put him on edge.

'My, er, friend, er, lady friend, that is, got off the train but I cannot find her. She has not left the station, yet there's no sign of her on the train: the guard has checked three times and I, twice.'

'A missing person?' The stationmaster looked concerned, glancing from one to the other. 'That's most worrying, and a young lady, you say?'

'I don't suppose she's *missing...*' Irons felt embarrassed. 'Not in that sense. You really don't need to be alarmed, it is just odd how she managed to be off the train so quickly, that's all.' He removed his hat and ran his fingers through his hair, feeling thoroughly exasperated.

The stationmaster furrowed his brow and stroked his thick beard. 'I, too am, perplexed. No young lady, lost or otherwise, left that train. Could she not have got off at an earlier stop?'

'No, we were sitting in the same compartment until the train arrived here.'

The train drew slowly forward into the siding, until it was clear of the points. A minute later the points scraped across and there was a quiet, metallic crash as the ground signal dipped, displaying its soft, green glow. With that the guard, leaning out of the window, swung his handlamp slowly from side to side and, with a short, shrill blast on its whistle, the engine began to push the carriages backwards into the station, the guard keeping a sharp look-out from the brake compartment in the leading end. Once the train drew to a halt alongside the platform he screwed down the handbrake, stepped out, lifted the paraffin tail-lamp off its bracket and walked the length of the train once more. As he did so, the fireman uncoupled the engine and, after checking the signalman had pulled off the ground signal, gave his driver the right-away to run the engine round to the other end of the train. The guard attached the tail-lamp to what was now going to be the rear of the train, and walked over to join Irons and the stationmaster.

'Like I told you', he continued, as though he had never left, 'I never saw anyone meeting her description board the train, nor step off at any station along the way. And she's definitely not still on there', he pointed a thumb over his shoulder to the engineless carriages. 'So how do you explain that, eh?' The guard spoke in a ponderous, pedantic voice with more than a hint of scepticism.

'She was in the compartment with me the whole time, as close as you are to me now! You must have seen her when you walked past! Are you saying you don't believe me?'

'You boarded at Marylebone. Alone. I saw you myself!'

'Yes, that's correct. She boarded at Amersham. I'm sorry but this is just wasting time, I must go after her...'

'But no girl boarded at Amersham. Only two middle-aged gentlemen, both bound for Calvert, and then there was Colonel Bradshaw, with his fishing rods.'

The stationmaster glanced from Irons to the guard and back, with a look of growing impatience. 'Is a young lady missing, or is she not? One of you claims she was on the train, the other denies she ever got on board. Gentlemen, kindly explain yourselves!'

'She must have darted off the train in double-quick time, raced up the stairs and evaded us all. Please, don't think anything more about it.' Without waiting for their response, Irons flew two-at-a-time up the long flight of creaking wooden stairs, hoping optimistically that she would still be somewhere within sight, or even on the station forecourt, waiting for a taxi, for her father — or even, dare he hope — for him.

'What a curious affair', remarked the stationmaster. 'Perhaps she's a fare dodger.'

CHAPTER TEN
On the London Extension
17th September 1950

Edward Earnshaw was worried about the rapidly-falling steam pressure and what the gauge glasses were telling him. He could see that water was sloshing about the glasses with the rocking and rolling motion of their rough-riding K3 type locomotive, giving the impression there was plenty left in the boiler, but he knew that once they settled into a smoother ride, the water would do likewise and show it to be dangerously low. He needed to get the injector on, but this would just pump gallons of cold water into the boiler and further depress the failing steam pressure, and if it went much lower they'd be out of puff. It was a tricky situation, and he needed to deal with it.

He glanced nervously across at his driver, half leaning out of the cab, his grizzled, weather-beaten face staring into the night, one arm stretched across the boiler back-head to rest on the regulator handle, the other crooked beneath his body over the narrow cab side.

Driver Boswell had been holding this position for the last twenty minutes or so, peering into the banks of mist rising from the fields and collecting in the gentle folds of the Buckinghamshire countryside, concentrating hard so as not to miss a signal light winking through these opaque clouds that indiscriminately spanned the twin tracks on their run north.

It was not raw, but the night still had an edge, sharpened by their forward movement, and Eddie reckoned Boswell must be pretty near frozen down one side and mightily sick of being pelted by the bits of char and burning cinders that bounced off his face and grease-top cap like a shower of tiny stones. But the old pro remained stoical, silent, intent on the job in hand, the glow of the fire illuminating his profile in brilliant orange when the fire doors were opened, at other times just a faintly-etched shape against the indigo night and the moving backdrop of smoke.

Eddie felt guilty for letting him down, but the fire simply would not burn properly and had not done so since they left Cricklewood. Now he was in danger of committing one of the cardinal sins of an aspiring fireman: not providing enough steam for the job. This would be a humiliating embarrassment and invite a barrage of derision and leg-pulling at the loco in the days to follow. As a cleaner with aspirations to making the next grade following an exam booked in for the following month, it was not going to look good if he ran out of steam. Even worse if he caused the boiler to run dry and drop the fusible plug, so releasing the remaining water in the boiler onto the fire to douse it. That would both cause damage to the engine and block the line until they could be rescued.

His predicament was made worse because this was the return leg of the first day on what he'd been promised was to be his roster for at least two weeks: working a long and fast trip to London and back. It was a significant step up from the usual grind of shunting around the yards at Woodford Halse or the short runs up to Leicester North Yard that was his usual diet. It had filled him with pride that morning when Shedmaster Saunders had chalked his name on the board beside this run, but now any such thrill had evaporated, rather like his steam, and he felt a helpless sinking inside as he realised he was going to blow it — rather than blow the safety valves.

'Damn this dirty, rotten stuff! It's bloody useless!' Eddie gave a rare curse and dug his shovel into the mound of poor quality coal and prodded and probed for something decent to feed the flames. Rivers of dust and tiny pieces of slack cascaded out of the tender front, flowing over the shovel and onto the wooden floor, adding to the many pieces crunching beneath his booted feet.

'What you doing with that fire? I need steam!' Driver Boswell had responded by glancing into the cab and his experienced eye needed only moments to register the situation.

'It's the coal — it won't burn!' He had to shout to be heard over the roar of the engine and the rattle of the unfitted freight coupled behind.

'Yeah? Looks like coal to me,' Driver Boswell's voice was sarcastic. He gave the steam gauge another sharp glance and pulled a face. 'That's no use. Put your back into it, lad!' He returned to staring into the night air. 'And get some water in the boiler!' The shout came from over his shoulder.

Eddie whacked open the fire doors and flipped his shovel over to deflect the worst of the fierce heat and bright light that made his eyes water as he peered into the roaring pit, searching for the reason he was losing steam. He groaned. Instead of the evenly spread incandescent bed of merrily burning coals, he could see a great mass to one side, sitting like an ugly dead weight licked by small blue and purple flames. Over half his fire was not burning properly and he could see clinker forming on the fire bars. It needed drastic action.

Taking a deep breath, he turned on the water supply and worked the steam injector until he heard the distinctive rushing sound as it engaged. He kicked the damper lever on the floor to open it wide, turning the blower on full before throwing a quick four rounds of coal onto the healthier side of the conflagration. He slammed the doors closed with an impatient clang and leant out of his side of the cab to watch the chimney. The smoke was not turning a filthy black as it should, despite being lifted clear of the boiler by the rush of air from the blower.

He ducked back and rattled the fire irons on the tender top as he tried to find the 'long pricker'. These irons were long bars, some up to twelve foot, with big, looped handles at one end and various shapes at the other. Eddie thought they looked like giant sardine can keys made for Gulliver. He found them hard to manoeuvre so that the far end — which was a sharpened point bent over at ninety degrees in the case of the long pricker — faced the firebox, whilst being careful to not let it poke out of the cab and risk striking a bridge or signal post. Fortunately, his engine was a type known to the men as a 'Ragtimer', probably because of their distinctive syncopated beat and unsteady gait, and these had a very open cab and tender that was useless for keeping the bad weather out, but did facilitate swinging the fire irons around.

Eddie started to riddle the lump of poorly burning coal and chip at the clinker gripping the fire bars. His arms were soon aching with the effort and the pricker refused to go quite where he wanted it. After taking too long in this task, he carefully eased the now red-hot iron out of the fire, concentrating with justified nervousness on the glowing tip as he swung it away from the driver, his eyes burning with great bobs of coloured light that swam in a disorienting manner, the engine swinging with its Scott Joplin-esque rhythm beneath his feet and rendering him unsteady. He gave it a mighty shove, intending to launch the long pricker onto the mound of coal behind, but stared, mortified, as it bounced once with a metallic twang, and then flew off the side and onto the line.

Oh heck! I don't believe it! He closed his eyes for a moment hoping this would somehow undo that he'd seen. He had to pray it had not landed across the rails of the other line. Should he alert his driver so they could stop and recover it? Eddie's stomach churned with apprehension that he might be the cause of an accident.

'Ach, it's no good. We're out of puff. Well and truly stuffed!' Driver Boswell turned to face Eddie at that same moment, giving him an inscrutable look as though challenging him to speak, but Eddie felt his nerve fail and he remained silent. The driver eased the regulator back a touch. 'I'll limp her along as far as Brackley then see what can be done. Sunday evening and all! Worst bloody luck...'

'It's the coal. And this blasted engine.'

'What about the blasted fireman?' He took a deep breath as if about to lay into Eddie, but seemed to change his mind. 'Keep your eyes on the road and holler the moment you see a signal.' Driver Boswell stood up and stretched his back for a moment, indicating that Eddie should take his place with a nod of his head. 'Let's see what a pig's ear you've made here...'

Eddie stepped over to the driver's side and leant out to look ahead along the line. Despite feeling sick at his shoddy performance, he got an instant frisson of excitement taking control of the engine, even if it was wheezing like a sick coal miner and coasting down a slight incline at no great speed.

The driver took his turn peering into the fire, rattling the remaining fire irons for a moment before expertly swinging one into place as though it weighed nothing and was but a few feet in length. It was soon put back in another deft move, and he started to hurl heaped shovels of coal onto the fire in smooth, almost lazy movements. Eddie glanced across and marvelled at the ease and confidence he displayed.

'Keep yer eye on the bloody road!'

Eddie quickly looked back along the engine boiler and at the plume of dark grey smoke, a rich flash of red occasionally licking at the rim of the chimney.

'Distant! All clear!' Eddie shouted as he spotted the black and yellow board pointing skywards.

'Uh huh,' grunted Driver Boswell, who banged the fire doors shut and squinted at the gauges. 'That'll be Brackley down distant. We'll make the station, any road.' He nodded his head to indicate that Eddie should now move out of the way. 'Bloody useless!'

Eddie cringed.

'Tubes are clogged; the fire arch dropped and the big end's knocking like billy-o. Can you hear that clunking? And she's leaking steam like a sieve.'

The young fireman nodded assent, but stayed quiet, staring mournfully at the steam pressure gauge. The fall plate he was standing upon occasionally banged against the tender as the tired engine swayed and rolled, whilst he listened out for the other, more ominous, knocking sound the driver had identified.

'When we get to Woodford, I'll sign her off failed. Remember the number — 61835 and avoid it like the plague! A friggin' disgrace giving us this, the little buggers. Sixty-one, eighty-three flippin' five!' Driver Boswell shook his head slowly in disbelief, but then suddenly stood upright in a movement that jolted Eddie out of his blue reverie. Boswell slammed the regulator shut with a loud curse, then rapidly started winding the engine back into neutral, whilst his other hand applied the brakes in a series of short, sharp applications, at no time taking his eyes off the road ahead.

'Bloody hell! There's a woman on the line!' His shout was harsh and cut through the noise of the footplate, the fear clearly audible in his voice.

The train was moving not much over fifteen miles an hour, but with a string of loaded box-vans behind; on a falling grade it was still going to take time to stop. Worse still, Driver Boswell needed to be careful not to cause a ripple down the train as each four-wheeled wagon collided with the next, creating a dangerous tidal wave of energy that could seriously injure the poor guard in his van at the tail, and perhaps also breaking some coupling chains along the way.

Boswell continued to work the brakes, expertly slowing the train, winding the valve gear into reverse. Both men on the footplate felt the jarring and banging of their complaining train behind, sensing the great weight of the vans pressing against them as a barely-controllable force. Making a rapid stop, even at this modest speed, was to experience a sickening sense of helplessness as the momentum carried them relentlessly forwards, aided by rails rendered greasy by the cooling night.

'Is she crazy?' Boswell held the whistle cord and gave a series of long and angry blasts. If an engine could adopt the emotions of a sentient being, then their Ragtimer was furious.

Eddie looked over the driver's shoulder and could just make out, some way ahead, the slight figure of a young woman in a dress partially covered by what might be a pale mackintosh. He could discern few details other than the equally pale oval of her face turned towards them and he thought one of her arms pointed to the side as if indicating something. He bit his lower lip and winced at the sound of squealing brakes and gripped the tender side.

Fortunately, the woman responded to the screaming whistle and stepped off the track. Eddie felt the tightness around his chest release. She ran towards the wooden fencing that protected the line in a fluid movement that gave Eddie the curious sensation she was little more than a shadow flowing smoothly and soundlessly across the land. He felt a prickle of perspiration form on his brow and a tremor of nerves as she paused to look back at them one last time, before disappearing down the embankment.

'Stupid cow!' Boswell thumped the cab side with a balled fist. 'We could have bloody killed her.' Despite his rage, the driver's voice held more than a trace of genuine relief, and as the train finally came to a stand and Eddie wound the hand brake down to hold it steady, Boswell took a moment to mop his brow with a grubby blue neckerchief pulled from his overalls.

'Golly — that was close!' Eddie realised he was shaking.

'Not half. Look out for Bob at the back, I'm going to see what that silly cow's bloody well playing at.' Boswell swung himself out of the cab and dropped on to the ballast whilst Eddie remained standing at the cab side. Now the danger was over and his initial alarm quietened, it seemed a bit of an anticlimax looking at the empty track.

Eddie liked this approach to Brackley, which in the 'down' direction was signposted by first passing through a deep cutting and dipping under the distinctively skewed Buckingham Road Bridge. He looked back along the train and could see they had cleared the black outline of the bridge and that the cutting was falling away on either side, leaving the locomotive exposed on top of the embankment that led onto the long, curving viaduct. The town was just a distant sprinkle of lights across a hill to his left, and Eddie could make out the belfry on the town hall. The Ouse Valley, however, was a mass of formless dark, pierced by a few dimly-illuminated windows peeking through a sheet of mist that had collected at the bottom. How the driver thought he was going to find the girl in all that, he was not sure.

The handlamp of Guard Bob Goodless was now flashing as he made his way forward alongside the train. At least he was OK, and no doubt coming down to enquire what they were playing at by slamming the brakes full on with little or no warning.

Eddie peered at the fire and saw it was burning slightly better and the needle at least steady, if not climbing across the pressure gauge. He dropped down onto the ground to meet the guard.

'That were a nasty surprise! What's up?'

'We were forced to slam the brakes on. There was someone on the line.'

The guard pulled a face and rubbed his shoulder. 'I see. Damn nearly ripped my bloody arms out.' He winced as he touched a sore spot. 'I felt summat was not right immediately, and when I heard the warning sounds coming down the train, I bloody well knew what to expect.' He rubbed an elbow. 'I had to hold onto the brake pillar for dear life, but no real harm done, all things considered.'

'We'd have run her down otherwise.'

The guard gingerly flexed a shoulder. 'Aye, well... Where's driver?'

'He went looking for her. She was just standing right in the middle of the track!'

'Not again! She's becoming a ruddy nuisance.'

'You mean she's done this before?' Eddie was incredulous.

'Oh aye. Last night and a few before that. It's been the talk of all the lads around here this month past.'

'Then someone had better keep a look out and arrest her. She's a menace! She needs locking up!' Boswell reappeared at the front of the K3, chuntering loudly and with a face like thunder. 'She's going to have a short life playing daft games like that. Jesus, Mary and Joseph...' He bent down and peered at a drift of steam softly issuing from somewhere between the wheels. 'Must be doolally.' His voice softened as he straightened up again, having vented his rage. 'You all right, Bob?'

'As well as can be expected. I'll be bruised blue by tomorrow, though. No sight of her, then?'

'Nah. Too dark down the bank to see anything. It's all trees and bushes.'

The guard grimaced and shook his head, 'It's a strange business, that much is for sure. Well, I'd best check the couplings are sound. I'll signal from my van when it's OK to move off.'

'Right. I'll just ease us into Brackley; we need to lay over for a bit of a blow. Soft lad here made a right hump in the fire.' Boswell grinned at Eddie. It was as though he wanted to lighten the mood with a bit of joshing, and so help dispel any residual shock.

'Hehe!' Goodless winked at Eddie. 'Thought it was a slow run.' He laughed again, and then winced as doing so highlighted an area that was sore from being thrust against the brake pillar. 'We're protected here — the signalman's dropped the distant peg and can no doubt see us from the box, so we won't get shunted from behind, at least. Give it a few minutes here and then see how it goes, eh?' With that, Bob Goodless stumped off, shining his lamp beam between the wagons.

Boswell pulled out a metal tobacco tin with *Craven A* on the lid and opened it. 'Smoke?' He handed a thin, hand-rolled cigarette to Eddie without waiting for a reply then selected a second from the pre-assembled collection.

They stood in companionable silence for a few moments. The sound of Boswell's lighter flipping open and the rasp of the flint was the only communication between them. Their engine hissed and dripped quietly, the metal occasionally ticking and creaking, the boiler gurgling, but otherwise all was still. A sickly green moon slid behind a thin veil of cirrus minor as a growling lorry on the climb through town missed a gear before settling back into a low murmur.

They both pricked up their ears at a series of strange, clear and yet breathy piping sounds, not unlike numerous children's toys being squeezed in rapid succession from somewhere high above.

Whee-oh, whee-oh, wheep...

Driver Boswell cocked his head to one side, his brow furrowing as he took a long lungful of smoke and held it inside. 'That explains it,' he exclaimed, smoke streaming from his nostrils. He surprised Eddie by crossing himself.

Wheep, whee-oh, whee...wheep

The plaintive sounds moved across the sky. They were soft, yet surprisingly audible, a complex series of high whistles and calls.

'Explains what?'

'All that's gone wrong tonight. Them whistlers warn of trouble. They know when there's something bad going to happen. A warning, and not a curse just as long as there's only the six of them!' Boswell made a rueful expression. 'Mebbe that's why she cleared off the line?' He looked troubled, tossing his cigarette to the ground as if he'd suddenly lost the taste for it and was staring into the ragged clouds stained green and silver by moonlight. Eddie thought he was trying to count the calls.

'They're widgeon. A bit early, though.' Eddie's voice was light. 'I'd normally expect them to come in next month.' He was born and bred in the village of Woodford Halse and, despite the overpowering presence of the locomotive shed and wagon works and the vast, sprawling acres of sidings, it was surrounded for miles in each direction by open farmland, woods, coppices and meandering streams and so, like any country lad, he could tell a widgeon from a teal or a mallard.

'Widgeon? That's what you think? Aye, they might look the part all right, I'll grant you that.' Boswell shook his head deliberately in an ominous motion, the whites of his eyes shining in the moonlight. 'Listen to 'em!' His voice was a hoarse whisper. 'They're soul birds, that's what they are. They send shivers down your spine.'

The strange, thin piping calls wheeled across the sky, and Eddie sensed a growing unease. It was indeed an odd sound, especially when disembodied from the birds that he could not locate amidst the clouds. He'd never thought the sound haunting before, but as the ducks wheeled above, sending their piping calls from first one direction then another, he could appreciate why his driver found it so. They were just ducks of course, strangely late on the wing and probably looking for water to roost upon for the night — but seeing this tough, experienced, railwayman acting so fearful was unnerving. If his grandmother was talking like this, he would just laugh at her silly superstitions and humour her, but coming from Boswell it made him question what was really happening.

'Look there — against the moon!' Eddie pointed, and they both tracked the unmistakable silhouettes of the waterfowl flying in a loose formation as the clouds ripped apart to create a silver-fringed gap. 'Could they be teal?' He asked the question in an attempt to break the acute tension palpable between them.

'Six... can you see the seventh?' Boswell was staring into the sky as if his life depended on it, his skin drained of all colour by the cold light. 'Lord help us we don't find another,' he muttered under his breath. 'There's a death when seven come.'

'I think there's just six.'

'Just a warning. Perhaps we've used up our bad luck for tonight, eh?'

'I don't know...' Eddie fiddled with his cigarette.

'We'd have killed her if the seventh had whistled.'

Eddie remained silent. The piping was growing fainter, but he was nervous. He wanted to be away from here.

Driver Boswell gave Eddie a hard look. 'It was a warning of a death if we don't retrieve that missing iron! Maybe that's what we're being warned about? She was pointing. The girl was pointing at something beside the track, did you not see? And then the whistlers came...it makes sense.'

'Er, yes, I suppose so.' Eddie tried to swallow, but his mouth was dry and bitter with the hard tobacco smoke. Again, he felt unsettled by his driver's surprisingly deep-rooted belief in something that sounded like silly superstition. But Boswell had a point, he'd not only rumbled the fire iron falling onto the track, but there was no doubting it had the potential to cause an accident.

'Was you going to speak up, or just hope I didn't notice?'

'I—I was. Honest! But then there was the emergency stop and the girl on the line, and then checking on Bob at the back....'

'Yeah?' Boswell shrugged this away. 'Well, now we've got time on our hands, *you* can advise the signalman at Brackley about what *you* did. Clumsy oaf. He'll have to send a man to walk the line and retrieve the pricker, you do realise that? One long walk for some poor old bugger. Let's just hope that's what they're whistling for and we prevent a nasty accident.'

Eddie felt an involuntary shiver down his body. A sensation his mother claimed happened when someone walked over your grave. The thin, reedy piping came again across the night air, but now far quieter.

'What are they? The soul birds?'

Driver Boswell fixed his beady eyes on Eddie for a moment as if trying to formulate a satisfactory answer. 'They're the Seven Whistlers. Some folk claim they're the lost souls of unbaptised children who died young and are doomed to wander the skies forever. I've always believed they are the undying dead. Unhappy and tormented souls of murdered folk whose bodies have never been found and properly laid to rest.' His voice was low and earnest. Eddie's eyes opened as wide as saucers. 'Really?'

'You might scoff, but ignore their warning at your peril!' Boswell wagged his finger at him to reinforce his point.

Eddie could think of nothing to say in reply to this. He hurriedly clambered back into the warm cab, muttering something about checking his fire, and busied himself with practicalities, trying to clear his mind of this strange talk by concentrating on earthly matters of coal, fire and water.

CHAPTER ELEVEN
Brackley
17th September 1950

It made no sense to Irons. He was standing at the open door of the booking hall, slightly winded by his recent exertions on the stairs, looking out onto the short, semicircular service road that turned off the A43 and which was empty save for a shiny, blue-and-black Austin taxi. The driver of this vehicle was leaning on the bonnet with one foot nonchalantly resting on a broad mudguard whilst he hand-rolled a cigarette, a cap pushed to the back of his head, allowing the lamplight to shine on slicked hair furrowed with comb lines.

'You the last one out?'

'It looks that way.' Irons ran a hand over his face. 'I say, did you see in which direction the young lady went? She was the one in green.'

'Sorry, no young women went past here in any colour dress — more's the pity. Except Mrs Mathers, of course, but as she can't be a day short of eighty, I can't think you mean her.' The taxi driver grinned. 'What's up, mate?'

Irons puffed his cheeks full of air then slowly exhaled, trying to release some of the tension building in his chest. 'Is there another way out of the station, do you know?'

'This is both entrance and exit, that's why I'm here. Well, saying that, I suppose you could always walk up the goods road. Bit of a drag and all dark at this time of night, though.' He wrinkled his nose.

'I see. And where does that come out?'

The driver pointed with his thumb towards town. 'Over that way behind the trees; it drops down pretty steep to the side of the station. She done a runner on you, then?' His voice was laughing, the little cigarette bouncing on his lip as he spoke and sending a cloud of smoke around his face.

'It rather looks that way.' Irons tried to keep the same jocular tone, but stopped from saying more. He had no right to be telling just anyone about his meeting with Miss Askew and reminded himself that this was a small town where word could soon spread. It would not do for a new teacher to get a reputation for being some kind of tearaway. 'She must have gone that way. That explains it. Thanks!' He made to start walking.

'Hop in!' The driver stood up and opened the front passenger door. 'I'll get no more fares tonight.'

'It's all right, thanks. Not far to Magdalen.'

'It's on the house. Gratis. I'm off home now and, since I'm going your way, we can look for your missing girlfriend on the drive. The name's Hancock — Dennis Hancock.'

'Richard Irons. Pleased to meet you.'

He gratefully accepted the lift. He rarely got the opportunity to ride in a car and the comfortable leather seat was a rare indulgence, even if only for a few minutes. On top of that, the taxi driver appeared to be a friendly face and perhaps more worldly-wise than either the guard or the stationmaster, and he might prove useful.

As the old Austin grumbled into life and pulled out onto the deserted main road, both men kept a watchful eye for Miss Askew as they passed the white-painted gate and dark blue enamelled sign that indicated that the inclined road led towards 'British Railways Brackley Central Goods Yard'.

'So what part of town is your girl from?'

'She's not *exactly* my girl, to be honest. We've only recently become acquainted. We've not even discussed where she lives — not yet, anyway.'

The driver glanced across at Irons, the fag still dangling from his mouth, and gave a throaty chortle that was heavy with suggestion. 'Good priorities, mate. You don't want to be wasting time on the domestic side of things when you can just go straight for the "how's-your-father". Haha!'

'Good heavens. Nothing like that; we're not much more than acquaintances at the moment. Botheration, I can't see her anywhere...' Irons was leaning forward in his seat looking out at the empty town. He felt disappointment building inside.

'She could have gone down any one of these side roads, that's your problem. What's her name? I know about every family in town. I certainly know which girls are the lookers!' He gave Irons a conspiratorial wink. 'Pays to keep an eye on the pretty ones.'

They had pulled to a stop at traffic lights protecting a junction, the sound of music and laughter spilling through the open door of The Plough and into the taxi as the dark presence of Magdalen College chapel loomed ahead to their left, framed in a gap between a long avenue of dark trees that had been disfigured by years of pollarding.

'I bet you do!' Irons felt his spirits lift. The man might even know her and offer some information that could prove handy. 'Her name is Betty Askew.'

The taxi driver misjudged letting out the clutch and stalled the Austin. He gave an angry puff on his cigarette, gunned the ignition and pulled away, making the vehicle express his impatience. 'She's not from around here, then?'

'Oh yes, she was born in Brackley. Do you know her? She must be about eighteen, perhaps a touch older. Brown hair, blue eyes...'

The driver frowned and swung the taxi to the left, turning off the broad thoroughfare and down the side road that ran parallel and gave access to the front of the school and the market place. He stopped the taxi under the overreaching arms of a tree that rustled with drying leaves, hinting at the coming autumn. 'I'll drop you here.' His chirpy demeanour had shifted in these brief moments to something darker.

'Perfect. Thanks awfully!'

'You sure about her name? You could have heard it wrong.'

'No, I'm quite sure I've got it right. Oh, one other thing, she told me that she works at Woodford.' He laughed, but for no particular reason, now feeling confident and less reserved about confiding in a stranger. 'She's one of a gang of girls that clean engines up there and...' Irons stopped because the driver had turned his head and glared at him with a look like thunder, the stub of his 'rollie' twitching in the corner of his mouth, a pulsing vein prominent on his neck.

'Listen chum, I don't know what your game is, and I've nothing against a feller chasing the local girls, but you're an out-of-towner, up from the big smoke, if I'm any judge of accent, so you listen to me. Be careful what you go around saying. You might think it's clever. but there are plenty of folk round here who could take exception to what you're doing. Decent people, who could be very hurt. So drop this stupid lark — and get out of my cab!'

'I'm sorry, er, I don't understand, what...?' blurted Irons, genuinely bewildered by the man's abrupt change of attitude towards him. 'What have I said?'

'You're a reporter!' He jabbed an accusatory finger towards Irons.

'No, I'm a schoolteacher.'

The taxi driver spat a piece of tobacco from the corner of his mouth through the opened window. 'You know what I think? I think you're here in the hope of stirring up a story to flog to the papers.'

'No, you've got it all wrong. I don't know anything about any story.'

'Do you know something about what happened to her?'

'I just wanted to meet her again and maybe...well, maybe take her out to the pictures.'

'That's hardly possible, is it? Just let it rest, will you? Forget about the Askews. Leave those poor folk in peace, or else I'll personally come looking for you.' He scowled menacingly. 'Now, hop it!'

Irons opened the car door but just before getting out he paused for a moment, turned to face the man and said, 'I honestly don't understand what I've said to upset you but, whatever it was, I am genuinely sorry. Well, thank you for the lift, and goodnight.' He climbed out of the car and closed the door, looking at Hancock through the open window.

The cabbie's final words to him were spoken in a tone now devoid of anger, but no less clear and forceful for being quiet and controlled. 'Betty Askew is dead — a long time dead. Poor kid.' With that he let out the clutch and the car gently pulled away. Irons stared after the car until its rear lights disappeared from view.

He stood alone on the pavement, feeling lost and mystified. The pollarded trees dropped leaves about him as a gust of wind rattled the stunted branches above. The big harvest moon was casting moving shadows on the ground through the stumpy limbs of the tree. An owl screeched from somewhere beyond the school playing fields and he heard the urgent, insistent whistling of a distant train. He should have heeded its warning.

CHAPTER TWELVE
Amersham
18th September 1950

'There's not a breath of wind, and yet those blessed French doors have still managed to slam and crack a pane of glass. It's beyond the limit, it really is. That must be the third time it's happened,' Isabella Liney looked pale with annoyance. 'I've been telling you to fit hooks and eyes to keep them open for I don't know how long.'

'Again?' Jocelyn Liney shook his head in frustration. 'And I keep telling you that, wind or no wind, a through draft can still cause the doors to slam. Oh, very well, I shall call Parker's later and get them to replace the glass and fit the hooks.' He looked at a ridge of ominous cloud boiling up in the distance, rising above the tall, mature trees that surrounded their garden. 'There could be a storm coming, best you keep the doors closed for now.'

Isabella Liney shivered, despite the strong sun and the humidity building in the air. She shrugged her shoulders as if trying to rid herself of a bad memory. 'It's still odd how the draft is only ever in the dining room and nowhere else.' She pursed her lips for a moment as she composed herself. 'It's always cold in here, have you not noticed?'

'Exactly my point about the doors.' Liney mopped his brow. 'Gosh, it's getting close. A hot day for digging.'

'I can never get that room warm, even on a day like this!' Mrs Liney continued on her theme, worrying away at it. 'I have Doris keep a fire in there every day, but to absolutely no effect. Well, if you get too hot with your digging, just go and sit in the dining room for five minutes! But mind you take your dirty shoes off first.' She still managed to get in a warning, despite her distracted thoughts. 'I'm sorry to say it's my least favourite room. There's plenty of light and such a lovely view onto the garden and yet… and yet, I feel quite ill at ease in there. Sounds silly, but that's the truth of it.'

'Wasnt that room was one of the reasons we bought this place?'

'I know.' She looked uncomfortable. 'But then I hadn't expected it to be as cold as a grave.' She shivered.

'That's a bit strong, old girl!' Liney gave her a funny look, sensing that his wife was not joking. He turned back to the herbaceous border amidst which he was standing and changed the subject. 'Never mind all that now, what I'm thinking is, why we can't get someone in to do this? Amersham must be full of willing tradesmen who would have it cleared in half the time it'll take me. I could arrange it at the same time I instruct Parker's.' Liney ended on an optimistic, questioning note that he knew would be futile.

'I'm quite sure there are, Jocelyn, but that's absolutely *not* the point. You know as well as I that they'll only prevaricate and the next thing one knows it'll be weeks before it's finished, just mark my words.' His wife made a thin line with her mouth. 'It's a perfect summer's day, at the moment at least, and so we must crack on. I've been dreaming of a Gertrude Jekyll style border since the day we moved in, and that was goodness knows how many years ago.'

'Don't I know it?' Liney muttered under his breath. 'Seven years, I think you'll find.'

'Now, if we can get all this horrid stuff cleared out, you can have a bonfire this evening whilst we have a well earned G and T.' Isabella Liney gave her husband one of her arch looks that brooked no dissent and placed a well-manicured hand upon her hip. 'And besides, the exercise will do us a power of good.'

'Hah!' Her husband looked at the long border running down one edge of their garden, thick with matted fronds of ground elder and studded with a motley selection of unhealthy hydrangeas that were once supposed to be blue, but which had long since faded to an unpleasant grey-pink, like bruised flesh. A large, stone bird bath sat in the middle of the border on a plinth, a thick mat of ivy clinging around the base. He grimaced. '*We*? I take it you are referring to me, singular? I can't see you digging this lot out, dearest.'

'It would ruin my manicure; but I'll put my gardening gloves on later and lend a hand making the bonfire — when I return from the nursery, that is.'

'Now that really takes the biscuit; you're swanning off choosing plants whilst I break my back digging this ruddy garden!'

'Language!' She gave a petulant frown. 'Someone has to choose the plants — and choose well. It's a fine art making a border that manages to look perfectly wild and carefree and not just a ragged mess. I have not had my nose in this—' she held up a well-thumbed copy of Gertrude Jekyll's *Colour in the Flower Garden*, '—for nothing these past weeks. You wouldn't know what to buy. And besides, it's *your* waistline that needs the most work. I don't know what they feed you on at the bank, but it must be off-ration, as it's expanding your midriff in line with your bonuses! Whilst the latter are to be welcomed, the former, somewhat less so.'

Liney glanced down at his rotund stomach and at the waistband of his trousers that dipped alarmingly low below its soft overhang. 'One simply has to have lunch, and in a style that befits our company. It goes with the nature of our work at Cazenova's.' He stood upright and made an unsuccessful attempt suck in his flabby belly. 'Actually, we do a lot of exceedingly good business over a bottle of claret and some fine dining.' He looked wistful, as if already dreaming about the substantial and leisurely meals awaiting him in the week ahead. His wife, however, was already walking towards their large, arts-and-crafts styled detached house.

'It'll be the devil's own job,' he called after her, waving an unseen hand at the border.

'Then the sooner you make a start, the quicker you can relax,' she tossed the words over her shoulder.

'I'm not moving that blasted bird bath!'

'I didn't ask you to. Just clear around it, and I'll see what I think once the plants are in. I'll be a couple of hours, so I'm sure you'll be all done by time I'm back.' She gave him a flash of smile. 'I'll tell cook to make us some nice lamb chops for dinner.'

'All done? In a couple of hours?' Liney pulled a sour face and shook his head, but his complaint was lost on his wife, who was now out of earshot. He was resigned to the task ahead, however. His wife insisted that the garden was a job they must to do themselves and absolutely forbade him employing a gardener, even though he could easily afford one, or even two, for that matter.

After staring sadly at the mass of green leaves and wiry fronds a while longer, he looked around as if checking that no one was watching him demean himself with manual labour, though this was highly unlikely, as the garden was protected by a high brick wall draped in sweet-smelling ivy, now alive with bees. He picked up the garden fork and jabbed it into the nearest matt of foliage.

Twenty minutes later he had already made a reasonable pile of grubbed-out elder on an old blanket he had spread out for that purpose on the lawn. He was now perspiring heavily and could feel his back and legs complaining, whilst his hands, that usually wielded little more than an expensive fountain pen, were rubbing raw. He'd been worrying away constantly at the many roots that seemed to lie like sinuous rat-tails through the soil and which would not give up their purchase in the earth unless he put his not inconsiderable weight behind pulling on them. After one especially hard wrestling match, he suddenly found his backside hitting the grass with a bump, with a clump of earth in his hand stuffed with broken roots sticking out like so many severed electrical cables, having unexpectedly snapped free.

'Stupid bloody weeds!'

He was about to toss this aside when his eye was drawn to something entwined within the twisted roots. Easing it out and rubbing most of the loose soil off, he discerned that it was a woman's bracelet.

It was cheaply made, from some kind of plastic, in garish orange and ochre. Liney wrinkled his nose at the poor workmanship and thanked the Lord that Isabella did not have to wear such end-of-the-pier trinkets.

Tossing it onto the blanket without a second thought, he resumed work, but soon ceased again and leant on the fork handle, breathing hard and taking the opportunity for a rest as he contemplated what he had just exposed. A bold robin skipped across the freshly-dug earth and cocked its head as if also inspecting the find.

Liney reached down and released a piece of green material that showed signs of having been extensively burnt before being buried. Despite this combustion, there was still a sizable portion left.

'How the blazes did that get there?' he muttered under his breath, glancing towards the robin as if seeking its opinion.

He stood upright and turned the cloth over in his hands for a moment or two as he considered this discovery, privately cursing the sluttish behaviour of people who could litter their own gardens in this manner. It looked like the remains of a dress, as part of the neckline and the opening of one shoulder could still be identified. He threw this onto the blanket in disgust and, as he did, he noticed that Isabella was fast approaching across their manicured lawn.

'You're back early, checking on me?'

'Not a bit of it. I forgot my purse. What a nuisance; I'd driven all the way there and only realised when I arrived. Oh, what's that?'

'It looks like a piece of dress.'

Isabella took a closer look. 'It's been burnt.'

'Very observant.'

'Is that not a bit odd?'

'Why? People are forever burning waste in their gardens.'

'I suppose not.' Isabella did not look convinced.

'There's a horrid bracelet as well. Here...'

'A young woman's, and inexpensive.'

'You mean cheap.'

'Do you think the dress and bracelet were owned by the same person?'

Liney pushed out his lower lip in thought. 'Possibly.'

'But, look, what's that?' Isabella Liney bent down and eased out of the disturbed earth where the dress fragment had lain, a metal buckle with a short piece of leather strap still threaded through. 'From a handbag, I'd say. Gosh, the little squander-bugs: they must have burnt a frock and a leather handbag, and during strict clothes rationing. Absolutely unforgivable!' The robin flew onto the top of the wall and started to sing, as though broadcasting her sense of outrage.

'We don't know that. It could have lain here since before the war. Besides, this is just a fragment of strap. Perhaps the rest of the bag was re-used for something. Liney looked dismissive. 'Not that we ever had to stoop to that ghastly make-do-and-mend malarkey.' He sniffed in a self-satisfied manner and exchanged a knowing look with his wife. 'The same goes for the dress. Most of it could have been cut up for re-use and they were just burning the leftover bits. I certainly wouldn't blame anyone for using *that* for rags! 'He gave a contemptuous laugh. 'What I do know is that it's turning into a ruddy waste heap around here! No wonder the plants look sickly.'

'I suppose you're right, but I still don't like it.' Isabella Liney pulled her thin, beige cardigan a little tighter around her body. 'I find it rather unsettling, though goodness knows why; it's just a bit of old rubbish.' She wrinkled her nose up at the belt buckle.

'Precisely. Now don't be so melodramatic, Bella, you've been reading too many of those ghastly crime magazines, if you ask me.' Liney made little attempt at concealing is disapproval of his wife's choice of reading matter. 'Those rags are just sensationalist, alarmist rubbish.'

'I don't see why you have to be so sniffy. I learn an awful lot about the workings of the criminal mind in them.'

'And why in heaven's name do you need to know about the criminal mind and its workings?'

Isabella did not reply to her husband's question. Instead she visibly shivered once again and hugged herself that bit closer. 'I do feel quite unnerved. I've got goose bumps all over. I know you think I'm being silly, but don't you find this a bit...suspicious?'

'Absolute rot! The chap's wife was probably having a clear out, that's all. Now let's have no more debate on the subject and let me get on. It's just some old junk, nothing more.' He looked her in the eye, 'And have a care you don't go gossiping around the close and letting your overly vivid imagination run riot.' He dropped his voice to barely a mumble. 'I'd never live it down at the bank.'

He closed his eyes for a moment as he imagined stepping into his regular compartment for the short electric train ride into the city and meeting the looks of self-righteous indignation he would receive from his bowler-hatted companions, each pointedly shaking their newspapers in disapproval before returning to studying the share prices.

'Keep a lid on it, Liney, and maintain the dignity and quiet professionalism of the business at all costs. Do that, and you could go far.' That was the advice he'd been given when he first started at the merchant bank, and he was not about to blow it now over some old rubbish.

His was a closed and highly ordered world where everything was expected to run smoothly and strictly without either fuss or bother. A chap soon learned not to rock the boat by attracting undue attention, especially when it concerned his private life.

'As long as you think it's nothing,' and Mrs Liney tossed the buckle on top of the scrap of fabric. 'But didn't you say we bought the place from a retired doctor?'

'What's that to do with anything?'

'He was a confirmed bachelor, was he not? I distinctly recall you stated that he was "a solitary old bird rattling around in this big house", or words to that effect.'

'Did I?' Liney laughed. 'Such men can still have lady friends, Isabella.' He raised a knowing eyebrow.

She gave him a disapproving look. 'That's as maybe, but do they burn their young floozy's clothing in the garden?'

'I really wouldn't know.' He felt the first tickle of doubt on the back of his neck. 'We really must be careful not to let our imaginations run riot. I'll burn all this later — and do it properly this time — and we can forget about it. Now, I simply must get on if you want me to finish before that thunderstorm brews up.'

CHAPTER THIRTEEN
Brackley
18th September 1950

Betty Askew dead? What was the man on about? Of course she wasn't dead — he'd sat talking with her during two train journeys. That cocky cabbie was badly misinformed. Typical. Think they know everything. Not just every road in town but the comings and goings of the townspeople, to boot. Well, he was spectacularly wrong on this occasion.

Despite this confident mental assertion, Irons was still dogged by the memory of the sickening sensation he had felt when he'd heard the man state so emphatically that Betty was dead. Coming hot on the heels of his bewilderment at the way she'd suddenly disappeared, it had upset him sufficiently to cause him to lay awake for hours in his narrow and lumpy bed. When he'd finally succumbed to a short and fitful sleep, his dreams had been unpleasantly vivid and upsetting, taking the form of a long and exhausting journey that felt more like a chase, although it was far from clear whether he were pursuer or pursued.

He was following Betty, but she was always just ahead of him, sometimes quite close, sometimes far off, but always out of touching distance. She was hurrying, though occasionally stopping and turning, as though checking he was behind. Her face was tense and nervous. Was she scared? Whatever her emotion, something in her expression urged him on. Were they trying to escape something — or from someone? He had a horrible sensation of dread. No matter how hard he tried he could never catch her up and when he repeatedly called for her to stop and wait it was in nothing more than a hoarse croak.

A very sinister taxi cab, without a visible driver, was always parked on a driveway or at the side of the road they were running along, and each fresh sighting of the car induced a sense of extreme panic within him. Sometimes its long nose could be seen pulling slowly into view around a street corner in a menacing manner, the windscreen reflecting the light in such a way that he could not see within. He knew it was malevolent, or at least its unseen driver was, and each time it appeared it forced him to slow down, or to duck into a doorway and lose ground on Betty until such time as it moved silently away, only to reappear somewhere else. Finally, and after all manner of twists and turns, he found her standing at the top of a steep, grassy bank, whilst he slipped and slid in a frantic attempt to climb up and join her.

As he made wild, futile attempts to reach the crest of the hill he was forced to watch in horror as she beat her arms frantically like windmills, whilst a flock of angry owls swooped, flapped and pecked around her head and hands, catching in her hair with their sharp talons, tearing at her flesh with claw and beak, her mackintosh coloured with bright red streams of blood, her screams piercing like a locomotive releasing steam from a safety valve...

Irons woke up sweating, a hand tangled up in the top sheet, and with the sensation that it was his own voice that had jolted him out of the nightmare. He lay, staring at the ceiling, perspiring and breathing in short gulping breaths, his mind seared by the dreadful images. As he lay and regained some composure, he realised there was an insistent little tapping on his window, as though someone wanted to attract his attention.

Tap tap tap. Gentle yet hard, like a finger on the glass.

Tap tap tap.

Could there really be someone outside? No, his room was on the first floor. The sound persisted, with three more little strikes on the glass, inviting him to pull back the curtains. He suddenly had the craziest notion: Betty Askew had managed to track him down and had come to seek his help! Like the high jinks of a first year student, she'd clambered up a drainpipe and was perched precariously on the ledge!

He leaped out of bed, rubbed his hands across his face to get the blood flowing and then, with a nervous sense of anticipation, eased a curtain aside.

It was nothing more than a small bird pecking at the metal frame. A blue tit, that now fixed him for a moment with one beady eye before darting away in a flash of blue and yellow when it saw his bleary face. He smiled at his foolishness then went to the bathroom at the end of the corridor to wash away any lingering memories of his nightmare.

Irons had to face Monday morning exhausted and in a disturbed frame of mind, despite his best efforts at pushing aside and washing away what was nothing more than a bad dream. His inability to fully concentrate on the job caused him to retreat into demanding of his class long periods of silent study or rote-learning from books, and any lad foolish enough to break these enforced silences was rudely punished by a surprising eagerness to cane their opened palms, and threats of worse hanging over their bowed heads.

He needed time to make sense of everything that had happened the previous night. The taxi driver's outburst was the easiest to resolve: it was simply a coincidence that two women with identical names came from the same town. One had, apparently, met with an untimely end, and the taxi driver was unaware she had a living namesake. Despite claiming to know every girl in town, he was clearly fallible on this point.

One lesson Irons had learnt from the incident was discretion. It would be wise to keep his interest in the living Betty Askew to himself for the time being. Whilst part of him wanted to make further enquiries and clarify this misunderstanding, he decided it might be wiser to play a more cautious innings henceforth. Only if his fledgling relationship with her managed to stand on firmer ground would he confess it to anyone else.

Discovering details of the tragic story of the other, sadly deceased, Betty Askew could wait. If the 'poor kid', as the taxi driver had called her, was dead, then she was past help — unlike *his* Betty, who not only appeared to be in distress, but had actually requested his help. And in that respect it appeared she had even left him a clue in the compartment after her sudden exit, although this curious document — if it could be so named — raised more questions than it answered and did nothing to suggest how he could help her to recover her engagement ring.

On numerous occasions during that tiresome day whilst his pupils were bent to their studies, Irons would lay the tiny slip of paper picked from the carriage seat on his desk, or hold it surreptitiously in the palm of his hand, and reconsider the few words it bore, in the hope he could make sense of them.

The Cobra's Eye
RC to BA forever
20th September 1942

They were written with a neat hand in black ink on a tiny square of heavy-laid, cream paper not more than an inch square. It was certainly not freshly written, judging by the slight discolouration at the edges and the spot of foxing on the back. It looked as though it may have been in direct sunlight at some point.

But what was the Cobra's Eye? It didn't sound like a pub. Was it a book, a film? Could it be a restaurant, or a club, where these lovers had a tryst? Presumably BA was Betty Askew. Was that the date they became engaged? The date was the strangest part of this enigmatic scrap of paper. How could the engagement have been eight years ago (almost to the day, he noticed)? He'd reckoned Betty at about eighteen. Perhaps twenty-one, at a push. She would have been far too young in 1942. No more than thirteen, at most. She explained that her beau died in the war, so... Oh, hang on, she must have been referring to the present Korean conflict. But no; 1942 placed this engagement firmly during the Hitler war. Had she become engaged whilst still a child? His head swam with the impossibilities and contradictions.

It was possible that Betty had dropped the note accidentally and he was not supposed to solve this riddle, but he felt certain it had been a deliberate act and part of her attempt to secure his help, so he persevered in trying to make sense of it, but to no avail.

As the day wore on his mood became increasingly fractious, as did that of many others in the school. The air pressure was dropping like a stone and the sky, that for so many days had been dotted with a collection of white, fluffy clouds grazing like sheep across a benign field of blue, was now turning dark and deeply oppressive. An ominous wall of slate grey, turning a livid purplish-black like a vicious bruise, was now creeping up from the horizon as though a heavy awning was being slowly winched over their heads. Great towering thunderheads brilliantly illuminated by the last high beams of sunlight stood tall above this deadening blanket, leering over the rooftops and chimneys like vast outriders driving the slow-rolling storm clouds forward.

The electrical charge was palpable, as was the increasing humidity that made the air hot like that from a furnace and which shortened tempers, and made sweaty collars stick to hot necks and sharp prickles of perspiration erupt beneath damp hair on pink foreheads. The boys were abandoning their caps, despite warnings to the contrary, whilst both master and pupil were surreptitiously loosening ties. Everyone repeatedly looked out of the ancient, mullioned windows at the premature darkness descending upon the town in advance of the gas lamps being lit, rendering the market square dark and drear, filled by the ominous presence above. The patient shoppers standing in the bread and meat queues that reached far out of the row of shops looked upwards with anxious and fretful expressions, praying they could collect their ration and be home before the floodgates opened.

The shoppers had their prayers answered. The storm just sat overhead and stewed a while longer, and as evening drew in and the shops locked up, everyone became desperate for the rains to break and the electrical storm to vent its pent-up energy and so release the town from its brooding grip. The ceiling of dense cloud was now weighing heavy in all directions without relief, stretching as far as the horizon, animated occasionally by distant flickerings and low grumbles that reminded many of the blitz nights when a distant town received a hammering.

The evening meal at Magdalen was over. Everyone emerged from the stifling humidity in the refectory, from the smell of boiled cabbage and braised meat that had challenged even the hungriest to consume the food before them. All anyone wanted was to flop in saggy, common-room armchairs or to lie on beds, too frazzled to pretend to look at their homework. The masters were desperate for the chance to finally shed their sweltering black gowns and mortar boards and have a restorative cup of tea or a cigarette whilst leaning against an outside door jamb in the hope of some fresher air.

After a day of deliberation, Irons knew what he must do to break his own mental storm. He was no closer to solving the riddle of the note, but he knew he must find Betty that very night. He sensed that she was in some kind of real and present danger and delay was not possible. As he had been excused dorm duty until later that evening, he seized his chance.

He idled away an hour or so in desultory conversation with half an eye always on his watch, then told Jim Duggan, the biology master, that he was 'going for a fag and a pint before last orders'. He rushed off promptly, before the flame-haired Scotsman could suggest joining him. With little thought of the rain that was surely to come, Irons raced straight out of the school-gates bareheaded, his jacket was tucked under one arm and became instantly clammy in the humidity.

He strode purposefully up the high street and past The Plough, not without considering that a swift pint was the more sensible option, but he pushed this aside and continued onwards towards Brackley Central station. The trees in the park were rustling anxiously and leaves skittered and circled across the broad pavements in wild dances. This gathering wind suggested that the storm was preparing to unleash its venom at any moment. The Scots pines in front of the little, red-brick station building sighed in the dark, relieved only by the light of a solitary gas lamp above the entrance. Irons found the sound of the wind eerie, like that of soft female voices whispering in the branches above, and fought to reassure himself it was just wind, wood and needle at play.

He had pulled up short in his approach to the station and stepped between two of these creaking trunks, heart pounding, for there was the unmistakable shape of the Austin taxi guarding the station entrance. To his unsettled mind it looked horribly reminiscent of his terrifying dream. He could not see if the driver was within because the windscreen was a sheet of reflections, exactly as in his nightmare. Why was he so scared? He'd been only too pleased to take the cabbie into his confidence the other evening, and yet here he was skulking behind trees, feeling apprehensive of meeting the man again. Even worse, he realised he was acting suspiciously and surely inviting a bad reaction, if not from Hancock the cabbie, then from anyone who might see him.

At that moment there was a series of brilliant flashes that starkly illuminated the interior of the vehicle in a hard, unflinching light, confirming that it was empty, followed by an ear-spitting bang that struck Irons physically to the core. The rain came moments later, pouring down in huge, heavy drops like a silver curtain that blurred his vision of both car and station, splashing noisily on the ground like so much gravel tipped down a metal chute. It was torrential and instantly soaking: a rain that demanded he took cover.

Hancock and one of the station staff appeared at the doorway and peered out at the sudden and noisy downpour, their faces momentarily bleached by another lightning flash, eye sockets black pools of shadow rendering their faces like skulls. They ducked back inside, and Irons saw a door open and both enter what looked like an office.

Holding his jacket high, head bowed against the heavy rain, Irons sprinted across the divide, his shoes wet and trouser turn-ups darkened with water in the few short moments it took for him to enter the little booking hall. He did not slow or risk a look as he passed the ticket window, just continued across the bridge that lay directly ahead, his feet loud on the wooden boarding and pounding down the stairs onto the platform below.

He paused to catch his breath, the rain still falling in torrents and beating on the glass canopy in a tremendous roar before gushing noisily through the down pipes. Everywhere was the sound of water, drumming, running, splashing and gurgling. The sky was being ripped apart repeatedly by sustained strikes of lightning followed immediately by a series of deafening cracks of thunder like a bombing raid. The lightning flashes allowing him brief glimpses of a rain-lashed tank engine crawling over the viaduct, hauling its short train of coaches, the steam from the chimney beaten down to one side like a soggy white pennant.

The last train. He was just in time.

A porter was leaning on a doorframe, his shadow thrown across the platform by the light from within. A distant bell tinkled, barely audible through the noise of the storm, but otherwise the station appeared deserted. It was battened down like a ship in a storm.

The smart Thompson L1 tank engine hissed and fizzed noisily as it clanked to a halt close to Irons, its gay, apple-green livery slicked and glossy like a dance band crooner's hair, reflecting the string of station lamps under the canopy as the rain bounced off the cab roof, from under which two pairs of eyes looked out from the darkness within.

The fireman stepped briskly onto the platform with a friendly nod towards Irons. After a momentary pause to steel himself for the task ahead, he trotted out from under the cover of the canopy and across to the curved metal arm jutting from below the tall, cylindrical water tower on the platform's far end. Doubled over against the rain, he pulled on a chain to swing the arm, and its dangling rubber hose like an elephant's trunk, across to the side of the engine. He clambered on the slippery side tank, getting drenched whilst doing so, and had the water filler lid open and the end of the hose in place in a matter of moments, holding it steady with one hand whilst keeping his cap firmly wedged on his head with the other, waiting for the driver to run out and turn the metal wheel at the base of the tower that opened the water valve.

The hose expanded and bucked once or twice as it filled. The fireman adjusted the angle of its entry into the tank until he was happy that it was completely secure, then he leaped back down onto the platform, brushing off the worst of the rain from his jacket. Meanwhile, the driver stepped back into the cab and fiddled with something that made a steamy, hissing sound from near the wheels.

Irons was keeping his eyes fixed on the length of the train, closely observing the few passengers getting out.

'What a night! I'm flippin' soaked!' The fireman beat at the legs of his overalls and flapped his sodden jacket to shake off the worst of the rain. 'Jesus, it could have held off a few more minutes!'

'It's been brewing all day,' Irons remarked, keeping his eyes on the passengers now hurrying along the platform and on the porter half-heartedly loitering beside his little two-wheeled trolley, although it was clear he expected no work tonight. 'The air pressure was giving me a headache, so I'm glad the storm has broken.'

Irons watched two middle-aged women carrying wicker shopping baskets and wearing impractical hats almost fall out of a carriage with an unfurling of umbrellas, giggling and screaming in mock anguish as they tottered on their heels through the rain. They were followed by a sober-looking businessman with a leather attaché case, an elderly gent and his wife, and four senior schoolboys, each wearing prefect's badges on the lapels of their Winchester House School blazers, reminding Irons that he must soon return to his own schoolmasterly duties. But there was no Betty Askew.

Botheration! He cursed under his breath. A feeling of intense disappointment flooded over him. It felt far worse than the drenching he had already endured.

The young porter sauntered across and exchanged greetings with the fireman before addressing Irons. 'You travelling up tonight, sir?'

'Er...no.' Irons was caught off-guard. 'I was just looking. Taking the number...' He pointed at the numerals on the side of the L1 tank. 'I'm developing an interest in engines.'

'And I'm developing an intense dislike for 'em on a filthy night like this!' the fireman laughed heartily, the porter joining in. There was a rueful smile from the driver inside the cab.

'Did you see her tonight on the way in?' The porter tossed the fag-end of his cigarette over the side of the platform and looked up at the tall fireman.

'Nah, not a dicky bird.'

'Thank the Lord. We'd have no chance of spotting her, not

until too late,' the driver added. One gloved hand held an oily cloth; the other rested on one of the locomotive cab's handrails. 'I know she's supposed to be crazy, but even she'd think twice about being out in this.'

'Who said she were crazy?' The young porter had his hands in his trouser pockets and was hopping from one leg to another with nervous energy whilst glancing at Irons to see if he was catching his attention. 'There's some as say she's not natural. More *super*-natural, if catch my drift.' He gave Irons a look laden with barely-concealed meaning.

'Poppycock!' The fireman flipped the porter's cap upwards with a swift movement of his hand, sending it tumbling down his back. The young man reacted with surprising speed, twisting himself around and managing to catch it before it hit the ground in a move that suggested this was not the first time he'd been so treated.

'Oy! Give over, that's my best cap!' He tried to make his young, fresh face look suitably grave, but merely succeeded in resembling a naughty schoolboy. 'It's true. God's truth it is!'

'Yeah? I don't hold with all that nonsense.' The driver stepped back into the gloom of the cab and did something so the engine changed the note of its constant hissing yet again.

'She's off her rocker. No more to be said,' added the fireman.

The porter was readjusting his hat with an unnecessary level of concentration, rather like a cat caught losing its footing and then preening with exaggerated fastidiousness to cover its embarrassment. 'Well, I've seen her! And she looked just like a spook to me.' His face flickered in the blue light of another lightning flash, head nodding with the weight of this revelation, and this time he caught Irons's eye. 'She proper gave me the shivers an' all!'

The fireman's response was lost by another thundering boom, but he was laughing and looked unmoved. Irons, however, was staring at the porter.

'Hey, watch the water!' The young porter pointed over the fireman's shoulder and laughed raucously, clutching at his stomach with exaggerated glee.

The fireman sprang into action as water cascaded from the tank filler in great, white streams that splashed, together with the torrential rain, over the edge of the platform in a foaming torrent. 'That's your fault, talking such tosh, you monkey!' He shut off the water and sprang back aboard the locomotive to free the hose.

'Give over! I was just telling you what I know.'

Irons had been listening to the exchange with interest. 'Excuse me, who are you talking about? It sounds most intriguing.'

'You not heard about the girl in white? Now there's a story for a stormy night...'

'Don't listen to him, he's full of tosh.' The driver grinned.

'No, seriously. She stands in the four-foot, forces the trains to stop, and then just vanishes into the night! Spooky.' He rolled his eyes dramatically in an expression rendered all the more grotesque by another flash of electrical charge.

'Where does she do this?' asked Irons.

'Here! Near the viaduct. Far side usually, but some say she even walks around here when it's locked up at night. What do you make of that? A real ghost prowling our station!'

The fireman had a half smile on his face, shaking his head in mild disbelief as he walked back to the cab of his engine.

'How odd.' Irons looked back along the now-deserted and rain-washed platform, the air still muggy, though rapidly cooling to a more pleasant temperature. 'What does she look like?'

'Thinnish, youngish and wrapped in a white death shroud.' The porter waved his hands in an action presumably supposed to suggest a ghost. 'Actually, I thought it looked more like a coat, but the scariest thing of all is that she just stands and stares, pointing at... Oh, er, I'd better jump to it or I'll get a flea in me ear!' He straightened himself up and nodded towards the open door, where the top-hatted stationmaster now stood, thumbs hooked into his waistcoat pockets and looking like a sombre funeral director. 'Gotta dash!' With that, he stepped smartly away with a cheery parting salute.

The fireman, having completed watering the engine, hopped back on board, looked along the train from out of the cab, his cap-peak instantly collecting a string of clear beads of water as he waited for the flash of the handlamp from the guard. A signal clonked into place, giving them the 'right-away', and the driver offered a short toot on the whistle to acknowledge he'd seen it.

'We're shunting over to the other side of the platform, then we'll run the engine round ready for the return leg,' the fireman offered helpfully, perhaps sensing that Irons was new to train spotting.

'Righty-o. Thanks.' Irons glanced at the station clock and decided he could wait until they'd completed this movement, the fireman's advice lending this idea legitimacy in his troubled mind. Perhaps Betty would still turn up to catch the return service, though he thought it unlikely she would be travelling south at this hour. Indeed, it looked unlikely there would be any passengers, as the station was now just an empty expanse, fizzing with curtains of rain.

He paced up and down under the shelter of the awning, watching as the short train was propelled into the opposite side of the island platform, the guard leaning partway out of the leading coach, guiding them slowly into place. The locomotive uncoupled, backed off and trundled off into the unwelcoming night, ready to run through the station and reappear on the front end.

It was growing steadily chillier and Irons now donned his damp jacket and stood gloomily watching this flurry of activity, wondering what on earth he was doing risking catching a chill by loitering on some God-forsaken station. He looked through one of the waiting room windows and saw a cheery fire in the corner, a padded leather bench and a table with brochures and a newspaper laid out, and immediately stepped inside and stood before the warming blaze, trying to dry himself. It was a wasted activity, for he was soon going to be soaked again during the walk back to Magdalen, but the smell of burning coal and the leather seats were suddenly terribly appealing, in a homely sort of way. He felt dog-tired, and as he stood with his back to the fire he closed his eyes for a few moments, wishing he were snoozing in the saggy armchair in his room. The adrenaline rush of the day had evaporated and the desperate belief that he must meet Betty — that somehow he *would* meet her — had gone as well. He felt foolish and embarrassed. If he left soon and got back briskly, he could probably hide this idiotic escapade from his peers and forget all about it, push it aside, and push any thoughts of that Askew girl away at the same time. He was acting like a fool.

Another series of lightning flashes crackled outside, the light so intense that his eyelids were no defence, blazing a bright orange and yellow. He opened his eyes in surprise and as he did so, he caught the last dying moments of the brilliant sheet of light and was startled to see a pale figure passing one of the rain-soaked windows. Even with just that fleeting glimpse and despite the rain being lashed under the awning and against the glass on that side of the room, he was sure it was Betty.

Irons dashed to the door and saw someone stepping into one of the train's four carriages: just a glimpse of leg, a swirl of coat and an arm swinging the door closed.

He ran to the nearest carriage door and climbed aboard, moving along the corridor and glancing into a succession of empty compartments. It must have been her! But where was she? He heard footsteps ahead and continued, but the corridor was empty. A toilet door swung slowly open with an eerie creak, but there was no one inside. He walked forwards, trying to keep his footsteps silent, edging up to each compartment and peering inside.

The engine, which had been reattached while his attention was focused on Betty, now gave a short toot on its whistle. This was followed by a shudder and a groan, and the train started into motion.

'Oh, heck!' Irons stared in consternation as a Brackley Central nameboard glided past the window, the pair of gas lamps that illuminated the sign distorted and refracted into many broken fragments of colour through the rain-and-soot-streaked carriage window. Having no ticket was the least of his worries: he was due back at school in the next quarter of an hour! Deserting dorm duty without explanation or warning was going to land him in hot water when he finally rolled up. But when would that be?

There was nothing to do until they reached the next station. He would have to make the best of it, but until then he may as well find Betty and try to salvage something out of this mess. With that intention in mind, he walked through to the next carriage.

Adrian Turvey was sitting on one side of the old kitchen table in his snug back kitchen. Geoffrey Austin, the silver-haired head librarian, sat opposite. A double spread of the *Weekly Dispatch* was opened between the two, upon which a series of small bones was carefully laid out. Austin was still making a few final tweaks to the arrangement; his curved briar pipe releasing an aromatic curl of smoke, adding to the scent of wood smoke from Turvey's little black range. The solitary bulb in the overhead light suspended on a brown cord from one of the low wooden beams was not bright, so Turvey had lit a large, brass oil lamp that looked as though it belonged on a boat, and the glass bowl protecting the burning wick now threw interesting shadows across the table.

Neither man had spoken for fifteen minutes. Austin just made the odd grunt or a contemplative sort of noise whilst sucking on his pipe as he worked, with Digger resting the tip of his nose on the edge of the table and sniffing continually, as if his sense of smell would help resolve the developing mystery, his tail constantly beating time.

Turvey had been supping at a pint of flat, home-brewed ale, hoping this would fend off a sickening feeling of dread forming in the pit of his stomach. His friend had barely touched his, concentrating instead on the clutch of little bones they had collected earlier that day and placed in a cardboard box that had once held *Rutland Stove Lining*.

On a sheet of newspaper, Austin was trying out various positions for these delicate objects, sometimes lifting and turning one to improve the fit, as though he were assembling a jigsaw puzzle, but instead of a helpful box illustration to guide him; he had merely the image of a man cheerfully trowelling stove cement into place. Turvey found himself staring at this cartoon-like illustration and wished they could talk about the glowing range that he had successfully repaired last spring using the contents of the box, or how low the Ouse was running these last few days, and that it would benefit from this downpour, or the price of beer; in fact anything other than think about the horror of what now lay on the table between them, unpleasantly juxtaposed against the newspaper's grainy monochrome images of British and American troops hunkered down under North Korean attack, south of Seoul.

'Well, there's no doubting it. None at all, I'm sorry to say.' Austin sat back in his chair and waved his pipe towards the table. 'Some bones are missing, of course. I dare say other creatures had them away, or maybe we just didn't look hard enough, but no matter. It's definitely a human hand. I'm rather better at dating Roman or even pre-Roman remains, but I'd hazard it's been there for anything between one and ten years. No more.' Austin sucked on his pipe and shrouded himself in blue smoke, his lined and creased face impassive, but his eyes betraying something between professional excitement and acute apprehension.

Turvey ran a hand across his face. 'Are the bones very old?' Turvey knew they were not, but was trying to stave off the awful reality a moment longer.

'I'm afraid not. Not *archaeologically* old. That would be quite impossible, as they were found in bushes on an embankment that's been there just a touch over fifty years.'

'Why would someone's hand bones be there?' Turvey stared at Austin, one hand now stroking the ears of Digger, who nuzzled close to his master's grubby brown trousers.

'It is indeed a puzzle. More importantly, whose hand is it?'

Lightning flashed behind the heavy curtains and the little cottage shook with the following clap of thunder. They sat in silence and glumly stared at the bones as the storm further dampened their spirits. 'To add an unwelcome touch of the macabre, one could also ask if the owner is missing it now?'

'Or past caring?' Turvey swallowed some beer hurriedly. 'If he —or she — is dead then...' He tailed off. Both men understood exactly.

'She, probably. It's quite small. A woman's, though it could be a youth's.'

Turvey groaned. 'I know it's illogical, but somehow knowing that makes it worse.'

'And makes it less likely to be the aftermath of an accident to a railway worker. Not a very credible idea, I know, but it is perhaps the least unpleasant hypothesis, and one that might not have quite such portentous implications.'

Turvey nodded grimly. 'I'd better call the police straight away. There's a telephone in The Greyhound. Look, I don't know about you, but this glass of home brew is losing its appeal with *that* in the room. What say we place the call then cheer ourselves in the snug by the pub fire with a couple of proper pints?'

'Yes... yes, I rather think that might help steady the old nerves. Going out in that—' Austin paused, and they listened to the relentless splashing of rain hitting the road, '—is going to be jolly unpleasant, but I still think it better than sitting here staring at this little box of tricks!'

The train was cold. Freezing, actually. If felt like too many windows had been left open allowing in the wet air, which was very unwelcome in damp clothes. He hurried along the dingy, swaying corridors past the stinking toilet with the banging door and across the noisy, concertinaed divide between coaches, chasing a shadow, a fleeting sensation, of the woman in white.

Irons stopped suddenly. There she was. Sitting alone in an unlit compartment. The bulb must have blown, rendering it nearly pitch black, so he was fortunate to even catch a glimpse of her pale face in the smoky blackness within. It was strange to choose such a sad, gloomy location when there were other empty, but illuminated, compartments close to hand.

He stepped through the doorway and greeted her. She looked up, and he thought she might have smiled, although it was hard to make out anything other than the rough outline of her features, her face rendered as little more than a series of dark hollows and shapes that emphasised the delicate outline of her skull.

'May I join you?'

'Of course.'

It was almost as though she had been expecting him. 'Gosh, it's awfully dark in here!'

'I like it like this. You can see outside. Your eyes soon get accustomed. It's preferable to having those blackout blinds drawn down and being constantly worried about showing a light.'

'Quite!' Irons was momentarily puzzled by the reference to blackout blinds. They had been taken down years ago, but this was a small detail and his obvious delight in seeing her immediately pushed this point aside. An icy coldness enveloped him.

He could now see her more clearly, aided by a flat flicker of distant sheet lightning. She looked gaunt and drawn, and her naturally pale skin was rendered the purest white.

She leant forward, not flinching from his gaze. Her voice seemed more urgent than before. 'We don't have much time because we will soon be in Finmere, where you really should get out and hope to flag someone down for a lift back to Brackley.'

Irons was surprised by both her directness and her appreciation of his situation. 'Heck, yes! I'm going to be in awful trouble. It won't be easy to get home at this time of night and in this weather. But never mind that now. You don't seem surprised to see me.'

'Nor you, in finding me.'

'True.' He gave her a smile. 'I must confess I was rather hoping you would be on the last train from Amersham, or even at the station. I nearly left when you didn't step off when it arrived.'

'You said last time you would try to help me.' She looked at him earnestly, the sense of urgency she displayed at their previous encounter having returned to her voice.

'Of course I will. But you left in such a hurry, vanished, so it seemed, without saying what I can do for you.' He sounded breathless and eager. 'Look, would it be dashed impertinent to exchange addresses? Or a telephone number where I could reach you? I know that sounds awfully forward, but...'

'I'm sorry if I appear a little strange and...unconventional,' she interrupted him. 'There are severe constraints on my time, and on my liberty. I have so very little time, so we must "cut to the chase", as the American airmen like to say.'

'Tell me how I can help.'

'I need you to recover my engagement ring. It's called the Cobra's Eye. A funny name, isn't it? It is a solitaire diamond set on a gold band, and a thing of rare beauty — and great value.'

Irons nodded, amused to discover that it wasn't a restaurant, after all.

'I know who has it', she continued, 'he stole it from me. He took it by force and menace and...let's just say he acted in a most brutish manner.'

'That's an absolute outrage', replied Irons, 'I could punch him right now!' He looked angry, but this soon changed into something more ambiguous. 'An eye for an eye? Hmm... a cobra's eye, in this case.'

Her face betrayed a painful memory. She had ceased fiddling with her ring finger; her hands were now folded in her lap. She spoke with the same sad voice, but now with an authority that made Irons listen intently. 'He gloats over it in secret. It also holds a sort of spell over him. That's because of how he took it from me — it will always have the potential to destroy him. He can never tell anyone about the diamond, never confess how he came to own it, and so it remains his guilty secret, gnawing away at his soul. He is an elderly man — far older in body and spirit than actual years. I can at least derive some satisfaction in knowing that he has already aged as a result of his guilt. I cannot say more. To do so will confuse and alarm you, perhaps even frighten you off.'

'You can tell me anything, really. I want to understand.'

'It is inadvisable, and I do not have time.'

'Have you reported this theft to the police?'

'That is impossible. There are... complications. The police cannot help me. This man knows many highly influential people: judges, politicians, senior police officers, aristocrats. He can bring influence to bear. They are in his debt and will go to any length to keep him free of scandal. It is my word against his, who will believe the word of a poor railway cleaner?'

Irons felt the injustice of her position of powerlessness like a sting to his heart. 'You cannot go to the police. Hmmm... ah, you want me to accompany you on a visit the old man, to try to reason with him?'

'No. I want you to enter his house, find it and take it. But you must not confront him! Do not challenge him nor give your identity away. Be silent and stealthy. Take the ring — and be gone!'

'Break in? Oh my goodness. You want me to *steal* it from his house?' Irons did not expect this development.

'Hardly stealing! He took it from me with violence.'

'Violence?' Irons gulped.

Betty Askew nodded. 'Yes.'

He ran a hand through his hair and pondered her request for a few seconds. 'I—I don't know, this is all rather...on the edge; rather, well, vigilante.'

'Yours will be a far lesser crime than what he inflicted on me. Think of it as helping to right a wrong.'

Irons realised that his dry tongue was sticking to the roof of his mouth and wished he had some water — or, better, a glass of pale ale. 'But there is my position at school to consider.'

'You will be careful. Nobody will ever know. Wear gloves so you will not leave prints. I could not bear it if you were held accountable. You found the note I left?'

'On the seat? Yes, I have it in my wallet.'

'Good. I need you to leave that in place of the Cobra's Eye. A straight swap. This is vital: you must exchange them.'

'Why?'

'It is the name of the diamond. The name is also written in Egyptian and English on the base of its box, so the old man is quite familiar with its name. He will understand the significance of the initials and the date of our engagement when he sees it in place of the missing ring.'

'You want him to make the connection with yourself? But aren't you simply inviting immediate retribution? You said yourself that he was violent. Surely it would be better to take the ring as surreptitiously as possible and leave it at that? No trace, no clue.'

She shook her head. 'It is imperative that you remain anonymous in this affair, but I need him to understand that I am behind it. He cannot reach me. I am quite beyond being hurt any worse than I have already suffered at his hands. That little note will complete my revenge in a most elegant manner.'

'Revenge?' Irons stared at the pale shape of her face, indistinct and blurred, despite being so close. He felt a cold sweat of dread on his skin, a slightly nauseous feeling that he was being drawn into something dangerous and disturbing. And yet he could also feel the adrenaline coursing around his body, and the unmistakeable urge of attraction and desire that made him unable to walk away, or to refuse her.

She leant closer towards him. 'He is an old man. Once he realises that note is about Raymond and I, the shock is likely to be too much for him to bear.' She gave a little smile. 'Death by natural causes, they'll call it. A heart attack, most likely, and impossible that any blame could be attached to a cat burglar who crept in a few hours, or maybe days, earlier. Perhaps a few weeks will pass, depending on when he discovers the exchange and how strong his constitution is. And remember, nobody knows he has the ring, so when there is an inquest into his demise, it will not even be mentioned. The note might be a little puzzle perhaps, but an enigmatic one, and quite impossible to connect with yourself.'

Irons stared at her, his emotions on a stomach-turning fairground ride that mixed fear with intense excitement. This was so bizarre and unexpected. Like something out of a film. She was a real life femme fatale! What a delicious thrill. He could almost hear zither music twanging in the background as they sat swaying and rocking in the colourless compartment, the scene inky black, except for their faces, which were illuminated from the side by hard flashes of lightning, their skin streaked by the shadows of the rain streaming down the window. It was pure Film Noir. Betty was now transformed from engine cleaner into someone more like the strangely alluring Marlene Dietrich, asking him to kill a man by proxy as the rain hammered on the roof and the thunder ripped the sky asunder...

'The man's name is Melcombe — Dr Melcombe. He lives alone in Ivy Cottage. The houses in Turweston have only names, no numbers. You could be in and out in no time.'

'I'm not so sure...' Irons could immediately see problems. 'It would be almost impossible to find a small ring in the dark. It could be anywhere!'

'He keeps the ring in a locked drawer of his desk in the study at the back of the house.'

'But how do you know all this?'

'No matter. Just make the switch, and then take some of his considerable ill-gotten wealth whilst you are there. He collects gold sovereigns. Take some as your reward.'

'The only reward I want is to help you! To make you happy and—'

'—don't say any more, please.' she interrupted, giving him an imploring look. 'Once you have it, you can just vanish into the night. He will never report the burglary once he realises the Cobra's Eye has been exchanged for that potent little note. That nasty surprise will gnaw away at him, rot him right to the core. Test the strength of his old, black heart...' Her voice grew in strength and Irons even detected a note of triumph as she ended. It did not make him feel reassured.

He rubbed his face with both hands and exhaled long and slow. There was something sickeningly dreadful — and yet utterly compelling — about this extraordinary plan. He could hardly take it in.

'Nobody but the old man, yourself and I, will ever know what happened.' She smiled and took a deep breath, as if steeling herself to make a great effort. With lungs filled and the air held inside, she clenched her fists for a moment, then reached forward with both hands and clasped one of his between them. They were as cold as ice and her fingers felt almost brittle, as though they could be snapped like frozen twigs.

'You're so cold, Betty! You must be catching a chill from the rain.' Irons was reeling from what she had asked of him, but the thrill of excitement almost like an electrical charge from the raging storm outside that accompanied the contact between them pushed aside any lingering reservations. He edged a little closer, his knee now gently pressing against hers, and as she did not recoil from this contact he wondered if he dared to risk a kiss.

'You must do it tomorrow evening.'

'Oh golly. Why so soon?

'The longer you wait, the more likely your resolve will fail.'

Her face was so close now and her voice seemed to surround him in a soft but urgent whisper that enveloped his senses. It was intoxicating. 'Strike whilst the iron is hot!' Her eyes widened for a moment.

He laughed. 'How appropriate: Irons is my surname.'

She smiled indulgently. 'It must be tomorrow night.' She met his gaze, her liquid eyes silvery. 'When you have the ring, come to the churchyard of St Peter's in Brackley, and place it beneath the little pot of flowers on the grave of Private Raymond Coulson.'

'RC? The same as on the note?'

'The same...'

'And "BA" is you, of course. But I don't understand the date. 1942? How can that be?'

She appeared to ignore, or perhaps not to hear, his question. 'The stone is easy to find. It is the first one in the fourth row as you enter the churchyard by the lych-gate. It is fresh and clean — although the grave below is empty.' She bit her lip and paused as if overwhelmed by a strong memory. 'We do not have his body; it lies in a simple grave in Egypt. A hard irony of the fate we both share: to never lie together.' Her hands clasped around his a little tighter, which gratified him, but the look on her face implied that even this simple act was taking great effort on her part. He was also feeling a deep, gnawing chill creep through his hand and along his arm, her body lacking the vital warmth he expected.

'I will be close, but hidden and watching for you. Place the ring under the pot and leave immediately. Then you must forget all about it, and me.'

His face fell in disappointment at her words. 'But that's impossible, Betty! He remonstrated. 'How can I? I hoped that you and I could... that's to say, well, we—' he searched her face for a sign of encouragement '—might become friends, or...' He tailed off, seeing her expression blank and immovable. It was confusing. She was clasping his hand, her leg still lay against his, it was intense and intimate — and yet she still seemed so unreachably far away. Despite their close proximity he was finding it hard to keep her face sharp and in focus. The lightning had ceased and the darkness was rendering her increasingly insubstantial, her face little more than a fuzzy charcoal drawing. 'Is there no possibility we could meet again?'

'I'm sorry, truly I am. But where I must go it is impossible for you to follow. Things are changing and cannot be stopped. And I am glad. In time, you may understand.'

Despite her words, he felt that her present state of mind was merely temporary. She had clearly undergone a painful bereavement and then the trauma of robbery with menace and violence, for which she could get no justice. No wonder she could not entertain or envisage herself ever courting again. He felt a definite glimmer of hope that, given a little more time to grieve, and having wreaked vengeance on the wicked old man and regained her property, she would soon begin to feel able to move on with her life and love again. And, of course, she would feel well-disposed towards the man who had risked all to recover her treasured ring.

'Well, OK, I will do it. But I cannot be sure what time I can get to the churchyard. We should have some means to contact one another...' He was hoping to secure her home address, to ensure that, after the deed was done, he would not lose contact with her forever.

'I will be there. I will wait for as long as needed. I will wait every night if necessary. Look, the train is slowing. You have to leave.' Without warning she suddenly gave Irons a kiss on the mouth, taking him completely by surprise. Her lips imparted a sensation of intense cold rather than warm, womanly flesh, and yet, despite this, Irons was thrilled. 'You *will* do this one thing for me, won't you? May I have your word?'

He nodded gravely, matching her mood, despite the frantic beating of his heart. With that kiss he felt bonded to her both by his promise, and by the faintest inkling that, despite her words to the contrary, he may also be on a promise of something more. He was rewarded immediately with a smile that captivated him, but which suddenly transformed into a pained expression. She continued, with what looked like an intense effort of will, 'I regret I cannot give you what you want.' Her eyes searched his, full of understanding, and regret. 'Especially as I know you would never break your word.'

'Never!'

'Now you must leave...'

'Perhaps I could see you safely home?' This was quite reckless, as doing so would make him even later and place his position at Magdalen in even more jeopardy. But it was his final chance to secure a means of finding her again.

'Please go, you must return to Magdalen.' The train ground to a halt at Finmere. Freeing her hands from his, she stood up. 'Please accept my sincere thanks. It means more than you can imagine. Goodbye, Mr Irons.'

Reluctantly, he unlatched the carriage door and stepped down onto the platform. As he closed the door quietly behind him, he looked through the glass, hoping to exchange a few parting gestures with her, even nurturing the hope that she would unstrap the window, pull it down and kiss him once again. But, to his dismay and bewilderment, in the few seconds his back had been turned, she had vanished. It was almost as though she had dissolved like smoke into the gloom of the carriage interior. He darted a few steps to the left and right to peer into the windows of the adjacent compartments, but they were empty. As the train slowly pulled out of the station he stood and stared through every window as it passed him, but she must have walked towards the front of the train because she was nowhere to be seen.

The red tail-lamp on the last carriage receded into the dismal, wet night, its flame flaring and flickering in the squally wind, and cursed the fate that had given him barely ten precious minutes in her company. Now he would have to pray he could find a taxi, though he felt this unlikely in such a lonely spot. Hitching a lift seemed even less likely. He would just have to walk. As he stared gloomily after the rapidly-diminishing speck of crimson, he became aware that a uniformed railwayman with a world-weary expression had materialised close to him. 'Your ticket, please?'

CHAPTER FOURTEEN
Brackley
18th September 1950

PC604 — Ian Dowd to his mates — was young and inexperienced and had the sort of face that looked as though it has been scrubbed raw with cold water and carbolic soap. His pimply skin was a dough-white colour, irregularly blotched with pink, and whilst the light golden down on his chin and upper lip had made a valiant attempt to grow during his long day on duty, it was unlikely to ever resolve into a beard or moustache — even if he were not to shave for a few months.

His uniform was new and fitted imperfectly, the jacket hanging loose across his narrow chest with the sleeves a touch too short, whilst his starched shirt collar looked tight, the whole effect made him self-conscious as he stood and listened. His stoutly-made shoes (a definite perk of joining the constabulary) squeaked quietly in the way only new leather can, whilst he rocked backwards and forwards in what he thought was an appropriate movement, aping the style of Jack Warner in *The Blue Lamp*, but in reality it made him look like he urgently needed to use the outside privy.

His limited police training had not given him any guidelines about what to do when called to a house late on a stormy night to look at a bunch of old bones described as those of a woman's hand. He couldn't rightly say if they were or not. They did look a bit like a human hand, but there again he was no expert and could not claim to have seen any part of a human skeleton until now.

And the two men had quite obviously had a pint or two. Both were really quite animated, perhaps even a little over excitable and he reminded himself to be careful not to get drawn in by their nervous energy and jump to hasty conclusions. He should try to maintain a suitable air of caution. Their talk was a confusing muddle, all about Romans and field excavations, and how these bones were too recent to be ancient, and yet nothing to do with a railway accident, (he was not aware there had *been* an accident on the railway at Brackley, so was even more puzzled by this revelation) and then they talked about how the land was relatively new on the embankment, so it could not be from an ancient burial, although there were some fascinating and ancient sites in the area including the remains of Brackley Castle, and how someone called Digger had dug them up, or was that the dog who'd sniffed them out? Oh heck, what on earth was he to make of it all?

His notebook was soggy and his feet were aching and he was supposed to be clocking off now and getting home to rest awhile before turning in. Yes, he was looking forward to loosening the shirt collar which was rubbing his neck raw, not aided by the dampness from the rain, and relaxing with a nice cup of cocoa in front of the fire (his mother made the *best* hot cocoa!) The longer he tried to make notes of their jumbled explanations, the more confused he seemed to become. And besides, the bones were obviously quite old, certainly as far as he could tell they were. This hand belonged to someone long dead. Did the older of the men, the one with the smelly pipe, say something about Romans? Then the Romans could jolly well wait until tomorrow, at the very least. It hardly felt like an emergency. Did they really have to drag him out to tramp all the way up town on a night like this? What was wrong with tomorrow morning?

Anyway, they seemed pleased enough that he was taking the bones away in a box wrapped in newspaper and secured with string, and after (somewhat reluctantly) refusing a glass of whisky 'for the road', he donned his heavy, rain-sodden, police-issue cape and, with head bent down against the rain and the package tucked under one arm, he trudged gloomily back to the police station.

Tired, wet and lacking the enthusiasm to log the box of bones in the ledger that night, PC604 placed the package out of sight under his desk, deciding that he could do the paperwork tomorrow, when he felt more in the mood. He turned off the office light and locked up, and promptly pushed all thoughts of this annoying diversion to the back of his mind.

CHAPTER FIFTEEN
Near Turweston
19th September 1950

He ran as fast as he could, heart beating so hard it hurt in his chest. Lungs gulping air in rasping breaths punctuated by the leaden thud of his officially-recognised flat feet in their brogues pounding on the road. Arms pumping as he drove himself forward. His whole body was screaming 'stop!', but fear and adrenaline drove him on, with little thought or logic as to where he was going and what he would do when he got there.

Irons just wanted to be as far away as possible and to put behind him the terrible reality of what had just happened. If he could just run and run forever and lose himself in the one thought of how to keep his legs moving and fight the burning in his muscles; if he could just shut everything out and become a running man, free of all responsibility, free of reason — and free from the retribution that was coming his way as surely as dawn was creeping towards the horizon.

He must be about half a mile out of Turweston and, thankfully, had encountered no one along the way. It was a sleepy village, populated by the well-to-do or older types exactly like Dr Melcombe, who could be expected to take to their beds not long after closing time at the Stratton Arms, so it would be unusual if Irons met anyone in the early hours. In that respect Betty had been correct, arguing that he had a good chance of being in and out of Ivy Cottage without being observed.

The problem was that Dr Melcombe was a light and fitful sleeper, often given to waking and reading in bed at odd times in an attempt to induce sleep to return. On these occasions he used a small and rather weak reading lamp that gave no visible clue from the outside that he was awake. The thick curtains across his bedroom window, a legacy of the blackout, allowed not a chink of light to escape; the pencil-thin line of yellow beneath his bedroom door was so narrow and dim it gave no warning.

And Irons was no stealthy cat burglar. Though he had come well prepared, armed with a pocket torch and a long and hefty screwdriver lifted from the toolbox of Magdalen's handy man (a misdemeanour that had given Irons a pang of guilt until he'd reminded himself that it would be returned the following day). He wanted this tool in case he needed to prise open a casement or work on the locked drawers of the doctor's desk.

It had, of course, crossed his mind that there was remote chance that the doctor might awaken and catch him in the act and he had formulated a contingency plan: he would run. If cornered, however, he would reassure the frail, elderly man that there would be no violence, he would simply leave. Irons was a well-brought up young man. He could no more use his superior physical force and strength against an old man than he could against a woman, or anyone weaker than himself.

The back door of Ivy Cottage was locked, but it took Irons only a minute's search to find the spare key under a plant pot. He had suspected that Turweston's inhabitants were the trusting type. However, even with a key, it was alarming just how much noise the lock made when turned, and how loudly the hinges squeaked and the doorknob rattled. Irons learned too late that a small can of oil was a handy addition to the cat burglar's kit. Every step, every cautious exploration he made inside the depths of the cottage seemed to be unnaturally amplified; even his breathing sounded horribly loud. If only it was thundering like last night, with a deluge of rain on the roof to help mask these sounds; but tonight all was still, with just a lonely hoot of an owl from the nearby woods, and the steady chunk-chonk-chunk of a grandfather clock to relieve the profound silence within.

After what seemed an age, he'd found the doctor's study and commenced groping around the room and colliding with chairs and jabbing the corner of the desk into a thigh along the way (despite deploying his torch) until he found what he was looking for. It was a risk to switch on the small, green-shaded reading lamp, but Irons decided that he would be able to search faster with both hands free and so hopefully be out of there that much quicker. It was a risk worth taking. Certainly he knew he couldn't bear much more of the tension that was winding up within him, like the coiled spring inside the towering grandfather clock in the corner of the study. He just wanted to find that ring and be gone.

And again, Betty had given him good information. There were six shallow drawers across the rear of the desk and three of these were locked. Irons thought it probable that the ring lay in one of those. He was unlikely to find a key, and so the hefty screwdriver proved to be the ideal tool for the job, offering the leverage needed to spring the locks.

The first drawer was filled with small, flat, square boxes, each containing a surprisingly large and heavy gold coin. There were at least twenty of them. He recalled Betty's suggesting that he take some as his reward. He stared in fascination at the coins, turning one or two over in his gloved hands and admiring the glorious patterns formed in the slightly worn and polished gold that had an attractive lustre in the warm light of the reading lamp. They reminded him of the chocolate coins covered in gold foil he used to receive at Christmas as a child, before rationing ended such extravagances. These looked good enough to eat, but there was no doubt they were real.

Perhaps it might look better if he made it appear as though this were a chance robbery, with some of these coins taken along with the ring. Or would that merely reduce the power of the shock Betty wanted to inflict on the old man? The coins were distracting and he could feel himself becoming confused about why he was really there.

He decided to take just two of the biggest and most exotic-looking examples. It surely made little difference in the grand scheme of things. Not now he was here and already guilty of a serious crime. Besides, he might need some cash reserves, because his tenure at Magdalen College School was hanging by a thread. Turning up dreadfully late the previous night had been a personal disaster. The headmaster had carpeted him ruthlessly that very morning and left him in no doubt that this was both his first and final warning. He could understand why, but wished he could explain that he was delayed by trying to help a lady in distress. He knew that was impossible without appearing to be a romantic fool.

Yes, a couple of sovereigns could be an insurance policy. He left the drawer open and scattered some of the little boxes across the desk before slipping two coins into a pocket, where they immediately clinked with a clear, sharp sound that cut through the stillness of the room. Had this tell-tale rattle proved to be his undoing?

Irons leant on the parapet of the bridge that crossed the railway and gulped deep breaths, head hanging, eyes staring at, but not really seeing, the station that lay still and dark below. His heart was banging, his thighs burning from the running and stars swam before his eyes. He couldn't keep running, no matter how much he tried to lose himself in the physicality of the act, and besides, he really did need to stop and concentrate on devising a plan.

Think! He panted in desperate, wracking gulps. *You need to find a way out of this mess...* He groaned aloud, then leant forward and retched over the side of the bridge, vomiting onto the track.

Why had the stupid old man not just let him run off and have done with?

Irons slapped the palm of one hand against the brick in frustration, before resting his head against the cold parapet stone, soothing the raw wheal forming on one cheek where Dr Melcombe had swung at him. He had been caught unawares and sent reeling with the bony punch from the old codger's fist.

He closed his eyes and tried to block out the images that followed, but like a *Movietone* newsreel, they continued relentlessly: the fists beating on his back, then on his chest, the doctor snarling at him in a voice thick with contempt and hatred. He'd shouted back, told the old man to back off and let him go... he would do him no harm, just leave. But, if anything, this had made the old man even more incensed, hurling a surprisingly heavy paperweight that struck Irons hard on the flank and yelling: 'Give it back! Give it back, you bloody scoundrel!' The man's face was contorted with rage as he had body-charged Irons, ramming his bald head into his chest, sending them both reeling across the room until Irons had felt the hard mantelpiece crash into his shoulder blades. The doctor was like a man possessed, fighting like someone many years younger.

Irons had at first been unable to respond. Not only was he taken entirely by surprise and thus caught off-guard, he was not a violent man and his natural gallantry inhibited him from fighting an old man. Added to that, the doctor's assault was utterly relentless, and Irons was soon in such pain from the beating that at first he could do nothing but try (unsuccessfully) to protect himself from the next blows. He again shouted at the man to back off, and at one point actually managed to push him away so hard that he fell backwards. For a second Irons thought it was all over, but Melcombe stood up surprisingly quickly and, swearing furiously that he would kill him, resumed his violence with increased vigour.

The young man stood up and gazed into the starry night sky and the cold moon looking down at him, its light illuminating the railway lines below. A barn owl glided past, silent and almost iridescent white, its flat head swivelling like a gun turret to fix a pair of beady eyes upon him as it cruised the night air.

He ran his hands over his face, holding his eyes closed against the penetrating look of this odd bird and wishing he could just shrivel up and disappear. As he slowly regained his breath, he heard a deep, regular panting from behind, a sound like the breath of a great beast approaching. He stood still, the hairs rising on his neck and not daring to turn around and face what was coming. But why worry? What did it matter now? He was ruined, finished, washed up and ready to be thrown to the lions, so if the Hounds of Hell were behind him, so what?

Huff, huff, huff. It drew closer, and his face was licked by a damp and cloying hot breath, smothering him and working between his fingers pressed to his face. He opened his eyes and for a brief moment could see nothing but a pale mist that completely enveloped his head, gently illuminated by the soft moonlight and smelling of damp steel wool. It swirled and caressed his aching head before clearing into smaller drifts and then tiny cloudlets as the sound of a rhythmic metallic clanking from below made sense of it, and he watched as two locomotives, coupled together but without a train in tow, gently chuffed their way through the night, travelling stealthily like two black beasts skulking along the line.

He lowered his hands and stared at them in disgust. It was not the steam from the engines that had made them smell of iron, but the blood on his hands. Was it the blood of Dr Melcombe, or his own? Yes, he did have a nasty cut to one cheek and he could feel something warm and sticky there.

The doctor had been like a man beyond reason, a madman with superhuman strength, pounding his bony fists anywhere he could reach. Irons was already in pain all over his body and the old man was inflicting new blows upon old, layering him with agony. Eventually the younger man's self-preservation instinct kicked in and, seemingly without even engaging his brain, his hand had impulsively shot out and grasped the first thing he could find within reach and smashed it down on the doctor's shoulder with a sickening crack. The man gave a squeal of pain, but then picked up the chunky paperweight from the floor and lifted it above his head as though about to hurl it like a cricket ball, his face crimson with wild fury. As he shrieked 'I'm going to kill you, you bastard!' and pulled back his arm in preparation for bashing the lump of heavy glass down onto Irons's head, the younger man reflexively swung the poker like a cricket bat, swiping the old man squarely across the chest and sending him sprawling backwards until he hit the wall. He crumpled down onto the floor, where he lay still and silent.

And now here the younger man was, on the dark edge of town, sweaty and aching, just a common, dirty little criminal on the run. He'd not intended to confront the doctor, let alone to hurt him. He'd even pleaded to be allowed to leave when caught. The doctor had attacked him both incessantly and viciously; any injury he might have inflicted on him was, therefore, in the eyes of the law, delivered purely in self-defence. Surely a court would understand.

He felt the two gold coins in his pocket and thought about the diamond ring in its little box, now stuffed into his sock, concealed by the broad legs of his Oxford bags. He'd made the swap before the old man had surprised him, so at least he had achieved his goal. He'd taken only the swiftest glance, but that had been enough to set his pulse racing. He could see why she wanted it back. But his actions had been dangerously reckless. He could hang if the old man was dead. And all because a girl on a train told him to do it.

He walked towards town trying to plan his next move. Could he sneak back into school, get cleaned up and into bed and hope the police did not come a-knocking in the morning? He felt it unlikely that he would have to wait long for them to feel his collar. If the man were still alive, then he was done for. Irons was bruised and cut. He would struggle to find an explanation for these injuries and his clothes, the same he wore for teaching, were torn and possibly bloodstained. He had no others: a newly-qualified teacher's pay did not allow for a fully-stocked wardrobe. Hell and damnation, he was in a terrible, dreadful pickle!

He still had the outstanding task of delivering the ring to Betty as instructed. But he no longer felt so inclined. He needed to think about self-preservation first. She had promised to wait as long as necessary. She might have to wait some time, because he needed to keep his head down and devise a survival plan.

Irons bent down and stroked his hands through some long, damp grass in an attempt to remove the blood, then reached for the comb still wedged in his back pocket and untangled his hair. His hat was gone. Bugger. Could that be incriminating? He struggled to think of any way his hat could lead police to him. His options were narrowing: stick or twist. Both held little appeal and he was going to lose the hand whatever he did at this rate. But he preferred the idea of getting out of Brackley, and, since both stations were closed for the night, that left him just the hitch hiker's thumb. The A43 was quiet at the moment, although he usually heard the odd heavily-laden eight-wheeler rumbling its way through the town of a night, so he might strike lucky.

CHAPTER SIXTEEN
Buckingham Town Station
20th September 1950

'We've got a right fruitcake here!' Sergeant Andrew Giles of the Buckinghamshire Constabulary chuckled, his rosy cheeks adding to the look of mirth on his rotund face. 'Bonkers as a broom.'

'Surely you mean daft as a brush?' Detective Sergeant Trinder raised an eyebrow at the odd turn of phrase.

'That's what I said. Completely nuts. Trust me, John, you're going to love this. That's why I asked you over, not because I'm expecting chummy here to try any funny stuff.' He gave the prisoner a sidelong glance and spoke the next sentence in a lower tone, as if the man seated just inches away might not hear, 'though it's always as well to have two on this sort of job, just to be on the safe side.' He lifted his voice again, 'No, it's because I knew you'd like to hear this gem of a story! Believe me, he is a card!'

Giles yanked at the handcuffs linking him to the wrist of Richard Irons who, for his part, was sitting staring vacantly at the floor of the railway carriage, ignoring the presence of either policeman. His face was grey with tiredness and there was a look of bafflement in his eyes as he studied a folded piece of paper in one of his hands as if it were an oracle. Giles's action made his other arm jerk and his limp hand flopped on his leg, but induced no other reaction.

'Oy, you going to entertain us, then? We've a bit of time to kill on this journey, if you'll pardon the insensitive mention of the operative word. Come on: don't go all quiet on me, not now I've invited the detective sergeant along especially.'

Irons gave Giles a filthy look. 'I'm not a performing monkey.'

'Could have fooled me.' The jovial Giles slapped his blue-serge-trousered thigh with his free hand and laughed. 'You could do a turn in a variety show.' Giles winked at Trinder, who was silently watching the scene from the opposite bench seat. 'Listen, liss-*en*, you horrible lot... No! Oh...you there, at the back, stop tittering, I want no tittering at my stor-*ry*, 'cos its all true! No, it is!' Giles made a decent attempt at emulating Frankie Howerd, a young, up-and-coming radio comedian just becoming a hit on the Light Programme and inspiring many to copy his distinctive diction. He removed his cap with his free hand to reveal a shiny bald spot and slapped his forehead in an exaggerated manner by way of emphasis. 'Oh do come along now, do tell us the one about your friend in the spirit world.' He winked at Trinder again. 'Tell us how some apparition got you to kill a man.'

'I didn't kill him.'

'Perhaps not, but you tried to.' Giles's tone suddenly became serious. 'That's attempted murder, that is!' Giles sucked air in between his teeth. 'He might pull through, if you are lucky. But then again...' He gave a shake of his head in the manner of a builder assessing a damp patch on a ceiling, hinting at unimagined complications. He then replaced his cap and carefully adjusted it, as though to reinforce the point that any joking was now over.

Trinder was watching the prisoner carefully and privately enjoying his fellow sergeant's blustering banter. He and Giles had been friends for years and he rather liked the man's style, though he knew that his guvnor in the railway police, Detective Inspector Vignoles, would not approve.

Admittedly, the jollier sergeant was perhaps a touch loud at times, but even when dealing with the stickier moments a policeman could expect to encounter he usually managed to bring a relaxed approach to the job, reducing the levels of aggression or tension in a situation, finding space for a sympathetic smile or perhaps even a joke. It was a technique appropriate to his posting in a quiet county market town and it had made him a much-liked and respected pillar of the Buckingham community.

The situation today was a perfect example, with Giles maintaining a stream of repartee that, whilst playfully mocking, was not malicious, even though the villain in custody was suspected of breaking and entering, and of inflicting grievous bodily harm upon an innocent, vulnerable, defenceless, elderly, respectable doctor. Banter was infinitely preferable to sitting for hours in excruciating silence.

Sergeant Giles had telephoned first thing to see if Trinder would assist with escorting a prisoner by train from Buckingham to Brackley, where the accused was to be interrogated, though it was likely he would later be taken to Northampton, where the court was situated. He was sure Trinder would accept the invitation.

Trinder was with the British Railways Transport Police, one of the small team working in a specialist detective department based in Leicester Central station, on what had once been the Great Central Railway, but was now part of the extensive, recently-formed Eastern Region. He was still feeling rather pleased with the recent addition of the word 'detective' before his title, conferring upon him the same status afforded his peers in the county constabularies and, more importantly, those in Scotland Yard. Added to which, he was very happily married and the proud father of a three-month-old son, Robbie. So it was with a feeling of considerable indulgence and wellbeing towards the world that he had taken the call that morning.

He had exchanged pleasantries with Giles and traded enquiries about the health of their respective wives and sons, discussed the lack of sleep that babies induced and the merits of a drop of brandy on a finger as a means to get the child to sleep soundly. Overhearing Trinder's side of the telephone call caused WPC Lansdowne, bent over a report she was writing at the adjacent desk, to smile and exchange a glance with her colleague WPC Benson. The two women were accustomed to their sergeant's eagerness to share the ups and downs of fatherhood with anyone prepared to listen.

Finally, Giles had cut to the chase. 'It won't take long, but you'll find him a fascinating specimen. I realise you're not working the investigation, so it will be purely academic, but I'd still enjoy your professional detecting viewpoint.'

'You have me intrigued.'

'He was discovered in the ladies' waiting room at Buckingham station. It seems the late-turn porter forgot to lock the room before he went home. But that's by the bye. He was found just after 6a.m. looking bewildered, staring at some old poster he'd taken off the wall and mumbling and shaking, like he'd had a right nasty shock. Looked like someone had given him a pasting, too. The station staff gave him some sweet tea, as you do, and tried to find out what was wrong. At first he didn't speak, but when he did, he just said he'd seen a ghost. Repeated it, over and over.'

'I didn't see that coming!'

'I told you it was good! Better still, he reckons he's even got a picture of her — of this ghost! Found it at the station, on the wall of the waiting room on some old poster about a young lass what went missing ages ago, back in the war years. Just kept pointing at it and saying as it were her. The stationmaster, Mr Jeffreys, decided they needed help. He's a dependable old cove is Jeffreys. Do you know the fellow?'

'Can't say as I do, but I know the name. Go on with the story.'

'Well, Mr Jeffreys decides to give yours truly a call and seek my advice; and, as luck would have it, he called not long after the balloon went up about a robbery with violence in Turweston. A telex had just come through about an elderly gent who'd been found by his charlady. He were badly hurt, though not quite dead. She thought he must have caught the robber in the act, as there were a door and some drawers jemmied open. We were put on high alert for likely candidates who might be on the run. And then this man fell straight into my lap, courtesy of good old Jeffreys.'

'I saw that telex', Trinder responded, 'and asked all stations in our patch to keep an eye open for the perpetrator. And you think this man is responsible?'

'Open and shut case. The doctor was a cultured man, a collector of rare gold coins, really unusual ones apparently, and knock me down with a feather, two such were in this chap's pocket! What's more, chummy's got a bruise on his cheek, a cut to his hand and looks rough as hell. There's no doubt he's the villain. Watertight case, aided by the fact that the doctor reckons he can identify his assailant. Furthermore, the scene-of-crime boys say the prisoner's hat was found in the house, and chummy here is bareheaded. But what's got us laughing are his statements so far. You've never heard anything like it. He's obviously planning to plead insanity, and he might just carry it off.'

'Why, what's he saying?'

'You need to hear it from the horse's mouth, John, but, in a nutshell, he reckons a ghost put him up to it.' Giles paused for effect, leaving the telephone line to crackle and pop as the silence extended.

'Yep, you heard me right John, a ghost.'

'You're pulling my leg.'

'God's honest truth! Swears blind that's how it is.'

DS Trinder was holding the fort at the Leicester Central office whilst his boss, DI Vignoles, took time off to attend a funeral in his home village, extending this into a weekend visit to his parents. Trinder should really have remained at Leicester, ready to deal with whatever might arise, and should by rights have sent a uniformed PC as escort, but looking around the office he saw a full complement of officers, and they were enjoying a period of relative calm with only a light caseload. Everyone was just catching up on routine paperwork or dealing with minor incidents such as loose cattle on the line and the usual irritating rash of pick-pocketing. He could risk a few hours away, and so decided to accept Sergeant Giles's invitation. He enjoyed his colleague's banter and the ghost story sounded like it could be amusing. So he took the next train to Brackley Central, from whence he walked to what was known colloquially as the 'bottom station', Brackley Town, where he caught a local service to Buckingham.

Trinder was glad he had made the trip. It was a glorious, late-September day that was both warm and windless. The air was loud with sparrows brawling in the eaves of the pretty station at Buckingham, which glowed with a yellow light on the stonework, making it appear more like a lodge or gatehouse for the great country house nearby at Stowe. He was getting hot sitting in the rectangle of sun streaming through the carriage window, but was enjoying the sensation, a last 'hurrah' for the memory of another summer past. He could hear the sound of muffled shovelling from behind his head and the odd hisses and clanks the crew induced from their engine before departure. The guard blew his whistle and waved his green flag, the engine gave a short 'pop' on its whistle in response, and the train jolted into motion with a series of creaks and groans that put Trinder in mind of a wooden sailing vessel.

He allowed a little smile to himself, wondering whether little Robbie was asleep in his pram in the back yard right now, and if Violet was managing to snatch a few quiet minutes of repose in this pleasant sunshine. He flipped open his notebook, licked the end of a carefully-sharpened pencil and turned his attention back to the captive man seated opposite and securely chained to Sergeant Giles. He deliberately adopted a more conciliatory tone than his county constabulary colleague, as he was feeling content with the world, and this made him mildly indulgent towards everyone these days, even the villains. Besides, he was looking forward to hearing his story. As Trinder was a tall man of slim build, he leant slightly forward to rest his little police notebook on one of his angular knees in anticipation of taking notes. He found this a more comfortable position for writing, seated as he was on a bench seat whose springs were long past their best.

'How about going through what happened, right from the start?'

'I did that this morning.' Irons stared at the dusty carriage floor.

'I appreciate that, Mr Irons, but in my experience what someone says in the first hours after arrest is driven more by nerves than common sense. It's only natural to exaggerate or emphasise things that sound like they might help one's cause, but which perhaps don't sound quite so good in the cold light of day. Or warm sun, in this case!' He gave what he hoped was an encouraging smile, whilst the sunlight entering the carriage and striking his short and carefully combed and brilliantined hair helped emphasise his observation. 'I'm merely an interested observer, but it would be in your own best interests to run through the story once more, to make sure you haven't missed out everything.' He exchanged a knowing glance with Giles who, in anticipation of enjoying Trinder's reaction to the ghost story, was barely suppressing a giggle.

'What are you suggesting?' asked Irons, who at long last had looked up and listened to Trinder.

'I understand you make reference to certain, er, ethereal occurrences. This might not play out too well in court.'

'But it's true! I can't tell a lie, can I?'

'Telling the truth is undoubtedly going to be your best, and perhaps your only line of defence. I understand you do not deny breaking into the house of...mister, um...' Trinder looked enquiringly at Giles.

'Melcombe. A retired doctor living at Ivy Cottage, Turweston,' Giles offered, helpfully.

'And then you assaulted Dr Melcombe once inside his house.'

'It was self-defence. He came at me like a mad thing. He might be old, but he is vicious. I had no choice but to defend myself. Please believe me, you have to understand, I honestly never meant him to get hurt.'

'You've got a blummin' cheek!' Giles dropped his sunny demeanour and glared at Irons. 'You'd broken into his house in the dead of night and were caught in the process of lifting his coin collection, what did you expect him to do but go for you?' A man has a right to defend himself and all that's dear to him.' Giles looked indignant. 'Had no choice, my foot! You chose to break the law.'

'Why were you in Dr Melcombe's house?' Trinder defaulted back to his conciliatory approach.

Irons did not reply.

'You may as well admit the reason, since you don't deny being there.'

Irons looked crestfallen, as if the stark reality of his appalling situation had sunk in. Trinder waited, he knew to be patient, and in his own time the young man would start to spill the beans.

'He looked the wealthy sort. A retired country doctor was likely to have plenty of money.' Irons was feeling his way forward with his fiction. 'It was pure chance; he was as good as anyone else.' He gave a long, wearisome sigh. 'I was motivated by greed.'

'You first identified Dr Melcombe as a victim, and then located his house?'

'Yes, er, no. What I mean is, his house looked promising. I just chose one at random and broke in.'

Trinder looked sceptical. 'You already knew about his gold coin collection?'

'No. I found it when nosing around…' The last word died on his lips.

'So how did you know where to look for the coins?' asked Trinder.

'I struck lucky.'

'Pull the other one!' Giles interjected, 'you went straight for the desk. There is no evidence that you rifled through any cupboards or touched any of the other rooms. You knew what you were after.'

Irons looked guilty.

'In my considerable experience of house-breakings, it rarely happens that a burglar wanders around and chances upon exactly the right locked drawer without touching anything else.' This statement met with silence from Irons. 'Come on, tell us the truth.' Giles gave Irons a sly look.

'Someone might have suggested he had them,' Irons mumbled.

'And that "someone" is?' asked Trinder.

'I'm not sure. I can't remember.'

Giles was irritated at his prisoner's refusal to repeat the ghost story to Trinder. 'Come off it,' he snapped, 'that won't wash, that's not what you said at first.'

'All right, I do know who she is. That's to say, I thought I did, until this morning, but now I'm not sure what to believe. I'm starting to doubt everything. It's just too strange for words…stranger than you can imagine.' Irons stared at the floor again and moved his head from side to side, appearing confused.

'You have a female accomplice?' Trinder asked, feeling that he was making some small progress.

'Accomplice? Yes, I suppose that's what she was. I had not thought of her like that.'

'What is her name?' enquired Trinder.

'Betty. Betty Askew.' Irons spoke the words quietly and turned ashen grey, as if he were about to be sick.

'And what exactly is your relationship with this Miss Askew?' Trinder wrote her name in his notebook, giving Giles a quick look to prevent him from making an ill-timed observation. 'She is a "Miss", I presume?'

'We met on a train. She was once engaged, but she wasn't wearing a ring. Her fiancé was killed, or at least that's what she told me.'

'So you met her on a train and discussed her marital situation. What happened next?' Trinder asked, a hint of scepticism in his voice.

'Nothing much. We talked for a while and she...' He ran his free hand through his hair. 'Oh God, it sounds so darned foolish. I hardly know her. We met by accident and got talking. She's a girl of about eighteen, though now I can't really work out her age.' He looked Trinder in the eye and asked him, perfectly earnestly, 'Tell me, sergeant, how old is a ghost? And do they get older?'

Trinder and Giles exchanged glances, Giles feeling gratified that his performing monkey had at last mentioned the ghost. He had promised Trinder some entertainment and hated to disappoint.

Irons fell back to staring at the piece of folded paper in his hands, which he kept turning over and over in a movement reminiscent of Betty Askew's worrying away at her naked ring finger. 'I suppose you could say I fell in love with her,' Irons gave a queasy smile. 'At least, I fell into a passion for her. I lost my senses and acted rashly. But I had made her a promise and tried to follow it through.'

'So this Betty Askew is... a ghost, is she?' Trinder asked the question slowly and with caution in his voice.

'It would appear that way. And yes, that realisation has come as a shock to me, as well.'

Silence fell in the compartment. The train rattled and huffed along the single-track line, threading its way between verdant hedgerows and rolling, sunlit fields, studded with cows and sheep.

'When did you first meet Miss Askew?' Trinder decided to set aside Irons's talk of ghosts for the time being and treat this like any other interrogation.

The man's mood brightened as he replied. 'Sunday, September 3rd. I remember it exactly, as I was on my way to start at Magdalen College on the Monday. I'm a mathematics teacher. Well, I *was* a teacher. I won't have a job after this.' The final comment coincided with his face falling into a picture of gloom.

'And how often did you meet?'

'Just three times.'

'And where did you meet?'

'On the train. Twice on the last train from Marylebone to Brackley, and the final time on its return to Marylebone. We only ever met on a train. I've tried to look for her in town, but she always eludes me.'

'She must be quite a striking woman to have such an effect on you in so short a time,' observed Trinder, giving him a sceptical look. 'Did you take liberties with this young lady? A quiet train, late at night — it must have been very tempting.'

'I didn't get *fresh* with her, if that is what you are suggesting.' Irons looked deeply offended, although he rubbed an ear lobe with his free hand as he spoke, causing Trinder to suspect that this was not the whole truth. 'I must set an example, what with being a teach—'

'—you speak of honour and setting an example,' interrupted Giles, glaring at Irons in disbelief, 'yet you burgled a house and beat up an old man! You're heading to be made an example of, that much is for certain. Who can believe this silly talk of ghosts? You and your fancy girl are a team, probably moving around the country, finding folk with stuff of value, robbing them in their homes then taking off somewhere to fence the goods.'

Irons looked shocked. 'That's utterly ridiculous,' he blurted.

'Not as ridiculous as telling us she's a ghost!'

Trinder took over the questioning with his gentler touch.

'Can you tell us anything else about her?'

'She was a puzzle. I could not get to grips with her circumstances. She was always so vague about everything.' Irons gave an odd smile that unsettled Trinder. 'Maybe ghosts don't worry about time and place in the same way we do.'

Trinder and Giles looked at one another. Giles rolled his eyes and mouthed 'fruitcake'. Trinder was starting to wonder if the man was indeed deranged. He decided to get the questioning back onto safer ground. 'Did you walk her home from the station?'

'No.'

'Not very chivalrous, for a man of honour.'

'How could I? She just vanished into thin air when we came to the station! Puff! Gone. Ask the stationmaster, he'll back me up. There was a guard, too, who helped search for her. No matter how hard I tried, and no matter that we sat close together in the same compartment, she succeeded with this disappearing act. Strange isn't it? She eluded me twice. The railway staff got a bit shirty about it.'

'Shirty?'

'They denied seeing her! Made me look a proper chump. But that was impossible: it's a small station with hardly any passengers and she must have walked right past them. Though it starts to make more sense now: I mean, ghosts can walk through walls.' Irons brightened up at the realisation that the railwaymen had not in fact been using him as the butt of their joke. 'If you want proof of what I'm saying, ask the young porter at Brackley. He's seen her! It was another occasion, when I wasn't there, but he told me he'd seen a spook, a "woman in white". From his description, it was the same woman, it was Betty. Now, Betty had a pale mackintosh, so that explains why she appeared to be "in white".'

'I see.' Trinder frowned and bit his lower lip whilst maintaining a steady gaze at Irons, careful to not encourage this over-wrought and possibly unstable man into any more delusions. However, for all his attempts at maintaining a level of sang froid, Trinder felt an unpleasant prickling to his skin. It was only momentary, but the prisoner's words had struck a chord. Despite all logic and reason, there was something compelling about how Irons was telling his story. The early part of his testimony rang false, but now he was in full flow, it felt convincing. But more than that, it touched on something else.

Trinder recalled sitting in the porters' cubby hole beneath the central support of the road bridge that spanned the tracks at Brackley Central. It had been just a week or so ago, and he had been entertained by the porters telling of a strange apparition of woman they claimed was haunting the line. She forced some of the trains to slow to a halt before neatly slipping away into the night and so far had eluded their attempts at apprehending her. The men had been certain this was something far stranger than a reckless local girl with a death wish. He'd laughed it off as nothing more than a chilling story to tell when swapping anecdotes over a mug of tea around the coal fire. But now he was not quite so sure.

Trinder tentatively wrote 'ghost' in his notebook, but then drew a line through the word with an impatient flourish and looked back at Irons. 'You seem quite determined on this point.'

'I can only tell it as it is.'

'Hmm.' Trinder chewed this over for a moment. 'Pleading insanity is not a defence I would recommend.'

'Insanity?'

'No jury would heed your testimony of a ghostly apparition. We can hardly haul her up to take the stand in your defence. They'll think you're barking mad. But perhaps that is your intention.'

'Of course not.'

'Do you wished to be judged of unsound mind?' Trinder continued. 'Claiming a ghost as your accomplice might just do the trick. Think again, Mr Irons. You might reckon it the lesser of two evils to choose an asylum over prison, but I would strongly advise you to reconsider. The treatment administered in such places can be extremely harsh and very unpleasant. Some call it cruel.' He looked Irons in the eye. 'The effects can be long lasting, far longer than the punishment you would get by pleading self-defence during a foiled housebreaking attempt. Do that with a good lawyer and you could reduce your sentence by quite a margin.'

'Here, don't go letting him off the hook!' Giles looked uncomfortable.

'I'm just stating the realities of the legal system.'

'I'm not insane. Foolish, gullible, even love-sick, but what I'm telling you is the truth. My truth. I was seduced into doing what I did by the ghost of a lovely young woman.'

'Saints preserve us!' Giles rolled his eyes.

'So Miss Betty Askew, either the flesh and blood or spirit version, told you to enter Dr Melcombe's house? Why would she do that?'

'I—I suppose she'd heard something... You know, about his coins? I don't know...' Irons was lying again and being unpractised, was spectacularly bad at it.

'Are you saying that she cased the joint in advance or got a tip off?' Trinder asked.

'Um, I suppose so. I can't remember.' Irons could feel the little box inside his sock pressing against his ankle. He was determined not to mention the ring, so he looked out of the window and clammed up. He was dog-tired and his head was aching and plagued with images of the doctor's wrinkled face contorted with anger, of his blood on the carpet, and of an increasingly-anxious Betty waiting for him in the churchyard.

'Poppycock!'Giles exclaimed. 'You two are in it together, and a pretty pair of crooks you make, too. The ghost stories are concocted to distract us whilst your girl escapes. You're a very unconvincing liar, Irons, look at how you are struggling with your story: it's plain as day.' He sat back, perhaps to indicate that he rested his case.

'My colleague has a good point there,' added Trinder, 'but would you explain to me why are you so sure Miss Askew is a ghost and why she wanted you to steal gold coins that are of no use in the spirit world?' Trinder smiled, knowing he had dealt a good hand.

'I know she is a ghost because of this...' Irons unfolded the poster that had been in his hands throughout the journey. Giles allowed him enough play on the handcuff to smooth it out. It was faded and had numerous pinholes and tears at the corners. Handing it to Trinder, Irons explained: 'It was on the wall in the waiting room. Look: Betty Askew, aged nineteen, of Manor Road, Brackley. That is the girl.'

Giles puffed air out of his lips, but Trinder stopped him speaking with a motion of his hand. 'So you do know her address and her correct age. Why did you not say earlier?'

'Because I told you only what she communicated to me during our three short meetings. When I saw the poster it was the most terrific shock, I can tell you. It says she went missing in 1943. And she's dead now, so that means she has to be a ghost.' Irons sounded quite adamant on this point.

Trinder looked at the poster for some time before speaking. 'This is definitely the girl you met on the train?'

'Not a shadow of a doubt.'

The photograph was a pale sepia, due to the poor quality paper and years of exposure to light, but the smiling fresh face, the curls of hair and the open-necked shirt were still clearly defined, as were the bold, black letters above that declared: MISSING. There was a short statement about how she had vanished without trace on 19th April 1943.

'She's missing, not dead.' Trinder was frowning and struggling to make any sense of this odd story. 'Are you reporting that you've found a missing person?'

'In a manner of speaking. But do you really think she could reappear after eight years and having not aged at all?'

Trinder squinted at the photograph. Some lucky people don't change much in appearance over a few years, and that explanation is a darned sight more plausible than your ghost story. Look, if you can help us find this woman it might work in your favour. You'd win support from her family and solve an outstanding case for us.'

'Tell me', asked Giles, in a challenging tone, 'why did you say she lived in Amersham? You've got her address right here on the poster — Brackley!' The sergeant was barely managing to keep his voice controlled. 'You are playing games with us, matey.'

'No. I told you what she told me, and what I observed for myself. I concluded that she lived at Amersham, because that was where, I believe, she boarded the train, and also because something she said implied that she "had to be there", or words to that effect. I got the feeling she did not much like the place, though.'

'And she was going where?'

'To Brackley, twice, though the third time she was leaving it, on the last train going south.'

'And why was she going to Brackley?'

'She didn't say. That's one of the strange things about her. I was never clear in my mind exactly what her circumstances were. She's originally from Brackley, born there. On that point, she was clear.

'Perhaps she worked at Brackley?'

'Oh no, she said that she worked at Woodford Halse.'

'But lived in Amersham? That'd be a devil of a way to travel each day. Sounds wrong.' Trinder commented, making notes.

'I know. But it was only this morning, sitting alone in that waiting room, that I saw her face looking down at me, saw her address, and that she went missing seven years ago. To be honest, I've been in a state of shock ever since, and struggling to see how it all fits together.' Giles and Trinder remained silent. Irons spoke with such conviction it forced even the sceptical Giles to give due consideration to his claims, and to all the implications of his tale.

'Ah, there's something else. A taxi driver in Brackley became very angry when I mentioned her name. He gave me a lift and I fell into talking about Betty. I suppose I was desperate to tell someone about her, you know how it is when you meet a girl? But he was livid when I mentioned her name. He told me that Betty Askew was dead. He was quite adamant about it.'

'Can you give us any more details about this taxi driver? A name, or a description, so we can find him?' Irons recited everything he could remember about Hancock whilst Trinder took notes.

'Oh, there is one last thing, I have just remembered. It says on the poster that she's an engine cleaner at Woodford Halse shed. Well, that is one thing she did speak about in great detail. She told me that she was a member of the Dirty Girls Brigade.'

Sergeant Giles bit his lip hard to suppress an intense desire to laugh out loud. Trinder, however, realised that he now had a lead that would settle this story once and for all. If Betty Askew was, or had ever been, an engine cleaner, there would be staff records, and perhaps someone who knew her back in 1943 still worked there.

CHAPTER SEVENTEEN
Dunton Bassett
21ˢᵗ September 1950

All Saints' was a plain church, perhaps even austere, constructed as it was from pale grey limestone stained in places with the ruddy brown of iron, like spots of dried blood. This was stone that could draw in the warmth of the summer sun and appear to glow from within, but which in turn could be dour and forbidding when darkened by rain. The square tower was topped by an elegantly pointed spire visible for miles poking above the yews and other trees surrounding the church. All Saints' was set upon a small hill, one of a series that formed little rolls in the blanket of rich farmland that spread across this part of Leicestershire.

The Reverend Mr Gerard Vignoles was conducting the funeral on the east side, his head bowed over the open prayer book to reveal the circle of sun-browned baldness in his silver-grey hair that gave him an appropriately monkish aspect. His gold-rimmed, half-moon glasses were perched at the end of a long and slightly hawkish nose, and his sharp but kindly eyes below their bushy white brows dropped their gaze only occasionally to the little book opened in his hands, for he knew the service by heart.

This easy familiarity with the burial service was a cause of private sadness to the reverend in that so many had needed him to officiate in this most final of rituals, but was also a strength, for he could speak the words with true feeling and not just read them by rote from the page. He was freed to lift his eyes and cast them across the family and friends of the deceased now gathered around the open grave, making contact with those able to look away from the highly polished coffin or from staring at the shoes of those standing on the opposite side of the rectangular hole so freshly cut in the graveyard grass. He offered support with this dart of friendly contact; seeking to help the words of comfort and reassurance of a glorious after-life in the embrace of God ring true and deep.

Today, the service had an extra layer of meaning for the Reverend Vignoles, for not only was his wife Caroline amongst the mourners, but so were his daughter Gwendoline and son Charles, accompanied by their spouses. This was no family funeral however, but that of a friend; not only to the Vignoleses, but someone much loved by a great many of the folk from the two adjacent villages of Dunton Bassett and Ashby Magna.

Young James Hoden — known simply as 'Jimmy' or 'Sunny Jim' to virtually everyone — was another victim of every parent's worst nightmare: polio. A horrid disease stalking the country in recent years with renewed vigour, like a silent, invisible and unbidden killer, though one that sometimes chose to leave its victims crippled until the release of an untimely death. Some escaped; touched by the killer's hand but left with manageable scars that allowed a full and long life. But they were the lucky few.

Jimmy had managed to hold out for fourteen years, but his lungs had always threatened to collapse with the promise of suffocating the life from his thin body with its withered leg. It was a sentence unimaginably cruel. His last months had been spent incarcerated in a monstrous Iron Lung; permanently encased from the neck down in a terrifying contraption that unceasingly wheezed and sucked like a broken vacuum cleaner as it forced his chest to rise and fall in a relentless torment and command his lungs to inhale the vital oxygen. It gave him life, but it was a soulless and unnerving machine that squatted on his frail body like a nightmarish metal toad, and which forbade Jimmy any meaningful movement, his life reduced to staring at a simple light fitting in the cream-painted ceiling, feeling the bedsores worsen as his muscles wasted. It had been a release when even this miracle of modern medical science had been unable to keep him going any longer. It was barely an existence, and one without a future.

Until his last, desperate months, Sunny Jim had been a surprisingly active lad with a joyful disposition, usually ready with a cheery smile and a greeting as he stumped around the two villages on his National Health Service crutches. He soon became adept at walking surprisingly long distances traversing the field paths and bridleways and enjoying the gentle rhythm of the rural community within which he lived. But he was to be seen most often heading to and from the railway station, with a knapsack slung across his shoulders, which contained sandwiches and a bottle of fizzy pop. Notebooks and pencils were stuffed in the pockets of his shorts. For Jimmy loved the railway, and spent the majority of his short life in one of two favoured spots at Ashby Magna, the station that both separated and served two neighbouring communities on the busy mainline from Marylebone to Nottingham Victoria and the north.

Jimmy knew everyone at the little station, and was waved and whistled at by the engine crews. Packets of gum were tossed in his direction from many a moving footplate; sometimes a Sherbet Dip was handed to him by a kindly guard. The handful of regular commuters often solicited Jimmy's view on the punctuality of their expected train, sure in the knowledge that he would be as well informed as the signalman. Come rain or shine, Jimmy was nearly always there, recording the engine numbers, timing the trains with his granddad's pocket watch and waving at the diners on the crack 'Master Cutler' express that raced through without a pause.

In what turned out to be his last year of life, Sunny Jim had started taking snapshots whenever he could afford a roll of film from his pocket money, using a camera that had quickly become his prized possession. This was a second-hand, ex-RAF model, given to him for his thirteenth birthday by Uncle Charles Vignoles and Anna, his wife. Vignoles was not actually his uncle, but it suited the lad to think of him as such, and Charles for his part did not mind in the least. This now lay across Jimmy's chest as he lay in the coffin, though the carefully-pasted books of his railway photographs serving as his lasting legacy for his grief-stricken family to cherish.

Sunny Jim was a boy after DI Charles Vignoles's own heart, and so it was with a mixture of sadness and a desire to offer a final kindness to the young lad that he now looked at his watch, carefully tracking the passage of the hands. He then met the gaze of Jimmy's father at the head of the open grave, and gave a little nod. It was time.

'We therefore commit his body to the ground: earth to earth, ashes to ashes, dust to dust...' The Reverend Mr Vignoles took a small handful of loam and tossed it onto the coffin, creating a sound like falling rain as it hit the lid. As he continued the solemn service, Jimmy's mother took a deep breath and followed suit, managing to watch with teary eyes as her husband then did the same, finally turning to rest her cheek on the lapel of his black jacket.

'And I heard a voice from heaven saying unto me, Write, Blessed *are* the dead which die in the Lord...'

Someone sniffed, a nose was blown into a handkerchief; the wind flapped a black dress hem and tossed a couple of leaves into the hole, where they spiralled above the coffin, another mourner tossed some grains of soil. Anna gave her husband's arm a gentle squeeze.

'Lord have mercy upon us, Christ have mercy upon us...'

There... Charles Vignoles tensed slightly. It was very faint, carried on the wind, that odd churning and almost turbine-like sound of a distant steam engine approaching at high speed. The constant, rapid-fire beats of the whirring cylinders and panting exhaust blending into a rising and falling note carried across the fields only to echo off the church, entwine in the trees and bounce between the rows of the distinctive slate gravestones or to slip between the holes in the simple, cast-iron Celtic crosses that were a peculiar feature of some of All Saints' grave markers.

As the Reverend Vignoles came to the end of the Lord's Prayer and fell silent, there came the whistle like an extenuated wailing like a lonely curlew above windswept moorlands. It stopped, but sounded once again, the powerful roar of the express noisily underpinning the wavering note.

The mourners exchanged teary glances as hands patted backs and arms held others that little bit tighter. Then came the final flourish. After the two heart-rending, keening wails like something from an Irish wake, there followed a ludicrously cheery 'Toot-tooty-toot-toot!' that broke the spell and caused a ripple of spontaneous laughter to erupt, helping release the tension that had become almost palpable.

It worked delightfully and the timing was impeccable. Sunny Jim's last request had been fulfilled to perfection: a send off by his favourite locomotive, Leicester Central's big Pacific *Sir Frederick Banbury*, driven by his favourite top-link crew and passing at high speed for full effect. As the rattle and roar subsided and the long rake of carriages flew past in a smooth whoosh of wheel on rail, the graveside gathering started to break up into huddles of people, all dressed in black, dark brown or lilac, in suits or sombre dresses cleaned and pressed especially for the occasion but still bearing a whiff of mothball from the back of the wardrobe.

Charles Vignoles and his wife left his father shaking hands and offering further words of condolence, and took the opportunity to slip away. They would leave the grieving parents to spend the remainder of the afternoon with close family. Vignoles had done what he could in arranging the steamy send-off, and both he and Anna, together with Gwen and her husband Michael, had helped arrange the wake. Now they had little more to offer.

They walked down the gravel path from the church and through the metal wicket beside the substantial black-and-gold painted gates that guarded the impressive entrance to church and rectory, and which had somehow evaded being melted down in the drive for metal for the war effort. Beside these gates there stood a Celtic cross carved from granite that was the village war memorial, which bore a surprising number of local names, each picked out in gold leaf. One of the names not included however, was that of Vignoles's younger brother Jack, who had been killed in Spain serving with the International Brigade. The government had not endorsed these anti-Fascist volunteers, and it was a source of some private sadness within the family that his sacrifice was unrecorded on a memorial outside their church.

Pausing for a moment of reflection, they walked down the short but steep hill into the heart of the village, Anna's arm linked through her husband's and Vignoles puffing on a pipe of sweet tobacco, both in that quiet frame of mind that funerals induced.

'Shall we walk to Dunton and back, then take a well-earned drink in the Jolly Friar?'

'Splendid idea! And I'd like to call in at the station on the way back and see how it went down there,' Vignoles agreed. 'It was probably quite a sight with the staff lining the platform.'

'How lovely. But how sad that the very person who would have most loved to have been there and seen it, was not.'

'Perhaps he was — in spirit?'

Anna smiled. 'I hope at least he was aware of the love the village folk felt for him. We can't really ask for much more.' They walked on in silence for a while. 'You know, Charles, I rather like the idea that he might come back and haunt the place one day. He could take up his usual spot at the platform end and keep watch on us all, and then in the night when it's all quiet and we're lying in our bed in the rectory, we might catch the distant sound of him stumping along the road.'

Her husband took a puff on his pipe and nodded approvingly. 'I like the sound of that. Though he might spook the passengers. There again, I'm sure they'd all recognise him as a friendly spirit.'

'A far cry from some of the visitations in that book you gave me.' Anna smiled up at her husband. 'It really is fascinating reading, but a bit unnerving at times.'

'I'm glad you can't put it down.'

'The stories are marvellous and I'm becoming really intrigued, although I do think we could do with Sunny Jim in the mix to add a more friendly balance. It's noticeable just how nasty most spirits and apparitions are! There are a small number considered benign, but the majority are downright terrifying. I wonder why they always have to be so dangerous, murderous and scarifying.'

'Dare I say, because they make for a better story?'

'Hmm. You don't believe in this sort of thing, do you?'

'My inclination is to say I do not. All delightfully diverting, of course, but I suspect the majority of these stories are either works of pure fiction invented to fill a long winter's evening or are based upon events that actually took place, but which have been misinterpreted or exaggerated over time.'

'You're just such a pragmatist, Charles!'

'It rather comes with my job, I'm afraid. It would be very remiss of me as a detective to take everything I was told in an investigation on face value and not question it.'

'But you don't completely dismiss the possibility of contact from the other side?'

'No—o, I suppose not.' He looked unconvinced. 'It would be foolish to insist that there was no such thing, especially when I've never had any contact with a ghost, convincing or otherwise, let alone been able to prove or disprove their existence.'

'And yet you believe in the Holy Ghost.'

'Of course.' Vignoles took a thoughtful puff on his pipe and pondered this apparent contradiction. 'But I'm not sure that's quite the same sort of ghost. Certainly not the sort you have in mind.'

'A force for good rather than bad, but otherwise why is it so different? Could there not be evil or naughty spirits stalking the world?'

'Ye—es...' Vignoles replied, but he looked even more unconvinced.

'OK, perhaps I am getting a bit fanciful, but I think I can understand how there might be unquiet souls about, doomed to wander the earth or cross the skies forever.'

'What a romantically vivid imagination you have, Anna!'

'You can blame the author for that.'

'All right, put me down as mildly agnostic on the issue, though I can assure you that if I ever hear something going bump in the night, I will assume it is an intruder and deal with him accordingly. We have far more to fear from the living than from the dead.'

'I shall try to find comfort in that statement.'

An hour later they descended the wooden stairway covered by an elongated glasshouse onto the island platform of Ashby Magna station, where Vignoles's attention was taken by an elegant, beautifully-presented, former GWR loco simmering at the platform end, waiting for the 'right away'.

The sunlight brought the oiled depth of the locomotive's deep green colour alive and the bright brass-and-ivory detailing was gleaming in tribute to some serious elbow grease by the cleaners. His eye was especially drawn to the curving nameplate that declared in heavily-serifed capitals that this engine was the 'Evenley Hall'.

He was asking Anna if she could remember the location of the actual hall after which it was named, when the stationmaster approached them. At that moment the engine pulled away with an almost aggressive barking sound that hurled neat puffs of steam into the air like punctuation marks.

'Fine engine. Looks like Banbury shed must have borrowed her for a few days. When an engine in that shape comes in you want to keep hold of her.' The stationmaster was shaking Vignoles by the hand and smiling as he spoke.

'A cracker. Not seen her before... Anyway, good to see you, albeit not in the cheeriest of circumstances.' The three exchanged the kind of looks one did after a funeral. 'How did it go off? Sounded wonderful up at the church.'

'Splendidly. We did the lad proud down here. You should have seen the engine, really bulled up a treat. They'd polished every inch and even put a few flowers on the buffer beam and wrapped a black crepe ribbon around the smokebox handles.'

'How sweet!' Anna smiled wistfully, her dark eyes becoming teary. 'Engine drivers can be softer at heart than they look.'

'Well, it cuts through everything, doesn't it? Makes you think about what really matters. And footplate men really know all about life and death, as theirs is a dangerous job.'

'Quite right. Though thankfully accidents are infrequent on this line - and long may it stay that way,' Vignoles replied.

'You watched the train come through?' asked Anna.

'Indeed. Everyone formed a line, hats and caps doffed. She was going like the clappers. He was really giving her the gun, as they say. She'd be in Rugby before they knew it!'

'Jimmy liked them going fast,' observed Vignoles, and they all smiled fondly as they recalled how the lad loved the crack expresses the best.

'Have you time for some tea?'

'Thank you, but we've rather worked up a thirst for pint of Tiger in The Friar,' replied Vignoles. Anna nodded in agreement.

'Can't blame you. Wish I could join you. Another time, eh? When do go back to Leicester?'

'Tomorrow. But we could call in for a cup of tea before our train.' Anna added.

'You'd be most welcome.' The stationmaster grinned as the couple turned to start the climb back up the steps. 'Oh, but wait a moment, There is something you must see. Back in a tick.'

Anna and Vignoles exchanged puzzled glances as the stationmaster entered his office and almost immediately came out holding a carefully-folded newspaper. 'Local rag left on a train. The guard passed it on: he thought I'd want to read the railway story inside. It's quite a tale.'

'Really?' Vignoles eyed the *Buckingham Advertiser* with curiosity. 'What on earth could be so interesting in Buckingham? It's on a rather sorry little branch line. Perhaps the news is that a train actually ran along it!' he laughed.

'Ho ho, far more interesting, Charles. You won't guess in a million years, but here: take it, look it over when you have a pint to hand. You might need a drink after that,' he winked. 'Page two. Tell me what you make of it over tea tomorrow.'

'Thanks very much. Cheerio!' Vignoles tucked the folder paper under one arm and they climbed the steps.

Half an hour later, Anna was seated on a bench by the window of the Friar public house. 'Charles, I really do think you should read this. It is most peculiar, though I'm not sure you are going to like it.'

'Oh yes?'

'Dear old John Trinder is involved with a ghost.'

'A *what*?' Vignoles had a glass of ale in each hand, the frothy heads bubbling over, dripping down the sides and splashing onto the table. 'What has my sergeant been up to in my absence, then?' He mopped up the spilt liquid with a bar towel then placed a half-pint before Anna. 'Might I need a fortifying dose of this first?' After swiftly downing a good quarter of his pint he pulled the opened paper across the table and started to read aloud from where Anna was pointing with one of her perfectly-manicured fingers. '*Robber's ghostly accomplice sought by police. Is she the long lost railway girl?*

The police are hunting for a woman they would like to interview in connection with a robbery that took place on the night of Tuesday 19th in Turweston. There is a mystery at the very heart of this apparently run-of-the-mill crime that has the otherwise sleepy village talking of nothing else and has got the police scratching their heads.'

Vignoles paused to roll his eyes at Anna, then continued. *'At first sight this appeared to be just another housebreaking. The criminal was disturbed whilst he hunted through the valuable coin collection of retired doctor Percy Melcombe, 70, of Ivy Cottage, Turweston, just a step across the county border in Northamptonshire. The burglar, Richard Irons, 23, a mathematics teacher at Magdalen College School for Boys, Brackley, assaulted Dr Melcombe and left the poor man unconscious and bleeding.'* He frowned. 'A schoolteacher at Magdalen breaking and entering? That does not sound right. *The attack has shocked the usually peaceful community. However, the story takes on a most surprising aspect following the arrest of Irons in Buckingham railway station the following morning. According to Sergeant Trinder of the British Railways Detective Department, the burglar's accomplice in this botched theft was the ghost of a young woman... "They are apparently working as a team", explained Sergeant Trinder.* What the blazes?'

Vignoles's eyebrows shot up. He turned to his wife. 'I leave the office for a couple of days and the next thing I know my sergeant's talking to the press about goodness knows what nonsense! I've never read such drivel in all my life. Has Trinder completely lost his marbles?' He carried on reading, agog at what might come next. *'Irons has advised the police that the apparition can only be seen on the late Marylebone–Brackley Central train. He claims that the spectral girl told him exactly who to burgle and when.* Oh, did she, now?'

He drank some more beer and gave Anna a disbelieving look, she in turn suppressing a laugh behind her own raised glass. *'Irons insists she is the ghostly spirit of a long-missing young woman. He has been cooperative and given us a name and description. We are withholding her name whilst we make further enquiries, as the circumstances are rather peculiar, added to which, the veracity of the prisoner's statement must be called into question.' The police would offer no further details about this incredible story leaving us to speculate on what it might mean.* Thank God for that,' Vignoles exclaimed, relieved. 'At least Trinder appears to have learned something about discretion.' He resumed reading. *'Is there really a ghost riding our railway and encouraging young men to become thieves? Or is the culprit trying to bamboozle the police? The Buckingham Advertiser will be keeping a close eye on developments and is looking forward to witnessing both Irons and his other-worldly lady accomplice when they appear in court. That should be a county session to remember! Dr Melcombe is recuperating in Brackley Cottage Hospital but he is expected to make a full recovery.* Well, that ends the story on a positive note.' He paused for a few seconds, staring into space, then drained the last few inches of beer from his glass and placed it on the table.

'What am I to make of all that?'

'You have to admit, it is intriguing. And how strange we should have just been having a conversation about ghosts, not an hour ago.' Anna was smiling, hoping to diffuse her husband's bluster and annoyance. 'I think it sounds awfully exciting and improves a dull housebreaking story no end.'

'I'm glad you think so.' Vignoles had removed his distinctive, rectangular, silver-framed spectacles and began wiping them with a soft cloth. 'Tell you what: you can lend Detective Sergeant Trinder your book.' He stressed the rank and title with irony, 'perhaps it might help him invent an even better story to fuel this paper's desire for cheap sensationalism. No, better still, let's rope in the shag-dog of Birstall and be done with!' He replaced his glasses carefully and gave them a last prod into position with a finger, then impatiently picked up the paper again.

Anna looked deadly serious. 'I suspect the dog only frightens off men and is no use for finding women in white.'

'Eh?' Vignoles tossed the paper on the table and stared at Anna, who now gave him a mischievous look, eyes twinkling. 'Oh, yes...' He realised she was pulling his leg. He shook his head again, this time with amused disbelief, then tried to drink the last dregs from his glass. '*Ghostly accomplice*, indeed...'

'Another?' Vignoles stood up with his glass in hand and waggled it in the air. 'I know I could do with one. Let's just hope I can keep a lid on it and stop it going national. I'll need more than a drink if the Badger gets wind of it. Can you imagine what that old stick-in-the-mud will do when I tell him we're trying to arrest the spirit of a dead person! Not that we should be joking about that. There is one aspect to this ludicrous story that concerns me: the reference to the missing girl...'

CHAPTER EIGHTEEN
Brackley
22nd September 1950

'Dr Melcombe, you really must rest. It's not right to exert yourself so soon after such a nasty attack. It could set you back and you'll only end up staying here longer.'

'Heaven forbid...' he muttered darkly.

'And I'm quite sure neither of us would want that, would we?' Matron Blackthorne was a chubby, buxom, rosy-faced woman with greying hair pulled into a bun, much given to bustle, chatter and fussing — everything a small cottage hospital might want in a matron. However, she had almost met her match in the intractable doctor. 'I think your telephone call can wait until tomorrow, at the very least. You have a broken collar and ribs that will only mend by rest, rest and more rest.'

'Nonsense! I'm perfectly fine. They're just light fractures. And since I've been bandaged up like an Egyptian mummy I am hardly likely to fall apart on the walk there and back!' He spat the words out with force, but privately was fighting to conceal the considerable pain in his chest and all down one side. 'I'm quite capable of walking down the corridor. Now, if you will just stop fussing and fetch me my dressing gown, you can point me in the direction of the telephone.'

Matron's mouth formed a narrow line as she fixed her gaze on the swathes of bandages and the livid bruising creeping from beneath them across his sickly skin. 'The doctor gave strict instructions. You wouldn't want to get me into trouble now, would you?'

'I don't give a fig what that drip has to say, and, frankly, unless I get to make that call, there will be a darned sight more trouble!' He glared at her.

Matron returned the defiant look. She was used to the odd difficult patient and had learned to develop a thick skin to enable her to let such ill-mannered behaviour slip by like the proverbial water off a duck's back, but even so, Melcombe was a particularly irritating man. Doctors were, of course, the very worst patients, inclined to argue about everything. She folded her arms as she delivered her final word. 'I shall allow you five minutes — not a moment more!' She wagged a finger. 'Don't think you are the only one who can kick up a fuss.' She lay his dressing gown across the end of the bed. 'I'll get a nurse to help you.'

It took him at least five minutes just to make his way to the matron's little office and shoo the overly-attentive nurse away to leave him in peace. He slumped in the wooden, round-backed chair and took a few laboured breaths, his temples throbbing. Being struck on the shoulder and in the ribs by a fire poker, then being knocked out by his head cracking against a solid wall had taken more out of him than he would admit to the matron. He could do with a stiff whisky; instead, he had to make do with inhaling the ever-present smell of surgical spirit and floor disinfectant.

However, what had really rocked his equilibrium was not the physical assault — he'd have a go at anyone who dared to break into his home and not care a jot for his own safety. The physical injuries would heal with time and he was not shaken up about stumbling upon an intruder. No, what had really left him reeling and on the edge of nervous collapse was the little square of paper he'd found in the top right-hand desk drawer that had been so crudely forced open. It had perhaps shocked him even more than the loss of his precious Cobra's Eye.

He'd regained consciousness sometime in the early hours of the morning. The thief was long gone and a cold draught from the open front door played across his face and neck, causing him to revive and awaken. The adrenaline had instantly kick-started his battered body, helping him find the strength to crawl across the floor to his desk, using it to haul himself to his knees, scrabbling with desperation through the disturbed mess on top of the desk, not caring for the valuable coins scattered across the green leather surface, which he sent carelessly spinning and cart-wheeling across the floor in his desperate panic to see if his secret was safe.

Almost immediately his worst fear was confirmed. Something truly dreadful had happened, something that went beyond a simple burglary and a cracked rib or two. The drawer that held his secret had been forced open. His blurred eyesight cleared sufficiently to detect the fresh, pale wound where a screwdriver had damaged the wood. He leant heavily on the desk and made a frantic yet futile search of the drawer, fighting against the agony of his injuries, his blind fear momentarily cutting through the pain. He felt physically sick at the awful emptiness of the drawer, the very lack of the small and ornate brass-and-ivory box and its precious content. He let out a cry of anguished despair, then noticed a small square of cream paper with an enigmatic message. What could it mean? All he could comprehend at that moment was the phrase *the Cobra's Eye*. He paused and thought for a few moments, and realised this meant that the ring had been taken by someone who *knew... Someone who had left him a sign that he knew about his dark and guilty secret.*

He had a confused recollection of stumbling and blundering about the room, the little note clenched in one fist, but eventually the effects of concussion and the mental and physical shock of this dreadful night had overwhelmed him, and he had slipped back into unconsciousness.

Melcombe still had the note, now crumpled and wrinkled with the force of his grip. He'd apparently refused to let go of it when the ambulancemen had come to take him away, after his housekeeper had discovered him at about seven that morning. The note had been the first thing he had seen upon opening his eyes in the hospital bed — instantly attracting his attention as if it were a red triangular warning sign on top of a black-and-white banded post on a sharp bend in a road — forcing him to instantly remember what had happened, and the recollection inducing yet another groan of dismay that had nothing to do with his physical injuries.

The handwritten words were like acid eating him away from the inside in a searing twist of fear, for this could mean only one thing; the ring had been swapped in a deliberate and calculated move. If he was not such a pragmatic, unimaginative sort of man, he might be inclined to think the note was like a voice calling to him from the grave.

But harsh reality was worse than any such wild imaginings. The physical reality of this scrap of paper meant that someone — presumably that young man who had broken into his home — knew about The Cobra's Eye and, worse, how it had come into his possession, even though he could swear blind that no living soul was aware he had it in his possession.

'I'm connecting you now, Dr Melcombe.' The operator's voice was clear and crisp, her diction immaculate. He grunted acknowledgment and gripped the receiver hard, the black Bakelite already clammy with his sweat.

'Yes? How might I help?' The voice was confident, the accent home counties underpinned by a richness that suggested a love of cigars and brandy. It was a voice of a man unlikely to be easily flustered. It was everything the doctor needed to hear right now.

'It's Melcombe. Percy Melcombe.' He was breathing hard.

'I realise that, or else I should not have taken this call at my club.'

'Sorry, it's important, I cannot speak for long, and we must be circumspect.'

'Of course.'

'I need your help. It's urgent, there's no time to lose.'

'I see.' There was a pregnant pause. 'What has happened?' The man's voice betrayed no hint of emotion, remaining as clipped and precise as that of the operator.

'I've been beaten about a bit. I disturbed a burglar in the night and he lashed out at me...'

'Oh, my goodness, I am so sorry to hear that.'

'It's nothing, and that's not why I'm calling.' He was breathing heavily, perspiration on his brow. 'What matters is that I don't think the intruder was just any old burglar. He was keen to make it appear like a straightforward attempt to lift my coin collection.' He paused to stifle a wave of pain. 'The police will think he was after that, but he actually took something of far greater value — and this is important — he left something its place. Something to mock me.'

'That is most curious.'

'He's taken something that absolutely no one knows about — not even you.' Dr Melcombe stared at the closed door of the matron's office, peering through the frosted glass panel to check there was no eavesdropper outside. 'To do with that particular *problem* of some years back.' He could feel his breathing quicken, heart pounding. 'This makes me fear our solution to that problem did not go completely unnoticed — it's the only possible explanation.'

'That's not good, not good at all.' The man cleared his throat. 'Let me get this clear, you *are* talking about that rather tricky matter in '43?'

'The same.'

'Ah.' He left a heavy pause hanging, as the enormity of the news sank in. 'And what makes you so sure this third party is aware of that event?'

'The message he left is quite unambiguous.' The old man felt his hand trembling as he held the handset and noticed a painful tightening around his heart. 'It refers directly to the person in question. I cannot explain more over the telephone.' He was gasping for air as he spoke. 'It would be ill-advised.'

'Quite so. And what of the thief? Did he escape after assaulting you and leaving this enigmatic calling-card?'

'Yes, at least at first; but I understand he was apprehended shortly afterwards. He is under arrest. I've been told to expect a visit from the police later today to give a statement.'

'He sounds little more than a rank amateur. Are you quite sure he's such a risk?'

'When I explain the exact circumstances, you will understand why he must be stopped. Damn and blast, this could jeopardise everything!' He banged the desk with his free hand and immediately felt burning flames of pain scream down his shoulder. 'Ow!... sorry... breath is short... He could destroy us. Do you understand?' Melcombe was failing to control his voice, his apprehension and the physical pain were now taking their toll. Beads of sweat formed on his brow and the air rasped through his constricted throat.

'Calm down and pull yourself together, man. Going to pieces won't help.' The other man's voice was terse and clipped, and if he shared Dr Melcombe's concerns, then he did an excellent job of concealing it. 'Very well, leave it with me. I will see what can be done with this burglar. Do you know who he is?'

'Richard Irons. A young man working in the town as a teacher.'

'Interesting. I shall make further enquiries. A suitable solution may prove costly, of course.' He left a suitable pause. 'That coin collection might need cashing in though, old chap.'

'Have them, have the lot if you can fix this... Just deal with this man and make sure you get the...' Melcombe stopped.

'Get the what, old man?'

The telephone line crackled as both men fell silent.

'He took some of the coins... get them back, that's what I meant.'

'I see.' The clipped voice made it clear the speaker was not fooled. '

Leave it to me, then. I shall come to speak privately with you as soon as I am able. In the meantime, this is what you will do...'

CHAPTER NINETEEN
Amersham
23rd September 1950

The man coughed quietly to attract attention, then rubbed the end of his nose and twitched his greying moustache, waiting patiently for Jocelyn Liney to look up from *The Financial Times*.

'Yes?'

'Sorry to disturb you, sir, but we've found something you might want to take a look at.' The man hovered near the open French windows, conscious that he must not step inside and onto the expensive Wilton carpet, something that he had already been warned against by Mrs Liney.

'Can you be more specific?' Liney's thoughts were already drifting back to the lists of share prices. He was not in the least interested in anything the man had to say. He'd convinced Isabella to allow him to get these chaps in to relocate the stone bird bath and having scored that satisfying victory he was not about to become involved in any more gardening, not unless he was absolutely forced to. He was paying the man to do the job, and he could jolly well get on and do it.

'It's a sort of box, sir. Buried beneath the bird bath.'

Liney flicked the paper with annoyance. 'What do you mean by a *sort* of box? It's either a box or it is not, man! More junk, no doubt. There was enough of the stuff littering the place when I cleared out the border. What makes it worth telling me about?'

'Well it's wooden, but rather good quality. Too nice to be stuck in the ground.' Liney just raised a quizzical eyebrow, but held his silence.

'Shall we lift it, sir?' The workman added, sensing he ought to be taking a stronger lead in the conversation.

'Why not?' He put aside his newspaper, folding it noisily and fussily to express his annoyance and stood up slowly, still feeling the effects of his gardening exertions even after so many days, silently reflecting that his wife may have a point about how cold this room is, as it had left his fingers chilled and his knees stiff. 'I suppose I'd better have a look.' He forced a hint of a smile, remembering how delighted he was to have this man and his mate to do all the work, and thinking perhaps he'd better not put the chap's nose out of joint by being too stern. 'Maybe it will contain something valuable to offset your fee — haha!'

'What is it, Jocelyn?' Isabella entered the room carrying a vase of flowers.

'Apparently they've found something buried beneath the birdbath now!'

'Is it more women's clothing?'

Liney pulled a sudden look of displeasure, though he hurriedly softened this, and darted a quick look at the workman as though nervous he might react to this revelation. 'Of course not. It's a wooden box. An empty one, I'm quite sure.'

'How intriguing.' Isabella put the vase on a crocheted mat protecting a small side table, then brushed her hands together as if to remove some imaginary dust transferred from the brilliantly-shiny piece of porcelain. 'It will certainly have to come out as I'm planning a magnolia to go there.'

The three walked across the immaculate lawn towards the border now partially filled with new plants placed in the recently-turned earth. Yet more plants were standing in a neat row, waiting to be planted, each still in its pot and with little paper tags from the nursery around the stems. A green tarpaulin was spread on the edge of the lawn, upon which lay the birdbath on its side beside the hefty stone base now resting upon two strips of timber to spread the load. A large wooden wheelbarrow holding tools was to hand.

A second workman, in grubby trousers and a cream-and-brown chequered shirt with rolled up sleeves was in the freshly dug border, bending over, hands on thighs, staring intently down a hole. He straightened up as they approached and gave a slight nod to the Lineys, whilst taking a deferential step backwards.

'If you walk on these planks you won't muddy your shoes. There you go... See, it looks like well-polished wood. Nicely fashioned, and with a little carry handle on the top.' The elder of the workmen took his place beside the hole as he was speaking. 'Any idea why its there?'

'None at all. The birdbath was in place when we bought the house. Well I never, that is indeed most curious.' Liney looked genuinely puzzled.

'I say, do you think it is one of those time capsule things? It looks awfully good quality and not just a common old packing crate.' Isabella Liney's eye's lit up. 'I've always wanted to know what people put in them. Just imagine!'

'Steady on, old girl, that might be raising our hopes a little far, but it's a surprise all right. Well, you'd better haul it up so we can take a closer look. I just hope it doesn't turn out to be a damp squib after the build-up you've just given it, Isabella.'

The younger of the two men stepped forward without prompting and knelt down, threading a strong piece of cord through the carrying handle before standing upright, wrapping the cord around his wrists and taking a firm grip with both hands and hauling hard. The muscles on his brown forearms bulged as he strained, and then the soil started to give a little, and he caused the box to jiggle from side to side to release the compacted earth. After a minute of pulling and rocking the box, he was able to lift it free.

The older man caught hold of it beneath the base and held it close to his chest. 'It's not heavy, though I'd say there's something inside. I'll take it across to the tarp.'

It looked like the sort of box that might hold a scientific instrument, perhaps a large microscope or weighing scales. The wood was dark and close grained, probably mahogany, with neat brass hinges that had discoloured green, though they looked as though they would polish up bright again. The older workman gave it a quick wipe over with a cloth and the dry soil dropped away cleanly. The sunlight brought the colour of the wood to life, but also revealed an ugly dark stain down one side that badly disfigured it in a series of splashes and smudges. He looked up at Liney with a questioning expression.

'Ugh. That stain's a pity, it rather ruins the box.' Liney wrinkled his nose. 'No doubt that's why it was stuck down a hole.'

'Come along, open it!' Isabella could bear the suspense no longer.

The man laid the box on its back, so the front could be more easily opened and reveal the contents to all at the same time. As he fiddled with the little key that was still in the lock and which had seized up during its time beneath ground, a cloud scudded across the sun, switching off its cheery and warming rays in an instant.

'Got it. Here we go.' He pulled the door wide open.

Isabella's face moved in a fluid slow motion through a series of expressions; from eager excitement into dawning disbelief and then finally melting into a mask of terror, with staring eyes, flaring nostrils and lips curling back from a mouth opening wider and wider. Her scream was long and piercing, one awful, blood-curdling, sustained note that was finally cut off as her knees inelegantly crumpled and she collapsed onto the lawn, an arm flung wide, one hand pressed flat across her mouth.

Nobody moved for what seemed an age, though it was probably no longer than a second or two. It was true that, in these extreme moments, time really did slow to a snail's pace and everything became intensified. The scene unfolding before them would remain vivid in the memory of each person present, as if burned onto the brain, and would prove impossible to dislodge. Liney was later able to recall, of all stupid things, that an earwig was slowly crawling up the side of the box.

How could he be enthralled by a mundane insect when the partially-decomposed head of a young woman stared out at them? Her empty, rotting eye sockets, sightless through a matt of pale brown hair, her waxy skin stained with brown blood or eaten away in ugly, stomach-turning scars and wounds, her teeth transformed into vicious points and ugly stumps, the flesh consumed to the bone around her delicate jaw.

The stench from the box was nauseating and, indeed, someone began noisily throwing up his lunch. Liney spun away and sought refuge from this nightmarish sight by trying to comfort his wife, cradling her head and feeling her stir in his arms as he knelt beside her. He became aware that his shoulder was being shaken.

'Do you have a telephone? Mr Liney, sir. A telephone? Do you have one?' The elder workman was ashen, his voice weak and lifeless.

'Er... yes... of course. In the hall... Oh God...' He rocked backwards and forwards on his heels.

'We must call the police.'

Isabella made a loud groan, rolled over onto her side and started sobbing, her shoulders heaving. Liney stared at her with an expression of incomprehension, his face drained of all colour. 'No, wait! Let's not be too hasty.' He stood up and gulped in some air, rubbing his temples with both hands. He made a supreme effort to not look down at the box. 'We need to think about this. What should we do for the best?' He looked scared.

'Do?' The workman scowled. 'What do you mean *do*? There's only one thing to do.' He was jolted out of his own state of shock and recovered some of his previous energy. 'We call the police right this minute and none of us touches anything until they get here, that's what we do!'

'Of course...of course. Yes. Oh dear God, but the scandal. I'll be destroyed. Ruined! Have you any idea? Have you any bloody idea what this will do to me?' His shock was presenting itself as anger, just as his wife's was showing as hysterics and the younger workman's with being sick.

Liney spoke gently to his wife. 'Bella, pull yourself together. Come on, stand up and go inside. I want you away from that... thing.'

'Are you going to make that call, Mr Liney, or shall I?' the workman persisted.

'No. I'll do it.' Liney replied, but made no move to do so.
'What was that about some clothing in the garden, sir? Your wife said you'd burnt a woman's dress and bag.'

Liney's Adam's apple bobbed and his cheeks flushed noticeably. 'That was nothing, just old rags. Yes, I burnt them.'

'A bit of a coincidence,' remarked the man, developing a suspicious tone.

'You've got a damned nerve! You don't think I have anything to do with...with this?' He was shaking, whether from a sense of outrage or shock was unclear.

'I don't know what to think, but the police have to be told about that as well. Take care of your wife, sir. She needs you right now.' His voice had lost every trace of deference and had taken on an authoritative tone that clearly would brook no argument. 'Right, sir, now I'm going to make that call.'

CHAPTER TWENTY
Leicester Central
25th September 1950

DI Vignoles was seated behind his desk, navy suit jacket draped over the back of his chair, pipe smouldering in his left hand and feet resting on the fat hot-water pipes running beneath his office window that overlooked the station concourse. In one hand he held the local newspaper whilst the other was spread open across the mounds of papers and files and other odd items that seemed to permanently clutter his desk, creating a gently rising and dipping paper landscape that could almost be a contour model of the land near Dunton Bassett. He did not look happy.

'First the *Buckingham Advertiser*; then the *Banbury Cake* and now today's *Leicester Mercury*. The genie is out of the bottle and this silly story is spreading. I've had Mrs Green shoo away at least two journalists this morning and the phone has not stopped.' He tapped the paper with his free hand to punctuate his sentence for effect, enhanced by the insistent sound of the telephone ringing, followed by the weary voice of his secretary as she answered it. 'It'll be the nationals next and then we'll really be in hot water.'

'Sorry, sir. I fear it has rather caught the public imagination.' Detective Sergeant Trinder looked chastened.

'For goodness' sake, what were you thinking of? Talking to the press about such idiotic twaddle.' Vignoles took a long pull on his pipe and turned his head to eye the embarrassed sergeant, whose lanky frame loomed large in the room.

'A slip in concentration, guv. I was just assisting Sergeant Giles in moving a prisoner, but when we reached Brackley Town this young reporter fellow had obviously got wind of what was going on and asked for a few words as we stepped off the train. He was right there, practically button-holing us. Caught me off guard, I suppose, guv.'

'It's your job as prisoner escort to be *on* guard, sergeant.' Vignoles closed his eyes for a few moments as if drawing upon a reserve of patience to face the next part of the confession. 'And then?'

'Giles only mentioned that we had apprehended a thief, but this cub of a reporter slipped in a question about a ghostly woman on the train and that rather threw us off balance. It took us by surprise that he already had part of the story. We should have whisked Irons away but instead I found myself saying something about this being an unlikely angle and requiring further investigation and...'

'In other words, you helped fuel speculation about the more lurid elements of this ridiculous tale.'

'In a manner of speaking, it would appear so, guv.' Trinder winced.

'Did Irons get a chance to say anything?'

'Giles forbade him to say a word, but we could not prevent him nodding in reply to some of the reporters' questions.' Trinder coughed to clear his throat. 'The problem is, Irons blabbed quite a lot in front of the station staff before he was arrested.'

Vignoles gave Trinder a long stare, but he knew his sergeant was right. There were other avenues for the press to explore if they made the effort to look. 'Do you have any idea what damage this has done? The unnecessary anguish it has caused the Askew family?' Vignoles spun around so that his feet were beneath the desk and took a moment to straighten his red-and-silver, diagonally-striped tie. He faced Trinder. 'I've had a distraught and frantic Henry Askew on the blower demanding that we tell him exactly where his daughter is. What the blazes was I supposed to say?' He tossed the paper on top of the others on the desk and jabbed a finger at the grainy image of a young Betty Askew printed on the page. 'The first I heard about her was when I saw this! Luckily, I'd bought the paper on the way to work this morning and read the story before I took his call.' Vignoles exhaled as if breathing out his frustration. 'At least I didn't sound like a complete imbecile,' he muttered ruefully.

'Sorry, guv. Her name leaking out was unfortunate. We did not mention it once, so I can only presume that after that first story in the Buckingham paper, other reporters did some digging. Perhaps one of the station staff at Buckingham told them about her. The staff found Irons at the station looking distraught and clutching that blasted poster, declaring that he knew Miss Askew, and that she was a gho...' He stopped mid-word, caught on the sharp end of Vignoles's disapproving stare. 'All this was before he was arrested, of course. At that point he was just an oddball in need of help so her name could have come out, anyway.'

Vignoles sat back in his ancient, curved-backed wooden chair, tipping it backward on creaking springs that allowed such movement. 'Okay,' he waved a hand as if blowing all this away. He spoke softly now. 'I will allow that her name was already in danger of breaking cover before your involvement, but you showed a lack of circumspection in front of the press. They have a job to do and they don't care a jot what upset they might cause by grabbing a headline. Nor do they care about how I'm supposed to explain all this to the Badger.'

'Has he spoken with you?' Trinder winced.

'Not yet. I can only assume the story has not yet hit the London papers, but it soon will, at this rate.' Vignoles stopped and fiddled with his pipe for a moment, taking another puff or two. As he did so, he observed Trinder's manful attempts at stifling a yawn and how his usually immaculate grooming had slipped that morning, evidenced by a slight kink in the usually ruler-straight side parting in his slicked-down hair, and the slight nick to one side of his jaw from a less-than-perfect shave. Trinder was sleepy thanks to a restless night with little Robbie, and even a rebuke from his inspector was failing to stop him feeling the effects. Vignoles knew a substance that could perk the fellow up.

Vignoles reached across to a bell-pull concocted from a grubby length of rope attached to a brass arm extending through the matchboard panelling that ran along one side of his office, dividing his part from the larger main room his officers shared. He gave the rope a sharp pull, and a bell clanged once on the other side. He'd been promised a proper intercom system years previously, but the signal and telegraph boys had yet to show any inclination to provide it, and so this crude but simple system continued in use, summoning Mrs Green to his door.

'Two coffees if you please, Mrs G. And make it strong. No, make us a pot: we'll be here some time.'

'I'll have to see if we have enough coffee first. It's been devilish hard to find this past week.'

'Do try your best. Cadge some off the refreshment room girls, if necessary. The poor sergeant here will nod off if he doesn't get some soon!'

Mavis Green rolled her eyes at the idea of asking for this precious commodity from the woman with the mobile drinks trolley parked outside their office. 'I'll see what I can do. And you have had a further six requests for an interview from various nationals and some of the seedier elements of the gutter press. I sent them all packing.' Without waiting for the response she knew was coming, she left and closed the door.

'They can all go to blazes!' muttered Vignoles, but he reined in his temper and cursed more quietly than he might. 'All right, John, the carpeting is over. Lesson learned, eh?

'Yes, guv.'

'And do stop calling me guv! Ever since you became a DS you seemed to have picked the habits of the Met. Now let's see what we can do with this—' he gestured at the papers between them '— muddle we've got ourselves into. First thing, I cannot see how the burglary has much to do with us in the railway detective department. It's a constabulary matter, surely.'

'Yes, though I understand there is already a minor dispute developing about which force should take on the investigation,' Trinder was cautiously feeling his way into the conversation. 'Irons was arrested in Buckinghamshire, but the crime took place in Northamptonshire and neither force seems eager to follow it through, using Irons's statement that he only ever met Miss Askew on a train. So both forces are trying to argue that this is actually the crucial link. The railway journey, that is. Both constabularies would prefer us to take it on.'

'You are joking.' Vignoles raised a hopeful eyebrow, then pulled a face as Trinder confirmed that he was not. 'That's probably because it has the potential to turn awkward, what with the unhappy parents now on the scene. God knows I'd prefer to avoid walking on egg shells whilst I try to explain how their long-lost darling daughter is being talked of as a criminal.' Vignoles puffed out his cheeks and exhaled slowly. 'A tough job that nobody wants. No, this is just a breaking and entering job that went wrong. There's nothing more to it. All this talk of ghosts, or whatever nonsense, is just smoke and mirrors signifying nothing. Pure *Wizard of Oz* stuff pitched perfectly to amuse the press, but nothing to concern us.'

'There *are* some puzzling aspects to the case, though.' Trinder was opening his notebook and wondering if this was the time and place to mention how the railwaymen at Brackley Central had told him about a woman haunting the station area in the past few weeks, and how their description bore an uncanny similarity to Irons's description of the ghostly woman he'd met on the trains.

'Just as there are at the start of many cases, and surely one of the constabularies can tease those out and make sense of them.'

Vignoles was not impressed. 'From what I've read and from what you've told me, they should have this boxed off in no time. Besides, never in a month of Sundays will Badger give us the go-ahead to take this on. Forget about this amateur burglar. However...'

Vignoles paused as Mrs Green entered carrying a tray holding a tall, green-and-brown pottery coffee pot with steam emerging from the spout, two mismatched cups and a jug of milk. There followed a lot of fuss as the newspapers were gathered up and more space cleared on the desk to accept the tray, prompting a file to fall off the edge and spill papers across the wooden floorboards. Eventually some semblance of order was established and Mrs Green left, but not before observing that she was planning 'to give this place a proper going over in the coming week.' A statement that sent shivers through Vignoles, who knew that he would be forcibly evicted from his own office for a day and would not be able to find anything until a good few weeks of intensive re-cluttering.

Both policemen now settled back in their seats taking sips of the hot and surprisingly strong coffee. 'I don't know how she does it, but this tastes good,' observed Vignoles.

'I understand your wife may have some bearing on the matter,' Trinder replied. 'Mrs V can always find a bag of decent coffee beans to pass on to Mrs G.' Trinder risked a smile, sensing that the worst of the ticking-off was over.

'You're probably right. She can find things to eat and drink no one else can, rationing or not. It's my father-in-law who tips her the wink about where to look. He has the contacts in the trade, and besides, no self-respecting Italian would serve the wishy-washy muck we in England usually call coffee! Now, where were we? Ah, yes: if we push this Irons fellow to one aside, what *is* interesting is his claim to have found the missing Elizabeth Askew. I feel duty-bound to follow this up for three reasons. One, I've had her father on the phone; two, she was railway staff; three, she was last seen on our railway back in 1943, and apparently she's back on it again now, so that places her firmly within our purview.'

'Good point.'

'Badger will take the bait on this angle. Get Blencowe and the Howerth lad onto it: tell them to dig out her case file. And they can take a look at what the newspapers had to say about her disappearance at the time.'

'Can you recall Askew going missing?' asked Trinder, sipping his coffee. 'I'm not sure that I can.'

'Vaguely, but it's perhaps too intangible to have lodged in the mind clearly. She went missing and was never heard of again. That was it, nothing more. I find it hard to hold on to so many negatives. Sad...' Vignoles waved his hands in the air as if trying to excuse this failing. 'I was not on the case first time around, although I do have a feeling that dear old Badger may have been. I think the Northants constabulary was driving the investigation back then, as our department was relatively new and still finding its feet.'

'Perhaps you could ask the chief superintendent about the case? It might help smooth things over with the newspapers.' Trinder was relishing a shot of caffeine that helped banish the effects of being woken at 3a.m.

'I shall. But one thing this department will be clear about is, she's not a ghost; so let's have no further mention of that.' Vignoles peered over the top of his spectacles to make the point, like a barrister in court, then poured them both some more coffee. It was going down fast.

Trinder was now relieved that he had not mentioned the woman on the viaduct, nor the story doing the rounds about the Seven Whistlers being heard in the night sky by a Woodford loco crew. He cringed at the thought of Vignoles's reaction. 'You think she's his accomplice?'

'It looks that way. A real flesh and blood woman doing a reconnaissance job, finding suitable victims with something worth stealing in their homes and tipping Irons the wink. A young woman is rarely perceived as a threat and could easily wheedle her way into the confidence of an elderly chap living on his own.'

Trinder was nodding thoughtfully. 'That follows. Maybe she worked for Dr Melcombe for a spell? In a domestic, or possibly a secretarial, capacity.'

'It would be worth interviewing the doctor to find out how she made contact. He might be able to recall when and where he met her, and if she entered his home. We must establish if this woman is the same as the long-lost girl as a matter of urgency. We have a moral duty to determine that point, one way or another. Once we've found her, she can be handed over to face due process of the law, but at least her parents will know she's alive. She worked for the LNER at Woodford Halse shed, so that makes her one of ours. Part of the railway family.'

'Is it credible that this woman is really the missing Betty Askew?'

'I don't see why not,' Vignoles shrugged. 'Returning like the prodigal daughter. The son in the parable was no angel, after all… But let's just hope she has come back. Crook or not, at least she would be alive. News of a missing teenage girl always sends a chill to my heart. It rarely ends well, but we can hope.'

'Why do you think she disappeared?'

'Why indeed?' Vignoles carefully placed his cup on the saucer and stared at the ceiling, watching a spider crawl along the dust-furred cable of the pendant ceiling lamp. 'There could be many reasons and one should not assume it was a result of something sinister. She was a grown woman, and…' he searched for an explanation, '… she may have eloped with a man deemed unsuitable by her parents, for instance.'

'A lot of our gals took up with Yanks and Canadians over here around that time, and sometimes it was frowned upon. Did you get any idea what her father was like?'

'Hard to say from one strained telephone conversation, but pretty down-to-earth was my impression. He was tense and brusque, but that's hardly surprising under the circumstances. We'll speak with both parents in due course. He sounded genuinely worried, but that does not preclude him from having prompted her to run away.'

'An unhappy home life, perhaps?'

'We should be alert to the possibility. Of course she could have been blasted to atoms by a V1 rocket or something. Were they coming over at that time? No, too early…well, a land mine then… no matter.' He looked doubtful. 'But surely someone would have remembered if she was in that part of town on such an inauspicious day.'

'Unless…' Trinder sat upright, looking eager, '…unless she was somewhere she was not supposed to be.' He held a finger up in the air, like a conductor might in order to direct an orchestra, but to hold Vignoles back while he tried to collect his thoughts. 'Maybe she deliberately concealed her true whereabouts that day. Slipped away, taking care to cover her tracks because she was having a secret affair, and sadly, ended up as one of those poor unfortunates who got so blasted to bits nobody could identify what was left.'

Vignoles nodded slowly. 'That might work. You see, John, any number of explanations present themselves when you set to thinking about it, and none of them involve the supernatural.'

'Point taken.' Trinder gave a sheepish grin. 'But let's assume for a moment she ran off with a thoroughly unsuitable man and has lived under another name these past years. Are we saying that she's now taken up thieving?'

'People do all manner of things. If it was indeed the case that her man friend was not to her parents' liking,' Vignoles puffed on his pipe and raised an eyebrow, 'well, perhaps he turned out to be a thoroughly bad egg and got her embroiled in a life of crime.'

It was now Trinder's turn to look unconvinced. 'But why would she choose to resurface on her home patch years later? Darned risky, as someone would surely recognise her.'

'That is a puzzling aspect, I agree, as indeed is Irons's desire to alert us to her existence. If he'd kept his trap shut we wouldn't even know she was part of the set up, let alone go looking for her. But for all we know, she's been working this operation for some time. Perhaps she became overconfident.'

'And this Richard Irons, guv, do you think he's the criminal she eloped with?'

'He is, apparently, only twenty-three. Seven years ago he would have been, what, sixteen? An artful dodger type who recruited a girl two years his senior. Hmm... it's possible, I suppose, and yet the man is a schoolteacher. Could he have been training for a respectable profession by day and out house-breaking by night? It just sounds so very unfeasible.'

'Maybe she became a criminal, and then recruited him. Maybe becoming a teacher was just a smokescreen to conceal his criminal activities. Same with the girl, she becomes an engine cleaner in order to appear to have a respectable job.'

'Well, it's all speculation, so get me some facts on the table. Dig out her file as quickly as you can, and anything else that might prove useful. I want a copy of Irons's statement and all that you can recall of your conversation with him so we can pick it apart. We'll interview the felon in due course; not about the burglary, but about her. When we have something concrete to work on, we'll go and talk to her parents.'

CHAPTER TWENTY-ONE
Brackley
4th March 1943

'Oh, but you must come, Betty. You simply must!' Rosalind Dale's eyes sparkled with excitement as she clasped her workmate's hands. 'It's promising to be quite a bash, not like the usual dreary affairs with that terrible old wind-up gramophone and rattling loudspeakers. They've got the Squadronnaires performing with a real band, and there's a cold spread included in the price of the ticket, and as the Yanks are paying for the whole kit and caboodle, it'll be wizard! They always have heaps of food — and top quality too. That alone has to be worth the price of the ticket.'

Betty Askew gave a pained half-smile. 'I'm sorry Ros, but I'm just not in the mood. I've not been in the mood for months. I sometimes wonder if I ever will be again.'

'Exactly my point! Look, no one blames you for feeling blue. God knows it's a cruel blow — but you still have the right to live a little. You can't just keep on working all hours and never let your hair down, not even once. It's not good for you.'

'Live?' Betty dropped her gaze. 'That's the problem, isn't it? I'm alive and Ray isn't. It just feels so darned unfair. Wrong.' She looked bitter. 'He was home for just a few precious weeks then forced straight back to that awful desert — and for what? To die. What right do I have to dance and laugh when he's lying beneath six foot of sand?' She pulled her hands away from Ros's and pressed a clenched fist to her lips, narrowing her eyes in an effort suppress tears. 'What do I care about anything doing me good?'

'Because we care about you. Your parents care, and I'm quite sure Ray's parents do, too. You look so tired and exhausted, Betty. You're so thin and down in the dumps. You can't just keep slogging away in the loco without respite.' She gave an encouraging smile. 'Look, it's just for a few hours, just one evening when you have a chance to dress up and put on a brave face, maybe even forget about everything, just for a little while.'

'Forget? Why would I want to do that?' She looked sulky.

Ros smiled sympathetically. 'No one imagines for one second you will ever forget Ray, it's just an expression. But you know what I mean: an excuse to leave your worries and cares at the door. They'll still be there the next day, I'm sorry to say.'

Betty gave a rueful raise of her eyebrows but looked less tearful whilst listening to her friend.

'Ray would do the same if it were the other way around, I'm quite sure of it,' Ros Dale continued. 'We all have our cares and others have lost loved ones, too, but we just have to carry on as best we can. How can any of us function if we spend all day thinking about the suffering in the world and this damned war, on what might happen to us any moment if a bomb lands?'

'I know...I know.' She sighed deeply and gave her friend an imploring look, searching for encouragement. 'I suppose I could do with a chance to stop thinking about the war and all that goes with it for a while. It makes my head spin sometimes.'

'There's nothing wrong with going to a dance. In fact, I think it's our patriotic duty to stay cheerful and not give in. That horrible Goebbels would like nothing better than to say he'd broken the spirit of the women of Britain, so we jolly well need to show him what's what!'

'I doubt he'll be watching a dance in Brackley Town Hall.' They both laughed at the absurdity of the idea, and Betty's mood noticeably lightened.

'Perhaps I am exaggerating, Betty, but there is something vital, something *necessary* about not giving in to these blue moods.' Ros took a deep breath, her voice adopting a casual tone, 'I find I can cheer myself up by thinking about all those young American airmen who'll be there...'

Betty raised a carefully-plucked eyebrow and gave her friend an arch look, which Ros noticed.

'Not like that, you silly goose!' She paused for effect, her eyes twinkling with a hint of mischief. 'Well, it depends,' she giggled. 'I've seen one or two around town who are quite dishy,' she gave her friend a coquettish look, 'But that's not the reason I'm going to the dance, of course.'

'Are you sure?' Betty gave a wistful smile, as if recalling happier times spent discussing the relative merits of a man in uniform.

'Come to think of it, that's exactly the reason!' They both laughed, Betty surprising herself in so doing. 'Some of them do look like they've been lifted straight out of school, though!' Ros put a hand over her mouth. 'They look too young to be sent over to fly a dirty big aeroplane to bomb Berlin. They look scared half to death, if you ask me.'

'Perhaps they are.'

'Probably with good reason.' They exchanged meaningful looks. 'They could be lost a night or so after the dance. Gone forever.' Ros looked thoughtful for a moment. 'Oh dear, and now it is me who's sounding defeatist and gloomy! Seriously, I just think they deserve a couple of hours of harmless dancing with the local girls. It seems the least we can do.'

'As long as it is *just* that!'

'Of course, Betty.' She flicked her hair. 'But if they behave *really* well, then maybe I could allow a little kiss on the cheek at the end of the evening. To wish them *bon voyage*.'

'You can jolly well count me out there, Ros!' But Betty's face had softened, despite her outburst. 'All right, you've persuaded me. I'll come along and I'll do my best. But I can't promise to stay to the end, it might be too much for me.'

'Attagirl! That's the spirit.'

Betty Askew toyed with the diamond ring on her hand. 'So, where do we get tickets? We'd better buy them before I lose my nerve.'

CHAPTER TWENTY-TWO
Leicester Central
26th September 1950

Chief Superintendent John Badger slapped his brown leather gloves on the side of the desk and watched the bluebottle fall dead to the floor. 'That's about the long, tall and the short of it, Vignoles. He's dropped all charges and there's no case to answer.' He gave an almost apologetic shrug. 'Not unless we decide to prosecute the young fool for trespassing in a ladies' waiting room.'

'Which was left unlocked, unlike the general waiting room, leaving him little choice but to use that room.'

'Eh? Actually I was not being completely serious, though between you and me, it sticks in my craw that a common criminal can just walk free. What kind of an example does that set?' Badger twitched his moustache, giving the edge of the desk another swipe as though he were slapping the young man in question.

Vignoles considered his statement. 'If Dr Melcombe is not interested in pressing charges, that is entirely his prerogative.'

'Seems to me being whacked about has removed his common sense.'

At that moment a locomotive waiting impatiently beside the platform outside let off a jet of steam from the safety valves with a sharp pop, like an over-shaken bottle of champagne releasing its cork. This was followed by a very loud hissing and roaring that filled the office through the partially opened window, fizzing about the walls with a sound on the edge of being physically bearable.

'Damn, how can you live with that infernal racket?' Badger tried to cover the fact that he'd jumped almost out of his chair by readjusting his position, twisting around and crossing one leg over the other, fingers carefully tweaking a trouser leg so the fabric did not stretch over his elevated knee. 'So that's it, though, frankly, I can't say I'm too sorry to see the back of the more crackpot elements of the story. Your job now, Vignoles, is to ensure the newspapers knock this childish yarn of a railway ghost on the head. I want it killed off, understood?'

'An interesting choice of words, but I agree with you.'

'You do? That makes a change.'

'The trouble is, this sort of lurid claptrap sells papers and the public appear to be lapping it up. I can't do an awful lot to dampen their enthusiasm.' Vignoles brightened up, 'but at least it's boosting ticket sales.'

'Is it now? The traffic department may well clap themselves on the back, but whilst the detective department is being linked to the hunt for some blasted phantom, it's making us a complete laughing stock. We'll be known as the *defective* department at this rate.' It was a rare attempt at a witticism by Badger, but Vignoles appreciated it. 'They can sell as many tickets as they like for their little train to nowhere, but cut us out of the picture, and make it snappy!'

Since the newspapers had picked up the story of 'the woman in white haunting the line', there had been a sharp increase in the number of people taking the last train to Brackley Central. Monday night had seen the usual handful of regulars boosted to a half-full train, and the following evening the three carriages were filled to capacity in both directions for the first time since the service was introduced. The crew had been made to work noticeably harder than usual to lift their train out of Marylebone and when it finally steamed into Brackley it was onto a platform unusually busy with yet more curious onlookers and a couple of press photographers who dutifully snapped anyone and everyone, including the bemused driver and his fireman. There had been a lot of noise and chatter, much hustling and bustling and loud complaints that there was nowhere to get a cup of tea during the twenty-five minutes turnaround. By the time the train arrived back at Marylebone not one person had seen a ghost.

'I suggest the most effective way to put a stop to this is to find Miss Askew. It works on a number of levels. Find her, and we placate her parents, plus solve a case long grown cold, and for a hat trick we end this silly tale with some positive publicity for our department. We could snatch victory from the jaws of defeat.' Vignoles, although surprised at the news that Irons had been set free, was pleased with how everything was playing out along the lines he was hoping to follow.

Badger nodded appreciatively. 'Yes, that would do the trick.' He placed his gloves on the desk and picked up the poster that Irons had taken from the waiting room wall. His eyes softened as he fell silent for a moment in contemplation. His voice lacked its usual bark when he added, almost wistfully. 'Do you think she's still out there?'

'I do.'

Badger stared at the faded photograph of Elizabeth Askew. 'If she is alive, that would fix everything very neatly', he remarked. He placed it carefully on the desk. 'Just because Dr Melcombe has, rather stupidly in my opinion, dropped all charges against that Irons fellow, and has asked that the investigation be called off, there's nothing to prevent us reopening a missing person's case and looking for this young girl. The question is, can we justify doing so based on this man's delusional ramblings?'

'I've only had the Askew file for one day, but I've read it through and considered the case. The trail is cold, but it strikes me it was never especially hot. I'm not convinced enough energy was expended looking for her back then.'

'Well, there was a war on, resources were stretched to breaking.' Badger sounded defensive. 'It was all hands to the pumps, literally at times. There was so much rail traffic and most of it war stuff, all needing our special attention...'

'I remember the time well.'

'Maybe we had insufficient time to devote to the poor lass. But the priority then was the war effort above all else...'

'Water under the bridge now, sir. Irons is adamant it was Askew that he met on the train, so, assuming he's sane, she's still alive. I have a copy of his statement and the notes my sergeant made when escorting him, and Irons is very convincing on this point. So with your permission, I think we should go on the hunt for her.'

'But Irons could easily have made it all up, based on seeing her name and image pinned to the wall,' Badger stabbed a finger at the poster laying on Vignoles's desk. 'After all, he knew nothing more about her than is written on this! Check his statement for yourself.'

'That is a valid point, sir.' Vignoles nodded in agreement. Badger had his moments of thinking like the detective he once had been, before he'd chosen instead to advance his career aggressively up the greasy pole of the police hierarchy. 'He's quite able to play games with us, that much is for sure. He's hot headed and a bit naive, but mentally sound, I think. I'm not sure what to make of his odd claims about Miss Askew, nor what he hopes to achieve by making them, other than to confuse us. We must find her as soon as possible and get her side of the story.'

'She could be an impostor. A doppelganger who's taken the girl's identity.'

'That's plausible, but either way, the family needs to know.

The parents will be suffering dreadfully, thinking their daughter is taking train rides to Brackley and not calling in to see them. We need to give them some sort of answer.'

'Darned right, inspector, so make it snappy! I'll give you until the end of the week.'

'That's not long enough, sir; the trail is going to be devilishly hard to pick up after so much time.'

'Nonsense, you've only got to follow that idiot Irons as he walks free and he'll take you straight to her. I'd put money on it, Charles! He strikes me as an incompetent fool and, as she's his fancy bit, he'll soon go running back to her. Anyway, you like all that undercover stuff, so here's your chance to tail him. I'm giving you carte blanche, what d'you say to that?'

'I also need to speak to the Askews. And to Dr Melcombe, as I need to quiz him about Betty Askew...'

'You'll have to cut the doctor out. He wants nothing more to do with the police.' Badger's attention was now being drawn to the sensuous lines of a bronze statuette depicting a lithe and virtually naked dancing girl. This had resided in Vignoles's office for more years than anyone could remember as an item of unusually attractive lost property that had never been reclaimed. 'He's got his stolen coins back, and that's it, as far as he's concerned. He was most insistent on that point. '

'I won't speak to him about the burglary, but as a witness in a missing person enquiry. I think she paid a call on him, maybe worked in his home. It's vital we get his statement in case there's a clue that could lead us to her.'

'Sorry, Charles, off limits. My hands are tied. You cannot speak with the doctor. So, time to put on dark glasses and a false moustache, and get on that young tearaway's tail. You'd better get your skates on, you've only got until Friday.'

CHAPTER TWENTY-THREE
Brackley Central
26th September 1950

As the train rumbled south Irons could feel his heart pounding with the same urgent beat of the engine, reminding him of that dreadful sprint from Ivy Cottage in the dead of night. His feeling of apprehension was increasing exponentially the closer the train drew to Brackley.

He felt as though he were on the edge of nervous collapse. The last forty-eight hours — or had it been longer? —had been a living hell. He could barely remember what day it was. It felt like a lifetime since he had been arrested. Day and night were rendered much the same whilst in custody, time taking on a whole different meaning when liberty was denied, each hour stretching to breaking point when seated on a hard wooden bench with just a square of barred and filthy window high in the wall that imperfectly differentiated between daylight and the lamp burning on its post outside the cell. His existence had been measured in cups of strong tea offered by burly men in uniform jingling keys and giving him strange looks, or worse, taking turns to peer through that horrid little sliding shutter in the cell door, whilst muttering and laughing like cheeky schoolboys at the zoo peering at a caged animal.

Thankfully he was now free, though he felt like a mariner back on shore after a long voyage, with the ground beneath his feet dipping and rising without warning, making him both unsteady and slightly nauseous. It was as though he was intoxicated by this newly-regained liberty, and yet he'd drunk just one pint of Sileby Bitter a few hours earlier in an attempt to gather some Dutch courage. One beer had not been enough. He needed the fuzz of inebriation to knock the edges off everything. He slumped into a corner of the compartment and hung his head, thinking gloomy thoughts.

The world that just a few days ago had been normal and ordinary now appeared alien and dangerous, populated by people who made barely-concealed comments behind his back or fell silent as he passed, their eyes pursuing him. It was a world filled with pressmen ready to pounce with pencil and notebook, demanding that he recite his story about the ghost on the train. Everyone was a potential threat, from the surly ticket inspector to the women with their huge wicker shopping baskets in the ticket queue who openly discussed his 'being mixed up with a girl who'd run away'. He even received a sly glance from a smart businessman with a sturdy dog.

Yes, by some extraordinary circumstance he was free and with no charges pressed, but he was guilty, and everyone knew it. He'd been released through the inexplicable kindness of a doctor he'd bashed with a fire poker, but he was not absolved of responsibility for his actions nor of the guilt he felt for what he'd done. It almost made him feel worse that the doctor had chosen to take back his property and let him walk. Such generosity of spirit was in stark contrast with his ugly criminal intent.

He'd lost his job, of course. Not that he'd dare to return to Magdalen College School for a while, but he knew full well, without having to suffer the humiliation of facing the headmaster, that he would be barred for life from teaching, either there or anywhere. Word would get around. To undergo the painfully embarrassing ordeal of showing his face at the school right now would serve no useful purpose other than to crush his spirit even further, and he was not sure he could take much more. In time he would send for his trunk, but for now he had literally nothing more than the clothes he stood up in.

Irons felt so angry at himself. He'd been a bumbling fool and woken the doctor. If he'd just taken more care and not made so much noise. He ran a hand across his face as though cleansing these thoughts from his mind, just like he used to wipe long division sums from his blackboard with a dampened cloth to reveal a freshly cleaned surface, like new tarmac slicked with rain. Waking the doctor was not the point. He should never have listened to Betty and allowed himself to be seduced by her tale of woe and loss.

So the doctor was an evil, thieving, brutish monster was he? A nasty man who'd taken a valuable diamond ring from her by force? Well, the old fellow had shown a willingness to forgive a heinous crime, and that flew in the face of her description. It's true that the old man had attacked him for all he was worth, but that was in defence of his property. She'd duped him, all right. Pretending to be the poor innocent, whilst wheedling away to get him to do her dirty work. The audacious cheek of it!

And how did a lowly engine cleaner come to own such a diamond, unless by devious means? It was laughable to think it was given to her by a humble army private. She'd even got her dates muddled, and the worst of it was, he'd spotted that before he'd committed any crime and yet that still had not stopped him! He didn't even challenge her. How could she have been engaged in 1942 and still look like a teenager today?

She was nothing more than a confidence trickster, a smooth and dangerous operator able to slip in and out of a railway carriage without being observed. Both he and that pedantic old guard had been looking for a woman walking down the platform in full view, not an agile trickster who might even have slipped out of the train onto the track. Or perhaps she'd changed her hat and coat, altered the way she walked and fooled them that way? Music hall illusionists were always pulling tricks like that, so why not Betty? For all he knew, she'd been close at hand each time, watching and laughing at his bewilderment. It made him angry and embarrassed in equal parts.

He remembered how she was deliberately vague with her answers and her eyes always so sad and doe-like and constantly on the edge of tears, pulling at his heartstrings in a cynically manipulative manner that he, idiotically, fell for, hook line and sinker. Had she not always sought him out in that virtually empty train? Chosen to be alone with him, a single man, when she could have had a whole compartment to herself? Oh, she really knew how to work on his emotions. She made a point of sitting enticingly close, arousing his senses and provoking his amorous interest, making sure their knees touched suggestively, cradling his hand between hers, kissing him. She'd worked on his intellect, too, leaving an enigmatic note that would compel him to stalk the same blasted train until the time and place suited her to reappear and deliver the *coup de grace*. It was all so bloody obvious now.

If that were not enough, he'd added ridicule to his ignominy by claiming she was a ghost. What a joke! Irons made a sound that could almost have been a bitter laugh. He lit a cigarette, exhaling a deep lungful of acrid smoke, his elbows on his knees, and stared at the dusty linoleum on the compartment floor.

A long night on a hard bed in a cold cell had given him a different perspective on events. That DS Trinder had been astute: he had indeed been changing his story after having time to think it through. This woman, whoever she really was, had obviously noticed a similarity between herself and the face on that old poster and ruthlessly exploited it to her own ends. It was a clever touch, a neat twist, in a perverse sort of way, and he could not help himself from feeling a grudging but enormous admiration for how well she'd played it. Someone should put her on the stage. MGM would pounce on acting as good as that.

Irons stared at the burning cigarette in his hands, turning it one way and another to make the smoke curl and loop as it rose towards the carriage ceiling. A slight, ironic smile started to play across his face and there was a mean glint in his eye. He still had the ring.

He was incredulous that the police had not bothered to frisk him thoroughly enough to have checked his socks. It was pretty obvious from his job that he was not really the criminal sort and his willingness to confess to the crime and offer up the coins in his pocket and blather on about ghosts and other daft rubbish had probably been enough for them. The sergeant had merely checked all of his pockets and left it at that.

So, he held the ace card, and now it was time to play the winning hand. The girl promised that she would go to the graveyard every evening and wait for him. Neither of them had imagined that this much time would have passed without his showing up, though. Nevertheless, he was sure she'd be there this evening. He'd go, but she was not going to get everything her way; he'd demand they sell the ring and split the proceeds. It was perfectly reasonable. He was due some recompense. He'd risked imprisonment and a criminal record, and had in all probability ruined his entire career in order to help her, so she could hardly expect to walk away into the sunset while saying 'thanks a lot' casually over her shoulder, and with a thousand or more pounds worth of diamond in her hand. A fifty-fifty split of its considerable value was only right and fair.

Irons felt the train brake and immediately tensed. The semi-fast stopper was approaching Brackley Central, where he would have to run the gauntlet of the staff and their disapproving stares. He would prefer to arrive unseen. He'd timed it so dusk was encroaching and he was hoping he might be able to keep his head down and skulk about in the shadows.

He stood up, stubbed out his the cigarette on the floor with his shoe and pulled his hat brim low, conscious that this same hat, until just a few hours ago was being readied to be brought as evidence against him. A small paper tag bearing a number was still pinned to the inside band like a curious memento.

Lowering the window in the carriage door on its leather strap, Irons leant out to look along the train, watching the fragile clouds of luminescent steam drift from the locomotive cylinders only to be beaten into little cloudlets by the spinning wheels and restless motion of the connecting rods. The train was approaching the station on a series of reverse curves, allowing him a fine, clear view of the locomotive and a brief glint of golden light reflected from the polished brass nameplate that he recalled bore the odd name of *Umseke*, until the train swung the other away, revealing the blue-brick road bridge spanning the tracks and the island platform with its necklace of twinkling lights glimpsed between its arches.

Irons was ready with his hand on the door handle, prepared for a speedy disembarkation, but he suddenly dipped his head and arm back inside and pressed his back against the vestibule bulkhead. On the platform stood a man in a long trench-coat, and Irons didn't like the look of him. Even from that short glimpse of his profile silhouetted by a gas lamp that threw a long shadow across the platform, he knew the man was waiting for him. There was something about his confident, almost menacing stance; the cigarette dangling from his lip, a hand in one trouser pocket that threw his coat open on one side, legs slightly apart. *The press!* If he were not a hack, Irons would eat his newly-returned hat. They had an unerring ability to sniff out a story and clearly this example of the breed had got wind of his return. That was a blow. Nobody must know he was in town and above all he must not be followed when he went to the churchyard.

He looked around, frantically trying to think of a solution. The train was almost at a standstill. He crouched low and kept his head down. Taking a leaf from Betty's book of tricks he crabbed his way to the far side of the vestibule, reached up to the door latch then swung the door open to reveal a view onto a grassy embankment studded with dark bushes, with a wooden fence running along the top. He sat on the floor and eased himself over the edge, then dropped onto the stony ballast, praying the sound of his feet landing was masked by the passing of a noisy luggage trolley along the platform.

Irons reached up to slam the door shut, then glanced up and down the line of coaches. The curve of the platform placed him out of sight of the engine crew and the guard would be occupied for the next few minutes, so this was his chance. Still keeping low and careful to place a hand on his hat — it had helped incriminate him once too often already — he sprinted to the rear of the train and crouched below the black-and-white painted edge of the platform, his head close to one of the oval-shaped buffers on the last coach. On the platform a couple of wooden boxes were being lifted onto a trolley, whilst a group of school prefects in their distinctive Magdalen blazers walked towards the stairs; Irons recognised one of them as Fernyhough minor from 4B. There was a surprising number of people milling about and he thought he saw a man with a camera which had a flash reflector mounted on the top. Perhaps the newspapers were out in force?

The reporter that had attracted his attention was striding up and down the platform and smoking aggressively in short, impatient gestures, and Irons allowed himself a satisfied smile that he had at least spoilt the man's evening. No copy would be dictated down the telephone from the kiosk in the station foyer tonight. He also noticed the stern stationmaster standing sentinel in his office doorway.

It was time for the train to leave and Irons needed to make his next move. He looked back at the embankment, beyond which there stood a sturdy, detached, brick-built house nestling in a corner between the road and the side of the railway and surrounded by a clutch of verdant fruit trees and flowering bushes. A short run of steps led from the edge of the railway up to the back garden and Irons guessed this must be the stationmaster's dwelling. The steps were but a few yards away across a length of siding that held a solitary open wagon, and masked from view by the train in the station. He heard a call, a door slam and *Umseke* hissing with anticipation. It was now or never.

He ran as fast as he could, hoping his sprint would beat the famously quick station starts on this line and he could be out of sight before the train cleared the station. It felt as though many eyes were boring into the small of his back and he awaited the urgent shout that would betray him. Behind him, the train made a great whooshing sound followed by a series of deep barks. The wheels spun for a moment until caught by the driver and the tremendous energy was converted into forward motion, followed by more roaring explosions from the chimney. The rhythmic beats grew faster, echoing around the station and sending a sulphurous cloud of smoke and steam tumbling over Irons and the steps he was ascending. It was the perfect smokescreen, and he was able to bound to the top and swing open a little wooden gate on a metal spring and step into a dusky garden filled by the scent of engine smoke and roses, hot oily steam and flowering ivy.

The garden was large and filled almost to bursting with plants. Fruit trees arched above his head and tall bushes flanked the brick path laid in a herringbone pattern. There were rows of vegetables, fruit bushes, a shed, a greenhouse and a little square of lawn spanned by a washing line. How the stationmaster's wife must curse the proximity to the railway as she hung out her laundry. He stood still, drawing breath. All was still and a blackbird sang loudly in a branch above his head. He could see a warm yellow light from a window.

He adjusted his vision to the rapidly-increasing indigo of heavy dusk that was creating darkening shadows between the thick bushes and flower heads. It was the light spilled from an open door that drew his attention, and the pinprick of orange that moved like a glow-worm through the air. He stared more intently and then started as though jolted by electricity as he realised that a pair of eyes was staring back at him through a gap between some hollyhocks and the lower branches of a pear tree.

It was a woman, her dark hair in an unfashionable bun on the back of her head and wearing a dark dress with long sleeves, all of which rendered her virtually invisible. She was standing with one arm across her body, cupping the elbow of her other. A cigarette smouldered between her fingers. Their gaze met and locked.

'Sorry, you can't come in here, mister.' When she spoke her voice was not loud, but it was strong and it carried on the still air. 'This is private.'

Like a cornered cat, he could think only to flee and instead of apologising and calmly walking away, he turned and ran blindly to the far end of the path. He felt plant fronds brush against his body and when a twiggy branch of a damson tree caught in his collar there was the dull thud of fruit falling.

'Hey! Where are you going?'

Irons was not listening as he scrabbled over a compost heap, releasing the sweet smell of warm moist lawn clippings as he did so, then tumbled over a bramble-covered fence, his hands torn with stinging lashes by thorns that snagged at his clothes, causing tears and pulls that were hard to escape.

'What are you up to? Come back!'

He was running down a steep grassy slope towards a rooky wood too dark for him to see into its inky interio and now loud with the birds at their evening roost. The great viaduct embankment was looming ever taller to his right as he drew closer to the mass of trees, his feet slipping and slithering on grass moistened with dew, barely in control of his movements and arms flailing like windmills to keep balance.

Irons guessed he should encounter the Great Ouse on the far side of the wood, and as long as the stationmaster's wife did not raise the alarm and send someone after him, he had succeeded in getting into a good position to approach St Peter's from the least-frequented route. He would lie low and wait for an hour or so, then pass beneath the viaduct and make his way to the church.

He leant on a fence post edging the field to draw breath. Looking back up towards the station and the house, the distinctive outline of the Scots pines etched black against the vast village of stars turning imperceptibly slowly behind, a gentle mauve glow indicating the proximity of the rising moon. The sound of the train in the distance was echoing faintly and a dog barked. But there was no obvious sign that he had caused a rumpus at the station, though he felt it sensible to slip beneath the trees without delay.

But he was not used to this darkly unfamiliar territory. Hampstead Heath or Hyde Park on a sunny day or a walk along a canal path about summed up the limit of his experience of raw nature, and the cover of night had rendered this alien world unappealing. He was grateful for the shelter the wood offered but having to enter it without so much as a torch was alarming, and it was filled by strange noises. There were odd rustlings and the trees made creaking sounds like old joints in limbs, the leaves murmuring and hissing like exhaled breath and then there was that cackling and cawing above his head.

He was not fond of big, black birds at the best of times. It was an irrational fear fuelled by childhood stories of witches and goblins, and he could almost imagine the birds were actually laughing at him. It certainly sounded like it. The wood just felt too alive. He knew there was nothing to fear except perhaps a twig in the eye, an ankle twisted on a gnarly root or a stubbed toe, but that did not prevent him feeling anxious. It was as though he were being watched. Whichever way he turned, he felt exposed; caught between the unsettling feeling that someone, some *thing*, was observing him from within the dark greenwood or watching him from the elevated station. He needed to override his fears and step under the trees.

Just as he was about to do so, his attention was drawn to a pale shape gliding silently down the embankment, caught in the first tentative beams of the ascending moon's light. It moved swiftly, and twisted in the air on fingered wings, turning its strange, pale face with dark, saucer-like eyes and hooked beak towards Irons. It now swooped closer, then expertly turned about in a move superior to a fighter plane, and as it did so he was sure he felt the touch of the air pushed his way by the owl's wings. Two flaps, and it accelerated away to follow the line of fencing edging the wood.

Irons was captivated, drawn to those unfathomable eyes. Was this how a little vole felt as it stared in up in the last moments before its life was snatched away? The bird had returned and it hovered a few yards from him, its wings scooping the air, holding its head as still as if clamped in a vice with its gaze locked on his. He felt a tremor of deep unease. Did owls attack humans? He could see the curled, sharp talons hanging like the undercarriage of an airplane and knew they could do him harm far worse than the stinging cuts from a bramble bush. There was something almost human, and yet so wild and untamed about the little heart-shaped face. He wished it would release him from its penetrating, unblinking grip. The owl flapped a wing, veered to one side and screeched with a sound that seemed to Irons to be full of anguish and pain. Then it flapped stealthily away to the far edge of the trees and out of sight.

He now felt an intense sense of foreboding as he trampled along a narrow cut worn down by the feet of others that had travelled the same way. It was ridiculous, but there was actually something about that bird that reminded him of Betty. Something about its pale face and those eyes...

He stumbled onwards, blindly finding his way, holding his arms before his face as protection as he made his way along a narrow footpath that took him in less time than he feared, to the river. The wood opened out at a bank edged with bull rushes and a vast weeping willow. The black presence of the viaduct dominated the quiet flowing water that held a thin veil of mist suspended a few feet above its surface. Irons sat on a log in a small clearing that he guessed an angler had made, and closed his eyes. He was exhausted and emotionally drained.

But his closed eyelids offered no respite, for his mind was filled by images of Betty's face looking at him in the darkened carriage compartment, eyes appearing to grow rounder until they resembled the barn owl's, her nose in the twilight gloom sharpening in the half-light into a beak...

Ugh! He opened his eyes with a start to see the owl on a fence post on the opposite bank. As he looked, its weird head swivelled and stared back. *For Christ's sake, it's just an owl. And a lovely one, at that!* He forced a little snort of mirth. 'Good evening Mr Owl!' He called across the water. 'Looks like it's just you and me, kid!'

The owl glared back, unblinking.

'Good hunting?' *I'm talking to a bloody bird.* 'Don't you know it's rude to stare?'

His palms were sweating and the owl seemed to be the source of this sense of unease, as if it held a curious radar system that was sending rays across the mist and water. He found a small stone and threw it so it hit the water with a loud plop just in front of the bird. It gave an angry screech, even more unpleasant than the last, before launching into the air with a few effortless wing beats and gliding low and straight across a misty water meadow.

Sergeant Trinder finished his cigarette, flipped the butt onto the track and walked back disconsolately into the stationmaster's office.

'No sign. He must have got off at an earlier station.' He pulled a rueful face. 'I knew we should have tailed him aboard the train. Stick like glue to the fellow, that was my suggestion, but who listens?' He slapped a hand against his leg in frustration.

'I was standing in this doorway the whole time and am certain he did not disembark,' agreed the stationmaster.

Trinder nodded, 'and I had an excellent view from the porter's room. Of course, what might have blown it is, I was not alone in waiting for Mr Irons. There were a few others lurking about that were not intending to travel. You saw that man on the platform?'

'I did. Don't know the fellow, and I don't think he was a local. A gentleman from the press I suppose, and another fellow had a camera.'

'If Irons got wind that they were waiting it would explain his baling out early. Did the reporter arrive by an earlier train?'

'No. He went back up the steps a moment ago. He'll have a car.' The stationmaster grimaced. 'All paid for on a nice, fat expense account, I shouldn't wonder!'

Trinder laughed. 'May I use your telephone?'

'Be my guest. I suppose you'll want to contact the other stations and see if any of them saw him get off?' The stationmaster was standing with his back to the little fire burning in the grate and which was taking the edge off an evening now chilling rapidly.

'Correct. The lack of resources is the problem. If we had the manpower, we could have someone on the train and at every station.' Trinder heaved a resigned sigh, 'but of course that would be hard to justify, and we were given a strong tip off he was to be on that particular train. We'll find him, just not tonight.' Trinder flipped his coat tails to one side and sat on the corner of the desk, picking up the telephone receiver, but paused before he started to dial. 'I suggested to the boss that we put one of our girls in plain clothes so she could sit in the same compartment, but he scrubbed the idea. Oh well, I'd better call and give him the bad news!'

Irons could hear his feet on the pavement and the rustle of the breeze in the trees. But there was something else. Perhaps that was the beat of a distant engine working hard behind the sound of his exhalation, but was there another sound lurking underneath, that of an animal panting and the heavy pad of paws? Or was that just his pulse banging in his ears?

The moon was unveiled. It cast its clear light on the almost glowing form of that dratted owl. It had tailed him all the way along the course of the river and the footpath towards the town. The silver bird skimmed the fields, flashing between the trees and sometimes he thought it had gone, only for it to reappear on a tree branch or gatepost, ready to turn and observe his approach. It reminded Irons of the menacing taxi that had stalked him through his nightmare. But strange though its presence was, as he neared the houses that demarcated the edge of town and could see the tower of St Peter's close to hand, the owl was no longer his main preoccupation.

Something was following him on foot, but every time he turned, there was nothing. Not a movement or a sound and yet when he walked on, there it was again, the sound of panting and padding and the tick of bestial claws on stone flags. He resorted to stepping lightly on the ground and holding his breath in order to hear more clearly... Yes, there it was, *tick-tick-tick*... It was tailing him and making the hairs on the nape of his neck stand on end.

He spun around suddenly and the dog stopped. Square in the middle of the road, its beady eyes fastened on his. Irons did not move, unsure what to do, but then it wagged its tail, swung its head to one side and trotted away up a drive.

Irons exhaled in a long slow breath and leant for a moment on an Alvis he happened to be standing alongside to regain some equilibrium. It had been a long and stressful day and he was done in. The dog had slunk off, at least, and it looked as though he was alone. A few leaves skittered across the street. Looking up he saw he was close to the rear of the church and the constricted entrance of the footpath that ran between two long hedges of dense box reaching above head height that would bring him out beside the main door at the base of the tower. The route was uninviting and the sharp turn part of the way along rendered the end of this leafy corridor invisible. His lack of enthusiasm for entering this gloomy space was not aided by the poor light cast by a solitary lamp that needed a new gas mantle, as the flame sputtered and burnt with a strange, sickly-yellow colour.

With one last, searching look along the road he marched boldly down the path, an elbow brushing against the leaves released the strange scent of box. He softly whistled to help dispel the tension, choosing the lilting Harry Lime theme that had lodged itself in his brain. It felt appropriate however, for it struck him this Betty Askew was not so unlike the Harry Lime in the film; He was supposed to be dead and buried, but was actually alive and well and working an illegal scam. Similarly, was the real Betty dead and the girl an impostor? Or was she alive and well and playing some kind of sinister game for her own ends? Either way, he felt he was an actor in an increasingly unsettling Film Noir that he wished would soon end.

Despite his valiant whistling he felt hemmed in by these impenetrable hedges and started to run, and again that ominous and dogged echo instantly matched the beat of his hurrying feet. He stumbled out into the open space before the church door and was thankful the gas lamp on its standard was burning bright. Looking around he saw the dark lines of gravestones like so many irregular teeth, each one kissed by pale moonlight. Some distance away, a statue of a kneeling figure was praying in the same cold light. But all was silent, and he was alone.

Never one to find well-tended graveyards unsettling, and as nothing appeared to be following him out of the narrow pathway, he relaxed. He was just acting stupid. If he really were being tailed then it was by the very person he wished to confront and it was high time they met, face to face. He certainly didn't fear her; if anything, he was relishing the chance to confront this clever, scheming girl and hammer out a deal. The only problem now was that she was nowhere to be seen, so Irons started to explore the headstones, trying to read the inscriptions carved on their faces and noting the vases of cut flowers with the colours leached out by sun and rain, and the withered potted plants and forlorn, unkempt graves lacking even these signs that someone still remembered.

He was trying to identify the resting place of Private Coulson. The girl had given him specific instructions to go there, so if he was going to find her now that was the obvious place to start. Thinking about the encounter, he stooped down for a moment and extracted from his sock the little box containing the ring. He clasped it in his hand. He did not notice the eyes watching him, monitoring his every move.

Now some way from the path, he identified a row of pale headstones that looked newer, one of which was piled high with fresh floral tributes. Another was marked by a short, squat tower surmounted by the life-sized kneeling angel he had spotted earlier, her bowed head and hands clasped in prayer skilfully carved from white stone. This looked worthy of closer inspection.

He blinked and held his breath, sure that the angel had just turned its face in his direction. The young woman was carved in sensuous, flowing marble that looked convincingly like soft fabric, curly hair and real skin, her hair veiled by what looked like intricate lace, although most of her face was left exposed. It was a masterful piece, but what stopped him in his tracks were her blank, sightless eyes, now challenging his. He was sure she had been looking down upon the grave, down past her hands pressed flat in prayer. He must be hallucinating through tiredness and an acute lack of food. At that moment the moon slipped behind a cloud and, as darkness closed in, he strained to make out the features that struck an unsettling chord.

It was Betty! It was the very likeness of her...it had to be! The shape of her jaw line, of her eyes, her hair... He suddenly felt a rush of anger, all sense of shock instantly replaced by fury; all the frustration, humiliation, fear and regret of the last few days now boiling up inside. So, she was playing a stupid trick, was she? Dressed up like a stone monument so she could observe the dumb mathematics teacher as he left the valuable ring and just walked away like a muggins. Well, he was going to teach her a lesson. He was not going to be spooked by these horror show antics!

He ran forward, all fear stripped away, and almost exhilarated that he had seen through her game of deception, his hand squeezing the ring box yet harder so he could feel the pain as the corners of the wooden box dug into his palm to remind him of what was real and what was not.

As he drew close, the angel moved. Her expression transformed from a beatific half-smile to a look of alarm, then into one of warning. Her white arm lifted and pointed to somewhere above his left shoulder as she loomed above him. The angel's face seemed to contort into an expression of acute fear, her white marble mouth opening in a soundless cry.

Irons was not fooled. She was real flesh and blood dressed up in stage paint for ghoulish effect... and yet... what was that?

The beat of what must be a large dog running hard and breathing heavily was now unmistakable. It was so loud that Irons could hear the feet pounding close to his heels and, as he tried to turn about, the great head with its fiery eyes and lips drawn back from rows of sharp, yellow teeth loomed inches from his face. He saw with awful clarity the dribble of saliva flowing from its jaws and the lolling, wet tongue, and he smelt the stench of hot, foetid breath.

The sharp teeth sank into his throat like pincers, his windpipe offering initial resistance as his knees bent and buckled under the weight of the beast. He was still breathing as he fell, his back twisting in the air, arms frantically scrabbling at the animal now locked onto his throat. They landed hard, the force of the impact forcing the dog's teeth through the strong gristle and the man's final breaths were a hideous whistling, gargling, sucking sound accompanied by a fountain of crimson spraying as if from a hosepipe, his eyes lifted upwards to meet those of the watching angel, the marble of her skin now spattered and streaked by his fresh, warm blood.

A short while later, a smartly-dressed man ran his hand through the grass and pocketed the little wooden box that he had seen falling from the dead man's hand, then called his dog away from the corpse. The animal panted heavily. Attaching a short leash to its heavy leather collar, he ordered the dog to walk to heel. Near the iron archway beside the board holding innocuous parish notices, he halted for a few minutes to wipe the dog's jaws and snout free of blood, and gave the beast a hard rub between its ears with his perfectly-manicured hands, a flash of expensive watch and a shirt cuff clasped by a platinum link winking for a moment as he did so. Then they calmly continued their evening 'constitutional' as though nothing had happened.

If anyone did see the man and his dog pass as they strolled quietly along the leafy road lined by fine houses in their perfectly-maintained gardens, they thought nothing of it. He was a respectable citizen giving his faithful friend a last turn before bedtime and this unremarkable event passed immediately from their minds. Neither did the drunk staggering down Halse Road pay any attention to the gentleman letting his dog jump onto the back seats of his car before carefully removing his black coat, folding and laying it on the red leather passenger seat and closing the door, all done in easy and unhurried actions that failed to induce interest or suspicion.

PC604, aka Ian Dowd, also paid no heed as the same vehicle smoothly changed gear and pulled away. Dowd was, sadly, unable to recall anything about it, nor indeed to bring to mind any suspicious activity that evening during his final circuit of the town before the end of his tour of duty. Which was 'a pity', as DI Vignoles gently put it when questioning him the following morning. It was indeed, for this young recruit was just about to encounter the most startling and disturbing incident so far in his short time with the Northamptonshire Constabulary. He was not to make such a discovery ever again in what proved to be a long and unspectacular career pounding the beat around a succession of small towns and villages until transferred to a dull desk job in Daventry, from which he was to eventually retire.

CHAPTER TWENTY-FOUR
The Gorse Hotel, Woodford Halse
26th September 1950

Whilst Irons was seeking refuge in the woods, a group of friends was enjoying a quiet drink in the Gorse Hotel. This drinking establishment lay in the small hamlet of Hinton-cum-Membris, a part of Woodford Halse in all except name. The 'Gorsey', as it was called, sat on the edge of an irregular-shaped village green just a short walk from the embankments and bridges carrying the railway that neatly bisected Woodford Halse from Hinton, and which probably helped preserve the sense of these being two separate places.

The Gorsey was a large, back-and-white timbered construction designed to look far older than it actually was, and whilst it aped a romanticised idea of the Elizabethan era, it actually dated from shortly after the opening of the railway at the turn of the last century. It was lavishly appointed with splendidly ornate fireplaces, high ceilings decorated with extravagant plasterwork that caught the cigarette smoke, a curving staircase and many leaded windows, just as one might expect in a modest country house. It was divided into a number of bars and saloons and there was a big entertainment space on the first floor that could comfortably hold most of the many railway men and their families who lived and worked in the town. If the sooty 'loco' and the clattering goods yards and busy junction station could be considered to now go a long way towards defining this as a railway town, then the Gorsey had to be included too, for it was the hub of nearly every railway worker's relaxation time.

If someone needed to find Driver Boswell or his mate 'Tanky' Burgess; get a message to Fireman Rowbotham; or share a pint with Goods Clerk Simmons or indeed any number of others, there was a high chance they would be in the Gorsey and, if not, someone propping up the bar would know where they were. So the little snug was the place of choice for three friends working for the Eastern Region of British Railways to gather after work and have a quiet drink.

PC467, otherwise Simon Howerth, with his mop of red hair slicked flat after a dash of cold water and the attention of a comb, was returning from the bar with three drinks. Seated beside his friend Eddie Earnshaw on the high-backed bench was Signalwoman Laura Green, with whom Eddie had been walking out for almost a year.

'I encountered Gerard Powys Dewhurst today,' remarked Eddie. It was one of those observations from out of nowhere that help keep conversations flowing.

'Yeah? Where abouts?' Simon placed two pints of Tiger and a port-and-lemon on the little circular table between them and sat down.

'Is he someone important?' asked Laura, innocently.

'Oh aye, very! He's a director on the railway,' Eddie smiled significantly. 'Called in at Woodford, unannounced.'

'You met a director? Gosh, the nobs don't usually have anything to do with the likes of us.' Laura looked surprised.

'He looked a bit rough, though.' Eddie winked at Simon. It was clear she had not twigged.

'He'd been drinking?' She looked shocked, but sensed there was something going on.

'You could say a bit worse for wear, but after a bit of care and attention he perked up no end and was given to me and Driver Woodcock to take to Leicester and back! Brilliant fun.'

'You did what?'

The two lads laughed. 'He's a locomotive, Laura,' Simon gave an impish grin. 'One of the Director class, and a bit of a rare bird around here these days.'

'Oh, you little monkey...' She gave Eddie a friendly punch on the arm. 'You had me thinking you were mixing in high circles for a moment.' She pulled a face at him. 'But of course, I can see the engine in my mind's eye perfectly now, I just didn't make the connection when taken out of context.' They were all laughing now. 'I knew the name sounded familiar, really I did!'

Laura Green loved the railway; the snorting noisy engines and the colourful cream-and-red carriages, the impossibly long trains of rumbling coal wagons; the periods of solitude between trains in her lonely signal box, punctuated only by the ringing bells of the equipment. Then there were the heavy levers painted in their gay, bright colours with polished handles. The exercise of throwing the signals and points kept her figure trim and fit. But most especially she loved the people who worked on this vast and complex network. She might not collect locomotive numbers as Eddie and Simon did, and she certainly could not name the years the Derby was won by the various racehorses the top-link express engines were named after, as Eddie could, nor indeed trot off the names of African animals that some of the others carried, as Simon liked to do, but she could still appreciate the finer points of the workings of a steam engine and the curious mixture of brawn and art needed to operate one efficiently.

'So how are things going in the job, Simon?' Laura pointedly changed the subject and took a sip from her port-and-lemon.

He supped his fresh pint, wiping the froth from his upper lip with the back of his hand before replying. 'Pretty good these last weeks. It was a bit slow for a time as I was doing awfully dull office stuff for simply ages. Making the tea, fetching this, finding that and of course filing, filing and yet more filing. You can't believe the paperwork we get through!'

'I suppose it's all part of the job.' Laura observed. 'You must have to keep records of absolutely everything. It's the same for me in a way; you might think I'm there to set signals and direct traffic through my block section, but I spend most of the time making meticulous records of every movement in a huge ledger or reading through mountains of new instructions for special workings for the week, and then filing those away.'

'Yep, that's about it!' Simon grinned. 'But at last I think the DI is prepared to let me loose on some real work. Investigative work!' He raised an eyebrow and paused to let this exciting piece of information sink in.

'Excellent,' Eddie nodded approvingly. 'Come on then, what's he got you on?'

'All in good time! I knew it would take a while and the DI did warn me I would start right at the bottom.' Simon was clearly enjoying spinning the story out. 'I had to work on menial stuff before I could step up, but that's all right. It's not often one gets a second chance in life, and I have to pay my dues.'

'You landed on your feet, to be honest.' Eddie gave him a serious look.

'I know. After what happened down at Marylebone last year, I could have been properly hung out to dry. I might have ended up in a borstal or even worse...' The three exchanged knowing glances and silently concurred. They remembered all too clearly how Howerth had become drawn into buying and selling counterfeit goods supplied by an especially dangerous and violent gang and how it had cost him his job as a fireman.

'So, come on! What's he got you doing?' Eddie was on tenterhooks. He loved detective work as much as Simon, although since those dramatic events of the previous year he had tried to rein in his investigative tendencies and concentrate on his proper job on the footplate.

'I've been assigned to work with PC Blencowe to look out some old case notes and see what other information we can dig up about the missing woman, Elizabeth Askew.' Simon paused again for effect, his friends looking suitably impressed.

Not the one the papers are writing about?' Eddie asked. 'Isn't she supposed to be working with another villain on some robberies? I was not too sure exactly, as the papers seemed to be muddling this up with weird stuff about a ghost.'

'The same! She left home one morning in April 1943 and was never heard of from that day until now when this chap reckons he saw her on the train to Brackley. They got talking and, as a result of something she said, he did a burglary job, which he bungled.'

'She put him up to it?' Laura asked, making a slight readjustment to a tortoiseshell-effect hair-slide holding her long, blonde hair in place.

'That's what the burglar is claiming, amongst other things.' Simon gave a cheeky grin. 'Now this burglar, one Richard Irons, has given us a very good description and swears blind he's met the missing woman. In fact she even introduced herself and told him her name and everything.'

'So where's the problem?' Eddie gave his friend a curious glance across the top of his pint.

'We can't find her. Not a sight anywhere. We've got the railway police, three sets of constabularies, plus of course her friends and family all on the look out. Zilch! Nothing. So now we have to wade through the original files and work forwards, trying to make sense of everything we know about her and what might have happened to her on that day, and see if there are any clues to where she is now.'

'But surely this Irons chap must know? Even if he says he doesn't?' Eddie asked. 'I reckon he's lying.'

'Spot on! Now I can't say too much, but some in the department are following that particular lead very closely!' He tapped his nose. 'Seriously, not a word to anyone, OK?' The other two nodded. 'But the DI said the same thing as you. He reckons that Irons will meet up with this woman soon enough, so it's just a case of waiting for him to lead us to her.'

Laura was listening intently, a puzzled expression on her face. 'Then it sounds like it will only be a matter of time before you apprehend her and she can spill the beans. So, why dig all the old files out?'

Simon raised an eyebrow and deliberately took time to sip his beer. 'Very perceptive. You will have read some of the more strange and oddball theories in the papers, and I can confirm that Irons has stated on record that the woman on the train was actually a ghost! The spirit of Elizabeth Askew.'

'I read something about that. So you're actually working on the railway ghost story?' Laura clapped her hands together in excitement. 'Now if ever there was a real mystery, that's it. How exciting.'

'And peculiar.' Eddie took a draught of beer and gave his friend an approving look. 'But what's the real deal? Clearly she's not a ghost...' He opened his arms wide and looked between Simon and Laura with incredulity.

'It is a bit far-fetched.' Simon grinned. 'We're actually not supposed to even mention that part, to be honest. I'd get my head bitten off by the sarge if he heard me say it.'

'So why is the man claiming this? Is it a smokescreen?' Laura asked.

'It could be. The DI ordered us to drop all references to the ghost angle and I can't say I blame him, as it is a bit embarrassing for grown policemen to be talking about arresting a spook!' They all laughed. 'We work with facts.' Simon now looked serious, adopting a tone of voice that implied he was already an experienced criminal investigator. 'So, she disappeared in '43 and not a peep from her until she reappears close to home seven years later, at which point she chooses not to get in touch with her family, but to meet a complete stranger and convince him to enter into a bit of breaking and entering. Now the question has to be *why* would she do that?'

'I can't imagine.' Laura looked flummoxed.

'What did Mr Vignoles have to say? Gosh, do you work with him every day, talking about the investigation?' asked Eddie, as interested in the way the detective department functioned as the case itself.

'Heck, no! I was told to sit at the back and say nothing, and he only spoke to us for a few minutes. Sergeant Trinder deals with us. He sent Blencowe and me off to the Northamptonshire

Constabulary HQ in Northampton to fetch the files and then we got to work in the library looking out newspaper reports from the time. It was jolly exciting to go on an important errand like that, and the county headquarters were fascinating. You know, they have a super canteen...'

'But what might be the reason for her odd behaviour?' Laura's eyes were sparkling with interest and she didn't want the conversation to veer off the point and onto gastronomic matter. 'You said she encouraged the burglar to commit the crime.'

'That's what he's claiming, and he gave a full confession, so we have to take it seriously. However, even that part of the story is strange, as all charges have now been dropped against the man and he's been set free!' Simon pulled out a packet of Player's Navy Cut and offered them around.

'How strange.' Eddie looked stumped, then took a cigarette, eyeing it suspiciously as these were a strong brand.

Simon registered his look. 'All I could get, Eddie, and at a high price, too. Bit rough on the throat.' He sipped some beer. 'It is a strange turn of events, but no matter, Inspector Vignoles said we were not interested in the robbery anyway, only in trying to piece together the story of this woman. Is she, or is she not, the missing Betty Askew, that's what we must find out. Going back to what you said, Laura, even if we do run her to ground in the next day or so, we can't necessarily trust anything she tells us, so that's another reason we need to get more background on her. Now, there are a couple of ideas the inspector shared with us. One is that she ran away from home, deliberately cutting off all ties, and has led a criminal life all these years. Or, two, the poor woman really is still missing, perhaps dead.' He grimaced and they exchanged serious looks. 'And if she is dead, then that means someone else is impersonating her. But why? Strikes us all as a funny way to work.'

'Or,' added Eddie, 'she committed a crime back in '43 and ran off to evade detection and never found the courage to confess to it. She's now forced to live a life of crime, living on the edge of society, like Robin Hood...'

'More like a real life Maid Marian!' added Laura.

Simon nodded approvingly. 'Yes, I quite like that.'

'Have you found much about her?' Laura asked.

'Not a lot. We've read through the interviews from the time she disappeared. They're mainly her friends, work colleagues, mum and dad. They're not much use. We're reviewing the various sightings that came in from the public; though there were not many. The sarge thinks most of these are rubbish, worse luck. Blencowe and me were laughing as some of the comments added by the investigating officer at the time are really fruity. There was one telephone call from Carlisle, and the caller was claiming to have seen her, but on the note recording the conversation is written: *Time waster. More interested in reporting the loss of his cat, Gerald. Worthless!*'

They all laughed. 'Another was from someone in Maidenhead, who the investigating officer described as: *three sheets to the wind and having problems remembering what day of the week it was. Unreliable.* But amongst the scraps, was one sighting of someone looking a little like Miss Askew at Amersham station, although the man, an ARP Warden, couldn't offer much about what she was doing or where she was going. Most interesting, is the statement of the booking clerk at Brackley Central. However, whilst she clearly remembers her, she can't tell us what happened after she left.'

'So Miss Askew was last seen on our railway line?' asked Eddie.

'The last accurate sighting was of her boarding a train heading south, presumably up to London, though we can't be sure. She worked here at Woodford. As an engine cleaner, no less.' Simon bent down and picked up his ex-army haversack from the floor. 'We found these. They must have been handed out not long after.' He opened a roll of handbills similar to the one Irons had taken from the wall at Buckingham station, though smaller. He took one from the roll and they positioned their glasses to pin the corners of the curling paper to the table. Betty Askew's young face stared back. 'There were a load of these, so we all took one to help jog people's memories.'

Laura bit her lip. 'I saw the same photograph in the paper but it seems more intense like this. More personal.' She looked at the grainy image a while longer, no one wishing to break the silence that fell. 'I don't know...I can't see her as a criminal. It seems hard to imagine. She looks a nice person and perfectly innocent.'

'Who knows?' Simon shrugged, but he also looked pensive. 'People can change.'

'But is she still alive? Whatever she may or may not have done, that's the most important thing.' Laura spoke softly.

'That's what we have to find out. Why she's like she is can come later, so my sarge says.'

'Why would she not let her family know she's alive?' Laura shook her head. 'I cannot accept that. It feels completely wrong. But there again I could not imagine in a million years wanting to run away, let alone doing something criminal.'

'How can we help?' asked Eddie.

'Like I said, Sergeant Trinder wants us to interview those originally spoken to back in 1943. Go back over old ground and all that. Now most are still living around Woodford, and they might have something new to offer.' He leant forward conspiratorially. 'They might even let slip they've actually *seen* Betty Askew in the intervening years.'

'Yes! If she's been lying low and living like Maid Marian, it stands to reason she's been in contact with at least one close friend who could be in on the deal!' Eddie beamed.

'Exactly. Now you can't be seen to be investigating her disappearance, in fact you should make every effort to not appear that way. We'll put these up around the place to jog memories, and if I slip you the names of her old friends and then if you were to come across any of them in this little village of ours and get talking... they might accidentally drop a clue.'

'Is that likely?' Laura pulled a cynical expression.

'Probably not. But that's what real detective work is all about.' Simon replied. 'Asking, asking and asking again, always hoping for that one scrap of information that we can add to another tiny scrap, and the two little fragments when joined together may make something bigger and more significant. A bit like a jigsaw puzzle.'

'Well, we can try. This story is certainly something to talk about over a cuppa and we might just hear something useful.' Eddie nodded as he spoke, already relishing the chance to help.

'Tell me the moment you hear anything, no matter how small.'

Eddie fell silent and looked at Betty Askew's face on the poster. 'I know that officially you can't consider this angle, but amongst friends having a drink, I don't see as it can do any harm.'

'Consider what?'

'What if this Mr Irons really did see a ghost?'

'Come off it, Eddie...'

'But I agree!' Laura chipped in. 'There's been all sort of talk of a strange character on the line and all manner of odd goings on. Eddie knows all about that. And now people are going to the station just to see that train, in the hope of seeing a ghost...'

'This is all silly talk. It's got nothing to do with the real crime.'

'You said Irons gave a formal statement saying it was so.' Laura dug her heels in. 'I know it's far fetched, but it makes you wonder.'

'And I did have a very strange experience the other night.' Eddie gave Simon a serious look. 'Near Brackley Central, and it was a woman that you could say looked a bit like her.'

'Get away with you.'

Eddie told Simon about the poorly steaming engine, the lost fire iron and the woman on the line. 'And the driver was seriously spooked, and I don't mean shaken up because he nearly ran her down, I mean he was spooked! Crossing himself and talking about the Seven Whistlers.'

'What are they when they're at home?'

'Soul birds that fly across the sky, warning of death.'

'Righty-o...'

'I know what you're thinking, but engine drivers don't normally talk like that,' added Laura, who had already heard the tale. 'And that's what has spooked me. It has quite put me on edge when working nights. There I am alone in my box with nobody for miles around. Imagine if a ghostly-looking woman was standing on the tracks, just staring back at me! Ooh, it curdles my blood!'

Simon sat there with his mouth open looking at each in turn. 'This is straight up?'

'Honestly, Si, I saw her, and it was just like I said. The lads on the station reckon she's been back a few times, as well. So those trippers on the trains are not as stupid as some are making out. Now, I think we need to have a look.'

'Go ghost hunting?' Simon asked.

'What's to lose? So we get a bit chilly and get to stay out late, but we don't have to tell anyone unless we do see her.' Laura shrugged her shoulders. 'I'm game.'

'Haha! Count me in! When do we start?' Simon's smile was wide and eager.

Ten minutes later they had conferred about shift patterns and scribbled some dates and times on a scrap of paper and agreed a strategy. They sat back with newly-refreshed drinks, exchanging conspiratorial looks.

'We only have a couple of nights over the next ten days, but it's a start. But please, don't let a whisper of this out to the sarge and especially not the guvnor. They'll kill me, and then I'll have to come back and haunt you!'

'Scout's honour!'

'I can't tell you how much I shall look forward to a bit of fieldwork. It will be such a wheeze!' Simon looked content and then gave Eddie a cheeky grin across the top of the glass. 'Though, to be fair, I'm also hoping I get a chance to sit in on some of those interviews with Betty Askew's friends. Not the important ones, but the routine stuff. You see, the sarge might send one of the WPCs to do these, and I'd like to help.'

'I'm sure you would!' Eddie exclaimed.

'What I meant is, that it would be good experience. From a detecting point of view.'

'Detecting what, Simon?' Laura asked, a twinkle in her eye. 'Discovering the pleasure of a pretty WPC's company?'

'Or the straightness of her stocking seams...' Eddie winked at Simon over the top of his raised glass and they laughed, happy to take their minds off the ominous presence of the face of Betty Askew still staring up at them in mute silence. 'So you got your eye on one, have you?'

'No! Anyway, who said anything about pretty?' Simon tried to look innocent.

'I did,' Laura instantly retorted. 'I've met Miss Benson and Miss Lansdowne, don't forget. One blonde; one brunette, one athletic; the other more voluptuous. And both very easy on the eye, do you not agree?' She and Eddie laughed.

'I suppose so...' Simon went pink. 'I sit next to them all day.'

'Lucky boy. We'll get you married off yet,' Laura observed.

'What?' He looked at her in mock outrage. 'Not that you two can talk! When are you going to tie the knot?' Simon threw the comment straight back.

'All in good time.' Eddie gave a sheepish look at Laura.

'Some things should not be rushed.' She flashed her eyes at Eddie, but shifted her body a fraction closer. 'And besides, we need to save for a lot longer if we're to have any chance of getting a home of our own.'

Eddie blew the air out of his cheeks. 'Too right! On a fireman's pay it's hard to save anything. And there isn't a house or flat to be had around here. I know why those families are squatting in the big empty houses in London. We might have to join them, at this rate.'

'Not on your life! No running water and filthy dirty. Ugh. I bet they're full of rats.' Laura shuddered.

'Some of those squats look really nice. I saw a feature in *Picture Post*. One family lives almost like royalty in the grandest rooms you've ever seen,' Simon replied.

'No, no and no! And don't encourage him. We just have to be patient a while longer.' She slipped her hand onto the seat cushion between them and Eddie gave it a squeeze, their clasped hands resting against her shapely leg, the curves of which were tantalisingly revealed by the thin fabric of her dress.

CHAPTER TWENTY-FIVE
Brackley
27th September 1950

The day was bright and cool by the time DI Vignoles and DS Trinder arrived in Brackley. Thin wisps of mist hung like smoke in the valley and pooled below Helmdon and Brackley viaducts like little clouds fallen too close to earth; however, the autumnal sun would burn this away once it had warmed the cold earth, and warmed the colder grave-markers in the churchyard of St Peter's.

Vignoles had been awakened hours earlier by the shrill ringing of the telephone on the table in the hall. It had been about four-thirty in the morning and he'd stumbled out of bed, reluctant to leave Anna, who had been pressed close to him, and who stirred and turned over nonchalantly, having long grown used to these unsociable calls.

It had been short and to the point. There was a body, and he was needed. Vignoles had dressed quickly, well practised in the art of throwing on clothes in the dark, and left Anna a scrawled note telling her not to expect him home until late. He let himself out of the house as quietly as possible and hurried to Belgrave and Birstall Station, his thoughts filled with unsettling images of dead bodies, haunted churchyards and strange, slavering shag-dogs stalking the empty lanes of his home town with murderous intent. His footsteps echoed on the deserted streets and for a moment he imagined he was being followed; symptoms of an unease prompted by his dreamy, still half-asleep state and the spare, but potent details given over the telephone about what awaited him.

With a set of keys, he let himself onto the station and used his special authority as a railway detective to arrange to be picked up by a goods train heading south. He travelled in the guard's van, collecting an even sleepier Trinder at Woodford Halse along the way. It was a short ride to Brackley and he let Trinder snatch a few minutes' nap whilst seated on one of the hard benches along the side of the van, aware that with a baby in the house his sergeant was probably suffering from chronic sleep deprivation and needed every opportunity for rest if he was going to be any use to the investigation.

As they approached St Peter's on foot, a fat man in a dark suit was easing himself out of an old Austin Ruby that was made to look even smaller than it already was by his considerable bulk. It was parked behind a black Wolseley 18/85 series 111 police car. His broad moon face beamed as he offered a disconcertingly cheery wave to Vignoles and Trinder before reaching onto the rear seat to retrieve his doctor's bag.

'Fine morning for it, what?' The doctor stopped to take a deep sniff of air. 'Glorious weather, so invigorating, don't you think?'

He waited for Vignoles and Trinder to draw close. 'Dr Halliday!' They shook hands. 'I may have had the pleasure before?'

'Indeed. Back in '46, if my memory serves me', replied Vignoles as they walked towards the churchyard.

'I remember. I do hope you won't make me climb over more filthy old locomotives this time, haha!'

'Hardly likely here, doctor,' Vignoles answered.

'That was a turning point for me as it panned out. I started to get a taste for the pathology side of things. Sounds a bit ghoulish to a non-professional, I imagine, but we chaps understand both the necessity and indeed, the fascination of the task, eh? Anyway, I moved across to doing it full time and am now relishing the role.' He grinned, 'So, let's see what horrible delight lies ahead for us this morning!'

Vignoles and Trinder exchanged glances, but remained silent, as their long and close association meant that they could sometimes read each other's thoughts.

A uniformed policeman guarding the entrance to the churchyard directed them around the tall box hedges towards a small group standing to one side of the church. There was a hush in the air, broken only by a loud group of starlings noisily hunting for food in the damp grass, their insistent bickering like the thoughtless chatter of young children oblivious to the horror that kept the men talking in hushed voices. As Vignoles approached he was on full alert, taking everything in and deliberately not hurrying, trying to assimilate the crime scene.

The sun cast strong, attenuated shadows across the dewy grass and burnished a marble angel a glorious yellow, picking out her delicately-sculpted nose and lips and drenching the elegant hands clasped flat and upright in prayer in rich warm tones. This same light made startlingly visible the splatters and rivulets of dried blood staining the stone like a poor experiment in expressionistic modern art. It was immediately obvious to Vignoles that this was a scene of violent death.

One of the men in the group was a police photographer. He wielded a camera with a silver parabolic reflector clamped on a bracket to one side. He was firing shots at something on the ground, the bulbs making little 'pops,' shortly followed by a tinkle as he dropped the spent bulbs into an empty red glass vase placed on a neighbouring memorial slab. The photographer stood in odd positions, his legs sometimes wide or a knee flexed, elbows jutting and body bent at the waist as he sought to capture every possible angle of Richard Irons's very dead body.

DI Bainbridge, of the local constabulary, saw the three men approaching and there followed a brief exchange of greetings and half-hearted pleasantries. They had met before, and curiously on the same case that had seen Dr Halliday clamber up the tender of a steam locomotive (at some expense to his suit). Bainbridge was still young, and though now more experienced, Vignoles sensed that Bainbridge looked relieved at the older man's presence. He was not going to create barriers, whether or not he felt slighted by a murder investigation on his patch handed over to a virtual outsider. 'Before we start, DI Vignoles, you may wish to read this —' Bainbridge passed a telegram across to him. 'I got something similar from my own superintendent.'

The few lines confirmed what Vignoles already guessed. The Badger had been busy that morning speaking to his peers in the Bucks, Northants and Oxfordshire forces, and the end result was Vignoles had landed the investigation into the death of Irons and the hunt for Askew.

'Has the potential to cut across too many boundaries, I suppose? I know how hard it can be to manage that, as Brackley lies exactly on the meeting point of three counties and it can be a right pain in the veritable backside if a case strays half a mile to one side or the other,' Bainbridge gave a weak smile. 'Makes sense if the railway pulls everything together and we help out as you see fit.'

Vignoles nodded, then looked at the body. 'Certainly puts the cat among the pigeons in our hunt for Miss Askew, what d'you think, sergeant?'

Trinder agreed. 'The plot thickens. This alters everything.' He, too, was now wide wake and aware this was likely to be an interesting morning ahead. No detective ever liked to see a body, nor witness the pain and hurt caused by violent crime, but there was no denying these events usually resulted in the most fascinating and super-charged periods of detective work, and to be part of the lead investigative team was a chance to be grabbed enthusiastically.

'A strange one.' Bainbridge remarked. 'Looks like a dog ripped his throat out.'

'But I suspect we have not been called here because a mad dog went wild?' Vignoles was holding his unlit pipe, a pre-requisite to some serious thinking.

'There's something odd about it.'

'Dear me, what a mess.' The doctor was shaking his head. 'I had better get to work, though I can see life-saving will not be a skill I need to use on the poor fellow.' The doctor's black suit with thin pinstripes served to exaggerate his considerable waistline, whilst conversely making his tiny feet encased in expensive, and possibly impractical, black patent-leather shoes look inadequate to the task of keeping him upright. He bobbed and wavered and looked almost ready to topple over as he peered down at the mangled body. He removed his hat to run a brilliant white handkerchief over his brow. 'So much blood... Dear, dear... rather brings to mind the words of Lady Macbeth, does it not gentlemen?' He replaced his hat, opened his doctor's bag and placed a stethoscope around his neck, finally slipping on a pair of rubber gloves.

Vignoles also took a good look at the body whilst the doctor was chuntering and instantly he could see the most probable cause of death. The man's neck was horribly mangled and torn wide open, showing marks that looked like they could have been made by animal teeth. A considerable amount of blood from the severed artery had pooled over the torso and into the grass, staining it almost black.

'Do you know who he is?' Vignoles sucked on his pipe.

'Richard Irons, a maths master at Magdalen,' Inspector Bainbridge replied. 'A formal identification will still be required, of course, but we know this fellow. Been warming one our cells this last day or so.'

'The coin thief. And, according to him, the only person to see Betty Askew since 1943.' Trinder looked at the man's face, now horribly contorted into an unpleasant mask of fear or pain, but could tell it was unmistakably the same man he'd questioned on the train from Buckingham. 'That's him, for certain.' Trinder looked grim, pacing around the perimeter of the crime scene taking a mental note of everything, a tall PC in an ill-fitting uniform stepping backwards to give him room as he did so.

'That's why I called you chaps over. As you'll be aware, he was set free yesterday with no case to answer, but this rather queers the pitch. I'm not sure everything was as cut and dried as it first appeared.' He looked at Vignoles. 'I know you lot are trying to find the missing woman he claimed to be working with, so I thought it best you were in on this from the start, and it looks like our bosses agree.'

'Good thinking, I appreciate your actions. Do you think his death has any bearing on the robbery?'

DI Bainbridge shrugged. 'It's a mighty strange coincidence he's dead less than twenty-four hours after he was released, and under curious circumstances. Feels darned suspicious to me.'

'Sergeant,' Vignoles looked at Trinder. 'It would appear he evaded you last night.'

'He could have taken a later train, sir. It's a small station and he could not have walked past me and the stationmaster without us noticing.'

'My sergeant was tailing this fellow in the hope he would lead us back to the girl,' explained Vignoles. 'He was a free man and not our target, so we aimed to be discreet. Perhaps we were too much so.' He darted another glance at Trinder, who looked pained. 'So he did not get off the train that we know he boarded, but he still ended up here. He gave us the slip along the way. But why?'

'We were in plain clothes, sir, so he should not have known he needed to evade us. But if he had got wind we were waiting, why the subterfuge?' Trinder was trying to make the best of the situation.

'Good points, sergeant.' DI Bainbridge nodded. 'Sounds like a man with something to hide. He was up to something more than house breaking.'

'It is starting to look that way. How did he die?' Vignoles directed the question at the doctor kneeling beside the body and working whilst they talked.

'You are quite correct. I can officially declare the poor fellow dead.' Halliday gave Vignoles a mildly admonishing look as he spoke. 'Intriguingly, there are a number of ways he could have died, going on this most cursory of inspections.' He looked at both Vignoles and Bainbridge with his beady eyes to ensure he had their full attention. 'Clearly the wound to his throat is the most obvious reason. A completely severed windpipe. Just here, can you see?' He pointed, and the photographer quickly leant forward and snapped the area the doctor was indicating with his podgy forefinger.

'Suffocation — actually, drowning in his own blood. Nice.' He smiled. 'Which brings me on to the considerable amount of blood you can see, some of which is splattered far and wide. This suggests the main artery was also severed and pumped for at least a short while after it was cut, so bleeding to death would have got him, if the drowning didn't. And then— ' he shifted and moved the head to one side, '—he took a severe blow to the back of the head, probably when he fell, and this may have knocked him cold and perhaps spared his suffering. Take your pick gentlemen for now. Until one gets him on the slab and takes a really good and proper look, it would be unwise to be more specific.'

'Time of death?' asked Bainbridge.

'Between say 11p.m. and 1a.m. last night. My PM report will try to be more specific.'

Vignoles took a step closer after acknowledging the doctor's observations with a slight nod of his head, and stood with chin resting on his hand studying the corpse. Irons was lying on his back, body twisted as though he had tried to turn around in the moments before he hit the ground. His head was pressed hard against the corner of a monument now heavily stained with rapidly-browning blood and what looked like a tuft of hair and scrape of skin stuck to the sharpest angle. One arm was thrown across his chest, completely red with blood and bearing visible signs of trauma, with ugly tears and cuts to the skin as though the animal had chewed and worried at it. His other arm was twisted behind his back in a position that only a dead person could maintain.

'And a dog did this?' he asked.

'I'm just the doctor; you chaps are the detectives. But I'd say from the injuries and his position, you are looking for a powerful canine which has been trained to attack. Perhaps a Boxer or Bulldog, a Doberman Pinscher, a Wolf Dog, a Mastiff or even an American Pit Bull Terrier.' The doctor started to peel off the gloves. 'The PM will provide a detailed examination of the wounds and perhaps I can try to narrow down the breed.' The doctor stood up, grunting as he stretched his thin legs, and commenced brushing at his trouser knees and straightening his jacket. 'My immediate concern is rabies. This was a violent assault and dogs do not usually attack in this manner. It's the first time I've ever seen such wounds.' He was now rinsing his hands in a strong-smelling disinfectant, tipped from a glass bottle he'd taken from his bag.

'A rabid dog, or one trained specifically to kill?' mused Vignoles. Something powerful and strong and very obedient to its owner, and able to be highly aggressive if so taught.'

'Could Miss Askew have been responsible?' asked Trinder.

'Only if she had a nasty dog with her,' the doctor replied. 'But a woman is quite capable of training a dog to attack, of course. I can see no obvious signs of direct human involvement, though I offer the usual caveat of waiting for the report on that point.'

'What have you found, sergeant?' Vignoles pointed to near where Trinder was standing.

'There are what could be footprints in the grass, sir. I think Irons came off the path and along this route towards the grave.'

'They are not ours. We also noted the marks because the low sun highlighted them, and took care to preserve their integrity. PC604 has assured me he did not trample his size tens across there, either.' The tall constable in question shuffled uneasily, but held his tongue, his eyes continually being drawn to the mutilated body in a mixture of fascination and revulsion.

'604, you found the body?' Trinder asked.

'Correct, sarge. It was just before midnight.' He stood bolt upright in response to the question, with his hands clasped behind his back, staring somewhere above Trinder's shoulder. 'I was finishing my round for the night and took a turn through here. I like to check the church is locked of a night. I almost missed him, but the moon came out and an owl flying low over that hedge there drew my eye to the side, and then I saw him.'

Vignoles was kneeling beside the impressions in the grass. 'It is very confused and muddled, but I could almost be convinced that two people were here, one of whom would be Irons. And here is a paw print...and another. Quite deep. That implies that a big, heavily built animal bounded past here at speed.' He moved closer to the body, now kneeling on the damp grass with his face just inches from the ground. 'The grass is churned up, probably where Irons was turning to face his assailant, then a skid mark made by one of his heels... So, the dog was chasing Irons. He ran off the path over there and towards this grave, but was caught about...here. Where presumably he tried to turn about and fend off the attack?'

'And the dog got his throat in the first bite. Bang, wallop! His head cracked on that stone and he was done for,' Bainbridge continued the story. 'Pumping out blood that poured into his lungs.'

'Sir! I've found some more footprints.' Trinder was peering closely at some impressions at the edge of the gravel path. 'The ground is still quite damp and this heel shape is distinctive.'

'There's a pattern on it too...' Vignoles joined him and pointed with the stem of his pipe, the low sunlight creating strong shadows that aided their task.

DI Bainbridge needed no prompting. Having checked that the photographer had completed his task, he removed one of the dead man's shoes and brought it across. He lined it up with the impression, although careful not to let it touch the marks in the damp earth. 'Slightly different shape, I'd say.'

'Yes. Can you show me the bottom of the heel?'

'Smooth and worn. A different shoe.' Bainbridge gave a grim smile. 'If a rabid dog is bounding about the place, I for one would not be standing nearby watching as it ripped someone's throat out.'

'Most unwise. Though I am not saying the dog is rabid, merely speculating on possible reasons for its viciousness,' the doctor added.

'The point being this might be the impression of the dog owner's shoe.'

'Possibly. If we can find another impression nearer the body it would be more convincing. As it stands, it could be anyone's and could be a few days old.' Vignoles was thinking aloud. 'Plenty of people pass here all day long.'

'I'll can get the technical lads over to make a plaster cast of all footprints we can find in the vicinity?' Bainbridge suggested, also indicating to the photographer that he should try his best with the camera.

'Please do so. You have the lab resources we lack,' Vignoles agreed.

Bainbridge addressed the constable. 'Guard this site with your life and don't let a soul walk anywhere near it! And watch where you stand! I'll send another officer to help. We'll have onlookers down here gawping any minute, so you mind you hold them back. Keep the whole churchyard out of bounds until DI Vignoles says otherwise.'

'No sign of a woman's shoe...' Trinder was carefully hunting around like a sniffer dog. 'I'm not getting a sense of Miss Askew being present, although I was wondering if they were going to meet here — it is private and quiet.'

'Perhaps he got here first and later she saw his body and fled? Was this an unfortunate mad dog attack that through tragic coincidence has been elevated to appear as something more sinister — in which case Bainbridge, I would suggest you get your boys out around town with a marksman to shoot the animal dead on sight. Or was this a deliberate attack by someone using a dog trained to kill? Someone who stood and watched as the dog did its work?'

'I took the liberty of having two men patrol the town in their car looking for a wild dog.' Bainbridge replied. 'Though I favour the latter interpretation.'

'Smart move. They could interview any dog walkers with especially- large dogs whilst they're at it.' Vignoles stood, resting his chin on one hand, eyes scanning the ground. 'I think this was a planned attack. Clever as well, because the real killer, the one with malice aforethought rather than the beast that was just blindly obeying a command, has not touched the body.' Vignoles then fired up his pipe and took a walk across to the bloodstained memorial. 'Quite a mess.'

'It won't wash out easily, I fear. Marble is porous so it will stain terribly. Water and a splash of Voltas might do the trick. Bleach the stains out.' The doctor was smoking a cigarette nearby as he spoke. 'Pretty ghastly. This poor angel looks like she's a murder victim,' he added, pointing with his cigarette at the bowed face with rivulets of blood like tears running from each blind stone eye.

Vignoles took a welcome puff on his pipe and read the inscription.

'Do you know anything about Private Coulson, inspector?'

'Can't say as I do.' Bainbridge thought for a moment. 'I suppose he could be the son of Richard Coulson who runs the motor garage up Halse way?'

'Sergeant, take a note of the names on all these graves. Just in the vicinity; not the whole place.' Trinder extracted his notebook and dutifully started copying the inscriptions.

'Coulson? Where have I heard that name recently?' Vignoles waved this thought away for the moment. 'And why was Irons in this particular place? Why run from the path towards a place that offers no means of escape if being pursued? This perimeter hedge looks impenetrable. If you were being followed you would stand a better chance trying to reach one of the houses on the road. Here, he was concealed, giving his assailant and his dog the perfect location to maul him unobserved.'

Vignoles knelt down and looked at the fresh flowers on Coulson's grave, some spotted with blood on the petals, an effect that looked especially disturbing on the white carnations. There was a bright red dribble down a small card affixed to another bunch of flowers placed in a glass vase. He peered at this, puffing aromatic clouds of Ogden's Redbreast tobacco into the morning air as he did so, before reaching forward and detaching the card. He stood up.

'Something interesting?' asked Bainbridge.

'Listen to this: *To the son-in-law we almost had. Trusting one day you and your darling Betty Boo will be united in Heaven forever. Maud, Henry and Betty — wherever you are.*'

'Betty Boo?' Trinder looked up from his writing.

'Henry? Henry and Betty...Is this a long shot, but could that be Betty *Askew*?' Vignoles raised an eyebrow.

'Ahem.' PC604 coughed to attract attention. 'Yes, sir. Henry Askew works at the brewery. He knows my father.' Ian Dowd sounded nervous as he spoke and fiddled with a sleeve of his uniform jacket.

'The same Henry Askew whose daughter went missing in 1943?' Trinder looked surprised.

'That would be correct, sarge.' His face turned pinker.

'Hang on, Irons was claiming that Betty Askew put him up to the robbery of Dr Melcombe, and now he's lying dead on the edge of her fiancé's grave,' Bainbridge looked animated. 'Rather a coincidence, isn't it? Maybe deliberate.'

Vignoles gave a grim smile of satisfaction. 'Ah, now I remember where I've heard Private Coulson's name. In Askew's file there was mention that she had once been engaged, though her fiancé had died some months before she went missing and not thought relevant. It was little more than a footnote, but I'm starting to wonder if there is not something more we need to look at.' He stared at the little card for a moment longer, tapping it against the fingers of his hand. 'Right, we need to pool resources and crack on. Bainbridge can dig out every last scrap of background on Irons. I need friends, family, work associates — the whole kit and caboodle. You all know the ropes.'

'Wilco. I can inform his family and arrange the formal ID if you wish?'

'Please. I would appreciate that, as we've got pressing work to do here.' Vignoles needed to keep Bainbridge sweet if they were to work together efficiently. He also needed the more extensive resources of the civilian constabulary to fall back on. 'We'll need to tease out his movements last night,' he darted a look at Trinder. 'Regular meetings to knot the loose ends together, and we'll crack this. My instinct tells me Irons was killed deliberately, and we need to discover not only why and whose dog did the deed, but why Irons was beside the grave of Betty Askew's long-dead fiancé at the time. Why *here*, of all places?'

CHAPTER TWENTY-SIX
Brackley
27th September 1950

'Have you found our Betty?' Maud Askew's eyes flitted between Vignoles and Trinder with nervous anticipation.

'I am so sorry, Mrs Askew; I regret to say that we have not. May we come in?' Vignoles removed his hat in anticipation of her acceding to his request. 'We need to ask you a few more questions about your daughter's disappearance, and perhaps the doorstep is not the best place.'

'Oh, I see.' Her face instantly lost what little animation it had as she stepped back to open the door wider, indicated they should enter the narrow hall. 'You'd better step in. My husband is soon to leave for work; he's taking his breakfast in the kitchen. I'll just go and fetch him.'

'That would be most helpful. We called early hoping to catch you both at home.' Mrs Askew ushered them into her front parlour and invited them to be seated. The closed room smelt stale and damp, yet held a lingering tang of furniture polish. It was unlikely to have been used since Christmas, and it felt cold and uninviting. Neither inspector nor sergeant sat on the uncomfortable-looking wingback chairs positioned either side of the unlit grate, nor on the stiff-backed sofa opposite the heavy and old-fashioned mantelpiece of dark wood that supported cheap pottery figures of a boy shepherd and equally young shepherdess, a 1930s Art Deco clock that ticked loudly, and two massive brass candlesticks. Both men noticed a framed snapshot of a young woman seated in long grass on a sunny day, the curve of a railway viaduct behind her being crossed at that moment by a smoking train. Vignoles leaned closer, guessing that this was Betty, and discreetly taking a moment to identify the type of locomotive.

Aside from the picture, which caught something of a treasured, special moment in the sunlit countryside, the room was as lifeless as the motionless figurines and the three plaster ducks flying in formation across the loud wallpaper. It was a parlour like so many others across Britain; reserved only for high days and holidays, for christenings, weddings and funerals. The door would be kept resolutely closed at all other times; the wasted space beyond forever waiting for an occasion deemed sufficiently special to see a fire smoke sulkily up the almost-blocked chimney, as overdressed relatives sat or stood uneasily in a room that felt abandoned and unloved.

They heard a gruff voice asking what was up followed by the scrape of a chair on tiles. A man in work clothes appeared at the door, the bib and braces of his dungarees hanging loose at his waist, a cup of steaming tea in his hand.

'Ah, Mr Askew, we are sorry to interrupt your breakfast.'

The policemen were taken aback at Askew's hostile tone and the voice that boomed: 'What brings you here at this unearthly hour, if you haven't found our girl?' His grey eyes narrowed suspiciously and he looked confident and self-assured, filling the doorway, while the face of his much-shorter wife peered around his bulky frame.

'Detective Inspector Charles Vignoles, Detective Sergeant John Trinder. We spoke the other day on the telephone. I'd like a few minutes of your time, please.'

'I'll make us all some tea...'

'No, thank you, Mrs Askew, and I would prefer it if the two of you would answer our questions together.' Vignoles responded quickly, sensing that Mrs Askew was likely to hide in the kitchen.

'Right, so you're the policemen who's going to find our daughter?' Henry Askew stepped into the room, making it feel cramped and overly full.

'I can assure you that we are doing all we can. There are some developments, however. I realise this is raking up painful memories, and I am sorry.'

'Aye, it is at that! My wife's not been the same since that ridiculous story in the papers. What the hell's going on? Where is she? Why has she not come to see her family?'

Vignoles spoke carefully, conscious of the man's anger and frustration. 'It was regrettable that you should read about your daughter in the morning papers. It was a most unfortunate example of the press running ahead of events in their desire for a scoop, prompting some hasty and ill-advised speculation...'

'Such as claiming she was dead and come back to haunt us?' Mr Askew almost spat out the words, his wife making a soft mewing sound like a kitten and fumbled for a handkerchief tucked in the sleeve of her cardigan. She sniffled on and off for the remainder of the interview.

'Can you imagine the hurt that caused us?' continued Askew, placing a cup of tea, on its saucer, beside the pottery shepherdess, careful, even though angry, not to spill the liquid on the spotlessly clean carpet, the fine state of which was further emphasised by its obviously pre-war design.

'I'm so sorry Mr Askew. All I can do is try to locate your daughter and discover the truth about what has been going on.'

'She would never just walk out on us. Never!' Maud Askew pulled the handkerchief away from her nose to speak and flopped down on the nearest chair as if her legs were in danger of giving way.

'She was a dutiful daughter. She never gave us any worry. Not until she... Look, something happened to her, inspector. Something—' Henry Askew took a deep breath, '—something bad. There is no other way to account for it.' He threw a glance down at his wife, who buried her face in the handkerchief, eyes screwed closed. 'She'd never just turn her back on us, and she would never get involved in thieving, either!' Askew's voice boomed around the room. 'You can forget that disgusting nonsense, for a start.'

'You have had no communication with her since the day she left?' asked Vignoles.

'Nothing. Not a word.' Askew paced across the room, taking a deep breath or two as he did so. 'Sorry, I'm forgetting my manners: please, have a seat, won't you?' He flicked a glance from Vignoles to Trinder, indicating that his invitation was extended to both, and as they sat he walked to the window, lifted his teacup from its saucer and gulped some tea as he looked out onto Manor Road. 'I don't believe for one minute that she's been travelling to Brackley and not stepped by to see us.' He continued to stare out of the window as he addressed them.

'Mr Askew', began Vignoles, 'may I take you back to the time you last saw her? To the morning of 19th April 1943. What was she wearing?' He had read the their statements given at the time, but wanted to hear if there had been any changes, seven years on.

'She were in her work overalls as she were due up at the shed,' Henry Askew replied.

'She had a white-and-blue chequered blouse underneath, and a navy-and- white polka-dotted scarf about her neck and a turban in mustard yellow covering her hair.' Maud Askew added, her voice almost a whisper. 'The yellow did not suit the ensemble so well, but it was only for work. And a splash of colour was welcome in such a dirty old place.' She sounded apologetic.

Henry Askew's voice whilst still loud now had a softer, dreamier quality. 'Looked good on her though, in a funny sort way.' He turned from the window and looked at Vignoles. 'Her working togs. Even though they was as grubby as anything, despite Maud's best efforts with the dolly-peg on washday, she still looked pretty as a picture, didn't she Maud?'

His wife nodded rapidly, handkerchief held to her mouth.

'I'm a working man myself, and there's no shame in my book wearing a worker's uniform.' He looked sideways at Vignoles. 'Of course, she could scrub up as smart as any for a dance or going to the pictures, but it looked right seeing her in overalls, she were proud of her war-work.' He managed the trace of a smile at the image in his mind's eye, genuine affection clear in his voice.

'You work at the brewery?' asked Trinder, pencil at the ready to make notes.

'Hopcroft and Norris's. Worked there since I were fifteen. Betty used to come along with me sometimes: you know, Saturday mornings, school holidays. I think that's where she got her love of machines. She used to sit in the engine room with Alan, the plant manager. He didn't mind her there as long as she kept out the way whilst he minded the steam engine that powers the brewery. She was happy as Larry down there, and before long was helping out with tinkering with the engine, filling the boiler with water and even taking a turn on the shovel at times.' He smiled at the memory and exchanged another look with his wife. 'Funny. I spent most of my life shovelling barley and malt, but she preferred shovelling coal.' A silence fell that neither detective was eager to break. Vignoles filed away a casual, half-suspicion that this plant manager, Alan, might have something to do with Betty's disappearance and wondered if he'd been questioned. Askew broke this chain of thought by concluding: 'So, like I said she was in her work clothes. Isn't that so, Maud?'

'Yes, of course. She looked at her husband. 'But... but remember she also had a dress with her. The green, summery one that she'd been saving up coupons for months, as well as her mac and a sun hat and sunglasses. It was a warm spell of weather, so that must be why she took those.'

'Was it usual for her to take a change of clothes to work?' asked Vignoles.

'Sometimes. If they were going out straight after,' replied Maud Askew. 'Though we only realised she had done so afterwards.

I suppose she must have put them all in a bag in the hall and I'd not seen it, what with rushing about filling her snap tin and getting Henry's breakfast on the go.'

'She never told us she was going out that night. I suppose she forgot,' added Askew, although he looked unconvinced as he spoke. 'She was on earlies, so I was still in the back kitchen with Maud when she left the house. That's why we didn't notice at the time. The odd thing is, we never did find who she were going out with that evening. All her friends denied any plans to go to the pictures, or whatever.'

'But she did not arrive at work, which suggests she had other plans for the day, not just for the evening.' Vignoles countered.

Henry Askew looked as though the wind had been taken from his sails. 'True... true enough. We've never been able to understand that bit of it.'

'What colour was her coat?' Trinder asked, sensing the need to change tack.

'Pale cream, and good quality.' Maud Askew answered. 'It was Aquascutum. Expensive. It was a touch too big, really, too long in the sleeves. Her Auntie Doris passed it on to her. It was still as good as new even though she'd bought it before the war. Doris thought it would be good for going to work in, but the colour was no good for railway work, so Betty usually didn't take it with her for fear of ruining it with the coal and oil.' Maud became more animated as she spoke of her daughter.

'Do you know if she took anything else?' Trinder was taking notes.

'What else would she take?' Henry Askew fired back, defensively.

'An overnight bag perhaps?'

An uneasy silence fell and Vignoles sensed an air of tension between the Askews.

'Just things for the one night. Well, it was not really an overnight bag, it was more a large shopping bag she could put the clothes in, but just the barest essentials, nothing more.' Maud Askew looked embarrassed. She blew her nose.

'What things?' Trinder looked directly at her.

'Hairbrush, some make up and...' she looked embarrassed, 'a change of underclothes. I—I only discovered exactly what after she didn't come back and was asked to search her room.'

'So she was planning to stay the night somewhere?' Trinder asked.

'We had enough of *that* kind of insinuation at the time! She is not the kind of girl to spend a night with a man, if that is what you are suggesting!' Henry Askew faced Trinder and folded his arms across his chest.

'No, no of course not', replied Vignoles, keen to reassure the Askews that the police were casting no aspersions on their daughter. 'Sergeant Trinder meant that perhaps she was staying with a girlfriend.'

Mrs Askew looked up at Vignoles, eyes swimming with tears. 'All her friends swore blind she was not with them, and I believe them. They're just as devastated as we are.'

'Can you tell us more about her fiancé? Vignoles sensed there was something not being said, something lurking below the surface reawakened by recent events and was straining to be voiced despite the best efforts of the Askews to conceal it.

Maud Askew gave Vignoles a look that was defiant, despite her reddening eyes and the little handkerchief at her mouth. 'He was killed at El Alamein, was Ray. Brave lad. We owe our freedom to men like him.'

Henry Askew nodded solemnly. 'Decent chap. They would have made a nice couple.'

'He was Private Raymond Coulson? I understand he was killed some months before Betty went missing.' Trinder was again making careful notes.

'1st November, 1942, in El Alamein. General Montgomery mentioned the crew of their armoured car in dispatches.' Mr Askew's voice took on a proud tone. 'They were pushed up deep, right on the front line, observing Rommel's tank movements. Took a direct hit, apparently. They didn't have a chance, poor blighters. One of the lads managed to crawl out, but he didn't last long, died the next day.' Henry Askew paused and they all remained silent. 'The date will stick with me forever. Poor Betty took it awful bad. Cut her deep it did. Fair shook us all up. How can we ever forget that morning when Dicky came over with the letter saying how his Ray was lost in action?' Henry Askew shook his head grimly.

'Betty went missing in April the following year. Had she —' Vignoles deliberately took his time asking the question, eying each parent as he mentally searched for the least offensive way to phrase the question, '— had she been seeing anyone else in between?'

'No.' Henry looked offended, but Maud stared intently at the carpet and her face started to blotch with pink.

'I know that Betty was grieving, but she was also young and full of vitality.' The atmosphere in the room grew tangibly tense. 'During those awful years of war everyone was encouraged to live for the day and not think about tomorrow.' Vignoles kept his voice clam and gentle and concluded, tentatively: 'She might have met someone.'

'She is not that sort of girl, inspector!'

'Perhaps she confided with you, as her mother?' Vignoles sensed the tension again between the two parents, and he gave her a long stare, willing her to disclose some long-held secret. But she shook her head and did not speak. It was now even clearer to Vignoles that something was being hidden behind their silence.

'I realise this is very painful, but we must get to the truth. Perhaps she fell in with a new crowd? Maybe she was invited to stay over somewhere with a new girlfriend you had not been introduced to?' Henry Askew made as if to speak, but Vignoles held up a hand and continued. 'And even a decent girl can strike up a friendship with a man, it happens all the time.'

'Do you think she met another man? And that this man may have done something...' Maud shook her head in denial at the thought. 'It's a possibility. It is vitally important that if you have any information, you tell us.'

'I resent what you're hinting at, inspector. She was a well-brought-up girl who went to church every Sunday!'

'Henry!' Maud Askew looked up at her husband, her eyes wide with alarm. 'They're just doing their job. They have to ask and we have to speak out. For Betty's sake.'

'Quiet, woman!'

'No! I won't be. Not any longer. Oh dear Lord, it's been seven long years. I just can't take any more.' She sobbed. 'I can't stand the not knowing.'

'What do you wish to tell us, Mrs Askew?' Vignoles gave Henry a stiff glare as a warning to keep silent.

She snivelled and then blew her nose, trying to regain some composure, not once looking up from the carpet as she did so. The other three remained silent, the clock marking the time relentlessly. 'She'd got in with a group of girls at the loco shed. They were a good bunch on the whole. Some still drop by at times and one of two even send a card at Christmas, which is sweet.'

'Maud, we don't need to be raking all this up...'

'Please, Mr Askew, will you let your wife speak,' Vignoles's tone was firmly insistent.

'Some of the gang were... well, they were a bit bolder, somewhat brasher than the others, the older ones anyway. I won't say anything bad about them, but they certainly did know how to "live for the day". Our Betty was young and naïve. She didn't know much about the ways of the world. I sometimes wonder if we tried to protect her too much.' She gave a furtive glance at her husband who was now staring at her sternly.

'That's enough, Maud.'

Vignoles became concerned that Mr Askew would prevent his wife from telling the truth. 'Sergeant Trinder, would you please take Mr Askew into the kitchen and put the kettle on, I think we could all do with a nice, hot cup of tea.' Trinder recognised his boss's ruse and, opening the parlour door, ushered Henry Askew outside and closed it firmly behind them. Mrs Askew frowned and looked concerned as the men left the room. Her obvious discomfort sent a clear message to Vignoles that her husband never made tea nor indeed lent a hand with any domestic chore. He invited her to continue.

'She became awfully withdrawn after Ray was killed', Mrs Askew explained, 'working all the hours God sent. It was not good for her to drive herself so hard and just mope about at home with only her gloomy thoughts for company. And of course, eventually, some of the girls did manage to take her out a few times, around March or April I think. It was when the American airmen were coming through the town, I remember that. There were lots of airbases around here in those days. They were coming over in great busloads.'

She stared out of the window, peering hard through the net curtains at the horse-drawn milk wagon that had just come to a halt opposite. 'She met one of them. A Yankee. Nothing serious, you understand? Just a dance or two, I suppose.' She gave a nervous laugh. 'She was always home on the dot. Always.' She emphasised her final word by looking Vignoles straight in the eye. The inspector felt the first twinge of excitement. Here was that little scrap of new information that every investigation needed.

'Do you know who he was?'

'She never said or, if she did, I can't remember.'

'Where did they meet?' Vignoles asked.

'At a dance. They held a series of them in the town hall. The USAAF paid for them, to help the locals and airmen get to know each other. "Welcome dances", they called them. I suppose, really, they were for the men to mingle with local girls.' She watched the delivery boy ladling milk from a churn into a neighbours' jug.

'Do you know what base the airman she danced with was posted to?'

'She told us nothing about him.'

Trinder opened the door discreetly and raised his eyebrows at his boss to enquire if he was ready for Henry Askew's return. Vignoles nodded briefly and silently, and the sergeant disappeared for a few moments before returning with a tray bearing a matching set of teapot, four cup-and-saucer sets, milk jug and sugar bowl. Mr Askew followed closely behind and glared grumpily at his wife, wondering how much she'd told Vignoles in his absence. Vignoles observed them both carefully as he formed the next question. 'Can you think of any connection between your daughter and Richard Irons?'

'Irons? You mean the crazy man on the train? The idiot who thinks Betty is a cat burgling ghost?' Henry Askew spun around and glared at Vignoles in disbelief.

'The same. Are you aware of Betty's knowing either Irons, or any of his family before she went missing?'

'The papers say he was a Londoner,' replied Mrs Askew. I can't see where she could have met him. Besides, they said he was, er, twenty-three, wasn't it? He would have been a schoolboy back then.'

'I agree it seems improbable, but perhaps he was evacuated to somewhere nearby.' This suggestion drew a blank. Vignoles shrugged. 'Could there be a link between Irons and Mr Coulson?'

'How on earth could there be? Why not ask that idiot to his face?' Henry Askew asked, tetchily. 'I'll gladly wring the bloody man's neck for the hurt he's caused us.'

'Henry! Don't speak like that.'

Vignoles raised an eyebrow. His expression stopped Henry Askew in his tracks more effectively than his wife's remonstrations. 'I would, but Mr Irons was found dead earlier this morning under suspicious circumstances. I will say no more at this stage about how he died, except that he was lying beside the grave of Mr Coulson.'

The couple, both visibly shocked, fell into a stunned silence. The mantle clock ticked loudly.

'Mr Askew, where were you between about ten o'clock last night and two o'clock this morning?' Vignoles asked.

'What? You don't think? Look here, what I said just now…I was angry at what was in the papers. I didn't mean anything by it!'

His wife answered the question for him: 'He was here, inspector. With me. We usually turn in about ten with a cup of cocoa. Unless Henry's in the pub, which he wasn't last night. He does the crossword and reads the sporting pages. I'm a light sleeper, and Henry was beside me all night. I'd know if he got up.'

'Do you have a dog?' Trinder asked.

'What?' Henry looked puzzled. 'No I don't!'

'Do you have a friend with one? Perhaps you take it for walks sometimes?' Trinder continued.

'I don't like dogs. I don't hold with any pet.'

'Have you had any contact with Mr. Irons since he was released?' Vignoles continued. 'Did you meet him in town last night?'

'I've never laid eyes on the man!' Askew's tone was that of outrage. And why would I want him dead? I want the bugger alive and telling me where my Betty is! Instead of accusing me of this and that, you should be thinking about the ring. Nobody pays attention to the ring! They didn't back then, either. Never mind what clothes she had with her, or what bloody pilot she had a dance with or this school teacher who's now got himself killed; you need to think about why she took her engagement ring.' He looked at Vignoles and then Trinder with a challenging expression.

Vignoles glanced across at Trinder, who indicated with a slight shake of his head that he knew nothing about a ring.

'It was lovely. A solitaire diamond. A real one.' Maud answered. 'It came complete with a tiny wooden box inlaid with metal.'

Her husband corrected her: 'It were ivory and brass.'

'Yes, ivory and brass patterns. A fancy, foreign design, it was.'

'Worth a small fortune, we reckoned.' Henry Askew added. 'She usually wore it on a chain about her neck to be safe and out of sight. But someone encouraged her to go off with both the ring and the box that morning. Surely that has to be significant.'

'She *always* kept the box on her dressing table, inspector. It held a little note written by Ray with the date of their engagement on it. It never left there. Never. Well, that is, not until she took it with her that morning.' Maud insisted. 'The odd thing is, she took both the ring and the box, but left the note behind.'

Her husband had his own thoughts on this: 'I wondered if someone might have robbed her of the ring, maybe she struggled and...' He tailed off, the next part of his theory being too painful to voice.

'Can I see the note please?'

The atmosphere froze. Henry Askew turned away from his wife with a snort of what sounded like disgust. She looked embarrassed and fiddled nervously with her handkerchief.

'I am afraid you can't. It, well, it went missing. Just vanished. A few weeks ago.'

'You probably threw it in the bin, not taking care what you were doing.'

'No, it just went missing. There one day, gone the next. Just like my little Betty...' She broke down in tears, pressing her handkerchief to her face. When she next spoke it was quietly and muffled, almost inaudible, 'It went the same day that I saw...' She stopped and blew her nose.

'Saw what?' Vignoles asked.

'Nothing, nothing!' She shook her head, but her eyes suggested otherwise. 'It has gone and that's it. I must have had a funny turn or something, not thinking straight.'

'You can say that again!' Henry Askew was unsympathetic.

'Perhaps we could look in her room? At her things, if you still have them? We could have another look for the note, just to make sure?'

She nodded her head, as her spouse fumed in the corner.

Vignoles looked grave as they walked up the narrow staircase. He was rapidly trawling through what he could recall of the case notes and was feeling a mounting sense of frustration that Henry Askew was probably correct in his assessment of the original investigation. It was sloppy, at best. Probably incompetent. What sounded like a very significant line of enquiry appeared to have been either overlooked or ignored. There was no mention of a valuable diamond ring anywhere in her case file.

CHAPTER TWENTY-SEVEN
Brackley
19th April 1943

Betty Askew walked briskly towards the entrance to the booking hall, the voluminous shopping bag with the long leather straps hooked over one shoulder. She could see a pale haze of smoke rising from an engine waiting in the station below. This was the train she usually caught to carry her north to the engine shed at Woodford and she knew she had judged the timing to perfection.

She was already dressed in her Dirty Girls Brigade uniform and looked much as she did on every working day. A voice in her head was screaming silently, *Just catch the train and go to work! Forget this crazy plan and lose yourself in scraping muck off those dirty old engines and joshing and joking with the girls. Carry on as normal!*

But the weight of the bag bumping rhythmically into her side offered a counter-point: And if you bury your head in the sand in the drying room? What then? If you don't fix this once and for all, what kind of future lies ahead? She pulled a pained expression as once more, perhaps for the thousandth time, she contemplated the shame that would surely follow; the contempt of neighbours and townsfolk, and perhaps even of the people she considered her friends.

And what of her mother and father? They would not be able to cope with the shame. It would humiliate them; shatter their world. She'd read that girls like her were sometimes declared mad by their own parents and family doctor then locked away in terrifying institutions far away from anywhere. Hidden from view behind barred windows in ugly, remote buildings shrouded by high walls, where severe, white-coated staff pumped them full of drugs and gave them electrical shocks that hurt like a penance, and so ensured they really were mad before too many years had passed, whilst their poor child was sent off for adoption, never to seen or heard of again. Perhaps this was just sensationalist nonsense; surely her own mother and father would never do such a dreadful thing, but she was not prepared put them to the test.

Betty patted the bag that held the change of clothes neatly folded inside. She hoped her hat and dress would not be hopelessly creased beneath her folded mackintosh. As she approached the ticket hall, a great mound of neatly-stacked sandbags protecting the entrance on either side, she prepared herself for the next stage of her secret journey.

As a holder of a railway staff residential travel pass, she had no need to buy a ticket. As she hurried passed the booking office she spotted Sylvia Geddes, the clerk, seated behind the little window. Forcing a cheeriness she did not feel, Betty gave a wide smile and an ostentatious wave whilst trotting past. She mouthed the word 'late' to Miss Geddes, who rolled her eyes and urged her on towards the waiting train with a shooing motion of her hands. So far, so good.

Betty clumped rapidly along the wooden bridge in her heavy work boots, deliberately making her steps boom and hopefully reinforcing the idea with Miss Geddes that she had run for — and caught — the train to Woodford. She had timed her arrival to give the impression of running and leaping aboard her train at the last moment. However, she halted near the top of the stairs and crouched low, silently descending a few steps until she had a narrow view of the platform below. The train guard's torso and legs were visible, washed in pale early morning light that threw a strong shadow onto the grubby, maroon carriage. He was calling 'All aboard! All aboard!'

She felt a twinge of guilt. She recognised the man's voice, and knew he was a decent, elderly fellow of the Old School, who'd stayed on past retirement to help with the wartime labour shortage. His type would never knowingly allow a train to depart if someone were rushing to catch it. He'd probably heard her boots clumping along the timber-floor-boarded overbridge and was holding the train out of kindness. Pulling herself back against the wall she waited, hoping she was out of his sightline. If anyone saw her now, crouched on the steps, it would be most embarrassing and awkward. Moments later she heard his whistle and a friendly shout to someone on the platform, a toot from the locomotive and the harsh hiss and bark of the engine.

After a few moments she ran down the stairs and darted across the open space to the far side of the platform buildings, away from the now-rapidly accelerating train. She was in luck, the platform was clear and she could get to the ladies' waiting room unseen. The transformation had to be made before the London-bound train arrived. Passing through the deserted waiting room she slipped into a toilet cubicle. Her swift change of clothes had a dramatic effect: she no longer looked like a member of the Dirty Girls Brigade, but the very picture of femininity in a green summery dress, a hat and sunglasses, short gloves, best shoes, a bangle about her wrist. She completed the look with some carefully-applied pink lipstick. Her diamond ring still hung from the thin chain about her neck. She could feel it swinging between her breasts when she moved, but she would place it on her finger once closer to her destination.

Once transformed she sat in the waiting room, fingers toying with the strap of the now considerably heavier bag, weighted down by her work boots and overalls. She heard voices from outside and also those preparatory sounds from signal box and station that presaged the arrival of a stopping train, then the gentle beat and clank of a locomotive and a rhythmic hiss, suggesting to her well-tuned ear that it was leaking steam from a gland. She stood up, nervously smoothing her dress, and looked through the glass pane of a door criss-crossed by strips of adhesive tape in diagonals to help reduce the effects of any possible bomb blast, just as the filthy-black locomotive streaked with dribbles of lime scale and burnt orange on the bottom of the smokebox clanged slowly to a halt, breathing like an overheated Pekinese dog. It had pulled in a rake of equally dingy wooden coaches, each stuffed almost to bursting with passengers, all of whom seemed to be dressed in muted shades of khaki or RAF blue, with the occasional flash of white from a sailor's cap. It was going to be standing room only.

She stepped out of the waiting room and had just placed a hand on the handle of the nearest carriage door when she heard a voice close by.

'Miss Askew! But I thought you were going to work?'

Oh botheration! What was she doing on the platform? She felt as though the ground had suddenly given way. She just stared back and could not speak.

'But... you've changed.' Miss Geddes stated the obvious.

'I—I have to go to London. On, um, business...' It was lame and unconvincing. 'A private matter. Hush-hush and all that!' She tried desperately to keep her voice light, to suggest there was really nothing that odd about her actions. 'But look, if you could keep it under your hat...' She offered her enigmatic reply with as much levity as she could muster, then opened the carriage door.

'Mum's the word', Miss Geddes winked knowingly. 'Won't breathe a single thing about it for all my living days, cross my heart and hope to die!' Miss Geddes made a heart-crossing gesture then raised a vertical forefinger to her lips to indicate that they were sealed forever. She understood perfectly. This was quite clearly the beginning of a thrilling, undoubtedly illicit liaison with a dashing beau — perhaps Miss Askew had taken up with a debonair army officer, a brave sailor, or a suave airman? She wondered if Betty was travelling to London without a ticket, intending to wave her staff pass and flutter her eyelids at the collector at Marylebone. She'd get away with it, too, the little minx. But she would keep her secret safe, and hope that, one day she, too, might have cause to slink off to the big smoke in her best dress for just such a romantic affair. It was like something straight out of the romance novels that she lost herself in during long, quiet evenings in the booking office.

'So, Miss Geddes, you are quite clear she was going to London?' Trinder gave her an earnest look.

'Oh yes. Told me so herself.' Had the ticket clerk remembered her promise to Miss Askew of lifelong secrecy she threw it aside. Not only was she thrilled to be the only living soul who knew where the now-famous missing girl went on the day of her disappearance, it was her duty to help the police with their enquiries.

'Perhaps because she wished to conceal where she was really going.' Trinder added, almost to himself, whilst he considered this. 'How did she seem to you that morning? Agitated? Nervous? Excited?'

'I hardly saw her, sergeant. She rushed past the window and just waved at me, saying she was late for work. Then I heard her tramping over the bridge in her big, heavy boots, rushing to catch the down train — or so I thought. What a minx! She looked exactly as she always did every workday morning. I suspected *nothing*.' Miss Geddes emphasised her final word then turned her attention to fiddling with the scone that lay half-eaten on the plate before her.

'But when you next saw her, she had changed clothes?'

'I could hardly believe my eyes. I had to take an urgent message down to the stationmaster because the telephone connection to his office was faulty, so I nipped down to the platform. Of course, she must have had the change of clothes in her bag, but even so it was like a conjuring trick. A complete transformation in under five minutes. I really was most impressed.'

Trinder could not help but smile at Miss Geddes's innocent excitement in recounting the story. She was as wide-eyed and excited about the event as if it had happened seven days rather than seven years ago. He paused in his questioning to take in the staid and utterly unremarkable interior of the Oak Cottage Café. This poky little establishment sat on the edge of Brackley market square, and if he was being uncharitable, the interior and ambience rather suited the plain, drably-attired woman seated opposite, with her dress the colour of milky coffee and a thin, grey cardigan over the top.

Her frowsy clothes did little for her. She was a pale, slightly shapeless woman in her mid-thirties, with eyes maybe just a little too large and prone to staring, and straight hair of indeterminate colour held back by two pale-blue plastic clips that made her look girly. Her mouth, however, was mobile and the upper lip nicely shaped. Trinder found himself thinking that, if she ventured to apply lipstick, it could look sensuous. He wondered if being the last person to admit to speaking to Betty Askew on that fateful day was still one of the highlights of this woman's uneventful life. She realised that her statement was important to the investigation and was perhaps deliberately taking her time, milking it for all it was worth.

'And how did Miss Askew react when you saw her on the platform?'

'Well…' Sylvia Geddes put a finger to her lips to suggest she was concentrating hard. She furrowed her brow. Trinder was struck with an image of Miss Geddes as head girl in school asked to stand before class and answer a difficult question. He could imagine her not wishing to appear too clever and so going through the pantomime of appearing to dredge up the answer before responding. Miss Geddes may have no sense of colour or style, but he had no doubt that she was quick-witted. 'I rather think Miss Askew was shocked, sergeant. She looked guilty, as if caught doing something she shouldn't.' Her eyes opened even wider. 'You do know what I mean?' She dropped her chin, and gave him an arch look, hands clasped around a teacup decorated with oak leaves and acorns.

'I think I do.' Trinder smiled indulgently. He was not confident of a startling revelation from this witness, but was prepared to be patient and take as long as needed, as there just may be something, a little detail that could help. And besides, the tea was perking him up and he had been awake since God knows what time that morning. 'Why do you think she was looking guilty?'

'Because she was up to something, of course!' She leant forward and both Sergeant Trinder and PC467, who were seated at the end of the table, involuntarily found themselves doing the same, as though they were hatching a plot around the teapot. 'I think she was going to meet a *man!*' She infused the word with meaning, as though a *man* was the most exciting thing on earth. 'I suspected that at the time, and I still think it now!' She gave officers Trinder and Howerth a knowing look that was hard to interpret as to whether she was disapproving or envious. She nodded her head just slightly to reinforce the point. Trinder glanced at her left hand that was conspicuous in lacking a ring.

'How was she dressed when you saw her on the platform?' Trinder asked.

She gave a surprisingly suggestive look. 'Exactly what one might wear if meeting a charming man for a date.' She raised an eyebrow. Her outfit was appropriate for luncheon in a good restaurant on a warm day. Though, of course, she told me it was *business*.' Miss Geddes put a hand to her mouth and giggled. 'What *business* do you think they were up to? She told me to keep it quiet, and so I have, all these years. I don't like to gossip.' Her mobile mouth took a sudden down-turn at the edges. 'When the police asked me about her back then, I told only the bare facts. She had missed her train and took a different one towards London in a change of clothes. One has to speak the truth when the police ask you, but I'm really not one for trading in speculation and so thought it wise not to judge or make unnecessary trouble for Miss Askew about her amorous goings-on. At the time nobody could have known that she would still be missing all these years later.'

'So, you thought Miss Askew was having a secret rendezvous?'

'Of course she was! Her parents are rather straight-laced. She could not have revealed anything about her tryst. You see, working at a station for many years, one gets to know just about everybody in a small town, and can form a pretty good idea of how people are, what they think, and suchlike.'

Trinder remained silent. This was mere speculation, but it was interesting to hear her thoughts. 'My parents died when I was twelve, so I can meet with any man I like and with no need to act like a femme fatale from a spy thriller!' She gave Trinder a meaningful, flirty stare across the top of her tea cup before taking a sip, as though she were hinting at her availability for a rendezvous with him. He gave Howerth a sharp glance to stifle what he suspected was going to be a snigger from the young PC.

'Do you have any idea who she was meeting?' Trinder asked.

'No, and that puzzles me. Let's be frank, I cannot imagine she *actually* had a lover in London, but then people are full of surprises. I mean, she's a poor worker in a God-forsaken little town in the middle of nowhere — how would she manage that?' She gave Trinder a challenging look. 'I thought she was meeting someone at the time, but upon reflection, I am perhaps not quite so convinced now. I am going to sound dreadfully catty, but perhaps she wanted me to *think* she had a man in the big smoke. Though why, I cannot say.'

'Are you aware of her seeing anyone locally? This could have been a deception to help hide a liaison closer to home?' Trinder kept his voice flat and unemotional. He needed to keep this woman dealing with facts, not enter into wild speculation. 'We know about her engagement to Private Coulson and his subsequent death, but we are interested in the time after Coulson was killed.'

'I suppose you want me to spill the beans on her fling with one of those young Americans?' Miss Geddes raised an eyebrow.

'If you have information then it is vitally important you tell us.'

She giggled. 'You are so dreadfully serious, sergeant. I hardly knew her, we just chatted occasionally at the station so I can't help when it comes to matters of her heart. Sorry.'

'Excuse me, miss, but what made you suggest she had been seen with an American serviceman?' Simon Howerth asked. He had spoken his thoughts aloud, and surprised himself as much as anyone.

Miss Geddes darted a look towards the young constable, who had remained silent until now. 'No reason. It's just what everyone was doing at the time... You must know the phrase made so famous Tommy Trinder during the war. Is he any relation to you, sergeant? Anyway, it was: *Over here, overpaid and over—*' She suddenly looked flustered. 'Well, I'm quite sure you don't need me to complete the line, young man.'

'There were a number of dances in the town around the spring of 1943. Arranged by the US Air Force. Did you attend any of them?' Trinder picked up the thread. 'They must have been quite a pull; an exciting event in a sleepy town such as this.'

'No. I did not.' Miss Geddes stared at the half eaten scone on her plate.

'I would have thought they would have been hard to resist.'

'I am no dancer, sergeant. I've never mastered the art, and as I rarely take a drink it would have been an uncomfortable and quite tedious evening. Being a wallflower sitting alone in the corner is nothing to enjoy, believe you me.' She gave a sad little sigh and Trinder sensed an aura of regret enveloping her. The spark of perkiness, verging on flirtatiousness, that had been visible moments before had evaporated. 'These dances were raucous and noisy affairs with far too much drinking going on and... all manner of other things! I suppose you want to know if I saw Betty at one of these dances.'

'Did you?'

'How could I, sergeant, if I was not there?'

'You speak of the dances as though you experienced them, that's why I asked.' Trinder looked puzzled.

'I do?' Miss Geddes coloured. 'I just imagined that's how they were...from what people told me.' She stopped. It was obviously a lie. Nobody spoke and in the lengthening silence, Trinder found his attention momentarily diverted to a noisy delivery lorry pulling up outside the bay window with The London Central Meat Co painted on the side in dark blue letters. Was she on the verge of telling him something significant?

Miss Geddes took a deep gulp of air, gave the young constable a glance that made him shut his mouth rather than speak, then faced Trinder. She looked as though she were making her mind up about something and he was prepared to give her time, pleased that his young assistant had the intelligence to do the same. 'What I told you is not strictly correct. I stood in the town hall doorway with a ticket in my hand, looking in. Can you imagine the scene? It was packed with people and thick with smoke hanging above the dancers and the music was far too loud. An awful racket, just a lot of banging and blaring trumpets. Despite invitations to step inside from a group of loutish young servicemen, I baulked. I confess my nerve failed me and I walked away.'

'Did your friends not encourage you to enter?'

'I was alone.'

A silence fell between them again. The noisy lorry suddenly cut its engine and put a blissful end to its noise. The quiet was punctuated only by the sound of teacups being washed in the back kitchen and the low murmur of a couple talking at a table in the corner. 'I find it easier to talk to people when I am behind my glass ticket window.' Miss Geddes spoke quietly but with the air of someone confessing a long-held secret. 'I don't find it at all hard talking and getting along with everyone when at work, and even talking to you is surprisingly easy. Even though you are a policeman. I'm just not very good at these social sorts of events. Well, I've said it now. Oh dear, you will think me awfully strange.'

'Not at all.' Trinder smiled indulgently. He sensed this was leading somewhere and wanted to keep her talking. 'So you would not have seen Miss Askew at the dance, but perhaps you did on the way there?'

'Not going to the dance. I came a little later, you see? About ten, I think it was. I dithered and delayed before walking down. Silly, isn't it?' She gave a wan smile. 'Look, I really don't want to trade in tittle-tattle. I absolutely deplore that sort of carry-on.'

'Indeed. But any information you may have could be vital. Anything you say will be dealt with sensitively and as discreetly as possible, but I fear the time for undue circumspection is long past.' Trinder looked serious.

'Of course.' She looked pensive. 'It was during the second of the two dances in town. It was a friday night, in March or thereabouts. You will be able to check this, I am sure.'

'Indeed,' Trinder agreed. 'And you saw Miss Askew?'

'I did. With a man!' She paused for effect. 'It was late in the evening and a little way from the town hall.' She now spoke in little more than a whisper. 'She was walking arm in arm with him.'

'What time was this, please?' Simon was making notes in his big open handwriting.

'About 11.30, but after so many years it is hard to be sure. It was a warm evening and I did not hurry home. I suppose I was all in a muddle with myself about not going to the dance. One part of me did wish to be there and yet... Anyway, I just wanted to walk around, to settle my thoughts.'

'Where did you see them?' asked Trinder.

'Crossing the humpy-backed bridge; the one over the railway. Near the "bottom" station.'

'That's be the A41, sarge, crossing the LNWR branch from Buckingham to Banbury Merton Street,' Simon Howerth chipped in, nodding confidently as he noted this down. Trinder gave him an odd look.

'Very good, PC467', praised Miss Geddes, reading the number on his epaulette. 'They were walking in the direction of Evenley Park, and none too steadily!' She gave a significant look at the two detectives. 'Both looked slightly worse for wear. Walking with arms around each other, and I am not sure who was supporting whom. I find it deplorable how people allow themselves to be rendered almost insensible by drink.'

Trinder was sitting bolt upright. 'Are you absolutely sure it was Miss Askew? There was a blackout and must have been very dark...'

'Quite sure. You cannot blackout a full moon, and young eyes soon adjust to the dark.'

'Eating carrots helps…Er, sorry, sarge, miss.'

Miss Geddes and Trinder both stared at the constable, who blushed.

'Indeed. And I can pre-empt your next question, sergeant: I have no idea who he was, except that he wore an American airman's uniform, with a cap on the back of his head. Oh, he had a thin black moustache and, I think, slicked down hair. Quite rakish — if perhaps a little young — and on the short side.'

'Your description is excellent and most helpful,' Trinder checked that Howerth was noting it all down.

'I never forget a face. I recall thinking he looked Italian and found that odd.'

'Why?' asked Trinder.

'Because they were the enemy back then, I would have thought that obvious. Although I understand many Americans are actually Italians. Or is it the other way around? Anyway, it stuck in my mind at the time because the last song I heard them blasting out all over the town was Chiribiribin. I always thought this a most unpatriotic song whilst our boys were fighting the Italians.'

Trinder smiled. He collected 78s, especially the cuts by the big dance bands. 'The Andrews Sisters with Glenn Miller. When the moon hangs low in Napoli, there's a handsome gondolier… I know it well.' He gave her an approving look.

'The words were apposite.'

'I can see why you made the connection. Where were they going?'

'I did not follow them. That would be most improper. But I suppose they were going into the park. There is a footpath at that end of the park and I've heard it is popular of an evening with couples.' She shifted her position in the chair, fiddled with her cardigan for a moment as if privately considering this fact before picking up the remains of the scone, from which she took a large bite. After making short work of this and wiping a crumb from her upper lip and her spirits apparently revived, she grinned at Simon. 'Personally I think the young Yank was quite in the mood for singing, Say si, si. What do you think, constable number 467?'

CHAPTER TWENTY-NINE
On the Marylebone train
19ᵗʰ April 1943

Betty Askew had expected the train to be crowded. They always were these days: permanently rammed to bursting with servicemen and women going to places they were forbidden to identify, on trains that took forever, as they crawled from one unnamed station to the next, the printed timetable rendered useless. However, there was a distinct advantage living close to the Great Central mainline as this particular route had few junctions along its run into London, and traversing the pretty, but sparsely populated, countryside allowed the trains to keep moving at something like pre-war speeds. It should be a straight run in from now on, she reflected. It could be worse.

The men standing shoulder to shoulder in the corridor smoking like chimneys were more than eager to help her squeeze past their kit bags, guns and other bulky equipment, past their hot and pungent bodies pressed unavoidably close, hands gleefully helping her along. These enthusiastic assistants helped her move along through two carriages until she was finally ensconced in a comfortable corner seat of what had in peacetime been a first class compartment. The young sailor snoozing in that particularly desirable seat had been rudely awakened and invited to give up his place in robustly unambiguous terms by a burly soldier, and so, despite her complaints that this was not necessary, she was able to travel in relative comfort.

In truth, she was grateful for the chance to sit quietly, and by pulling her hat brim low she could hide more of her face and close her eyes behind the dark sunglasses. She was aware of the men in the corridor nudging each other and whispering comments they imagined she could not hear, whilst throwing appreciative glances in her direction, but she managed to shut this out.

There was no doubt she had cut a memorable figure on her way through the train, but she banked on the passengers being out-of-towners transported somewhere distant for the war. They would all be far way, perhaps overseas, in a matter of days and it was unlikely any would recognise her and pass word back. Besides, if everything went well she could even be home that same evening and no one need suspect anything. She was unable to tell if she really was expecting. She'd got herself so worked up about the possibility that she'd made herself physically sick with apprehension. Perhaps all the doctor need do was reassure her there was nothing to fret about and all would be well again.

If she had to stay over, then she would need a half-decent story to tell mother and father, and luckily she had a willing accomplice to provide an alibi. But hopefully it would not come to that and Pearl would not need to say anything. She was young, fit and strong, and so perhaps it would not knock her sideways too much and she could manage to get home the same day. She groaned silently and felt nauseous at the thought. She prayed silently: please God, don't let it be so. Please, please make everything OK.

If it wasn't, would the doctor help her out? Pearl had sounded confident when they'd talked last night, but she was only working from the tittle-tattle garnered from the domestics up at Tingewick Hall. The servants had gathered information over a period of time from snatches of overheard conversations, but this had been enough to establish what had happened with Lady Finmere as a result of her clandestine liaisons with her supposedly secret lover. It had been too scandalous a story for tongues not to wag and rumours and gossip not to be spread. And so, according to Pearl, details of the establishment their lady had visited one weekend were leaked out.

Could she trust what she had been told? Pearl was insistent that the information was reliable and the address — scribbled on the back of an envelope — was correct. And she had stressed the most important aspect, that the doctor was a very competent man, and not some dangerous backstreet operator armed with a dirty needle and a pint of gin. It was still a dreadful risk to arrive unannounced, but what else could she do? Telephoning was impossible, not only because the switchboard girls at the local exchange might recognise her voice and overhear everything, but the doctor would probably just put the receiver down, refusing to even speak to this unknown person.

Opening her voluminous shoulder bag, she extracted a small purse and checked the cap badge Ray had given her last summer and her precious ration books. The three five-pound notes taken from her post office savings account and a handful of coins represented the sum total of her savings. Seeing this doctor was likely to be quite expensive. She had no idea how much such a 'procedure' usually cost, but she hoped ten pounds would cover it. After all, she had to put in ten hours a day of hard graft at the loco for two long weeks to earn that much. It would sting a lot to part with all three of the fivers she'd brought with her.

She reviewed her strategy for negotiating with the doctor. She must present herself in the best possible light, and that meant making no mention of her American beau. That would not aid her cause one bit. She was well-dressed and well-groomed and, most crucially, able to prove, by the beautiful ring on her finger, that she was formally engaged to be married. This would demonstrate how serious and committed her fiancé had been to their future life. The doctor surely must see that it was forgivable to spend a night with her beloved before he returned to the theatre of war, only to be killed in action. She could be suitably vague about dates, places, times; after all, this was demanded of all citizens during this war, making it easier for her to tell a little white lie that concealed the true identity of the father. The doctor would sympathise with her plight, agreeing that cruel Fate had ended the life of this father-to-be whilst doing his patriotic duty for the nation; he would appreciate the appalling difficulties that bringing up a child alone would present, that it would also prevent her continuing her vital war work. Of one thing she was sure: she would need to deploy every one of the meagre selection of bargaining tools she could muster, hoping she could pull at his heart strings and gain his sympathy.

Then, with beating heart, she looked at the decorative wooden box. She turned it in her hands, taking in every curve and curlicue of the ivory and brass design, running her gloved finger over the edges and recalling how Ray had told her that one of these corners had stuck in his back, and that was how he had discovered the Cobra's Eye.

She had left behind the little note that usually lay inside the ring's box. She did not want to sully the memories associated with this precious little scrap of paper written in Ray's neat handwriting with the emotional and physical ordeal that lay ahead. The hard, cold diamond was lovely, but these few inked words were the closest thing she had of the shattered remains of their love, of their hopes and of their dreams. And she had shattered the memory of those as effectively as death had taken him from her.

Putting the box away, she snapped the purse shut. She'd betrayed his memory in exchange for a drunken romp on the wet grass in Evenley Park. And what about Mancini? What did she think about him? He'd been kind, almost caring, in a nervous, fumbling, groping sort of way, and yet what did it all mean? It was little more than a desperate search for comfort and physical contact between two lonely people. She was unlikely to hear from Mancini again, although when he'd parted from her in the early hours, his shirt wrongly buttoned and the combed slickness of his hair tousled into something wild and unkempt, he'd promised over and over to write, to keep in touch.

But what was the use? Were they intending to become lovers? She did not think so; besides, they did not have the luxury of time to even consider the idea. Words in a letter in her hands didn't mean he wasn't dead. By the time she read them he could be now little more than burnt flesh and broken bones in a field in Germany. Ray was dead, and yet she'd received his last letter a full two weeks after the dreadful telegram, a painful time-capsule he'd slipped into an envelope whilst seated on the edge of a narrow camp bed in a khaki-coloured tent somewhere in a far distant desert, his sweaty hand causing the ink to smudge one of the words. It had sat unopened on her dressing table for days before she could bring herself to read his words of love and longing from beyond the grave. Perhaps that funny, wise-cracking Yankee rear gunner was already no more...

She didn't want or need another letter like Ray's. She couldn't even start to think if she cared, or even wanted to care, about Mancini. All she wanted was for the war to end and to lie in the comfort of someone's arms and try to forget everything...

After taking a few moments to fight back the stinging, salty tears, she turned to face the window and, partially concealed from prying eyes, eased the diamond ring from beneath the neck of her dress and unfastened the chain. Slipping the ring off, she refastened the chain then removed the glove from her left hand and slid the ring into place. The morning sunlight set the stone afire as she held her hand near the grubby window. She stared into it, time slowing and all thoughts of her surroundings momentarily forgotten as she drank in its beauty.

It was lovely, and yet, perhaps there was something almost unsettling about it. Or was that simply because she was aware of its great value? It was not a comfortable ring to live with, at least not for a humble working girl who spent most of her day clambering over steam locomotives, and whenever she did wear it on her finger she felt dreadfully self-conscious. She felt that sensation now, almost as though she were sitting in the compartment naked and everyone was staring at her, but nobody saying anything, nobody acknowledging the fact, each sharing in the lie and that was almost worse. Just like the emperor in his new clothes in that odd story she used to read as a child. One thing she could be sure of, the diamond was now inextricably linked with Ray's violent death. As she stared into the stone's centre she tried to imagine what his last day may have been like, hardly daring to think about how his life might have ended in that burning tin can in a searing desert. It was nauseating, and all she could really pray for was that the end had been quick.

Private Coulson stared through the narrow, letterbox-shaped slit, the armoured cover of which was lifted and propped open. It acted like a sun visor but offered no respite from the unbearable heat. It was so hot he hardly knew where blood, skin, metal and the sweltering desert air met. Everything was far too hot, and the air he breathed whilst somehow sustaining him, offered no comfort, just tasting of diesel fuel and unwashed bodies, of stinking feet, overheated rubber tyres, sump oil and the bitter tang of steel. Deep inhalations or gentle sips of air made no difference, and experience told him the best thing to do was to sit as still as possible and try to slip into a semi trance-like state, shutting down his faculties to a level where he could almost forget the acute discomfort of the hard driver's seat, the intense claustrophobia of his position deep in the heart of the vehicle. He must try to ignore the sweat pooling at the base of his spine and his almost complete restriction of movement and vision. Just sit and wait and hope. Wait until Captain Anderson told him to fire up the engine and drive, and only then, with a welcome breeze caused by their forward motion and with throttle under foot and the hard steering wheel clamped in his hands, could he feel released, able to finally exert some control over his destiny, steering them away from this crushing boredom and into the wide spaces of the desert, bowling along in a deafening roar of engine with the wheels bucking and bouncing beneath him.

But that had been hours ago. He'd followed Anderson's instructions and parked the Humber in a slight depression that hopefully would prevent their being spotted from the ground. Anderson was now scanning the horizon, using field glasses fixed to a bizarre periscope attachment that made it look as though he was swivelling a massively elongated pair of very tall and tubular ears, like some grotesque rabbit.

The captain broke the silence every so often, quietly feeding coordinates and cold facts about tank movements to 'Bounder' Baker on the radio set, who in turn repeated everything into the mouthpiece. Occasionally, the radio would crackle and a distorted and disembodied voice could be faintly heard replying. Otherwise, they maintained long periods of silence, punctuated by the odd dry cough, a rumbling tummy, a belch or a half-hearted comment that raised a murmured response.

They were men confined and pressed close, locked inside their cramped vehicle, pushed dangerously close to a front line that was now a pitched battle of staggeringly intense ferocity. The danger was palpable and the usual humour and banter was replaced by a quiet edginess.

Coulson stared at the narrow rectangle of sand dune and the equal measure of intense blue sky now increasingly stained by smudges of black oily smoke, and listened to the sounds outside, trying to identify the low murmuring rumble of heavy engines, the squeak and squeal of sand-abraded metal on caterpillar tracks, the rapid whump-whump-whump of guns and the buzzing of aircraft engines. As the hours crept by these sounds grew ominously closer, the constant noise of gunfire prompted one or other of the crew to identify the probable source and type of artillery.

'That's an eighty-eight.'

'Yep. Close an' all…'

'There's a battery of them. Keeping up a steady rate.'

'Good guns. Jerry knows how to make a gun. I feel sorry for our lads on the receiving end.'

A droning note wavered above the relentless crump and bass boom of shellfire.

'What's that? Hurricane?'

'Think it's one of theirs.'

'Shit.'

The crump of intense shellfire continued, the buzzing aero engine drifting in and out of earshot.

'Moving away.'

'Thank fuck for that.'

Coulson nodded agreement and spat on to the bonnet, watching the spittle fizz and evaporate.

'Sitting ducks, we are. Let's hope they've not got much up. If one of them tank-busting Fokkers comes over, we're done for. No chance.'

'Quiet down there!' Anderson's voice was not loud, but it commanded obedience. The periscope squeaked on its mount as he swivelled it to one side. The radio fizzed with a blast of interference, causing the operator to pull off his headphones and curse, wiggling a damp finger in his ear.

Coulson licked his cracked lips, and for the hundredth time that morning focused his eyes on the little photographs above the windscreen slit. One showed her sunbathing, he was not sure where. It was a picture taken a few years ago, but she had cheekily written on the back that it might give him 'something to dream about'. She looked happy, and beautiful, and he could admire her lithe limbs and trace the faintest line where her breast was not quite covered by her one-piece suit. It was a lovely image.

And then there was Betty seated in the sun with outstretched legs and one of her favourite trains crossing the viaduct behind. She'd sent these snaps to him in her latest letter, telling him how she'd made prints of each picture they had taken on the Box Brownie in Boots the Chemist, even though it had cost her an extortionate price and taken ages to get them done. He stared hard at the little image and tried to will himself back there, trying to step inside the tiny rectangle of blacks, greys and whites and lie beside her on the rug.

'Can still hear it.' Gunner Harrington's voice was almost a whisper, his desert-booted foot and bare leg close to Coulson's face. 'Like a friggin' wasp.' He fiddled nervously with the breach on the armoured car's gun. It was useless against air attack, but it was all he had. It was their only line of defence; apart from the not-especially-thick armour plating that encased them. 'It's coming around. I'd swear it is!'

Coulson knew from when he'd taken the hit in the leg last year, that war when it struck, happened too fast to take in, and yet, conversely, seemed to unfold in slow motion. It made no sense, and he could never properly explain this contradiction, but that was how it was. Too fast to know anything until it was too late, and yet there was still time to take stock, to see an edited newsreel version of one's life flash by. A final review...

As the aircraft engine screamed into a note that could only instil fear and terror, and as the cannon shells started to rip into the sand, he knew instinctively it was over. He would never get out in time and their vehicle could not protect them from a Focke-Wolf 190. Anderson was yelling 'Bale! bale!', knowing their best chance was to lie prone in the sand some distance from the Humber, but even as legs were scrabbling for purchase, arms fighting to move in a space too tight to allow easy movement, unable to disengage from the clutches of gear lever and gun breach and any number of sharp angles, his friends were screaming, and something red was spraying onto the side of his face. There was the horrible sound of metal being wrenched apart, the Humber lifting bodily from the ground, the smell of cordite and burning flesh and petrol in his nostrils and an intense, completely overwhelming, searing sensation that made even the desert sun feel cool. He was floating in the air, freed of this life, free of all earthly concerns, flames white hot and golden yellow and some even a searing blue from electrical sparks, all crowding around his head. He fixed his eyes on the little images of Betty that now curled, then cracked, as a bloom of brown appeared on her face from below the emulsion which then bust into a sunflower of flame and peeled apart in layers of slate grey dust.

She snapped out of her reverie by meeting the eyes of a WAAF girl seated opposite. The uniformed servicewoman was reflected by the strong sunlight in the carriage window and she grinned at Betty the moment she realised she'd been caught looking. 'Lucky girl!' The young woman's eyes flashed appreciation.

'I suppose so.' Betty mumbled the reply, not risking her voice cracking.

'Is he far away? Mine's in the Med somewhere. Naval officer. Can't say exactly, of course.' The young woman spoke softly, her voice kind.

'He's very far away. It's all I have now...'

'I know the feeling. A snapshot or two, a few letters, his cap badge and a bunch of memories, that's about the sum of it.' The WAAF gave a rueful smile, full with understanding. 'Not a lot, really.'

'Not enough.'

'When will all this end?'

'It already has ended. For him...'

'Oh my dear, I'm so, so sorry.' The WAAF looked genuinely apologetic.

Betty shook her head. No apology needed. Already her interest in the woman opposite was fading, replaced by the overwhelming fear that the price she might have to pay could be as steep as handing over the ring. Was she ready to do that? No, not unless there was absolutely no other choice. She looked out of the window, signalling that she wished to be left alone with her thoughts, and the WAAF seemed to take the hint.

It was painful being surrounded by so many men in uniform. It made it desperately hard to stop the flood of memories crowding in of the time spent with Ray; of their sunny picnic on the rug, with him in his army fatigues and the woman pilot waving to them.

And, if she was honest, all the joshing and joking and banter of the men in the corridor as she had pushed her way through to her seat had reminded her of those even louder, crazier, wild nights at the dances, of the music and endless chatter and noise and everyone acting as though this was their last night on earth, frantically cramming as much enjoyment as they could into a few short hours. It had been a kind of collective madness, with strangers suddenly acting as though they were lovers. Catching the occasional twang of an American accent somewhere along the corridor, Betty felt a dart of remorse and turned her thoughts to Tony Mancini.

Betty pinched the bridge of her nose and held her fingers there, determined not to cry tears of shame and anger, or of regret and fear for that young man. It surprised her to discover she was thinking about Tony, and actually wishing she could see him again. Was he still alive? It seemed improbable. She had long since got over her initial anger about what they had done, realising in the relentlessly enduring light of day they had both been culpable. She was guilty, just as much as he, and it was too simplistic to curse him for taking advantage. She had agreed to walk out of the dance, and it was she who had suggested going to the park. To be brutally honest, she'd wanted him, too; she'd wanted to lie in the damp grass and lose herself, to forget everything in a rush of passion, set herself free from worry, work, loss and longing and just live, and cry out in a moment of pure pleasure when nothing else mattered…

It was the drink, of course, and she had too little experience of rum and cola to handle it. God, how that Andrews Sisters song told the story! *Drinking rum and cola whilst working for the Yankee dollar.* Ha! Well, he'd given her enough presents, so she supposed he deserved something in return. She must have gulped down glasses of the stuff with an abandon that shocked her now. She would never get drunk again. Never. Although as she laid her head against the musty seat cushion, she thought how a stiff brandy might steady her ragged nerves.

Betty caught the reflection of the diamond in the glass. The ring had started it. Feeling shy and unenthusiastic about going to the dance, she'd made a point of wearing it on her ring finger, wanting to signal loud and clear that she was spoken for, that she was strictly unavailable, and hoping and praying that Ray would — through some form of divine communication — realise that he was still in her thoughts every waking moment and understand that this was not a betrayal of his memory.

But young men far from home and full of beer, and equally full of fear and apprehension, give scant regard to such signals. To Tony Mancini and his pals it was like a homing beacon; a pale light pulling them towards her and the perfect excuse to fire questions from all sides in their exotic, New York voices; questions that grew ever more cheeky and bold as their confidence grew and the intake of alcohol increased.

Mancini had been in a group of loud and gregarious men, their accents strong and characterful. They swaggered and they boasted and they threw their money about and the pockets of their well-cut uniforms seemed to be filled with unlimited quantities of scented soap, cigarettes, Hershey bars, precious nylons and all manner of other desirables now impossibly scarce in a country rationed to the bone.

Askew soon discovered this crowd were from various parts of New York State, some of Italian extraction, a heritage betrayed by their skin tone being noticeably warmer than the typical rain-leached British. Their hair was usually black and worn slicked to a shine with razor-sharp partings, with moustaches pencil thin and eyes dark and liquid and full of vitality. They were annoying too, and buzzed around like flies and at first she had been angry that the other girls had encouraged them.

But these young men were undoubtedly exotic, almost alien, and it was hard not to be intrigued. They spoke differently, and they quipped and joked at a speed that at first she found hard to follow, but this also made them like something from a movie. Their quick-fire routines reminded her of Abbott and Costello, their witty and flippant repartee was not unlike talking with a Marx brother. It was all rather bothering and bewildering, but oddly infectious, and so, encouraged by her friends — who seemed to be lapping it up with little concern for where it might lead — she found herself relaxing and actually starting to enjoy the encounter.

'C'mon, babe, how 'bout we take a turn on the dance floor, huh?'

'I—I'm not sure...'

'Say, why not?'

'I think perhaps I had better not...'

'That dress looks like it was made for dancing...'

'I'm happy sitting.'

'Gee, miss, but it's mighty remiss of me not to say how sweet you look. You look such a picture in that swell dress, I could sit right down an' paint you!'

'I thought you wanted to dance?'

'I thought you'd never ask.' He held out his hand.

She averted her eyes to check the hemline of her dress had not ridden up just as the band launched into a raucous rendition of *Oh Johnny! Oh Johnny!*

'No kiddin' Miss Betty, you look swell and I'd go as far to say it accen-tu-ates those positives, n' what's the point of a positive if ya' don't accentuate it, huh?' He gave a cheeky grin as Betty blushed. 'C'mon, doll, put this guy outta his misery and jitterbug with me. You do know how to jitterbug?'

'I like to dance of course, but this is all so new...'

'Sure you can, babe. Tony's got the moves...'

They danced for a couple of hours, maybe longer. She loved dancing and it had been a regret that she and Ray had only done so on two occasions and then only briefly. He was reluctant to take to the floor because he lacked confidence. A slow, lurching sway around a half-deserted floor to a record poorly amplified through tatty speakers was about the best they had managed. But Mancini knew the moves and was only too happy to sweep and swirl her around the floor as best he could in the space available. The jitterbug was a whirl of adrenaline and raw excitement on the back of the driving beat of the live band, the drums pounding and bass strings throbbing, giving her little time to think about anything other than staying on her feet and leaving her hot and flushed when they stopped, and to her surprise, smiling like the Cheshire cat.

As the Squadronnaires played *Little Brown Jug*, *the Beer Barrel Polka*, *Youssel Youssel* and any number of other favourites with the Yankee hosts, they lost themselves in the strong rhythms and their own thrilling proximity, and if sometimes his hands strayed across her bottom or brushed the side of her breast, well, it was surely excusable now all the couples had become pressed so tightly together as more crowded onto the floor, the dancing reduced to variations on a cramped intimate shuffle, during which it was hard not to be jostled and caressed and feel the hot eager lust of his body pressed hard against hers.

He'd walked her home as part of her equally loud and raucous group loosely formed into 'couples', although everyone was at excessive if slightly drunken pains to make clear that no such relationships had been established. Mary's escort held her tightly around the waist and pecked repeatedly at her neck, but she still maintained a noisy banter that encompassed the group, everyone laughing and giggling as a group and so preventing any attempts to lure one or other of the girls away for a more private encounter, although Pearl's lipstick had still become badly smeared by some enthusiastic snogging.

It was an evening of fun and nothing more. Betty had allowed Mancini a peck on either cheek, gently but firmly resisting his almost desperate plea for one on the lips. But his hands had still given her bottom an unambiguous, exploratory squeeze, and as she stifled a cry of outraged complaint he turned and walked away, tipping his cap to the back of his head and waving the fingers of a hand over his shoulder.

'See ya around, doll!'

And despite the best efforts of her rapidly-fading willpower, she did see him again, at the second dance a week later. If she'd just left it at that and resisted temptation, all would have been well.

The Dirty Girls Brigade had rolled up as a group in even higher spirits than before. The thrill and excitement of the previous encounter had been enhanced by a week of washing with a new block of fragrant soap, enjoying the sugar rush of unrationed bars of sweet chocolate and developing a taste for smoking Lucky Strikes and Camels. With new stockings proudly worn beneath best frocks and extra care lavished on their hair and make up, they were anticipating an evening as the centre of attention from these young and fit men. Men, they discovered, who were both excessively polite and attentive and yet bold and freed by distance and a different culture from the excessive reserve that prevented the British from expressing what they really thought, stifling their interaction with women into awkward, stilted affairs. The Yankees were eager to make it clear they considered the women attractive and exciting and yet were polite almost to a fault. The air of unreality that seemed to permeate the dancehall made this contrast strangely appealing and acceptable.

Knowing the airmen were due to leave town the next day and with no expectation of their returning lent the evening an even more reckless and carefree quality, and Betty had been unable to resist its infectious attraction.

She and Mancini had danced with gusto for over an hour, she now feeling more confident of the steps and making the most of the relatively empty floor in the earlier part of the evening. She had fallen in love with the jitterbug, if not with the young airman, and, unsure of when she might get another chance, wanted to make the most of the opportunity. Mancini was delighted to oblige.

The drinks flowed throughout and the presents he'd brought from the base swelled her hand bag to bursting, Mancini explaining that the base PX store gave him a generous allowance so she could take it all without feeling bad. Then, as the music took a quieter turn, giving aching feet a chance to rest whilst the pretty vocalist in her tailored army uniform with pencil skirt and cap set at an angle on her blonde curls sang a medley of softer, dreamier Vera Lynn numbers, they fell into talking. Leaning together across a battered card table covered with beer-stained baize and a candle stub in a jam jar set between them, it was not long before the conversation took on a more serious aspect, the realities of their situation impossible to keep at bay any longer.

'I heard you leave town tomorrow. Is that true?'

'Sure is, doll. Tomorrow, at seven, right on the dot.' He flipped an unlit cigarette into the air, catching it on his lower lip and making her smile. 'Two, three, mebbe four days later I'll be on my first run over Germany. Might be my first and my last.'

She stared at him as the statement sank in, then screwed her eyes closed for a second, the cigarette smoke that hung thick on the air making them sting. Mancini spread his hands wide, the cigarette now between two fingers. 'I can't fool myself no longer. Heck, I could be dead before the end of the week, and there ain't a whole lot either of us can do about it.'

'No! No, it can't be that bad. Don't you have escort fighters and guns to shoot back with?'

'Don't misunderstand me, I'll do my bit, and I plan on taking a few Jerry with me before I check out.' He took a deep swig of beer to ease a drying throat that was threatening to make him cough, his voice now quieter and more thoughtful. 'But I can only tell it like I see it, and things ain't lookin' too rosy right about now.' He popped the cigarette in his mouth, then placed a second beside it, flipping his lighter open and the flame flared between them as he lit each one in turn, Betty's eyes watery in the bright light flickering on their faces. 'See, I'm a Tail-end Charlie, Miss Betty. You know what those goons are?' He handed her one of the Lucky Strikes.

She nodded silently, concentrating on inhaling the smoke. She'd heard this moniker, and she'd also heard the stories attached to the least desired position on a bomber plane. 'I think so,' her voice was barely audible.

'It's 'cos I'm short, see? It ain't a job for the taller guys, so guess who gets the short straw, yours truly, little Tony Mancini! Yup, give the little wop the job, doo flippin' wop...' He dropped his voice so low, she had to lean closer. 'You know what the percentages are for Charlies? I'm tellin' you, it's worse for the dumb schmuck sitting at the back than the rest of the guys in the crate put together. Hell, we get it in the neck even if they get on home.'

She reached her hand out and grasped his. It was cold and clammy.

'It takes another man to strap me into that Perspex coffin. I can't even get or out on my own. Like a stupid baby, I can't even take a pee without their help. Sorry to be so crude an' all that, but you see what I'm sayin', Miss Betty?' He shook his head, smiling as if the idea was amusing. 'Then, I gotta hope my electric suit stays working or else I freeze to death, or, if the electric screws up, I fry. I heard it's like death row if the wiring goes nuts. Nice touch, eh?'

'Oh God, no...'

'But that's not all, doll. There's the oxygen line that runs halfway down the old crate that's busy bein' busted up by some Nazi in his Messerschmitt, so I gotta pray it stays in one piece or else I suffocate, and if that weren't enough, they prefer to shoot us up from the rear. So yours truly gets the full and undivided attention of every goddamned fighter over Germany.' He puffed smoke and bit his lower lip for a moment. 'If by some miracle I'm still in the land of the living but we have to bale out...' His eyes met hers, pupils wide and black the tall flame of his lighter reflecting on the glassy surface. 'Yeah, well... There ain't no baling out for a Tail-end Charlie. There ain't time enough to get me out.' He cut off the flame instantly and it fell dark between them. 'Puff!'

'Please don't say that.'

'Betty, you may be the very last woman I ever look at...'

'I can't bear to hear this...'

'I'd sure like it if...' He swallowed, his Adam's apple bobbing. 'If you'd let me kiss you. Just the once, y'understand? I mean a real kiss, one that counts. So I can take the touch an' feel of a pretty gal's lips with me into that damned Boeing before I check out. I want to remember the smell of your hair against my face, instead of that stinking rubber mask.' Betty Askew felt her heart almost stop. She hardly dare breathe, raw emotions screaming through her. 'Hell, Betty, I need to confess something, because I figure if I don't do it now it'll be too late: I've never kissed a girl before. Not *really* kissed, not like they do in the movies with my arms around your neck an'...'

'Shh... Stop. Let's take a walk. I need some quiet. The music feels too loud now and I think I've lost the will to dance anymore.' She smiled. It was weak and hid a range of emotions of which intense nervousness was probably the strongest, but it was still a smile. 'Just one kiss then. That's all.'

CHAPTER THIRTY
Brackley police station
27th September 1950

'So, inspector, who has an interest in Richard Irons being dead?' DI Bainbridge fired the question at Vignoles as he selected a slice of hot buttered toast from the plate between them. 'And do tuck in — they've been generous with the old roll-in-the-gutter!'

Vignoles was also munching hungrily, careful to not drip the hot butter Bainbridge was referring to in army slang. 'I'd say suspects are limited. Irons claimed he worked with Miss Askew over this house breaking. Possibly they've worked this before, though his amateurism seems to argue against that. What we *do* know is, he made a hash job of the burglary and was caught. Perhaps Miss Askew wanted him out of the frame, maybe he'd become a liability. And please, do call me Charles.'

'Right you are, Charles, and I'm George. But Irons was let off without charge, so why not be thankful for a close shave and leave it at that? Why would Askew take the risk of being caught for his murder when at best all we can do is implicate her in aiding a housebreaking? We've got nothing on her.'

'Beats me, George. It only makes sense if Irons discovered something else, something important. Perhaps he stumbled on it by accident...and it became imperative that Miss Askew keep him quiet.' Vignoles chewed over this idea along with his toast, but looked thoroughly sceptical about his own hypothesis.

'Hard to imagine what? He only lifted a couple of gold coins before he was disturbed, but I suppose he could have found something else? It would have to be darned small.'

'Perhaps he saw something? This is crazy, but let's imagine he was actually doing a spot of espionage, the robbery being nothing more than a cover story. He is there to read something, find some information, but once he passed this on, it got him killed.' Both men sipped from their mugs of tea as they tried to imagine what could get a man killed by a young woman with a vicious dog. Neither looked inspired.

'What about Henry Askew?' asked Bainbridge after munching on his toast a while longer. 'He had a grievance with Irons.'

'He has to be a suspect,' Vignoles replied. 'His alibi is supported only by his wife and, as she shares the same grievance, her word is of limited use to us.' He puffed out his cheeks in a slow exhalation. 'Now I can imagine Henry Askew and Irons meeting and tempers flaring. Perhaps things get out of control and a punch or two being thrown, but I'm struggling with the scenario we discovered. Let's not forget Henry Askew had to borrow a suitably ferocious dog from somewhere for the evening, so that sounds unlikely.'

'Agreed. And how did he contact Irons to arrange the meeting? It has to have been premeditated, and yet when and how did he do it? And why would Irons agree to see him alone and in a concealed location? It does not stand up to scrutiny,' Bainbridge looked crestfallen.

Vignoles took another slice of toast. It had been a long morning and he'd readily agreed to a late elevenses and a chance to review the morning's events in the relative comfort of Brackley police station on the Banbury Road. The toast was easing his hunger and the melted butter was surprisingly delicious. He was no nearer unlocking the puzzle of this death, but the toast was welcome.

'What do you know of Dr Melcombe?'

'Not much, Charles. A retired family GP, who's flown well below our radar. Keeps himself to himself and is comfortably off, possibly more than just comfortable, thinking about his collecting hobby,' George Bainbridge shrugged his shoulders and took a bite of a blackened edge with a satisfying crunch. 'But he was laid up in hospital when Irons was killed, so that has to put him out of the picture.'

'I want to know more about the doctor. Why was he so keen to let Irons off the hook? After such a traumatic experience most people want justice, whilst he appears to jealously guard his privacy above seeing Irons punished.'

'Some people just want a quiet life. Perhaps he thought there was no point in sending Irons to prison.'

'Perhaps. But it is a curious detail, George, and it has to be explored.'

'Correct. However, if he is just an innocent victim, that rather uses up our meagre stock of suspects.'

'Let's hope my men can find someone more promising.'

DS Trinder, together with PC Howerth, who had rushed down from Leicester to lend a hand, had been sent to interview Miss Geddes, the ticket clerk at Brackley Central and the last person to admit seeing Betty Askew, way back in 1943. They were also tasked with speaking to Mr Hancock, a taxi driver, who seemed certain that Betty Askew was dead, according to Irons's statement. Vignoles wanted the man to explain himself and he could be called in for more questioning if they deemed it necessary.

One thing was for certain, if this intriguing plot was to be unravelled, then more background information was needed and Vignoles had set further wheels in motion. PC Blencowe and WPCs Benson and Lansdowne were tasked with tracing any evidence of a valuable solitaire diamond being sold in 1943; with identifying the organising committee of the dances Askew attended; and, if possible, the identity of the particular squadrons of the USAAF present on those nights. It was a long shot, but they might even hold a list of names of the men who attended. In the next day or so, they were also to speak with all of Betty Askew's friends who had been at the same dances, Trinder having made a note of their names at the end of their interview with the Askews earlier that morning.

Vignoles might be feeling temporarily stumped, but the morning had been filled with activity, and whilst no lead had been uncovered yet, it was surely only a matter of time before they made a breakthrough. Admittedly, the wild dog hunt organised by George Bainbridge had drawn a blank and the house to house visits around the streets surrounding St Peter's had not yet yielded anything promising, nor indeed had an interview with the distraught vicar and his churchwardens, but it was still only a few hours since the discovery of the corpse.

However, Bainbridge was proving a useful sounding board. On the face of it, Miss Askew appeared to have done a runner and left of her own free will, perhaps even eloped overseas with an American serviceman. Her valuable ring could have funded their new life, and this lent some credibility to the idea. There were problems, however, the most obvious of which being that the airmen would have been shipped out of Brackley in 1943 to airbases in the east Midlands or East Anglia and certainly not home to the States. Both men felt it unlikely that she would try to follow him to one of the British airbases. This would be an unusual thing for a young eighteen-year-old to do, made harder by the restrictions and hardships of war, and surely someone would have recognised her during the long period of time before her beau was released from action to return home? It was implausible that she had remained invisible throughout this time.

'Do you actually think Betty Askew is back from wherever she's been lying low?' asked Bainbridge.

'If so, then where is she?' asked Vignoles. 'I've had uniformed officers and station staff up and down the line on the hunt, and we've had not a glimpse.'

'So, was she just a figment of Irons's imagination, Charles?'

'Sergeant Trinder was convinced by Irons's insistence that he'd met her. He saw how genuinely shocked the man was by that poster in the station waiting room. All of this makes little sense, other than lending credence to the idea the man was going doolally. Irons may have sounded convincing, but he could have been delusional. We cannot actually discount that idea, as nobody has come forward who actually saw them together, including a train guard who insists Irons was alone on the train. I just don't know...' Vignoles looked nonplussed. 'Damn and blast it, George — I need to find this missing girl!'

'Assuming she exists.' Bainbridge gave a knowing look. 'If she is just a figment of Irons's fevered mind, then she has no part in the robbery, and if you can find no trace of her emigrating with a Yankee, then...' Bainbridge left the sentence unfinished, confident Vignoles would be thinking along the same lines.

'I know. When a young woman has not been heard of in seven years, the most likely reason is that she's dead. And that grim possibility does nothing to help me understand why Irons was killed!' Vignoles looked grim. He leaned back in his battered old chair. He needed a break, something to take them beyond the impasse they appeared to be in.

The telephone rang and Bainbridge answered it. As he listened to the caller his face changed by degrees from neutral through puzzlement into mild shock, then horror and finally into a more professional expression of intense concentration. After a fairly lengthy call, during which he fired off a succession of short questions but in the main listened to an urgent voice at the other end, he replaced the receiver. He whistled low and long before speaking, raising both eyebrows in an expression of surprise. 'There has been a most intriguing development, Charles. A rather disturbing one, too, and, whilst I cannot say how it ties in with the death of Mr Irons, I know it will interest you.'

'Did I hear you mention Dr Melcombe, George?'

'Correct. That was the Amersham police. There has been a gruesome discovery. It was reported on the afternoon of 23rd, but only now have they made the connection to Melcombe.' Bainbridge formed his fingers into a steeple as they rested on the desk and tapped his fingertips together for a second or two. 'The head of what appears to be a young woman has been discovered in a distinctive wooden box buried in the garden of a private dwelling. The house has now been identified as that previously owned by Dr Melcombe, from where he once ran his surgery.'

'Good Lord!' Vignoles put down his now-empty coffee mug. 'Any indication how long it had been there?'

'They waited for the post mortem to offer guidance on this point, as the date is clearly going to be vital. Dating is proving a challenge, apparently, but it could have been put there when the doctor was still in residence. He retired as a GP that summer, moving out in late July 1943. However,' Bainbridge raised a hand as if to forestall any instant reaction from Vignoles, who put his pipe in his mouth, chewed the stem and remained silent. The date was intriguing and his mind was whirring. 'The decomposition rate', continued Bainbridge, 'is affected by being in a well-sealed box plus some other factors, so the best time they can offer is between six and nine years. Not accurate enough to let the current occupants off the hook, either, and questions have been raised about them, apparently. They may be irrelevant, but the connection to our doctor is a most curious coincidence.'

'Yes George, and Dr Melcombe surprised everyone by insisting on dropping all charges against the man who attacked him, a man found dead not far from the cottage hospital where the doctor is recuperating. What is more, he was killed right beside the grave of the soldier who was going to marry the woman who urged him to break into the doctor's house. The coincidences here are piling up and are quite mind-boggling. I fear it will take quite a few more than Sherlock's three pipes.' Vignoles lit his pipe, which he had filled whilst Bainbridge was on the telephone, sending puffs of aromatic smoke into the air as he spoke. 'If all that were not curious enough, we're looking for a young woman that one witness placed on Amersham station. It was not enough to offer any meaningful leads at the time, but now I wonder?'

'We've been asked to make some enquiries about Melcombe. See if he has any more pieces of that skeleton in his cupboard! Sorry, rather a bad joke.' Bainbridge apologised.

'Just the head? That lends a gruesome twist to what is already a dreadful discovery.'

'There are signs of acid burning to the teeth and lime thrown over the skin.'

Vignoles looked surprised. 'Thereby destroying any chance of dental records helping identify her, presuming she even had any, and instantly disfiguring the face in case it was discovered soon after burial. Someone has gone to great lengths to eradicate any identifying features. I suspect if we do find the body, the hands will be missing as well.'

Trinder looked shocked. 'Good Lord, why do you think that, sir?'

'A killer so determined to prevent the identification of their victim is unlikely to have taken the risk this woman has a criminal record and her prints being on file.'

'Gosh yes. Perhaps she has.'

'Indeed.' Vignoles looked pensive. 'But where on earth might he have taken two severed hands? The problem is he could have thrown them almost anywhere, but finding them is important. I don't hold out any real hope of them being little more than bones by now, but the location might just thrown up some clue...'

'Separate all the body parts that aid identification and it makes our job almost impossible. I'm assuming Dr Melcombe is still in the cottage hospital?'

'I believe so. He was in pretty poor shape.'

'It would be useful to keep him there, until tomorrow at least. I want to get down to Amersham immediately, then deal with the doctor when I return.'

'604!' Bainbridge stood up and called to the front desk. PC Dowd hurried into the office.

'Sir?'

'Get on to the cottage hospital and confirm that Dr Melcombe is still there, and constable, you know some of the staff there, I understand?'

'My aunt is a nurse, sir.'

'Good. It would serve everyone's best interests for the doctor to remain there until tomorrow. He must not leave today, is that understood?'

'Very good, sir.'

'But use discretion. He must not know this came from us.'

'Very well, sir.'

'And make us some more coffee, but put some blasted grounds into it this time. The last pot was dishwater!'

Vignoles had been enjoying his pipe and thinking about the latest revelations. As Dowd was turning to leave he voiced his thoughts aloud to Bainbridge. 'Depending on where the hands were disposed of, there is a remote chance of fingerprints. Where on earth might he have taken two severed hands? He could have thrown them almost anywhere, down a drain, into a river...'

Dowd had stopped in his tracks and spun about, gawping.

'What the devil is it, constable? You look like you've had a nasty fright!' Bainbridge gave Dowd an irritable look.

'Hands? Did you just mention severed hands, sir?'

'A pair of them, to be precise. Why d'you ask?'

'Oh Lord, I must apologise. It's — well, because of all that's happened these last days. What with the body, the wild dog and so much out of the ordinary. Once I'd — well, you see — once I'd put the box under the desk it just went clean out of my mind and...'

'Pull yourself together, man! I hardly need remind you DI Vignoles is in the room, so try not to make us look like a pack of fools. What are you wittering on about?' Bainbridge looked furious.

'Beg pardon, sir. With permission, if you will allow me to retrieve the box in question it will make more sense. It's underneath that desk, on the floor...'

A few minutes later the three were looking at the jumble of small bones now laid out on the desk, a variety of expressions on their faces. Bainbridge's was one of controlled annoyance, and in between darting reproachful glances at the young constable he had taken to sighing loudly or pointedly muttering 'I don't believe this!' at irregular intervals. The constable looked mortified, a not inappropriate expression under the circumstances. He had dug himself deep into a hole and could see no way of extricating himself.

Vignoles, however, was nodding enthusiastically whilst peering at the bones, occasionally moving them around as he tried to recall his basic grounding in anatomy. If he felt anger or annoyance at Dowd's forgetfulness, he did not show it.

'We need some tests done, of course. These need expert analysis, and in conjunction with that head in the garden, but my instinct suggests we may have stumbled upon another part of that poor woman's body. This is an extraordinary breakthrough, and the timing is fortuitous. I am not sure what we would have made of this discovery a few days ago, but now we have a clear objective: establish if these are from the same body as the head in Amersham, and then ascertain if these are the remains of... Well, we need to determine who this was.' Vignoles chose not to make too big a jump and name the woman as Betty Askew.

CHAPTER THIRTY-ONE
Amersham
19th April 1943

Betty Askew stepped off the crowded train, out of the hot fug of cigarettes and sweaty army uniforms, of Brylcreem and cheap perfume and sooty railway carriage onto a narrow rectangle of sun flooding the gap between the shadow cast by the train and the long, multi-gabled platform awning with the dog-tooth edging. She took a moment to inhale a few breaths of fresh Buckinghamshire air and enjoy the slight breeze caressing her face.

A wail of wolf whistles aimed in her direction heralded the train's departure, the whistling louder than that blown by the guard on his Acme 'Thunderer', and she bowed her head to send a diagonal band of shadow across her face from her hat brim. She wanted to keep a low profile, but these lads at the carriage windows whistling and blowing kisses were ensuring the opposite. Luckily there appeared to be almost nobody else on the platform, and these men were soon to be sent far and wide. The train groaned and squeaked into motion as she turned her back on the soldiers and walked briskly towards the exit.

She'd run through the drill enough times: walk confidently and look as though you know exactly where you are going, but with head lowered to avoid eye contact. She made it across the booking hall vestibule without any problem but had to step aside to hold open one of two narrow entrance doors to allow an air raid warden to wheel his bicycle through. His tin helmet was slung from the outside of his shoulder bag, and this bulk forced her to press herself flat to allow him to pass.

'Thank you, miss. Sorry to be a trouble, miss.' His eyes crinkled at the edges as he smiled, a long, brown moustache turning up at the edges. 'Hope I didn't spoil that lovely dress with my dirty old bike.'

'No. You're welcome,' She dropped her eyes and instinctively pulled at the brim of her hat, the bracelet at her wrist sliding along her arm as she did so. The action was pointless as the warden had a perfectly clear view of her face.

'You'll need that in this sun. Keep the rays off that pretty face of yours.' He eyed her appreciatively for a moment, until his expression took on a more serious aspect. 'But that won't be much use if there's a raid. Do you have your gas mask with you?'

She had already turned to leave, but was still holding the door wide with an extended arm, not wishing to let it swing back and collide with the wardens' bike. 'Yes, I have it here.' She patted the bulbous bag filled by her work clothes and boots, hoping this would satisfy him. She had long since abandoned the vile, smelly mask, keeping it slung on a hook behind her bedroom door just like most others since the blitz had ended. The threat of poison gas had never materialized and everyone had grown heartily sick of carrying the things.

The warden gave her a long, sceptical look, considering whether to challenge her assertion, but then nodded. 'All right, miss. Too many people are slacking these days; but you can't afford to dice with gas! It's for your own protection, you know.' After giving him a sweet smile she let a little Morris motor car with crudely-painted panels of what looked like white distemper on its wings pass her, then hurried across the open turning space in front of the station building and fell into step behind two young mothers pushing large prams with heavy shopping bags slung from the handles.

Having studied a street plan in WH Smith's in Banbury on the previous Saturday afternoon, Betty had memorised the route. It looked simple enough on paper. She just had to get her bearings. Along Station Road, but don't go under the railway bridge, instead keep going up to the big road junction to the right. Following this route, a mini-convoy of delivery lorries and a depressingly grey 'austerity' bus with filthy windows trundled across her path in a cloud of exhaust fumes, whilst a horse-drawn meat van approached from the opposite direction, the horses' hooves clunking as the heavy metal shoes struck the ground in measured treads.

At the junction she knew not to bother to look for road signs to Aylesbury or High Wycombe (they'd been taken down long ago to slow the progress of enemy invaders). Instead she must double back on herself down Rectory Hill. This road dipped under the railway, the abutments of the bridge heavily sandbagged and a small machine gun post created to one side, presumably by the Home Guard, although it was presently unmanned. The road followed a gentle descent to the river in the valley bottom and offered a charming glimpse of fields filled with ripening crops and hedgerows studded with trees on the distant valley side.

She now walked past a succession of large dwellings set in elegant gardens and backing onto a mass of broadleaved woodland. She should find Dr Melcombe's surgery close by, and if he took his patients from the sort of houses along Rectory Hill, they were going to be wealthy and more than able to pay his fees. Askew understood why Pearl Cooper had warned her that he was going to expensive.

Melcombe's house was a beautiful, rambling, Art-and-Crafts era construction set behind a walled garden and guarded by gracious wooden gates painted duck-egg blue. These gates alone must have cost the equivalent of a railway cleaner's wages for a year. The house was all orangey-red brick and dark wooden beams with festoons of hops trailed across the front that were pruned to reveal diamond-paned windows. There were tall, barley-twist chimneys and a great roof swooping low in a gentle curve to extend over a side extension with an oaken door bearing a bright brass knocker and a polished plaque on the wall beside two windows veiled by startlingly white curtains that covered the lower two thirds of the glass. Askew guessed this was his surgery.

As she stood at the gate, a little car motored up the hill towards her, driven by a woman in a nurse's uniform. Perhaps she worked for the doctor? For some reason this felt like a problem, and Betty rummaged in her handbag and pulled out a compact to check her makeup. As the little car passed she gained a clear view of the woman in her blue cape. She made no reaction, however, and motored on. As the reflection of the car diminished in the circular mirror in her hand, Betty was surprised to discover that she had been holding her breath. She flipped the compact closed and steeled her nerves.

All was quiet once inside the gates. The sound of the traffic passing on Rectory Hill was masked by the high perimeter wall and mature trees that rustled in the occasional puff of warm wind. What if he was not at home? She'd not considered that possibility. She closed her eyes for a second, praying that her journey was not wasted, then approached the door, shoes crunching on the honey-coloured gravel. She lifted the huge brass doorknocker in the shape of a fox's head and banged it twice. The sound was heavy and resonant. Only then did she see the little sign made from cream Bakelite with black painted letters screwed to the door frame demanding that she:

PLEASE RING. DON'T HIT THE FOX.

After pressing the bell button as well she waited and wondered why the doctor retained the highly polished knocker if not for use. She decided it was probably affectation, giving the right impression of an expensive country residence. The door did not open, and she stood on the step, trembling with nerves, uncertain what to do. She jabbed her finger on the bell again, just as a voice boomed from behind the door, 'All right! All right! I can hear you!'

The door was flung wide and a florid face reddened by broken capillaries across the cheeks and a nose edging towards purple stared back at her, his eyes suspicious behind his horn-rimmed glasses. 'I can hear the bloody bell! There's no need to bang on the blasted door...' He stopped. 'And who the hell are you?'

'Are you Dr Melcombe?'

'It's my name on the plaque.' He used his eyes to indicate the polished brass plate to one side. 'It's also my day off, and I'm busy.'

She tried to make her voice steady. 'Doctor, I so urgently need to see you. I've come a long way today. I—I know this is an awful imposition, but it's an emergency, at least I think it is an emerg—'

'—Yes, this is an imposition,' Melcombe interrupted, 'and you've got a darned cheek banging on my door like this. You need an appointment.' He peered at her, sizing up her clothes and her oversized handbag, her makeup, scanning her face. 'Do I know you?' Although still fierce, there was a hint of doubt in his voice, eyes narrowing. 'If you do have an appointment then you have the date wrong.'

'No. I don't. I—I was given your name. In absolute confidence, you understand.' She was shaking with nerves. 'Nobody knows I am here.'

He scanned the road beyond the entrance gates, checking there was no one passing. 'Inside!' He ushered her into a spacious entrance vestibule that was cool and smelt slightly of surgical spirit and strongly of a bouquet of white lilies in a vase on a low table. He shut the door and stood facing her, arms folded across his chest. His eyes looked guarded. 'Who gave you my name?'

'My friend, Mrs Cooper, recommended you...'

The name meant nothing to the doctor, and he fired off more questions. 'Who are you? Who sent you?'

'I'm Betty Askew... I can pay...'

'Step in here.' Melcombe's voice was commanding. He strode towards an open door and indicated that she should enter first. It was an elegant office flooded with light through small-paned windows, with expensive furniture, including a desk that looked antique and chairs to match. The limed oak floorboards were glossy with polish, where not covered by a vast oriental rug. In one corner there was a hand basin and a set of folding screens concealing a narrow consulting couch covered with a crisp, white sheet. More white lilies scented the room.

He indicated that she should sit on one of the two Sheraton chairs before his desk whilst he took his place on the other side, a scowl of intense disapproval on his face. His eyes remained cautious, calculating, continually sizing her up, studying her gloves, shoes and dress; trying to assess this strange, thin woman who'd just turned up on his doorstep. He was suspicious and acutely aware that she had the potential to cause problems. He would need to assess the situation carefully before deciding now to deal with her. He sat in silence for a moment, making her squirm with self-consciousness, then asked who Mrs Cooper was.

'She's my friend, Pearl.'

'And how do you know this lady?'

'We're cleaners at the loco in... I should not name the place, of course!' She gave a nervous, apologetic laugh. 'We work at an engine shed, on the railway.' Her voice was weak and on the edge of breaking.

'*Cleaners*? In an *engine* shed? His voice was dripping with a mixture of contempt and surprise.

'Yes. To help with the war.'

He gave a snort that suggested the war was not a pressing matter in his life. 'And why have you come here?'

'Because... because I'm *in trouble*, doctor.' She suddenly started to cry. When said aloud, the enormity of her situation overwhelmed her, the appalling consequences of what it meant proved too much to stem the tears. She reached into her bag for her handkerchief and continued. 'Pearl knows someone who's a maid in a big house near Tingewick, and this maid told her that... well, that Lady Finmere had this same problem one time, and you... you were kind enough to help.' Her cheeks burned with embarrassment. Dr Melcombe, conversely, went pale at hearing the lady's name linked to his in relation to an illegal operation. He picked up an expensive fountain pen and started to roll it between his fingers in an attempt to conceal his agitation.

'It was just the once, honestly, doctor. Is it possible... you know, to fall... the first time you do it? Mary says you can't, but I don't know. He was my fiancé, you see, and he was just about to return to the Front. We were to be married. I loved him so much... and well, it just happened, and now, well I'm late... more than late, I have missed my monthly completely, and I think I am in trouble and I can't be, doctor, I simply *can't* be, this is a disaster, because, you see, he was killed. I can't bring a baby into the world without him, really I can't! My dad would go berserk, he'd throw me out, and...'

'Perhaps you should have thought of all that before you took your knickers off?' His reproachful words cut her like a knife and stemmed the relentless flow of words spilling out between sobs. 'And do stop snivelling! You deserve everything you get and you won't find any sympathy from me, and certainly not by crying. I can't abide all this self-pity and false remorse.'

She blew her nose and composed herself, placing her gloves on the doctor's desk as she did so, for fear of making them wet with her tears.

He waved a hand to encompass the evidently wealthy surroundings of his consulting room. 'I hardly need mention I don't give the time of day to just any common-or-garden shop girl or railway cleaner. My patients come from a quite different background to yourself.'

'I'm very grateful to you for seeing me, doctor, really I am.' She made a great effort to compose herself.

Melcombe had no intention of helping her. The girl, clearly, could not afford his exorbitant fee for that particular service, but more importantly he would not consider doing so unless she had been vetted very carefully by his partner, Barney Ringham. However, he was worried about her unannounced arrival and about her friend blabbing what they knew. Clearly there had been a serious breach in their usual tightly-run operation that would need dealing with, and urgently. He needed to show her the door, and whilst his inclination was to just bundle her back on to the street, he realised this needed handling carefully. He could not afford for this emotional woman to blow the whole shooting match apart. He decided he would emphatically deny having ever carried out any illegal procedure, either on Lady Finmere or on any other patient, and intimidate her into keeping her mouth firmly shut with threats of a legal action for slander.

'Do not mention that quite baseless rumour about Lady Finmere ever again. Is that understood?' His voice was hard and decisive, but even as he was speaking his eye was caught by the light striking the heart of a diamond ring she was wearing. It flashed and winked at him as she dabbed at her eyes, and he frowned momentarily, as if distracted. He reluctantly pulled his gaze away from the Cobra's Eye and leant forward, resting his forearms on the desk, still twiddling with the pen. 'I cannot imagine that you would wish your name bandied about with no thought for who might hear it.'

'No doctor. I'm sorry.' She blew her nose.

He gave a perfunctory nod then sighed wearily, before slapping the pen down and leaving it there. 'How far gone are you?' He thought she might have already told him, but he was feeling slightly less inclined to terminate the conversation immediately. He needed to better understand with whom he was dealing, but more than that he was trying not to stare at that little stone. But it just kept pulling at his attention. It surely could not be a diamond, but the way the light played off it was mesmerising. He'd never seen anything quite so good outside of the V & A. He wanted a closer look.

'About two months, maybe a bit less...'

The doctor nodded again. He knew he could not confirm or refute it that early, but he was not about to share that information with her. It was clear she was inexperienced and lacked any understanding of the situation, and he could exploit her naivety to his advantage.

'I must inform you that I charge for a consultation.'

'*Consultation?* Oh, I see what you mean.' Betty realised that a respectable doctor would, of course, have to speak in euphemisms. 'I have money!' She scrabbled with her large, cumbersome bag, hands shaking, finding her purse and opening it. She offered him two of her five-pound notes, hoping he would not demand the third.

Melcombe did not even look at the cash. He was instead becoming increasingly captivated by the ring, which sparkled enticingly as she moved her hand.

'Is that enough to cover it, doctor? I could send more next payday.' Her hands were shaking and setting the light quivering within the Cobra's Eye.

He was not interested in her meagre monetary offerings; he was staring at the diamond on her finger, trying to assess its true quality. Incredible though it seemed, this poor, working class railway girl owned something very desirable. He realised he wanted it, and he would have it.

'Go behind the screen please, Miss Askew.' He stood up and moved from behind the desk. 'Remove your undergarments and lift your dress to your waist, then lie on the couch. My nurse has the day off, so you're going to have to make do with just me. But then, that's the risk you've chosen to take.' He gave a cool smile that was anything but reassuring as he walked to the washbasin.

A few minutes later Betty was struggling to make a small readjustment to her stockings, face burning with shame, hands fumbling as she tried to get a shoe into place that was refusing to behave. Dr Melcombe sat on the edge of his desk, arms folded, looking down at her, watching with an eager, unblinking gaze that was rather disrespectful, as she hurriedly put herself in order. He was enjoying her discomfort, and there was a sinister light in his eyes behind the lenses of his spectacles.

'It would appear that you had good reason to be concerned.' He lied.

'No! Oh no, no...' Betty pressed her hands to her face and wept bitter tears, gulping deep, painful breaths of air. He watched her sobbing, her face streaked, eyes already starting to turn red and puffy, and felt nothing for her or her feelings, nor even for the young, lithe and healthy body he had so recently explored in the most intimate way, but he cared a lot about that diamond.

'My fees are way beyond the means of a railway cleaner', he said, coldly.

'I've another fiver here, and about another pound in change.' She looked at him optimistically, but the face that glared back at her displayed contempt. He remained silent. 'I—I could pay you weekly, I promise, every week I will send you ten shillings, or as much as I can spare.' Her words poured out in a desperate plea. 'And I'll do overtime, too: we get time-and-three-quarters on a Sunday, I'll tell the roster clerk to put me down for every Sunday till I've paid you—'

'—that is quite out of the question,' he interrupted, abruptly and adamantly. 'I do not offer my services on the never-never, like some tallyman. Payment must be made on the same day as the consultation.'

They both sat in silence for a few seconds while she dabbed at her damp eyes with her lace-edged handkerchief, giving him another clear view of the diamond.

'That really is a very pretty ring you have', his voice now softer, almost gentle.

She looked at her third finger, caught by the intense shaft of sunlight that made the Cobra's Eye burn especially bright, its strange, yellow heart displayed to perfection. A sudden, strong flood of emotion welled up: the memories of kissing Ray and lying on the blanket on the grass assaulting her so vividly she could almost smell the grass and his aftershave and hear the drone of a bee on a clover flower. Her chest heaved as she tried to hold back a sob.

'It really is astoundingly good, for paste. I really had no idea they'd got so good at it.' The doctor leaned closer towards her, a dark presence looming over, his voice quiet and almost breathless.

'But it's real.'

'Impossible! A stone like that would cost a small fortune.' His face was one of intense interest, almost of excitement.

'My fiancé got it in Egypt. It even comes in its own special box, I have it here in my bag.'

'Egypt? Interesting… Let me take a closer look, if you don't mind. I know something about gemstones.' He peered at the ring for a few moments, turning her fingers one way then another, his hands moist and soft and yet his grip steely. 'Slip it off please.'

Betty winced as she did so and, with a shaking hand, passed the Cobra's Eye across. She was not sure where this was leading, but she could see that she now had his attention and the longer this continued then surely her chances of enlisting his help would increase. He rootled in a small pocket on his waistcoat and pulled out a magnifying loupe that slotted over one side of his spectacles. From her seated position Betty Askew looked up into his eye, now massively magnified, staring, unblinking and flicking from side to side like something from an American science-fiction magazine. An eerie, stifling silence fell, punctuated only by two soft grunts of approval, his breathing becoming noticeably quicker. After what felt like an age, he pulled his face away from the ring, flipped the loupe upwards on a hinge and stood up, pacing to the side of the desk. 'Yes… yes this is really quite a nice little stone. Perhaps not quite as valuable as I had hoped,' he lied again, 'but it should suffice.'

She was emotionally overwhelmed. The shock of the diagnosis, the fear of the looming 'consultation', her feelings of shame and guilt, and now knowing that she was going to lose Ray's ring in order to extricate herself from the mess she had got herself into with another man caused tears to flood into her eyes. She started to weep again.

'In that case, take it!' she blurted, her face a picture of misery. She knew in her heart of hearts that this was her punishment for going with that American airman.

He nodded and looked away. He seemed uninterested, just gently moving his fist almost as though weighing what was enclosed within it.

'So...do...do I get ready now?' She flushed red, quite terrified of the horror that she was about to undergo, doubly scared because she was utterly ignorant of what the sickening procedure would consist of, how he was going to do it, and with what drug or... apparatus. She felt cold and clammy and shivered all over, wracked with fear and foreboding, her red eyes now dry and staring as the horrible reality of her situation hit home. The time had come for her to face her worst nightmare.

'Get ready for what?' Melcombe's voice was light and carefree.

'The—er, the *consultation*,' she said, in a low, conspiratorial voice.

'But you've just had it, Miss Askew. He frowned.

'I—I don't understand, doctor. You were going to help me.'

'Oh, but I have. I have performed a very thorough physical examination and given you my expert opinion that you are most definitely with child. And now it is time for you to leave, so let me see you out.' He stood and began to usher her towards the door. 'What more could you possibly expect me to do?' His voice was almost mocking and heavy with meaning.

She fell into a stunned silence for a few moments as the terrible shock hit home, her face as white as paper. 'How can you be so cruel?' Her eyes flashed. 'Give me my ring back!'

'It is to cover my consultation fee. You understood that.' He smiled smarmily and opened the door, beckoning her to go through.

Betty Askew was shocked to the core. It was as though someone had thrown a bucket of cold water over her head. He was treating her with contempt and ridiculing her. She could feel her skin crawling with the terrible realisation that he had taken her ring under false pretences.

'But doctor, the ring was to get rid... To get rid of the problem! Like you did with Lady—'

'—how *dare* you!' he interrupted, indignant with fury, his face breaking into a flush of corpuscles that coloured his cheeks like tiny pink lines marking roads on a map. 'You have the dashed cheek to come here and make this kind of appalling insinuation. This is an absolute outrage! I am a respectable family physician, I'll have you know, with the best names in this town on my books. I will not have my name besmirched by ill-formed, malicious, railway-shed gossip!' He narrowed his eyes, his voice now low and surprisingly menacing, 'I should warn you that your suggestion that I might be prepared to undertake an illegal operation, or that the lady you named has had such an operation, constitutes criminal slander. I shall not hesitate to press charges, and I have excellent legal representation who can wipe the floor with you.' His free hand, still balled into a fist around the ring was shaking, the knuckles white and bony lumps. 'And I am sure the same goes for the distinguished lady whose name you had the goddamned temerity to speak out loud. Now I suggest that you get out of my house, and don't ever come back.' He almost hissed the last words, like a snake.

The lenses of his spectacles reflected the pale light flooding the floor, transforming them into two pale moons, his mouth a thin-lipped leer below.

'You tricked me! You lied!'

'Tricked you?' He laughed in a harsh explosion of sound that held no mirth. 'Come now, I do not recall making any promise that I have broken.' His voice was now slow, as though talking to a particularly dim-witted child. 'Perhaps in your fractious and hysterical state of mind you have misunderstood me.'

Betty felt her face burn with indignation and a boiling anger, the like of which she had never felt before. Dredging up some words she'd picked up in the loco shed she almost spat at him. 'You bastard! You horrible, lying, cheating, bloody bastard!' The words sounded particularly ugly and vicious coming from her pretty mouth, and the doctor was visibly shocked.

Then she flew at him like a scalded cat.

CHAPTER THIRTY-TWO
Woodford Halse
27ᵗʰ September 1950

Whilst Vignoles and Trinder were travelling to Amersham to investigate the discovery in the garden, PC467 Simon Howerth (much to his delight) was sent back down the line to Woodford to rendezvous with WPC Jane Benson, who had spent the morning tracking down the whereabouts of Betty Askew's work colleagues and friends.

The Dirty Girls Brigade had over the intervening years ceased to be engine cleaners, but most of the women had stayed in touch and none had moved far. Conveniently, two were still employed on the railway within the noxious surroundings of the loco.

Mary Bennett had made the grade as a fitter, the last of her sex left in what was now once again becoming an exclusively masculine world, owing to the mass dismissals of women in the years after war ended. Susan Gibson was sewing tarpaulin covers for open wagons in the adjacent wagon shop, having been replaced as a riveter's mate by a surly ex-marine just back from the Far East. It was cooler work, and Susan no longer suffered the stress of being on the receiving end of a heavy hammer pounded against the red-hot rivets she held in place with massive tongs, but the canvases were still extremely heavy and she remained sinewy and strong, with biceps bulging below the rolled-up sleeves of her shirt, her nails cropped short and dirty, her hands calloused and lined by the continual handling of the coarse material.

Mary and Susan were now seated on a rickety bench along the outside wall of the running shed. WPC Benson was offered the relative comfort of a beaten-up wooden chair, and the young constable was forced to risk his uniform on an upturned oil barrel covered with a piece of sacking to prevent the worst of it staining his trousers. There was soft grey and white ash all over the ground mingled with fragments of coal and clinker; in places this was congealed into sludge or formed opaque pools of spilt oil and water. The air was heavy with coal smoke and a light breeze was whipping little scurries of dust across this dead landscape, lifting the soft ash from the edge of the inspection pit that lay like an open grave beneath the wheels of a big Thompson 01 eight-wheeled freight locomotive. From the other side of the blackened brick shed wall, a hammer rang out in a sonorous rhythm as one of Mary Bennett's fellow fitters beat seven bells out of something. The hammer bouncing in two lighter strokes after the initial impact, *Dong, ding ding... Dong, ding ding...*

'Of course we remember her disappearing. It was awful. We couldn't understand it. Still can't, really.'

'That's right, Mary. It was so out of character. I suppose something dreadful must have happened, not that you want to think like that, but you have to be realistic. Have you any news?' Susan gave Benson an anxious look. 'There has to be a reason for stirring things up after so long.'

'We can't say much at this stage, but there have been developments. I just want you to ask you about the days before she vanished. How Miss Askew seemed to you? Who was the last person to see her?'

Dong, ding ding...

'Last to see her? Now, that would be Pearl. God rest her soul.'

'Was she was part of the group working here as cleaners?' asked Benson, quickly looking at the list of names she had made in her notebook. Dong, ding ding... Dong, ding ding... The relentless hammering continued.

'That's right. Pearl Cooper. Life and soul of the party, she was! She always got us working and laughing together, you know, to help make the working day pass that bit quicker. She could gee us up no matter what.' Mary paused, breaking into a fit of coughing, interspersed with attempting to inhale cigarette smoke. 'She's dead now, of course.' The hammering stopped with accidentally dramatic timing.

'Dead?' Benson instinctively touched her round-lensed glasses back into place as she looked up from her notes.

'That's one of the other weird things about it.' Susan took up the story as Mary finished coughing. 'Betty goes missing and the very night before, Pearl was out on the town in Banbury and got hit by a lorry. Run over on the street due to the blackout. Driver couldn't see her.'

'Pearl was the last of us to spend time with Betty,' continued Mary. 'They went off together straight after work for a drink in the White Hart.'

'Was that unusual?' Benson asked, hurriedly trying to readjust to this unexpected discovery.

'Well, it's thirsty work in this place, you see. Though mid week it was usually just a cuppa in one of the cafés, as we've all got to get back and get the supper on the table, then get the laundry ironed and all the mending done. We can't sit around drinking all nights, worst luck! Betty and Pearl were perhaps not the most likely pairing, but that evening, they had a drink, just the two of them.'

'I don't think we clocked Betty was missing until about lunchtime, as it was only then it hit us she was absent. We were so cut up about Pearl being killed.' Susan added.

'Well, I knew Betty had been with her that evening and thought perhaps she was at the hospital, or consoling Mickey — that's Pearl's old man. I was thinking maybe she had been with Pearl in Banbury.' Mary placed a booted foot on a locomotive brake block and rested her elbow on her crooked knee. 'I've often wondered about that. You know, how the one died and the other vanished at almost the same time. Strange.'

'We believe Betty Askew left Brackley on the morning of 19th April 1943. That might be some time after Pearl Cooper died, however. Do you know of a connection between these events?' Benson asked.

'No. No connection I ever heard of.' Susan shook her head and looked at Mary, who agreed.

'Pearl's death was fully investigated, I assume?' Simon Howerth chipped in a question.

Susan leant back against the grubby brick wall of the shed and gave Howerth a weary look. 'Oh yes. From what I understood, the man driving the truck was very shaken up about what happened. Claimed he never saw her until too late. No one doubted his word.'

'It happened all too frequently, I am sorry to say. The blackout was a menace.' WPC Benson remembered it well. She glanced across at Simon, who nodded enthusiastically and made a note. 'So, the last person to speak with Betty, outside of her home, was killed later that night. That is frustrating. Do you have any idea what Betty and Pearl could have been talking about? Any clue at all?' Benson knew she was sounding almost desperate.

Mary Bennett drew thoughtfully upon her cigarette, the butt of which was now stained pink with her lipstick, and gave Susan Gibson a sidelong glance, as if seeking approval. 'Look, we don't know for sure, and stirring stuff up is not nice. Especially after so long and about someone who's no longer with us, but we've often wondered if Pearl was offering Betty some advice. On the quiet, like.'

'What sort of advice?' Benson was curious.

'Let's say that Pearl was quite a character. Lived her life to the full, and then some!' Mary laughed and then coughed with the effort. 'Let's just say that she enjoyed the company of men, and not exclusively of Mickey.'

'Can't say I had much time for him, either. No matter. So she'd... Lord forgive me saying this, she'd been round the block a few times, then?'

Simon was grinning. Benson, however looked serious.

'I heard Pearl had got herself in the family way. It was a while back now, before the war started. But no thanks to hubby, Haha! So of course she had to get rid.' Mary gave Benson a wink. 'On the sly, and we've all heard how bad than can be. Go and see some old biddy living in the back of beyond, and God knows what she'll do to you, ugh!'

The young constable flushed red with embarrassment.

Susan Gibson, seeing his crimson cheeks could not resist teasing him: 'Remember that, young man, when you've got your sweetheart's drawers off!' The two railwaywomen laughed raucously, enjoying the look of acute discomfort on his face.

When their mirth and fits of inevitable coughing died down, Mary continued. 'The point being, she had experience and was willing to share it and help others. And she was not averse to passing on a few tips about keeping their men happy in bed as well.'

'Especially after she'd had a few glasses of port, Lord bless her!'

'And you think Betty might have spoken with Pearl about something like this?' Benson suggested.

'No. Betty was young and inexperienced. I'm sure she and her Ray never did it.' Susan gave Simon a cheeky look. 'Keeping herself for the wedding night and all that. A very traditional sort of girl. But she was starting to get into the swing of things a bit more when the Yanks came over. She was seeing one of them. Well, let's be honest — and don't write this down — we all had our little moments.' Susan gave Benson a challenging look. 'Don't look at me like that, there was a war on...'

'We're not here to judge, just to establish facts.'

'Were you there when she met this American? We've heard

that the Dirty Girls Brigade went to some dances in Brackley.' Simon decided it was time he tried to act the role of constable and regain some composure as he formed the question.

'We were. We had such a time of it, didn't we Sue? Betty was with Tony, I think?'

'Tony Mancini. I'm good with names. I wondered at the time if he had anything to do with her disappearing.'

'And did he?' asked Simon.

'Well you tell us, young man. You're supposed to be the detectives! Find out for yourself.' He squirmed. 'Listen, my old man did a bit of asking around as it happens, and the poor blighter bought it on his second run over Germany. Raid on Hamburg. Dead and gone before Betty vanished.'

'Not much more than a kid. Loud and full of himself like all of them — but he danced well. Treated her all right, too, I reckon; gave her lots of presents, but then they all did.'

'Not all he gave her! Haha!' Mary flipped her cigarette butt away to land on a pool of water, where it smouldered for a moment. 'Be honest, we were happy to enter into a bit of give and take for a few pairs of nylons, some fags and a good night out!'

'Speak for yerself!' Susan laughed. 'Anyway, they went to the park together. I know that, as I was there as well,' Susan put a hand to her mouth. 'Look, you won't go telling everyone all this? Folks don't need to know, you know. Not now. It's long past, ancient history. Most of us have got our lives back to something like normal and settled down again. But we liked a man in uniform and our lads were away for years. Men like a girl in uniform too, for that matter,' Susan gave Benson a knowing look, glancing across at the PC on the oil drum. 'As I'm sure you've noticed!'

Simon could not resist giving Benson a surreptitious admiring glance, silently agreeing that his colleague suited the black uniform with its silver buttons surprisingly well. It was austere and rugged and yet, through some careful tailoring, offered a tantalising hint of what delights lay beneath. Benson was a good six years older than he, but that did not stop him thinking what a fine figure she might look in an evening gown, although he was not so convinced about the practical, National Health Service glasses and the heavy, police-issue shoes she had to wear to work. Perhaps aware of becoming the unwanted focus of attention, Benson fired off another question. 'And Betty, what was she like?'

'She was a sweet thing. Kindly and genuine. She was so cut up over losing her Raymond. Went into a right glump for a month or two. But we snapped her out of it and took her out. I just think she might have got herself a bit carried away and not taken enough care in the heat of the moment. It's just a hunch, but Pearl knew people who could sort things out. Maybe she knew where Betty could go? You know? I'm only saying, mind. We're as stumped as anyone.'

On the short journey south to Amersham, Vignoles brought Trinder up to date about the discovery of the woman's head and the bones of a hand, then questioned his sergeant about his morning's work. Vignoles was satisfied with the progress being made.

'Miss Geddes's account is interesting. She appears to confirm what the girl's parents said, that Betty met a man, and then a month or so afterwards she goes missing.'

'And planned to head south, probably towards London, deliberately duping her parents and her friends about her real intentions.' DS Trinder looked pleased with himself, as he studied the notes PC Howerth had made of their interview with the ticket clerk. 'Looks like she was planning to run away then?'

'Planning on something she wanted to keep quiet.' Vignoles was settled in the corner seat of the compartment, one leg crossed over the over, his pipe in full steam. 'We don't know much about this young woman and I think we need to spend more time trying to understand her. But even with the little we do know, I'm not getting the feeling she's the kind of gal who would do a bunk. Surely she would confide in at least one pal about such a momentous decision?'

'True. But she was going for a clandestine meeting of some description.'

'Yes, John, you're right. It was a rendezvous, and a pre-planned one, because she took a few overnight things and her engagement ring, complete with its little box, if we believe her parents on that point.'

'And do we?' Trinder asked.

'On balance, I think so. At least in as much as I feel certain they had nothing to do with her disappearance, though I sense there is still something left unsaid, something lurking in that house they don't want to admit. I would like to speak to Mrs Askew without her husband present. I think she knows more than she was willing to say in front of him.'

'She's covering for her husband?'

'Hmm…? I think not. At least as far as the murder of Irons goes, Mr Askew is no more than a very long odds bet for the killer. But what about the cabbie? Any joy there?'

Trinder flipped through his notebook. 'Not a lot, I'm afraid. Hancock is a cocky bugger who has an opinion on everyone and everything, and at first I thought we'd really struck the jackpot, but after a while I realised at least half of what he was saying is just hearsay mixed up with arrogant bluster. Teasing out the facts from his fiction won't be easy.'

'Ok, hit me with some facts you think might hold up.'

'His assertion that Miss Askew is dead is not based — and I'm convinced of this — on his knowing one way or another. It's common belief around town that she's probably met with a sad end, and he's taken this as a fact and spread it. He's a chum of Henry Askew. Claims he drove the poor man around in his cab for weeks searching for her. Used all the petrol coupons they could beg, steal or borrow and scoured every village and town asking after her. I think this part rings true.'

'That explains why he reacted badly to Irons's claim that he'd met her.'

'That's the feeling I got, sir. It would explain his outburst. Both Dennis Hancock and Henry Askew are long resigned to the fact she's never coming back, and I feel he almost takes it as an affront to suggest she's riding our railway line and not lying in a shallow grave somewhere, despite the fact he actually wishes passionately she were alive.'

'This gruesome discovery in Amersham just might prove his suspicions correct. Does Hancock have an alibi for the night Irons was killed?'

'He does. I've got 467 checking it out, but it would appear strong; a fare to collect in Banbury — Brigadier Manton, who is a regular, wanted collecting from a dinner engagement. Hancock left Brackley Central at about eleven twenty to drive to Banbury, but on the way back had a blow out in Farthinghoe. Took him a while to change the wheel then it was over to Sulgrave to drop the brigadier off. Then he went straight home to his wife.'

Vignoles nodded assent 'I can't see him doing all that and still having time to bump off Irons or even to collect Henry Askew so that he might do so. Does the cabbie own a dog?'

'He says his wife has a little Yorkie. I could send 467 to check the doggie out, just in case.'

They both smiled. 'We can forget the cabbie as the killer unless something goes badly wrong with his alibi,' Vignoles concluded.

Their train was slowing and came to halt. The window next to Vignoles was filled by the maroon shape of a humming electric locomotive named *Sarah Siddons*. It made odd little clicking sounds, as if Miss Siddons was clucking her tongue in annoyance at something. The presence of this electrical box of tricks confirmed they were in Amersham, the farthest outreach of the electric Metropolitan line that had given these leafy and distant outreaches of London's suburbia the nickname 'Metroland'.

'Look here, this is an outrageous intrusion into our lives, that's what it is!' Jocelyn Liney's temper had not improved. 'Another bunch of detectives. Why the hell do we need any more of you, for God's sake?' He squinted at Vignoles, face pale and florid in turns. 'And I have as little to do with British-bloody-Railways as I can; sitting in a over-stuffed train to and from work is my limit, so I really don't see why you of all people are here — trampling your clumping great feet over our carpets.'

Vignoles remained impassive during this outburst, but observed the expensive carpet in question and the other accoutrements of a conspicuously wealthy lifestyle, the air smelling of elegantly-arranged cut flowers in extravagant vases that could be Lalique, and of the *Ronuk* furniture polish used recently and liberally, probably by the maid who had answered the door. It was a house that smelt of money. Anna and he were unlikely ever to afford even a sofa like the one he was standing beside, let alone the room it sat within. But there again, they didn't have a dismembered head buried in the garden and a dining table laid out with the charred fragments of a dead woman's life.

'Have you heard of Elizabeth Askew? Betty, to her friends.'

'Never. No idea who she is.'

'Can I ask you and your wife to look at this photograph? Do you recognise her?'

Liney shook his head decisively, 'Sorry, you're asking the wrong man. Never set eyes on her. Here...' He handed the print to his wife, who was sitting very stiffly on an upright chair beside the fireplace and staring morosely at the floor. 'Ever seen this funny-looking specimen?'

'No. I have not.' Mrs Liney gave the photograph a look that suggested it was dirty and soiled. She refused to touch it. 'This... this murder, clearly happened before we moved in. It has nothing to do with us.'

Vignoles made a movement with his mouth that implied he might agree. 'Mr Liney, you discovered some items of clothing when you were working in the garden. What were they?'

'Just rubbish. Burnt bits of fabric.'

'A piece of a dress was mentioned in your statement,' Trinder spoke up.

Liney shrugged. 'I suppose so. It was just a bit of green fabric. Was it a dress?'

'It was, you could see the neckline. And an orange bracelet. And a piece of leather strap and a buckle.' Mrs Liney's voice was flat and lifeless. 'I recall I was irritated that they had destroyed a leather bag.'

'They?' Trinder asked.

'They, he, she...I have no idea. Just a turn of phrase.' Mrs Liney looked flustered.

'You burnt these items and threw the metal parts away? Why did you do that?' Trinder continued.

'It was junk! I didn't know they were important, why on earth should I? Do you preserve every little thing you find on the ground in case it might be evidence of a crime you know nothing about?'

Vignoles nodded slightly, it was not an unreasonable observation. 'When the, er, the head was discovered, you were initially reluctant to call the police?'

'I was? I don't remember. I was in shock, I suppose. My wife had just fainted and was in some distress. I can't say I was feeling exactly chipper myself!' Liney mopped his brow with a handkerchief.

'For heaven's sake, I was hardly thinking straight. What are you supposed to think when you see something like that?'

'The bird bath was in that location when you bought the house from Dr Melcombe?' asked Trinder.

'Yes. We'd not touched that border since we moved in.'

'And what can you tell us about the doctor? Did you meet him?'

'Can't tell you much. We were taken around the house by the estate agent. The owner was not at home. My solicitor made the arrangements. I met the doctor once, a little later the same month, and then only briefly. He seemed rather old for his years. That's probably why he sold up and retired to the country. Failing health or something. He was well spoken and polite. Can't you find him, question him?'

'Did the neighbours have anything to say about the doctor?'

Mrs Liney answered. 'We do like to talk, and one gets a sense of how people are perceived, but they didn't say very much. That he lived alone and never married Of course, one *speculates*, but nobody knew his private affairs. They seemed to quite like him, despite his being a loner, and all expressed sadness that he retired and left so suddenly. Sold up in a matter of months. It was completely unexpected, apparently.'

'Did any of your neighbours mention the doctor having a young lady friend?' Trinder asked.

'No, they did not.' Mrs Liney smoothed her skirt and fiddled with her cardigan.

'You moved during the war,' Vignoles asked Mr. Liney. 'From where? And why?'

'Life did carry on for most of us, you know? The war was a blasted nuisance, but one could still function pretty normally. The house was on the market for a good price and I'd just secured a promotion.' His voice converted his sense of wounded outrage into something approaching smugness. 'So we took the opportunity to take on a place more to our liking. We'd been roughing it in a smaller villa on the edge of town until then.'

'You were not in the services, I understand.' Trinder's look was impassive, but the implied criticism hung in the air.

'Peace or war, someone has to look after the money, sergeant. Wars are expensive and without the likes of us working our guts out balancing the books, I'd like to know who'd pay for it.' Liney parried the observation robustly.

'Some might question if you succeeded. Life is stretched pretty thin even now, for most of us.' Trinder gave a little smile.

'The devaluation of sterling was a measure forced upon us by circumstances quite outside of our control. If the United States had not reneged on the Lend Lease Agreement, then...'

'Thank you. Most helpful.' Vignoles called the sparring to a halt. 'We shall be in touch if we need any further assistance.' He gave a perfunctory smile that made it clear he expected the couple to leave the room so he and Trinder could inspect the items carefully laid out in readiness of their visit. A uniformed constable held the door open for the Lineys, another stood guard beside the table.

The items had been recovered by the Buckinghamshire Constabulary, who had done an excellent job of ripping out almost every shrub and flower from the extensive borders in the once-lovely garden, turning it from an elegant oasis of calm filled with colour and loud with insects, into something more akin to the Western Front after a preliminary mortar attack.

'A piece of a ration book. All that's left is the end of an address. Could this *"ley"* be "Brackley"?' Trinder queried.

Vignoles peered at the scorched paper. 'And this could be a fragment of blue overall. Miss Askew wore overalls like these.'

'Yes. Pretty standard kit on the railway. Liney stated that they'd found a bit of green frock as well, and we know she wore green the day she left.' Trinder picked up a smoke-tarnished cap badge and considered it for a moment. 'Was her fiancé a desert rat?'

'Private Coulson?' Vignoles looked across at Trinder held it up. 'That's the 7th Armoured Division insignia, and he was killed in El Alamein. A keepsake? Do you know, the PX stores must have despaired at how many of these were given away by men to their girls. And they all needed replacing pronto, before the next parade.'

'It stacks up. Surely these must be Miss Askew's things. Are we working on the assumption that the, er, the head, is hers?'

'It is looking that way.' Vignoles sighed wearily. It was not unexpected, but it still felt like he'd been sandbagged. There was a lot of forensic work to be done before they could say for certain, but already Vignoles was anticipating having to break the news to Henry and Maud. 'So she had this little badge and the engagement ring with her. Fond memories of her lover, the man she intended to marry. Her new American friend however does not register, at least not from amongst what fragments we have to work with here.'

'Her engagement ring hasn't turned up here, though,' Trinder remarked, with disappointment.

'Tell me, Sergeant Trinder, why in your opinion would a young woman secretly leave home with an overnight bag and things that reminded her of her long lost lover, and visit a doctor miles away?'

Trinder flipped a blackened penny into the air as if about to call heads or tails. He slapped the spinning coin onto his forearm and removed his hand to reveal the head of Queen Victoria.

Either she is looking for employment, or... she is in trouble. My money's on the latter. She couldn't tell her mum and dad. No chance. They had enough trouble admitting she even had a dance and a cuddle with the airman, so I can't see them taking the idea of her being in the family way too well.'

Vignoles nodded. 'Mr A seemed the type to go berserk.'

Trinder turned the penny in his hands, a look of deep concentration on his face. 'So, she had to keep it secret. She applied for a job miles away, to work for this doctor. She'd work there till the baby came, have it in secret, give it up for adoption and go home.' Trinder put the old penny down and rubbed his hands together, 'Brr! But is dashed cold in here!'

'There is another possibility, of course,' Vignoles suggested, quietly. He moved away from the table and looked around the elegant drawing room with the tall French windows opening onto the wrecked garden. 'This is a very fine house. It must be worth, what, a good nine hundred pounds? Perhaps a thousand. I've been wondering how a GP became so wealthy, even working in a town like Amersham. It seems surprising.'

'He had an expensive hobby too. Those two coins Irons had in his pocket were worth nearly twenty-five pounds apiece! Leads me to suspect he had been earning extra, on the side. All strictly hush-hush.'

'You think he was helping unmarried girls to get rid of their, er, little problems, guv?'

'It's possible. A lucrative sideline, under the cover of his respectability as a doctor. But two questions immediately spring to mind. How did a Woodford railwaywoman come to hear about this — er — "service"? And more importantly, was her visit here connected with her disappearance?' Vignoles walked through the open French windows into the garden. 'You're not wrong, it has to be warmer outside than in here.' He glanced around to make sure they were not being overheard, then turned about, hands plunged in his pockets, and looked directly at his sergeant. 'Perhaps the operation went wrong.'

'And he dismembers her to hide what he's done', reasoned Trinder. 'If the hands found near Brackley Viaduct really are hers, he spread her far and wide.'

'Doing that reduces the chance of discovery. Although it would appear that his attempts at concealment have failed.' Vignoles took another look at the room. 'Something very bad happened in this house. I've seen enough for now, let's get out of here.'

'Gladly. The place gives me the heebie-jeebies'

'We need to speak to Dr Melcombe. Urgently!'

CHAPTER THIRTY-FOUR
Amersham
19th April 1943

Her furious assault caught him off guard. Betty Askew took the few steps to where he stood, with his arm still holding the door handle, in a matter of seconds, her cumbersome bag swinging forwards with the weight of her heavy work boots inside, adding to her momentum. She grabbed onto his free arm, her fingers scrabbling and tearing at his fist to try and reach the ring concealed inside, her nails biting into the taut flesh on the back of his hand making the old man wince, whilst her other hand pulled on his forearm with a strength borne of long hours working in the tough environment of the loco.

'Get off me! Let go, you vixen!' Melcombe did not know how to react. He had never grappled with a woman in his life, and was unsure how best to fend her off, pressed so close as she was to him, her face a mask of undiluted fury. In the first moments of her attack she had gained the advantage, managing to pull his arm between them as she attempted to prise his fingers open. Her nails started to draw blood where they tore at the pale taut skin dotted with liver spots.

Melcombe was not going to give in easily. He brought his free arm around and pushed at her shoulder, hoping to force her away. They were about equally matched now, and locked together in a strange and painful embrace, each straining against the other. His breath was blowing on her face as she tried to pull back one of his fingers. Their faces contorted with the pain and exertion, neither speaking, the room filled with just the sound of their breathing as they strained against one another, their scuffling feet setting motes of dust dancing in the shaft of sunlight penetrating the room. Then the doctor had an idea how to break the deadlock. He suddenly withdrew his hand from her shoulder and this unexpected movement put her slightly off balance; at that same moment he jerked his other arm sharply upwards, lifting his scratched and bleeding fist high into the air and using his other arm to smash upwards and help release her grip.

Betty Askew fought to remain upright, but the shock of this decisive move sent her reeling backwards and to one side, her awkward bag dragging her around in an uncontrolled lurch, just at the same moment as one of her feet caught on one of the doctor's legs.

Freed from gripping the doctor's arm, she was sent flying backwards. The back of her head stuck the edge of the open door square on and at just such an angle that it gave not an inch to either side, but shuddered on it hinges. Her face registered shock for but a split second and then she fell like a rag doll. It was only a few feet to the floor, nothing more. On any other occasion she would have been unceremoniously dumped to the ground to be left looking indignant and embarrassed (and no doubt cursing him with more words learnt from the enginemen at the loco) and nursing a nasty lump forming on her head. But the shock of the impact rendered her unable to make any recovering move, and so the back of her skull smacked hard straight down onto a brass doorstop in the shape of a long-eared owl, with an ugly, sickening crack that instantly turned Melcombe's guts to jelly.

She lay immobile, her eyelids closed but fluttering slightly. Her legs were almost straight and one of her arms now lay across her brow as though she had slipped into a restful sleep. Her chest rose and fell once, twice, three times and then, from between her slightly-parted lips, there was a long, slow sigh and she became completely still. A little pool of bright-red blood oozed from below her tangled hair, matching a trickle running from the point of a brass ear. A grandfather clock counted the passing seconds that Betty Askew would never experience as a living being.

He tried smelling salts; he pounded her chest rhythmically with both hands; he blew air into her lungs for long, endless minutes at a time. When this failed, in an act of appalling desperation he even slapped her face whilst simultaneously praying and cursing in equal doses until finally beating his fists on the floor with impotent desperation. It was all to no avail, and no matter what techniques he tried, whether expert or simply driven by the waves of intense anger and sickening fear that enveloped him like a blanket of ice, he could not revive her. Betty Askew was dead.

CHAPTER THIRTY-FIVE
London Marylebone
19th April 1943

Dr Melcombe mopped his brow with a handkerchief before removing his spectacles to give them a wipe, an act he immediately regretted as the now-dampened cloth served only to smear the lenses with a fine coat of perspiration. He was agitated, his heart pounded uncomfortably and he was sweating profusely, partially due to anxiety and partially because it was a hot day. He should have worn a lighter suit, but he'd deliberately chosen the Harris tweed with the intention of appearing staid, respectable and forgettable. Nobody was likely to remember an elderly man in a dark suit and hat who resembled countless others coming and going about the station, although he feared his now-florid complexion and shining brow might attract the unwelcome attention of some meddling busybody with a medical kit slung across his shoulders in a haversack. He had better pull himself together.

Marylebone station was busy. Each platform was occupied by a hissing locomotive at the buffer stops, heading trains of filthy coaches. Those closest to him were varying shades of soiled teak and looking as though they were assembled not from one of the most beautiful of woods, but from planks of burnt and charred timber rescued from bombsites. The train shed overhead was acrid with lazily-billowing smoke and alive with jets of fiercely-escaping steam illuminated by strong diagonals of light scything down from the unglazed bars, the glass long since removed for safety in the summer of '39.

Everywhere was noise and activity, with platoons of men in the uniforms of the armed services standing, sitting, talking or shouting and moving mountains of heavy packs and equipment from one place to another, in what appeared to the doctor's inexpert eye to be nothing but a hopeless bustle and only adding to the confusion all about. Orders were barked, doors slammed, whistles blown, porteresses trundled trolleys heavily laden with mail sacks, whilst young, insolent boys dressed in threadbare clothes with dirty knees and faces hustled to carry luggage 'for a sixpence', keeping step beside overburdened passengers and wheedling away at their resolve with a cupped palm.

If this relentless noise was not enough for Dr Melcombe's fraying nerves, everywhere he looked he was assaulted by enormous posters demanding his attention and exhorting him to do, or not do something for the war effort.

DON'T LEAVE IT TO OTHERS!
Register for Civil Defence Duties!

DON'T ask for bread unless you NEED it!

Keep your children in the country!

It was relentless, and he closed his eyes for a moment to shut out this assault on mind and conscience. Conscience? What was one of those? He took a deep lungful of dirty London air and his face contorted, not with physical pain but mental anguish. Did he have any shred of human decency left in his body?

Know how to behave in an Air Raid Shelter...

The strident demands were ubiquitous; the giant black letters banging at his forehead, drilling into his brain.

He opened his eyes and stared at a four-wheeled trolley being hauled along the platform by a pretty woman porter. His attention, unlike that of a gang of soldiers close by, was not drawn to her shapely legs and calves defined by honed muscles, nor by the tunic pulled taut across enticingly-curved breasts as she leant into the effort, but was transfixed by the bulk of his old wooden trunk sitting full square on the trolley deck surrounded by a host of smaller parcels and what was clearly a garden spade wrapped in brown paper. The things people sent by train never ceased to amaze him. He snorted, finding something laughably macabre in the realisation that he was now surely topping the list of the unexpected — and the abhorrent. A clammy trickle of sweat ran down his spine and he looked away whilst shaking his head, as if that action alone would free his mind of the appalling truth.

If that young porteress only knew... But enough of this maudlin introspection, it was time for action. He could not stand around feeling sorry for himself.

Less Light — Less speed: Look out in the Blackout!

He needed to look out, all right. He had a job to do, and the quicker he completed it, the sooner he could try to push aside this nightmare and seek to eradicate all memory of this terrible day. Many a night alone with a bottle of scotch and some self-prescribed sleeping pills might do the trick, but right now he needed to remain calm and unhurried. Less speed...

As the porteress drew close he fell into walking alongside her, leaning heavily upon a walking stick and adopting a limp. He only used this stick on nature rambles, but felt in need of a prop, both physical and mental. It was also a useful identifier, people would notice the stick and limp if they noticed him at all, and he would ditch this as soon as the job was done, and walk upright, thus altering his appearance instantly.

He requested she wheel his trunk to the portico outside the station, and as they picked their way down the crowded platform they exchanged small talk about the fine weather the capital was enjoying. Belying her slightly-built appearance, she enthusiastically joined him in lifting the heavy wooden trunk off the trolley, swinging her end of the trunk with enviable ease, whilst he fumbled and almost dropped his end to the ground, his palms greasy and arms suddenly going weak. By the time they had finished, he was panting and looked even more hot and bothered.

'Are you all right, sir? Can I get you a glass of water?'

'No, no, don't bother, my dear. I'm fine.' He flapped a limp hand towards her. 'Just a little hot.'

'If you're quite sure. Can I be of any further assistance?'

'Thank you, but no,' Melcombe insisted, pressing a coin into her hand then waving her away impatiently. He could ill afford her to remember him too clearly.

He sat on the trunk to regain his breath, leaning on his stick and eyeing the many people standing in groups and loose queues, all waiting for the taxis constantly pulling to a halt in a space reserved between a row of coaches and some chunky army trucks that relentlessly poured acrid exhaust fumes into the hot, still air. Despite the headache-inducing pollution, he received a slight lift in his spirits as he realised that the next stage of his plan might prove easier to finesse than he'd feared. He felt inside his jacket pocket to reassure himself that the envelope he placed there before leaving home was safe, whilst looking around for someone suitable to approach.

Three Negro solders were smoking and talking nearby. All were tall and smartly uniformed, their conversation muted, their laughter noticeably lacking the harshly raucous edge that every so often exploded from the far larger groups of white servicemen keeping some distance from them, as though there was an invisible line chalked on the pavement that neither group might cross.

Dr Melcombe had never seen a black man before because they were a rare sight, even in London. It was highly unlikely Amersham had ever witnessed a man with dark skin. To be honest, he would probably have steered clear as he preferred to avoid mixing with foreign types whatever their skin colour, but right now he had need of assistance and they could prove to be a satisfactory choice. He needed someone who would be far away before too many weeks had elapsed. Preferably someone who may never return to London, and black American solders fitted the bill perfectly.

He stood up and approached the dark men. 'Excuse me intruding like this, but I was wondering if one or more of you strong fellows could help an old gentleman?'

'We sure can try. What can we do for you, sir?' The nearest soldier gave him a friendly grin. His teeth were perfect and the doctor was pleasantly surprised.

'I have a very heavy trunk.' He indicated it with a hand. 'Full of valuable medical equipment and reference books. Utterly irreplaceable, of course, in these difficult times and they need careful handling. I'm a doctor,' he offered by way of an explanation, 'I'm in the process of relocating my practice, so I must place this in storage until I can get moved in and settled.'

'A doctor. We sure need more of your sort right now!' A broad smile followed this observation.

'Ah, well...I'm just a general practitioner, nothing more than that, I'm afraid. I cannot pretend to be of much use on the front line. Now, the problem is, I need to get my trunk a short way across town and into storage at Broad Street railway station. That's one of the other London stations. The trouble is, I have another pressing engagement to attend out of town and my train departs very soon. It's all terribly awkward and so I was wondering if I could impose myself...'

'You want us to deliver this some place?'

'I would be awfully grateful. If you don't mind helping an old man, that is?'

'Well... We gotta a little time on our hands...'

'You sure, Denzil? We don't exactly know our way about town.' One of the others spoke up, his voice dark and soft.

'It's really not far. Look, I realise this is a dreadful imposition and of course what with the war and everything, you might be suspicious of a chap accosting you like this.' He forced his warmest smile. 'I could be an enemy parachutist stashing equipment aside for an invasion, but my legs are really not up to the jump!' The three soldiers laughed pleasantly. 'No, I really would do it myself, but I just cannot get there and back in ten minutes, so I'm in a bit of a jam...'

'And it looks heavy for an old timer like you to be hunking around.'

'Indeed so.' He made a point of leaning on his stick. 'Those books are rather heavy.' His throat was now parched and his stomach cramping, and he looked convincingly ill.

'You probl'y guessed we're new around here and I can't say as I ever heard about nowhere else 'cept Piccadilly Circus, but you say this Broad Street is easy to find?' The first soldier was speaking.

'I will pay for you to go to the other station and back in a taxi. It's only ten minutes' ride. I will see you right for your trouble, of course. How about ten shillings?'

The three men exchanged pleasantly-surprised glances; it was a tidy sum for little effort. One shrugged, another asked 'Why not?'

'So we take it to this place, and then what we do?'

'Just leave it in the left luggage office. I have here a self-addressed envelope complete with a stamp. Just pay for three months storage — I'll give you enough to cover it — and place the little numbered ticket they will give you in here and pop it in a post box. You need do nothing else.'

The first soldier took the proffered envelope and looked at the address. 'Sounds simple.' He shrugged. 'It's a deal.' He offered his hand for Melcombe to shake.

One of the others had already secured a cab and had the rear door open. 'C'mon guys, what you waiting on?' Barely noticing the weight, the trunk was lifted by the other two and carefully placed in the back of the vehicle. With a nod and wave to the elderly doctor, who was now mopping his brow, they were gone in a trail of oily exhaust.

How long until it was discovered? A week? A month? A year? The lime and the rubberised coating of the gas cape and the heavy tarpaulin should contain the worst of the stench. It was possible it could go undiscovered for at least a few months, and by then no one would be able to recall who brought the trunk in. Even if they did, three black soldiers long since shipped out to some distant place were going to be impossible to trace. He smiled at that happy thought, then his face dropped again when his mind added the hope that the left luggage porter would not demand they open the trunk upon deposit today.

He mopped his brow again, and walked back into the hurly-burley of the station concourse, glad of the noise and confusion that would swallow him as effectively as any camouflaged uniform in the battlefield, his right hand fumbled once again for the little brass-and-ivory topped wooden box inside his jacket pocket. Dr Melcombe's eyes met those of the porteress who had wheeled the trolley a few minutes earlier, and he realised that she was speaking.

'Feeling better?' She gave a cheery wave as she dashed past.

'Much!' He suddenly became aware that he was smiling.

CHAPTER THIRTY-SIX
Brackley Cottage Hospital
27th September 1950

'I cannot seriously be expected to remember when I took a holiday in 1943. It's quite ridiculous.

'It was wartime, Dr Melcombe. Everyone was encouraged to travel as infrequently as possible. A holiday would, therefore, be a memorable occasion.'

Vignoles asked the questions as Trinder took notes, one standing on each side of the hospital bed.

'I can recall the week we had at Mablethorpe in '41 as though it were yesterday. The journey took five hours and we stood most of the way, but the sun was cracking the flags when we got there and the sea was lovely. How *could* I forget?' added Trinder with exaggerated enthusiasm.

'You might fill your head with frivolous nonsense, sergeant, but I do not', snapped the doctor. 'Besides which, your argument is deeply flawed: someone could have done this dreadful deed whilst I was at my club in London, out playing golf, or even in the dead of night whilst I slept soundly in my bed. Heaven forbid! I can assure you I was neither aware nor part of this evil act.'

'Why would someone unknown to you come into your garden to bury such a grisly thing?' Vignoles asked. 'Barely credible, surely?'

'How the blasted hell should I know? I cannot even start to comprehend it. It's a complete waste of time, your questioning me.'

'Your appointments diary would be a great help. It would confirm the times you were away and help us determine who you saw around that time. Hopefully this will remove you from the investigation and perhaps give us some pointers as to who was responsible,' Vignoles continued, his tone helpful and encouraging.

'We feel it must be someone who knew you or your home well.'

'I don't have the diary. I threw everything away with the move.'

Trinder made a note and sucked air between his teeth. 'Unfortunate.'

'Why did you take early retirement?' Vignoles fired the question from the other side of the bed.

'My health was not good. Still isn't, no thanks to that thug Irons, and now this! I have a dodgy heart, if you must know.' He waved a hand at a bottle of pills on the bedside cabinet.

'That's not what your neighbours and patients say. They were surprised, even a little disappointed at the way you just upped sticks and left, all in a matter of weeks.'

'What would they know? I kept the exact details private. I don't have to share everything with patients or meddling neighbours. Privacy is everything to me.'

'You live alone?'

'What of it?' Melcombe gave Vignoles a reproving look. 'I never married, but I cannot see that's any of your business.'

'Why were you disposing of a young lady's clothes in your garden?' Trinder asked. 'We found the remains in a bonfire.'

'Nothing to do with me! The chap who bought the place from me must be responsible. He had a wife, I think.'

'Do you own a set of scales? A rather fine, precision set as might be used for weighing tiny amounts of powder or pills?' Vignoles asked, both detectives keeping the questioning lively, deliberately dancing from one subject to another.

'Of course. Anyone in my profession is likely to have just such a weighing balance.'

'Are yours made by Oertling?'

'Let me think… it's a long time ago since I bought them. But, yes, mine are by Oertling. One of the best manufacturers of these instruments. Got mine second-hand but in perfect condition. Still, cost me a week's wages when I was starting up in my first practice.'

'Are they still in their box? I would imagine such an expensive item needs careful protection. It could be easily damaged, and during your house move you would wish to take great care…'

'Um… They didn't come with a box. The drawback of buying second-hand, inspector. I'm tired and need rest. My cracked ribs make it hard to talk. I have no interest in discussing the packaging of some old medical equipment!'

'Of course. But one last thing for now; have you seen this woman?' Vignoles showed Melcombe the photograph used on the missing person posters.

'No.' But Melcombe took a sharp intake of breath, causing him to wince and touch his ribs. 'Never. Sorry, I'm very sore.'

'She didn't visit you recently?'

'What? Why would she do that?' Melcombe's pupils widened and he made his voice crack with pain. He appeared to be having problems with his breathing.

'I wondered if she might have entered your house in advance of the break in. Perhaps she called at the door and you let her in?'

'I've told you, I've never seen her.' He took a few fast, shallow breaths then shifted his position on the pillows, wincing and his face deathly pale.

'You are quite sure? This photograph was on posters up and down the line, including Amersham, for quite some time.' He unfolded the poster in question. 'Do you not remember seeing this?'

Melcombe's Adam's apple bobbed. 'No... maybe... I could not say for certain. You're grilling me like a common criminal, inspector!' He glared at Vignoles, perspiration on his temples. 'If you persist in interrogating me like the bloody Gestapo, I shall insist on my lawyer being present.'

'We need to get to bottom of two suspicious deaths and that entails asking all manner of questions of all manner of people, Dr Melcombe.' Vignoles used his most placatory tone of voice. 'It is unavoidable, I am afraid.' The doctor mumbled something and retreated into looking pained. 'We would like to have a look around your cottage.'

'Absolutely not!'

'I can get a warrant because you and your house are a part of an investigation.' Vignoles made an apologetic shrug.

'How so? The robbery was nothing. It's of no consequence.'

'Interesting you should say that.' Vignoles smiled. 'I'm almost inclined to agree with you; Irons made very little attempt to take your collection; in fact it appears all rather half-hearted.' Vignoles observed Melcombe carefully. 'Perhaps he was seeking something else? Can you suggest what that might that be?'

Melcombe remained silent, his eyes flicking between the two detectives, but Vignoles noticed that he kept giving the little photograph of Betty Askew surreptitious glances.

'What is the Cobra's Eye?' asked Trinder.

Melcombe looked stunned. He coughed and reached for a glass of water on his bedside table and sipped it. 'Sorry, throat's dry.' His voice was forced when he next spoke. 'Do elucidate me sergeant, what is the Cobra's Eye?'

'It was mentioned during our enquiries, that's all.' Trinder offered.

'Who told you about it?'

Trinder smiled as if to say, *nice try, but hard luck, chummy*.

'You've never heard of the Cobra's Eye, and yet are more interested in knowing who mentioned it than in what it is.' Vignoles paused. 'Ah, but then, you already know, don't you?' He was giving Melcombe a hard stare. 'Was Irons interested in it?'

'I have absolutely no idea what you are talking about.'

'Did Irons break in to take it? Or perhaps you were going to strike a deal with him, but he reneged or disagreed and there was a scuffle between you both. Either way, someone got to him later, didn't they?'

'You really are clutching at straws now, inspector. I'd never seen that fellow before the night he attacked me and, as you know, I was laid up in here whilst he met with his unfortunate end. Cobras and a dead housebreaker: it is quite obvious you have no idea what you are looking for, nor indeed what you are doing here. Now, please leave.' Melcombe gave Vignoles a cold, mirthless smile. 'And I suggest you go away and think a bit harder before you return.'

'Oh, I shall. And don't worry, I will be back.

'Take your shoes off and relax, I'll get your tea ready. It won't take long.' Anna put her arms lovingly around Vignoles's neck, deftly removing his hat with a manicured hand and holding it behind his back. She planted a warm kiss on his mouth, her curvaceous body flatteringly revealed by a skin-tight turtleneck tucked into a flared skirt with a nipped waist. She pressed herself close. 'A beer?' Cocking her head to one side she observed that he looked tired. 'It's been a terribly long day, I suppose.'

'Long, but productive and intriguing.' He was enjoying feeling her breasts against his chest and ran a hand down the clearly delineated curve of her hip, feeling the corset beneath the fabric, his fingers playfully tracing the fastening of her suspender belt. 'But yes, a beer would be lovely.' He smiled at Anna, now tasting lipstick. 'Am I red?' He turned and glanced in the hall mirror. 'I look like a clown!'

Anna was laughing. 'More like one of those louche variety performers, haha! It's only a smudge. Come along...' She gently ushered him into their small living room. 'As it's late, I've decided you can have something on a tray. I've got some steak that I can fry and serve with chips I cut earlier.'

'Just what I need! Steak? You actually managed to find *steak*? Am I dreaming, or have you blown both our ration books for the month?'

'Well, it's horse, of course. But it looks good and will taste wonderful. Anyway, you like horse.'

'I do, though I think I'm the only one who admits to it. There's always an outbreak of horrified moral outrage if I tell the office we've eaten horse!'

'More fool them.'

Being a fraction of the size of the large and chilly space inhabited by the Lineys, their room was rendered cosy by curtains of an interestingly-patterned material that were now holding back the night, and a small fire taking the edge off any encroaching coolness, offering friendly little clicks and ticks as the coal burned in the grate. The furniture was of the most up-to-date 'Beautility' brand, suitably austere and inexpensive, yet clean and functional in a way that pleased their sense of design. There was new wallpaper on one wall in a bold design of greys, blacks, pale greens and yellows that had been described as seed heads, but which could be mistaken for splitting atoms, the other walls were simply washed with plain, strong colours that matched the atomic fission of the paper. It was a far cry from his parents' house, Dunton Bassett rectory; that was a rambling pile decorated with fussy wallpapers patterned with stripes or flowers and overstuffed with heavy sofas, oppressively dark furniture, long plate racks edging the walls and gilt-framed hunting prints. Not only that, but every flat surface was covered in a multitude of trinkets and knick-knacks that his mother Caroline loved to collect, apparently whenever she left the house.

Vignoles turned the 'on' switch of his prized radiogram and waited as the valves warmed up, the sound of dance music slowly rising as the radio got up to speed. Listening to Harry Roy's band for a moment or two, and deciding it was to his liking, he slipped his shoes from his aching feet and flopped into one of the armchairs beside the fire. He closed his eyes for a few moments. Anna had retreated into the kitchen and he heard the soft clink of a bottle and glass. He smiled. It was a reassuringly pleasing sound and a delicious escape from the horrors of looking at the butchered remains of a young woman and the horribly mangled throat of a dead schoolteacher.

Anna returned with tumblers and two bottles of Everard's Tiger on a tray that she placed on a low, black-lacquered, oval table. Carefully pouring the beer down the inside of the glass, Vignoles detected the first hint of the hoppy scent and enjoyed the sound of the amber liquid flowing into the foam of bubbles now forming on top. He held the full glass high and let the light from a standard lamp shine through the liquid, admiring the clarity and colour in patient anticipation. Anna also lifted her glass and they clinked them together.

'Chin-chin!'

'I needed that.' Vignoles nodded appreciatively after a slow and satisfying first draught. 'It's been a funny old day, really. Rather short on the funny, though. It started with a body in the churchyard in Brackley.'

Anna gave him a look.

'Yes, I know, you would expect bodies in a churchyard, but this was a suspicious death: one above the ground. Rather grisly. I will spare you the details. But if that were not enough to keep us occupied, we were off to see another body, well, part of a body. I cannot say more, it is far too ghastly for your delicate sensibilities my darling wife. Now that was buried, but this time in a private garden in Amersham.'

'Ugh! And are these events related?'

'There is a link. And, to my surprise, the Badger has put me in charge of the investigation — of both investigations — until I can be sure they are one and the same. A bit of a surprise really as we're working well off railway territory.'

'Shows he appreciates how good you are. About time, too.'

'Thank you darling; however, the fact is, no one else was prepared to take it on. So it was passed to muggings here. But, actually, I don't mind, because it's a curious case, or should I say cases, crossing different boundaries that will cause all manner of operational headaches.' He gave a little smile at Anna in appreciation of her company and drank more beer. They were silent for a moment or two.

'We have someone in mind as a suspect, but there's still an awful lot of work to do before I can make an arrest. He'd wriggle out with a good lawyer, perhaps even with a bad one, based on what little I have at the moment. I've got the Buckinghamshire boys taking apart a house in Amersham looking for clues, and tomorrow Trinder will get the Northants lot doing the same in the suspect's cottage in Turweston. Our suspect is heavily implicated, but I don't actually have any evidence of him committing either murder, you see. In fact, when it comes to the suspicious death in the churchyard, our suspect was laid up in hospital at the time!' Vignoles gave Anna an almost apologetic look.

'Early days, Charles, early days.' She patted his hand encouragingly. 'It's always like this at the start of a case. You are often telling me nothing seems to make sense to start with, but slowly, as you discover a bit more and tease out the strands, it always comes together in the end.'

Vignoles leant back in the chair. 'You're right. Everything is too raw right now. I need a good night's sleep to think it over and start afresh tomorrow. Hmm, I like this song...' Sinatra started singing in his wistful, late-night voice a song about loneliness, stepping across the rhythm of the band with consummate skill, phrasing the lines perfectly.

'He's an incredible singer,' Anna agreed. 'Probably the best.'

They listened together for a while in complete silence. Anna stood up as the song ended, placing her beer glass on the table. 'I'll get your steak and chips on.' She walked across the room into the hall but reappeared immediately at the door. 'I'm sorry, I forgot. There was a call. I made a note and left it on the telephone table in the hall and just noticed it.'

'Oh yes?'

'A Mrs Askew. She sounded terribly apologetic about telephoning and explained how she'd got the number from the directory as you'd left her one of your calling cards and so had your name and...'

'What did she say?' Vignoles was sitting upright in the armchair, all tiredness apparently forgotten.

'Just that she wanted to speak with you. To explain something private.' Anna gave a mischievous look. 'She was most insistent.'

'Then I must call her immediately.' Vignoles stood up. 'This is no laughing matter.'

'Slow down, it can wait. She said not to call at their house this evening when Henry was at home. Is he her husband?'

'Correct.'

'Anyway, they don't have a telephone and she insisted on seeing you face to face to explain properly. She wants you to come to her workplace, the Merry Chemist, in Brackley.'

'I know it. What could it be?' He was talking almost to himself whilst leaning an elbow on the mantelshelf. 'Something about her daughter, I suppose....'

'Is she the poor thing who went missing? I don't suppose you've found her.'

Vignoles looked pained. 'Possibly. Probably. Too early to be absolutely sure, though it looks like bad news.'

'Oh my God, is she the body in the churchyard? Oh no, you said that was a man. In Amersham, then?' Anna winced and Vignoles had no need to say anything. 'How dreadful. Mrs Askew sounded such a sweet lady, and hearing her voice makes it feel all the more real. What will you tell her?'

'I shall call the pathologist first thing and see if they have an identification. I'd rather stand on less shaky ground before I put her through that.' Vignoles was speaking softly. 'It will be a terrible experience for them to see the remains. I've only seen photographs, and that was bad enough. However, until we have something positive I might play this carefully and only allude to a discovery. Heck, I hate this part of the job, Anna. Trying to judge what to say and not to say for the best, when ultimately there really is no "best".' Vignoles took a deep swig of beer and stared into the flames in the grate. 'I had a suspicion Maud Askew was holding something back. Is it too ridiculous to hope that she has found her daughter alive and we can seek an alternative name to pin on the gruesome discovery? Of course, I'm just wishing to avoid a painful interview tomorrow. Ultimately, those body parts belong to someone deceased, and all I would be doing is transferring the pain onto another family.'

'I'll get you another Tiger', said Anna, sympathetically.

CHAPTER THIRTY-EIGHT
Brackley Central
27ᵗʰ September 1950

'My leg is getting cramped.'

'And I'm cold.'

Eddie Earnshaw was lying on his stomach peering beneath the lowest slat of the wooden fence edging the railway line. In front of them stretched the twin lines crossing the great, curving viaduct. Close to his right was a thick telegraph pole that reeked of creosote mingled with the light tang of oil, wood and a suggestion of flushed toilets wafting from the track, all softened by a stronger odour of grasses and damp loam. 'Any more tea in the can?'

Laura Green stood up gingerly, wiggling her foot to get the blood flowing. She retrieved the cream, enamelled tea can from her haversack and unscrewed the top. 'Enough for a cup each. And I've two squares of Dairy Milk. I bet you'd like one?'

'Chocolate? Top hole. You kept that quiet!' Eddie rolled over on to his side and even in the dark of the night she could see he was grinning.

'I've been making the bar last all week.' She handed over the lid of the tea-can, filled with hot, sweet tea, then shook out the cold dregs from a spare mug and poured the last of the liquid for herself. Sitting back down on the little square of rug they had laid on the grass, she cupped her hands around the mug, gladly absorbing its warmth. 'A cup of tea really helps lift one's spirits!' She took a sip and then, securing her mug in a tuft of long grass, unwrapped the chocolate. 'I hope Simon's ok. Any signal from him?'

'Thanks. No...no, I can't see a thing.' Eddie looked along the silver rails to the far side of the viaduct where their friend was hunkered down on the steep embankment a little below the sight lines of the station staff and signalman. 'I'll send the "no" signal to him as a test. Just to keep him on his toes.' He clicked on his flashlight and wiggled it from side to side, their pre-arranged signal that indicated 'no sign of her'. Almost immediately a tiny pinpoint of light did the same from a spot about a yard below rail level. The torch beam went out and near-darkness returned, relieved only by the little station lamps and faint red stains cast on the shiny rail tops from the oil lamps behind the signal spectacle plates.

'I suppose we can't be too surprised. It's not everyday, or night, that one sees a ghost. Assuming there really is one,' Laura observed. 'What shall we do? Give it another half hour?'

'I think we should wait until the down stopper from Marylebone. It reverses here and that's the one Si reckons she travels on. It has to be our best chance. We can hang on another twenty minutes after, as I arranged for us to get a lift from the newspaper train. But if we miss that, then it's going to be a long, cold night.'

'No, thank you!' replied Laura, 'I'm game for a while longer, but not all night.'

There was a thin, reedy twang and the creak of signal wires tautening followed by the heavy *chonk* of the arm lifting. A cool, green light replaced the red and a tiny bell sounded in the signalbox.

'Here comes something...'

They both lay prone, side-by-side on the blanket, hot drinks in their hands, the steam brushing their faces. There was a faint whistle and then the measured tread of a slow and heavy train.

Eddie listened a while. 'Heading south. A heavy goods?'

Laura nodded. 'A coal train or perhaps iron ore. I know that sound well because they pass my signal box all day long.' They exchanged looks, enjoying sharing the experience, faces close. 'I bet there's eighty on the back, by the sound of it.'

He nodded, reckoning she was better at this than both he and Simon combined. 'She might stop the train! That's what happened to me that time.'

'I'm in two minds about this now.' She bit her lower lip and watched the pale efflorescence bloom like a series of giant white flowers above the station canopy, the black monster snorting and breathing in deep gruff exhalations with its train clanging and banging in a riotous cacophony behind. 'It's one thing to want to see a ghost, quite another to do so.'

'An O8. No wait, I think it's a Western ROD. What a rare cop, Laura!' Eddie kept his voice barely above a whisper. 'A Great War survivor. Built for the Railway Operating Division around 1917, up in Gorton. They can pull a whole town, as long as you don't want to go faster than a snail! I can't see the number...is that 3023?'

'Shh...never mind train spotting. Look!' Laura Green was pointing, her outstretched hand quivering with nervous excitement. 'Oh, but quick, you must signal to Simon!' Her eyes narrowed as she tried to get a better look.

They watched as a slim, pale figure of a woman stepped up from the far side of the embankment, moving both smoothly and silently onto the viaduct and apparently oblivious to the thunder of the great train approaching from the other end. She wore a long coat and a hat, her face of the palest skin beneath the brim. She seemed to have no fear and stood on the track pointing her arm as though at something over the side of the viaduct parapet.

'Exactly what she did when I saw her!' Eddie exclaimed.

'There's something strange about her...Oh, she's got no hands!'

'That is a full coal train, and on a down gradient! There's no point in even attempting to stop!' He leaped up, sending his lid of tea spinning to land with a clatter on the edge of the permanent way.

'Hey, hey — you! Get off the line! Get out the way!' He was waving frantically above his head, but the pale creature stayed rooted to the spot with one foot on either side of a rail, facing certain death.

'I thought we were supposed to just watch... It can't hurt her. Oh God, but the train's going to strike her!' But Laura was also unable to suppress her own natural instincts and was soon standing, darting a quick glance to the far side of the viaduct, where a torch beam was frantically flicking up and down indicating 'YES!' Simon had also seen the phantom lady in white.

There was no time to reply as the lumbering train, probably eight hundred tons of unstoppable steel, coal, fire and water ploughed onwards, the crew hanging on the whistle and leaning far out of the almost-open cab, quite powerless to do anything. As the train hit the girl there was no sound, nothing but the relentless huff and rumble of the engine. Her slight body could not check the heavy goods train's progress, but this lack of sound was doubly disturbing.

Laura held her hands in front of her face whilst Eddie stared, open-mouthed. Somehow the engine did not mangle the woman into a hideous mess beneath the wheels, but rather the big 2–8–0 freight engine appeared to travel through her, the pale figure melting into the steam leaking profusely from the low-slung cylinders as though she had been vaporised into oily atoms. Almost immediately this cloud reconstituted, twisting and curling into the shape of a running figure. The young woman was now miraculously running across the tracks, her feet moving soundlessly on the ballast as she came straight towards Eddie and Laura.

She passed so close they could have touched her. Neither moved. They were frozen to the spot and could only stare in mute fascination as she passed, her face a death mask, her eyes were filled with a silvery-cold light that spoke of a deep, pure loneliness that coursed straight into their hearts.

The woman moved smoothly down the embankment side, now tracked by a thin torchbeam from afar. Eddie snapped out of his stunned inertia and clicked on his own torch and like searchlights on a German bomber, their two lights traced her pale, now almost luminous shape. She reached the riverbank and stopped, turning her head back whence she came and, despite the gloom and her apparent indifference to them a moment earlier, Eddie and Laura sensed she was trying to engage their attention.

'Look!' Now pointing into the Great Ouse, her arm still appeared to lack a hand;, but this may have been a trick of the desperately poor light.

Laura clutched Eddie's arm. The torchbeam was unsteady in his hand. The woman called again, in a faint, sad sound they felt more than heard. It was almost completely masked by the cacophony of the passing coal train. Their vision was impaired by great cumuli of smoke and steam rolling down from the passing engine, but they watched as the strange woman in white flowed into the water, appearing to melt into the damp, dank mist.

CHAPTER THIRTY-NINE
Brackley
28th September 1950

'We must leave now, it would be the height of folly to delay a moment longer.' Barnaby Ringham checked his exquisite Cartier wristwatch with a decisive movement. Having done so, he instinctively adjusted the lie of the sleeve of his hand-made suit.

'Yes, yes... but I'm really not sure I'm up to a long haul. I seem to have taken a bit of a setback.' Dr Melcombe was rubbing his heavily-strapped torso with painfully slow movements. 'Being grilled by that inspector has knocked me for six, and my neck and ribs are playing up like nobody's business.'

'You do look dead beat, but my car is comfortable and I have a travelling rug if you get cold. The Armstrong Siddeley *Hurricane* is a dashed fine car and comfortable.' Despite his concerns, Ringham allowed a moment of self-satisfaction. 'I've primed matron. Hopefully she'll keep her trap shut long enough for us to put some miles between us and the hospital, thanks to a generous donation to its funds. We'll refine our plans once we're underway, but take this. It's a ticket to Glasgow. When we get there we might go on to Rannoch Moor. Scotland's a good place to keep one's head below the firing line.' He slipped Melcombe a small, buff envelope with 'British Railways' stamped on the top left corner in red. Ringham then looked around the small private room and wrinkled his nose. 'You have the change of clothes as instructed?'

'Yes. My housekeeper, Mrs MacKendrie, fetched them last night. That's the case, in the corner.' Melcombe leant heavily on the arms of the one comfortable chair in the room and eased himself upright. Getting into his day clothes had been a lengthy process and he'd needed to sit down after doing so to both tie his shoelaces and regain some composure, aided by swallowing a couple of painkillers. 'PC Plod was standing guard over Ivy Cottage, but he was quite obliging and let her in. But look here, you still have not answered my question.' Melcombe's voice had a whining quality, like a little boy nagging at a parent. 'Have you got it? You must hand it over, Barnaby. I've got to have it back!'

Ringham ignored his demands, concentrating instead on pulling on a pair of smooth, black leather driving gloves with a button fastening on the back. 'Quite right, you're not under caution—' he paused to allow the implied 'yet' to fill the space. 'Chop-chop!' Ringham picked up Melcombe's bottle-green leather suitcase with P.M. blocked in gold letters on the lid, and held the door open for the doctor, who shuffled past. 'The car is parked around the corner, just a short walk away. I'd rather it had been somewhat further, but you sounded all done in on the telephone last night.'

'I'll manage. But the *ring...*' Melcombe almost hissed the word, his face so close he could smell Ringham's cologne and see a little nick where his solicitor's hand had uncharacteristically slipped when shaving. 'You do have it?'

'All in good time, Percy, old boy.' But his wink convinced the recalcitrant doctor to continue walking, implying that he did indeed have the object in question. Ringham had to throw the old man something to pacify him, or he'd just argue the point and refuse to cooperate, and they could ill afford to be overheard discussing such a potent object. Things were in a pretty delicate state and they needed to make their getaway.

The retired doctor's nerves were uncharacteristically frayed, however. He looked but a shadow of the blustering, arrogant fellow who'd bullied matron into letting him telephone Ringham at his West End club. Perhaps he'd been running on adrenaline at the time, because now he was completely washed out, with almost every bone and muscle aching and his mind frazzled by a disturbed and largely sleepless night. His red-rimmed eyes looked like those of a hunted man, restlessly roving about the room and flitting anxiously between the ugly wardrobe in the corner, then over to the window fringed with copper-burnished, rain-sodden Virginia creeper.

Since the moment Vignoles and Trinder had left, he'd hardly slept. As he lay in his narrow hospital bed, restrained by the starched sheets tucked hard under the mattress, he found sleep eluded him. He jumped at any little noise and, although only small, the building was still a hive of muffled footsteps and murmured conversations, a closing door here, the distant cry of a newborn baby there. These should have been comforting sounds, signals that nurses were close at hand and ready to offer help and reassurance, but instead Melcombe came to dread each new disturbance no matter how soft, fearing they heralded the presence of something unwelcome, something sinister. The retired doctor had opened his eyes wide from a brief moment of sleep and stared at the door in horror. He had the most intense feeling that she was right outside, at that moment, just standing there, eyes boring through the glossy, cream-painted wood. Although he'd been dozing he was sure he'd heard her walk along the corridor, her shoes making a soft sigh as they turned on the linoleum. It was as though his senses were heightened to an almost painful level of amplification, the blood buzzing in his ears, every tiny sound jangling loud like a warning bell.

His stare fixed upon the Bakelite doorknob, convinced that at any moment it would turn, and he had hardly dared breathe as the minutes stretched on. What was that? It was her voice. But how could it be? It was impossible, and yet he was sure it was her, outside on the street below. How could he forget the sound? He tugged angrily at the sheets that were stiff as cardboard and flung them back. Driven onwards by a sense of mounting dread he stumbled across the room, fighting against the pain burning all over his body He stared down at the pools of light cast on the damp road below. A soft rain was falling, forming halos around the flaring lamps as the leaves of the trees edging the park boiled and stirred in the gathering wind, their branches dipping and rising and throwing moving shadows. But where was she? He opened the metal casement and peered further out, not caring about the drizzle.

A thin, reedy piping sound came from above. He looked up and felt the rain splash on his face, spotting his lenses, but he continued to seek the source of the sound, compelled to look for the soul birds on their tireless migration, but the blanket of rain cloud had blotted out the moon.

Wheep…whee wheep…whee, wheep wheep…

Just a few birds on the wing, yet their calls were so mournful and laden with sorrow, cutting through the swish and rustle of windblown leaf, the patter of rain and the distant hoot of a passing train.

I'm so lonely…find me, find me…

Their reedy piping triggered something in his mind and instead of hearing the call of a curlew or the piping of a duck, it sounded like her voice…

Wheep, whee wheep…they will find me…

He banged his fist on the metal window frame. Stuff and nonsense! But who was that? He was shaking now, his body wracked by shivers, probably from the chilled damp air, and he gripped the windowsill. That pale figure moving along the pavement…in the deep dark shadows by the high wall. No...he almost collapsed with relief. It was just a thin man without a hat taking a walk. How could he have thought it was the young woman? Was he hallucinating? And yet he still had the feeling she was close by, watching him in dreadful proximity.

It was quite impossible. He knew only too well where her mutilated remains lay, each part deliberately placed far from the others, although her hands lay closer than he'd planned. That was dreadfully unfortunate. How he had dithered and delayed on that fateful train ride! The appalling remains, small and slender, wrapped in greaseproof paper like something from the butcher's shop, had nagged away at his conscience and at times he was sure her fingers had tapped lightly on the brown leather attaché case, rapping at the cardboard and leather, asking to be released, drawing his eyes and reminding him of what it contained. He had been unable to even look at the packet lying there all day, let alone open the clasps, lift the lid and toss this loathsome cargo away, as he knew he must. But the little sounds from within had drawn his attention and finally forced him into action. A loose pencil that had been rolling against the side was the innocent explanation of the sound. He tossed it onto the carriage seat in frustrated anger. The sound had goaded him into grasping the packet and hurling it through the opened window. And about time, too. He'd walked around London for an hour, from one gloomy, weed-strewn bombsite to another, thinking to toss the packet beneath the tumbles of broken beams that looked like a giant's game of spillikins, or drop it down any number of gaping holes into the rubble-filled cellars of these destroyed dwellings. And yet there were always some grubby-faced lads larking around or a group of youths stripping salvage and firewood, or a homeless figure ranting at the earth, seated like a shabby Lear on the skeleton of a baby carriage surrounded by empty bottles and horribly-stained bits of rag and blanket. It was impossible to commit the act unseen. There was always someone watching, walking past, and so many windows looking down onto these open spaces.

And so finally, in a fit of blind panic and rage, he'd tossed the repugnant package from the train window, intending it to tumble into a river far below. But it was going dark and he was not sure of his aim. Had he missed? He could not tell, but the shape and length of the viaduct was distinctive and a few weeks later, when he'd completed the house purchase in Turweston and was travelling up one evening to finalise some details, he realised he'd disposed of her hands in a place as close to his new home as the railway would reach. How could he have been so foolish? Had some unseen force guided his hand?

His fevered imagination was playing tricks on him now, and yet no matter how hard he leant upon his years of medical practice and rational argument, he could not shake off the feeling that she was right there, watching him, and he again wondered about what had compelled him to finally act and jettison her hands from the train at such an inauspicious location.

Feeling cold and foolish, he closed the window, fastening it with the latch, eager to shut out the haunting calls of the night birds. He drew the curtains tight together, and lay down, pulling the sheets up to his chin in a childish attempt to find comfort.

What was that? A scratch of a fingernail on wood — again! She was in the wardrobe! Must have slipped in whilst he was looking out of the window.

'Come out! Come on. You don't frighten me.' His heart was fit to burst, pulse dangerously high, palms sweating profusely. 'You fell. I didn't touch you. I just wanted to see your diamond ring, that was all… I meant you no harm. It was an accident. You were not even supposed to be there…' His voice was weak and the words barely audible. 'I wish I'd never set eyes on you, or your cursed diamond!'

Silence.

The catch on the wardrobe door make a little metallic click and the door swung open half an inch with a creak. He stared transfixed at the black slit in the gloom. He waited. Nothing. Eventually he found the courage to cross the room and fling the door wide. It was empty. He repeatedly tried to secure the door with its catch, closing and opening it. It looked in perfect working order, and yet every time he returned to his bed, after a few minutes it would click open again. He knew the wardrobe was empty, yet could not shake off the feeling of being watched. Finally, he wedged a tall chair against the door, which prevented it door from opening again.

Melcombe settled for a short time after this, but then the curtains across the bedroom window became the focus for his deteriorating state of mind. The pale light leaking in from outside sometimes flickered and moved along the floor beside his bed. He became convinced there was someone outside. Someone or something was flitting silently to and fro past the window, the street lamp opposite casting a shadow. He tried closing his eyes and ignoring these movements, but all he could see was the face of that young girl in his consulting room, lying on her back, eyes closed, no breath from her lips...

She was tapping on the windowpane. Or was it on the door to his private room? In his mind, he could hear the brass, fox-shaped knocker resonating and calling him to the door on that fateful day. Why had she chosen him? Damn and blast, what ill luck had brought her to his surgery? He didn't deal with working class girls; he only ever sorted the problems of the rich and the famous, and only when arranged through Barnaby. He was just given a name (probably false), a day and a time and everything was ordered and organised, all strictly hush-hush and handled with supreme delicacy and consummate professionalism. Technically the procedure was illegal, but they were educated, private patients and they paid handsomely via one of Barney's clever and complex ruses that ensured nobody would ever know, not least the taxman, and it suited everyone just fine. But someone had talked and his name had slipped out and so this blasted bloody train cleaner had come knocking.

He opened his eyes and stared. But the little hospital was now quiet and peaceful, as it should be. He could hear the clock of St Peter's chiming two. His attention was drawn again to a dark shape sliding across the floor. She was seated on the windowsill, hands feeling around the frame. He could imagine her face outside looking in, contorted with outrage as she asked him to let her go, let her leave. Why, oh why had he not just pushed her out the door and sent her packing? Idiot, idiot, idiot! He rubbed his eyes and banged his palms on his forehead, but the image of the Askew girl just would not leave.

Eventually, driven half mad with torment, he forced himself out of bed yet again, adrenaline cutting through the pain and stiffness. He flung the curtains wide so they jingled on their brass rings, but what he saw was just the complex shapes caused by a branch of a tree bouncing in the wind in front of the gas lamp. He had stood and stared out of the window for a long time, growing colder and colder.

His night terrors had left him drained and now Melcombe gratefully lay back in the front passenger seat and enjoyed the cool smoothness and the intense smell of the ostentatious red leather, trying to relax and let Ringham take control for a while. Barnaby was good at fixing things, just the man when in a tricky situation. He'd worked a minor miracle back then. He'd come to the rescue and barely missed a beat when confronted with the sight of a dead girl stretched out on the floor. He'd been a rock and dreamed up their plan to dispose of her remains.

But any lasting sense of relief was ruined by a nagging worry about something the inspector had raised, something vital that he needed to thrash out with Barnaby. He was also disturbed by the constant heavy breathing of Ringham's big, ugly Alsatian Wolf Dog.

The creature panted its reeking breath in noisy huffs like a steam engine, its long, brown-and-black snout thrust between the front seats, tongue lolling unpleasantly pink to one side of its wet lips. Whenever Melcombe gave it an impatient glance the dog moved its feet about on the rear bench seat, as if about to pounce, and fixed its overly-alert eyes on him, an ear flicking. It was unsettling. Then the creature would suddenly close its mouth and the infernal pant-pant-pant would cease, followed by an audible gulp as the dog presumably swallowed more of the excess of saliva, accompanied by a roll of its eyes, before starting up the rhythmic panting again. Melcombe was finding it stomach-turning.

'Doesn't that drive you mad?'

'Hades is my faithful companion.' Ringham's gloved hands slid smoothly on the steering wheel in calm, measured movements as he pulled away. 'One gets used to it, I suppose. Annoying you, is he?'

'Yes. And its breath stinks!"

'His name is Hades. Impolite to call him it, old chap. He might take offence.'

Dr Melcombe shook his head impatiently. 'Can't you make it… make *him* lie down, at least? He can sleep on the back seat like other dogs.'

'Hades likes to watch the road and to keep an eye on things.' Ringham gave the doctor a sly look as he changed gear and the great motor under the long bonnet roared. 'I like him alert to any eventuality.'

Melcombe had to be satisfied with this enigmatic reply, He turned to look out of the passenger window at the edge of Brackley town as it melted into a succession of fields and hedgerows, and at the Scots pines grouped around the entrance to Brackley Central passing to their right, the parapet of the road bridge they swung across causing the note of the car to change. The doctor caught sight of a steadily-chuffing goods train heading northward, a huge white cumulus of steam hanging in the air and the infernal panting of the dog offering a suitable soundtrack to this fleeting image.

'Where are you taking me? You mentioned Scotland.'

'We have tickets and reservations on the Mid-day Scot. I have a small shooting box on Rannoch Moor. It could be wise to hunker down there and take stock. It's in a darned lonely place: your inspector won't find us in a hurry.' Ringham gave Melcombe a sideways glance as he changed gear. 'But I've not made a final decision on the best plan. Need to have bit of a chin-wag and consider the options first.'

'Yes.' Melcombe glanced back across at his companion and then resumed patting his pockets and peering into his wallet, an action he had commenced soon after the car had pulled away from the Cottage Hospital.

'Need to get a few things straight in my mind,' Ringham smiled and Melcombe caught the sight in the rear view mirror. He was reminded of the skull on the life-sized skeleton he used to have hanging, as though on a gibbet, in his consulting room. It was cast in some kind of hard, cream-coloured plastic and articulated by metal hooks and eyes; whilst realistic, he always felt the teeth were implausibly perfect and regular. Ringham's teeth had something of the same perfection, enviably free of fillings, but this also gave his smile an unsettling quality, as though he was just too perfect to be true. In many ways Ringham was a true friend, but Melcombe had always retained the thought that he was not completely to be trusted. The man was just too ruthless and efficient to ever allow emotions to stand in the way of looking after number one.

'Then we can start with your handing the ring over. You do have it, don't you, Barnaby?' Melcombe asked, his voice irritable. He was jittery and anxious and had been brooding about the loss of the Cobra's Eye since the moment he had seen that odd note left in its place, the same note that he had scrunched into a little ball in his hand, but which now he could not find, despite the constant searching of his pockets and wallet. 'You did find it? I know Irons took it.'

'I have it. It was easy enough to follow him and choose an opportune moment to retrieve it.'

'But did you have to kill him, for God's sake?' Melcombe almost spat out the words.

'He was a liability. We couldn't risk his saying any more than he'd already blabbed to the press. They were turning him into a minor sensation. Still, the diamond is quite a beauty.' Ringham raised an eyebrow. 'Clearly you have an eye for quality. I can see why you are so interested.'

Melcombe felt his heart almost miss a beat. 'Hand it over! I must see it at once!'

'I think not. Sorry Percy old boy, but I shall take care of it, for now. You managed to lose it once, and we really can't risk that a second time, can we? And besides, things are a touch dicey at the moment. If you were caught with it on your person, they'd hang you without a second's thought, and there'd not be a lot I could do to save you. Far better I hold on to it until we're out of the woods, eh.'

'But it's mine! I want it back…'

Hades emitted a low, deep growl, his ears held back.

'Yours?' An eyebrow was raised. 'An interesting interpretation. And how exactly did you come by it?' Ringham gave Melcombe a sideways glance. 'One is coming around to thinking that you took it by force from that unfortunate young woman. That does rather alter the situation, you must admit.'

Melcombe gave no reply. The engine rumbled and the dog emitted a similar low note, though it was barely audible as they passed a convoy of three scarlet-painted British Road Services articulated lorries, each carrying long, sheeted loads of steel from the Corby Steelworks, the sound of their straining motors intruding on their conversation and the car immediately filling with choking exhaust fumes.

'Are you quite sure it was an accident? I have my doubts, frankly. The word "murder" keeps coming to mind.'

'How dare you!' Melcombe's eyes bulged behind his glasses, but he was trembling. 'Murder! How could you imagine it? It—it was an unfortunate piece of bad luck, that's all. Tragic, quite terrible, of course, but she fell awkwardly and hit her head. I never touched her.'

'So you said. I was never fully convinced from the start, but I needed you free of scandal and I couldn't allow an investigation at any cost, so we just brushed it under the carpet, so as to speak. Haha! Under the garden ornament, more like!'

The car swept past the Green Man, an old roadside pub set beside fields on the edge of a woody area, the car park packed with exotic and brightly painted motorcars, many in British racing green, though there were others in red, pale blue or even silver, and most bearing white roundels with bold, black numbers on their sides. Young men in fur-lined pilots' jackets leant against their vehicles, smoking, drinking and chatting, some revving their engines; others tinkering beneath open bonnets. It was the first day of a big race meeting at Silverstone, the racetrack a short distance away down a narrow approach road, and so the racers were gathering good and early at their customary watering hole, the air around them filled with the smell of petrol and loud with burbling exhausts.

Ringham looked past Melcombe at the cars and noticed that his stylish two-seater drew some admiring glances. 'A little more candour would not have gone amiss.'

'I'm very grateful for your help, Barnaby. But I paid you well for services rendered, don't forget. I sold four of my finest to raise the necessary funds. My God, Barney, I even parted with an Ecu au Soleil of 1574 and that lovely Genoa Quadruple of 1617!'

Ringham snorted. He was not sounding suitably impressed.

'And don't forget I gave up my practice and moved away.' Melcombe continued his complaint. 'You cannot accuse me of not playing ball. And now you suggest that I killed her?'

'But you kept the real reason she died a secret. Naughty.'

'The ring was irrelevant to what happened. She fell awkwardly, as she was leaving…it was just a tragic accident.' Ringham narrowed his eyes and remained silent. 'Look, the ring was no darned use to her by then…why not keep it?' Melcombe was trying to edge himself closer to the passenger door, away from the trails of saliva dripping from the mouth of Hades, who in turn, was staring back with beady eyes and occasionally emitting a sound that Melcombe could feel resonating deep from within the Alsatian's chest. 'What does it matter now? What's done is done. God, how I wish I had never set eyes on it. I think that ring is cursed. It brings bad luck, I can sense it.' His voice was weak, he was tiring again and the enormity of the situation was starting to overwhelm him. 'I never spoke a word, not about her, nor about the work I did.'

Ringham was slowing the car. He swung it smoothly across the now-empty road and into a gravelly lay-by, where a black-and-yellow Automobile Association telephone box was set back into the grassy verge. It looked not unlike something a guard might stand within on sentry duty, but with the addition of a door. The car's signal indicator ticked loudly and made an orange light flash on the dashboard. There were tall stands of dank trees lining either side of the road, edged by a narrow, open area of rough, scrubby bushes and lank grass holding drifts of recently-fallen leaves. They could just detect a faint, distant growl of high-performance engines blazing in short, staccato bursts as the men burned scarce and valuable fuel in wasteful dips of the throttle. Though they were a few turns of the road away from the Green Man, it felt still and even strangely quiet in the lay-by, with just the gentle drip of water from the night rain plopping from the soggy trees. A clammy mist was curling around the dense regiments of trunks, weak sun skimming the tops, but barely penetrating the dark interior, lending the scene a mournful quality of soft, wet colours and muted sound.

'Is that so?' Ringham twisted in the seat to face Melcombe square-on. 'Before that burglary I might have been inclined to agree, old boy. Your discretion was a credit, and you were rewarded accordingly.' He gave Melcombe a steely look. 'The scandal would be incalculable if word got out.' His voice hardened. 'Don't forget, some of those girls are dashed well connected; one was minor royalty. It was not our job to comment on their loose morals and apparent inability to keep themselves out of trouble. Our job was to fix the situation in which they had carelessly found themselves, and to keep silent.'

'I know all this. I don't need a bloody lecture, thank you!'

'Does no harm to reinforce the point. There could be far-reaching effects. The gutter press would have a field day. One slip up, one leak that you'd helped Lady This or Dowager What's-Her-Name lose an illegitimate child, and you can just imagine the reaction. An absolute rout.'

'Change the record. Nobody has heard a thing from me!'

'You say that, but these last days I've wondered how that idiot Irons knew to enter your house and find the ring? A ring you kept so quiet that even I knew nothing about it until you asked me to recover it. Strange, don't you think? And don't fob me off about your beloved coins. He wasn't after those, and you know it. You let the cat out of the bag. How else could he know? So I need a name, a time, the place you let your defence down. It's confession time Percy, old boy.' Hades now growled with an alarming sense of timing.

'I don't know. He must have stumbled on it by accident.' Melcombe's voice was weak and hoarse and there was perspiration on his brow.

'You're not convincing me. And you look scared to death. What's got into you? You're acting like you've lost something; you're fidgeting like you've got fleas. What is it?'

Melcombe looked ashen, and stopped rootling for the umpteenth time in the pockets of his tweed jacket. 'Er... There is something, actually. I must have dropped it when getting dressed. Look, I think we must go back, we must find it. I rather fear it could be significant.'

CHAPTER FORTY
Brackley
28th September 1950

The Merry Chemist was run by a Mrs Merry and Vignoles concluded, after only the briefest of encounters, that whilst she may have chosen her husband for all manner of reasons unknown to himself, the fact that she would adopt his appropriately cheerful surname may just have swung the balance. Certainly everything about her radiated a sense of contentment, from her apple-red cheeks, creased by an open smile across a rotund face, to her broad, bare arms folded across a vast bosom encased in a white cotton short-sleeved coat and bright floral printed dress that heaved and flowed with her laughter at any opportunity. Even the tight bun, held in place by two hairpins that could cause considerable damage if used as a weapon, did nothing to diminish her pleasant demeanour.

Her bright clothes and personality were much needed within the dark and claustrophobic interior of the chemist. The shop was part of a short row that included the Oak Cottage Café and all were ancient structures of local stone with sagging rooflines and dropped window arches. The row was leaning more than standing along one edge of the small town square presenting a most decrepit feel to an area dominated by the elegant, Christopher Wren-styled town hall and the collegiate aura of Magdalen College School.

The Merry Chemist's window was bowed and multi-paned, with some of the glass rippled and distorted, betraying its antiquity. The door required a hard shoulder-shove to release it from its frame, which was skewed out of true. Inside, the walls were lined from floor to ceiling by dark wooden shelves jam-packed with packets and packages new and faded, with bottles both dusty and clean, and of glass, clear and coloured, containing strange liquids identified by rectangular, blue-edged labels. There were rows of tinctures, oils, lotions and tubes of embrocation, ointment and toothpaste. Curled cardboard adverts for Dreene Shampoo and Calvex Carbolic Compound cluttered the glass-topped counter and whole areas of shelving were stacked with medicines and pills and rolls of bandages and emergency slings in sealed packets. It smelt of Fiery Jack and menthol, of dust and brown paper and powerful cough drops. Vignoles wondered if he would live a longer and healthier life just by inhaling this heady mix, but after an exploratory lungful or two, decided he longed for fresh air and his pipe.

Maud Askew, perhaps in contrast to Mrs Merry, was looking smaller than he remembered. She appeared somehow diminished in height and character, a slight and shrunken figure in her overcoat and almost overwhelmed by the dark shelves laden with medicinal products. She hovered near a low doorway, but managed a little smile before dropping her gaze to the floor. After Mrs Merry had cheerfully greeted the two detectives and asked how she might help, Mrs Askew stepped forward and quietly attracted her boss's attention.

'This is the gentleman I told you would call this morning. Inspector Vignoles, wasn't it?' she looked at him enquiringly and, receiving a nod in confirmation, continued, 'and this is Sergeant—er—'

'—Trinder, ma'am.' He lifted his hat.

Vignoles showed his warrant card to Mrs Merry.

'An inspector calls!' Mrs Merry gave a conspiratorial smile, but then immediately attempted to look grave. 'You may use the back room. I do so hope you have news... I can hold the fort here, and you take as long as you need, Maud.'

Mrs Askew gave her employer a brief look that was difficult to interpret, then lifted up a hinged section of the counter and invited the men to follow her. As Trinder passed Mrs Merry she touched his arm and whispered to him urgently, 'She needs you to find her. Just *find* her!'

The back room was tiny. Vignoles squeezed himself behind a careworn table that betrayed a lifetime of smoothing by continual scrubbing. He shifted a carton of St James's Balm to give him more elbow room, whilst Maud Askew perched on a straight-backed chair. Trinder elected to stand, and he leant against a Welsh dresser crammed with yet more packets and boxes and piles of bills and receipts skewered onto tall, metal spikes.

'Would you like some tea?' Maud Askew held up a teapot encased in a knitted cosy.

'No, thank you. We should not keep you longer than is absolutely necessary.' Vignoles had eyed the lethal-looking gas ring in the corner and was pleased to have a valid excuse to prevent the three of them having to shuffle positions and share the space with an open flame. 'You wished to speak with me?'

'Yes. I want to confess something to you.' She glanced at Trinder.

'Please don't mind my sergeant; it is better to have two sets of ears in such an investigation.' Vignoles tried to be reassuring.

'Yes, of course, I meant no offence.' Trinder gave her a nod. 'You must take notes, of course. Write it all down.' She looked flustered and pulled a handkerchief from her sleeve and gave her nose a blow. 'I didn't want to say anything in front of Henry. He's a good man at heart, but he'd take it the wrong way.' She fiddled with the lid of the teapot. 'He's a practical man. Down to earth, like Betty, really.' She smiled fondly. 'He likes things in black and white does Henry, so he would only tell me to stop talking silly nonsense. There's no room for ambi...ambig-you...'

'Ambiguity?'

'Yes, that's it. No room for any of that in his world.' She smiled sadly. 'I hope you understand. You do need to know this.'

'Any information is vital. Detective work rather depends on facts, demonstrable facts, but we are open minded and willing to listen to anything you have to say...' Vignoles was curious. Was this to be a vital revelation or a wild goose chase? He could not imagine where it was leading.

'That's true...' Mrs Askew looked nonplussed as she considered Vignoles's response. 'You may find what I am about to tell you hard to believe. You might dismiss it and tell me my nerves are frayed, that I need a dose of that Vimaltol.' She pointed to a cardboard box near Trinder's right elbow. 'But I can assure you I am perfectly clear-headed and would swear on the bible this happened.'

Vignoles made a gesture with his hands. 'Understood...'

'You will remember that my Henry mentioned a note Betty had in the ring box, but which she left behind on her dressing table.'

'And which subsequently went missing.'

'Yes. Well I can tell you when and how it went. I didn't accidentally throw it away. It was far too precious for that to happen.'

'I can appreciate that.'

'But what could I tell Henry?' She dropped the teapot lid on the table and hurriedly replaced it, before folding her arms tight, the hankie balled in one fist. 'Sorry! It's just so upsetting. Right, I have composed myself now. It was ten days ago, on the eighteenth. There's no possibility I would forget. I can tell you what time, as well. It was 4.30p.m., because we have a half-day and I was home by then, after queuing at the butcher's and got us a bit of brisket for the evening meal and then managed to get a tin of Bird's Custard Powder. I was nervous the whole time I was queuing because there was the most dreadful storm brewing. It was so close, all sticky and oppressive. It made me feel headachy and I was glad to be home and not still out when the heavens opened. Anyway, I had this tin of custard powder and was feeling really pleased with myself as I'd collected some blackberries the evening before, and with a couple of cooking apples I thought to make a nice crumble. I'm only telling you all this because I want you to appreciate that I can remember everything very clearly. Accurately.' She nodded at Trinder, who had started making notes but had left his pencil hovering above the page the moment she started discussing her meal options. 'So there I was in the kitchen with the door open into the hallway having just putting the shopping away and thinking to start making the crumble.'

She stopped, dabbing her nose gently and gathering herself for the next stage. Vignoles nodded indulgently, urging her to get to the point.

'Well, I had my back to the hall, rootling out a suitable dish for the crumble and so, there I was, head in a cupboard, when I got the most strange sensation. I felt so cold it made me shiver all over. I was almost convulsing with the shakes and my teeth were chattering. When you catch a chill it usually starts with sneezing, or your throat, doesn't it?'

Vignoles inclined his head in agreement. Where was this going? He was starting to regret leaving the search of Melcombe's cottage to the constabulary and was wondering if he ought to get back.

'This was more like an icy finger down my spine and such a contrast to the clamminess of the day, it being so oppressive with that storm. I was unable to do anything but hug myself to try and stop the shivers. But then I realised someone was looking at me.'

Trinder pulled himself upright and Vignoles took a sharp intake of breath.

'I was staring at the back of the cupboard and I thought, someone's come in and they've left the door open making a draught. Maybe that's why I'm so cold. But they're up to no good, creeping up on me like that. So I picked up the rolling pin and I turned around and stood up so fast. I'm not having someone come into my house uninvited. I'll give 'em what for!' She nodded to reinforce the point and held Vignoles's attention. 'I was not prepared for who was there.

Jesus, Mary and the saints preserve me, I swear, I swear on my life, she was there. Just standing in the doorway and looking at me, as close as the sergeant is to me now. Oh, I nearly died of fright!' She pressed the handkerchief to her mouth, her knuckles whitening with the pressure, her eyes brimming.

'Who was there?' Vignoles asked.

'Betty! My daughter. Just looking at me.'

Silence fell in the room, allowing the sound of the shop bell to ring softly from behind the closed connecting door. Mrs Askew kept the handkerchief tight against her mouth, her expression that of someone fighting to keep their emotions under control.

Vignoles face lit up. 'What wonderful news! You and Mr Askew must be so relieved. Whatever difficulties she may have got herself into, the most important thing is that she's—'

'—Stop! Stop!' Maud Askew waved a raised hand like a drunken traffic policeman and blew her nose, gulping in air. 'No. She's not alive. It was not the flesh and blood Betty I saw.' She sobbed and clawed for more air as Vignoles and Trinder watched in stunned silence. She regained her composure and after one last sniff, spoke in a quiet — if slightly shaky — voice. 'It was her spirit, inspector. She was hardly there and at moments she was almost see-through, at other moments as clear as you are here. But it was Betty. She came back.' There was a conviction in Maud Askew's voice that could not be ignored.

Vignoles glanced up at Trinder, who had a look of astonishment on his face that was almost comical. Vignoles managed to hide any emotion by resorting to the old standby of removing his glasses and polishing them, frowning as he did so. 'You saw the ghost of your daughter standing in the kitchen doorway,' he recapped.

'There, I knew you would believe me, inspector.' Mrs Askew looked as though a burden had suddenly lifted. Her face started to regain some colour and her shoulders visibly relaxed. 'I cannot tell you what comfort I gain from sharing this, and especially as you are the police. That means a lot. She came to see me, to let me know she'd not forgotten us, that we were uppermost in her thoughts.' She gave a strange, faraway look. 'At first it upset me and I was disturbed and frightened. It knocked me sideways. But then you came around asking questions and I knew that something was happening, that things would work out.' Mrs Askew made a sad little half-smile. 'Something terrible happened to her. I know that now. I realise now that I always thought so, but you don't want to give up hope, do you?'

'No.' Vignoles swallowed with difficulty. Trinder shifted his weight onto his other foot.

'She's lost to us in this world, but I know that soon you will find her, find her cold bones, and she can be laid to rest. And I can't really ask more than that, not now. You will find her and we can place her in the same grave that... that one day I hope we can also lay poor Ray's body in.'

Vignoles was trying to keep his voice level. 'Did she say anything to you?'

'No, but she showed me something. Her hands were cupped as though she were at the communion rail.' Mrs Askew demonstrated the action. 'And in her hands was that little note, the one from her dressing table. I saw it as clear as day, then she clasped it tight in one fist and asked me to forgive her.' Askew dabbed her nose and took a deep breath. 'Now I get a bit confused, what with all the emotion and the shock... but I think I ran towards her, just wanting to hold her, hug her; but she said, "No! Please stop!" Oh, and she looked so pained, so distressed, that I did stop — though all of me so wanted to hold her.' She then smiled, a fond, warm affectionate smile that surprised the two detectives. 'She looked me in the eye and said, "I must go. I cannot hold on any longer. I must, but I need this — it will help explain everything. Forgive me! Help me rest..." And then, inspector, she vanished. Just faded away, like steam clears from a window.'

'What on earth am I to make of that?' Vignoles took a long sip of beer and wiped his mouth. 'It's a touch early for a pint, but quite frankly I need something stronger than milky coffee right now.' They were seated on one of a number of benches outside the Red Lion, just out of view of the Merry Chemist, as a welcome gap in the clouds allowed the surprisingly strong sunlight to dry the ground around the market place and warm their backs.

'I didn't see that coming,' Trinder agreed. 'It makes you wonder, though.' Vignoles eyed him suspiciously. 'After all, that

Irons fellow was adamant he'd met the ghost of Betty, and now her own mother is saying the same thing.'

'We cannot dismiss there have been sightings of the woman herself or a look-a-like, but a ghost? Come off it, John!' Vignoles sounded contemptuous and Trinder remained silent whilst they sipped more ale. 'You're saying a ghost took that little note from the girl's bedroom?'

'You heard what the mother said.'

'She was, but despite her reassurances to the contrary, she was also emotional and upset. All that's happened these last days has reawakened the loss of her daughter. It could be a mixture of hallucination and guilt over losing the piece of paper that's making her imagine this.' Vignoles stared into his beer. 'I don't want to sound hard on her but, being charitable, we still need to overlook the improbable physical difficulties involved for a spirit-being to handle a real piece of paper, let alone understand why the ghost of Betty Askew would do that.' A wasp danced around the top of his glass and he flapped at it with a hand. 'OK, let's review where we are in the case. We're waiting on a firm ID on the head, but early indications from the debris we found in the bonfire and the fact that it is the head of a young woman with the correct hair colour indicate this is likely to be Betty Askew.'

'Agreed.' Trinder nodded, also wafting a wasp away.

'The hand found adjacent to Brackley Viaduct could well be that of a young woman. We await further analysis, but I am not expecting much. There's a limit on what they can they determine from some long-cleaned bones.'

'There is still a possibility they could be Betty's.'

'Based on what evidence? Simply that they were found not far from where Dr Melcombe currently lives. A far-fetched premise, and even if it were true we'd still be shot down in flames presenting that as evidence.'

'True...' Trinder looked crestfallen. 'It is more a gut feeling than anything else, but I still think we're on the right track, literally. The railway line links the two locations and the doctor moved here soon after Betty disappeared, upping sticks in a hurry. Look, what if the hands were thrown out of the window of a moving train? I could imagine he was aiming for the river. It was a decent attempt to conceal body parts that might help identify the body whilst still covered in flesh, but now, picked clean and with no body attached, they are virtually impossible to identify with any certainty.' Trinder looked pleased with his hypothesis and drank some ale.

'It's a decent theory. The trouble is, that's all it is, and all but useless for building a case against him. I think we're right to identify Melcombe as prime suspect in this heinous crime, but so far we don't have a darned thing that will stick.'

'But her head was buried in his garden! In a box that can be clearly linked to him.'

'And his defence will say he was out of the house at the time and knew nothing about it. The box was presumably close to hand and used by whoever committed the crime. Unless the lab boys can find his fingerprints, preferably bloody ones, we may struggle to prove he actually put her in there. It sounds plausible, even probable, but is it enough to convict him of murder? We need something that literally places his hands on her remains...and we need a body as well. However, we've got the Bucks Constabulary stripping Dr Melcombe's former home down to the floorboards and the Northants chaps doing the same in Ivy Cottage. Let's hope we find the other remains of that poor woman or some clue to her whereabouts. So far we've got nothing more than suspicions...oh drat these wasps!' Vignoles narrowly avoided swallowing one crawling along the top of his glass.

'They're dozy in the autumn.' Trinder was observing the next table, where over-attentive wasps were causing a similar problem. He then shook some coins from his pocket and selected three half pennies. He laid them out carefully in a triangular shape. Vignoles observed him with a puzzled expression, but held his tongue. Trinder continued discussing the case as if they were not there. 'We have nothing conclusive to prove he is a killer, and cannot arrest him.'

'Don't forget, he was laid up in hospital when Irons was killed,' Vignoles replied. 'If he was involved, then it was at arm's length. Someone else did the deed. Someone with a dog.'

'An assassination?'

Vignoles winced. 'Hmm, put like that, it sounds far-fetched, but Melcombe could have paid someone to do it. Or Melcombe has an accomplice, the two working as a team.'

'The man with the vicious dog.' Trinder nodded in agreement. 'What strikes me is that there is always someone else, unknown or unseen, lurking nearby.'

'What do you mean, John?'

'I went to see *The Third Man* again last week, I went with Violet. She needed a few of hours rest from looking after the little lad, so Jenny came over to babysit and we went to the pictures. Only up the road and just for an hour and half or so, and a swift drink in the White Hart after. You know the film?'

'Of course, I've also seen it, twice!'

Trinder grinned. 'Well, you know that the Joseph Cotten character thinks Harry Lime is dead, and is working on that assumption for much of the film, but things only start to make sense once he realises that Lime is actually alive and kicking? Well, until we identify Melcombe's accomplice, if he has one, we can't make a breakthrough here. It's as though this other person is the more important player in this drama. And it's the same with Irons. We've been looking for his accomplice and failing to find her. It's as though there is a third man — or third woman — just outside the frame in both cases.'

Vignoles started to fill his pipe as he considered this observation. He looked intrigued. 'Go on...'

'Now don't shoot me down on this, but I think the key is the ghost of Betty Askew—'

'—John, really!' Vignoles groaned in exasperation.

'Bear with me, sir, just indulge me for a few seconds', replied Trinder, 'she knows what really happened in Melcombe's surgery, who dismembered her body and where the parts are now concealed; and she — the ghost, that is — also convinced Irons to break into the murderer's house and do... something. I don't know what.' Trinder looked apologetic. 'But he was disturbed whilst doing whatever it was, and so the plan went wrong.' Trinder held up a hand to stop Vignoles speaking. 'Please just hear me out, guv — er, sorry, I mean sir. Betty's ghost also went to her parent's house the day of the break in and took something that potentially could incriminate Melcombe. Did she show this to Irons? I'm not sure what happened between them, but she did something that convinced him to turn into a burglar.' He paused and was encouraged by Vignoles's silence. 'It also struck me that this was a curious detail for Mrs Askew to invent or imagine. So, like Harry Lime, has Betty somehow risen from the dead? I don't know... But she's there all right, deep inside this mystery.'

'I cannot disagree with the last part of your argument, but as for the rest...' He tilted his head sideways and frowned sceptically.

'Yes, yes, sir, but stick with me. I think she gave the note to Irons. I'm not sure why, but finding both ring and note is vital. The ring is a possible motivation for Melcombe's killing Askew. If he is found with it, surely this proves he took it in 1943 when she was at his surgery.'

Vignoles exhaled long and slow, blowing air from between his lips so they made a sound. 'Or he bought it from a dealer in the intervening years. But I agree, it suggests he had contact with her and will help our case. Going back to your hypothesis, I can appreciate that, if Melcombe killed her for the Cobra's Eye, he would be shocked to discover something that related directly to this ring appearing in his new house, like a warning. Telling him that someone else knows his guilty secret. But how on earth can a shadowy imprint of a long-dead person do all this?' Vignoles looked stumped. 'Is she supposed to be befriending young men and travelling on trains whilst carrying pieces of paper?'

Trinder shrugged his shoulders. 'It's like these coins. They drive the wasps away. I cannot explain how or why, all I know is it works.'

'What?' Vignoles drained his glass and stared at Trinder.

'Have you noticed they've all gone? The wasps.'

'That's just coincidence!' However Vignoles noticed the wasps were still pestering a couple at the next table. The woman had resorted to standing up and waving her arms at an especially intrusive insect in a manner likely to get her stung.

Trinder stood up, walked across to their table and had a brief conversation with them. At first they looked puzzled, then both laughed. The man jingled some coins into his hand and selected three as Trinder returned with an empty jam pot, the last remnant of the jam, scones and cream they had been eating, three big ugly wasps crawling over the traces of raspberry jam left inside. He carefully placed this unappetising receptacle inside the triangle of copper coins and sat down. 'Watch this!'

'John, if your little experiment works,' a wasp flew into the air, angrily circling like a noisy fighter plane, then flew off on a wobbly flight path, 'I might *just* countenance your crazy theory.'

Trinder grinned. The other two insects soon followed, and there was a shout from the couple nearby. 'I say? It bally well worked, can you believe that? Thanks awfully!' Trinder touched the brim of his hat. 'Remember, only copper coins!'

Vignoles looked flabbergasted. 'Of course it really could just be coincidence...'

'I agree. But we are free of them and that's all that matters. My grandmother taught me how to scare wasps like this and it's served me well. Look sir, you always tell me to work on facts, and the fact is this works. I can't tell you how or why, just as I cannot explain the ghost of Betty Askew, and won't try to. But the facts of the case suggest that she, though dead, still has an active part to play and I think we need to follow that trail.'

Vignoles was toying with his empty glass, in the act of convincing himself that another beer was not a good idea and should return to Ivy Cottage to see how the house search was progressing. 'And how on earth to I tell Badger all that?'

'Perhaps keep it under our hats until we get something more definite. We could explore this angle quietly, not shout about it like those adventure-seekers on the late train. I admit we could be literally chasing shadows.'

'Low key...yes, that has something to recommend it,' Vignoles shook his head in disbelief. 'Can you find me something tangible? Something physical we can bring to bear against that doctor?'

Their attention was drawn to the sound of a black Wolseley approaching at speed. They saw DI Bainbridge in the passenger seat, a uniformed officer wearing a flat cap behind the wheel, both men evidently searching for someone. Bainbridge glanced in their direction and signalled urgently to Vignoles and Trinder as the car swung into the market place, the unlit blue lamp flashing bright as it was struck by a shaft of sunlight.

'Something is wrong,' and both Vignoles and Trinder stood up and walked towards the car as it screeched to a halt. Bainbridge was speaking through the opened window before the car had stopped.

'Troubling news, Charles: Melcombe has gone! Discharged himself a little over half an hour ago. He was collected by his lawyer, of all people. A smooth-talker, apparently, who was trying to buy matron's silence with a ten shilling note, but she was sufficiently annoyed by his arrogant attitude to call us.'

'She was not to know Melcombe was a murder suspect.' Vignoles looked grim. 'They left by car? Any details?'

'Yes, and that's the better news. A very distinctive vehicle; a two-seater, soft-top, all white, Armstrong Siddeley *Hurricane*. White and chrome wheels and red leather seats.'

'Phew...' Trinder whistled softly. 'Very flash.'

'We have the licence plate. It will stand out like a sore thumb.' Bainbridge tried to look optimistic.

'But half an hour's start... Which direction did they go? No matter, they can easily lose themselves and double-back along innumerable country roads.' Vignoles balled a fist and tapped it gently on his palm, thinking hard.

'There's more.' Bainbridge stepped out of the car. 'There was a dog, a big black-and-tan fellah seated on the excuse for a back seat in these sports cars.'

Vignoles and Trinder exchanged looks. 'Interesting. Do we know who the lawyer is?' Vignoles was impatient to get moving but this needed consideration.

'Wait, I think PC Blencowe found a name...' Trinder was flipping through his little black notebook. 'Yes, got it! Mr Barnaby Ringham. Has a Belgravia address.' They exchanged meaningful looks. 'Apparently he's awfully expensive and with a reputation for winning unwinnable cases for the rich and powerful. According to PC Blencowe, anyway.'

'He might prove a powerful ally for Melcombe,' Vignoles observed.

'We have a clear description of this chap from matron and he sounds like the same man. His clothes were immaculate and probably bespoke and apparently he wore a watch that looked like it cost a fortune.' Bainbridge gave Trinder an approving glance. 'Good work in getting a name, sergeant.'

'But undone by my not placing a guard on his room. I slipped up.' Vignoles looked grim. 'I didn't want to appear heavy-handed at this stage and considering his physical condition did not envisage him doing a runner. The hospital could not force him to stay, so the fault lies at my door.'

'Ringham was very persuasive. But look, there's something else you might be able to shed some light on. Melcombe's room was empty of his things as you'd expect, except a nurse found this under the bed...' Bainbridge handed Vignoles a tiny ball of paper. It was soft and the paper betrayed signs of excessive handling. The three men gathered around as Vignoles teased it open.

'It's a curious message...' Bainbridge sounded puzzled.

'I could almost believe in coincidences now.' Vignoles allowed a little smile of satisfaction.

'It has to be what was taken from Betty's dressing table! I have the text written in my notebook… just a moment…' The ever-efficient Trinder riffled through the pages. 'It was dictated to us by Mrs Askew.'

'The same,' Vignoles was already convinced. 'Written by Private Coulson to go with the engagement ring he presented to Betty.'

Bainbridge peered at the square of paper again and shook his head. 'You have the advantage of me here, Charles.'

'We can confirm its authenticity in a trice.' Trinder nodded his head in the direction of the Merry Chemist.

'Do so! But quickly.' Vignoles took a last look before handing it to his sergeant, who instantly strode off towards the wonky apothecary building. 'Perhaps Irons left this in Ivy Cottage. But could Betty Askew really have given this to him?'

'You've really lost me, Charles.'

'Sorry, I'll explain later, but right now we need to apprehend Melcombe and Ringham. George, we must pull out all the stops and find them! As soon as my sergeant returns, would you be good enough to let us have use of your police station? We can mobilize a search operation and I can get word across the railway system to watch out for them boarding a train.'

'But they left by car, remember?' Bainbridge looked puzzled.

'We can hardly set up road blocks as we have no idea in which direction they are headed, it would be futile. But if their car is as eye-catching as you describe then they will have to abandon it sooner or later and choose another mode of transport. My hunch is, they'll park up at a station and take a train. It's not only faster but less noticeable, and they'd blend in with the other passengers. Either that or they have a bolt-hole nearby and will run to ground for a while.' Vignoles was holding his unlit pipe, a sure sign that he was pontificating.

'I think you're right. Gosh, we're really up against it now!'

'We shall find them. It's only a matter of time. Their breaking cover has worked to our advantage, in some respects. Innocent men don't go on the run.' He watched as Trinder strode purposefully back towards them, the diminutive figure of Maud Askew in the chemist shop doorway, a hand pressed to her mouth. Mrs Merry joined her, a robust arm encircling her narrow shoulders that were now visibly shaking.

'Go back? Out of the question, old boy.'

'It's a tiny thing from inside the box that holds the ring. It would fit perfectly. It just has to be from there. It even names the diamond!'

'It has a name?'

'Yes, the Cobra's Eye. An odd one. When a stone is that valuable there's a penchant for giving it a flamboyant title.'

'*The Star of India…*' Ringham was nodding his head.

'Exactly. The paper is exactly the same size as the box when folded. But listen, I'd never seen this before, not until after Irons robbed me. This is important! She did not have it in the box, nor on her person back then. Do you understand what I am saying? It was left in place of the ring, in the same drawer where I kept it. Irons must have put it there!' Melcombe was starting to sound frantic.

'Are you quite sure?'

'Of course I'm bloody sure!' Melcombe's frightened expression convinced Ringham.

'What did it say?'

'Just the name of the ring, a date and the initials of Betty Askew and Raymond Coulson.'

'Who's the Coulson chappie?'

'Her fiancé. She told me about him. She claimed he'd given her this ring for their engagement. I was surprised, perhaps rather sceptical and insulting about the fellow, but the note confirms it. He was killed in El Alamein.'

'You are remarkably well informed.'

Melcombe's eyes were wide, his breath coming in short inhalations that seemed to give him pain. Glancing briefly at the dog that had now stopped emitting threatening sounds but was observing both men intently, the doctor leant forward and gripped Ringham's forearm. 'Believe me, there's something very wrong here. Coulson and Askew were both from Brackley!'

'What?'

'I swear I did not know before I moved. What ill fate brought me here? What made me choose this, of all places? I don't want to know anything about her, let alone walk around her home town! I tried to forget everything, to banish her name from my memory. We burnt her belongings and I was glad we did so, and I made a point of not looking at her address or anything that would remind me she was someone's daughter, someone's fiancée. I just didn't want to know! It was too horrible, too awful to see her as a real, living person...'

'Get a grip, man. Calm down and explain. And cut the emotional stuff.' But even Ringham's *sang froid* was starting to slip, his voice now less forceful, less confident. His eyes were continually distracted by a number of rooks that had launched themselves into the air from the treetops in a squalling, cawing, ragged explosion. They circled above the road like vultures looking for carrion. He freed his arm and reached into his suit to extract a silver case, chased with a monogrammed design on the lid. He flipped it open to reveal a gold interior, then extracted two cigarettes as Melcombe continued his story. The doctor's voice was little more than a hoarse mumble.

'I moved to Turweston because it looked like a quiet, respectable sort of village. Filled with well-to-do types, most of whom were in retirement, like me. Nobody was going to question my being there, no one would ask impertinent questions. The perfect place to keep my head down, maybe do some fishing and live a quiet life...as we agreed.' Melcombe gratefully accepted the proffered cigarette. 'But only then, only after I had given everything up, did I discover that I'm living right in the eye of the storm! Her name was everywhere. Brackley is only a small place and so her disappearance was big news. There were posters with her face plastered all over town. I've even seen her parents beside the grave of that Coulson fellow. Slowly, I started to hear bits and pieces of the story and to make the connections.' His hand shook that was holding the cigarette. 'It's been a living nightmare, a daily penance. And then a man breaks into my house and he not only takes the ring, but he leaves this damned message. It's a warning! Someone knows everything.'

'Yes...' Ringham's matching silver lighter flared as he held the flame for Melcombe to light his cigarette. 'Yes, that would be most unfortunate.'

'Unfortunate? It's more than *unfortunate*.' Melcombe wound the window down and puffed a jet of smoke outside. 'Is that all you can say? That inspector what's-his-name, the one who came visiting, well let me tell you something about him: he's rumbled us.'

'What do you mean?'

'He's found her. Well, part of her.' He glared at Ringham. 'But you'll know all about that! He's found her head buried in what was once my back garden. Christ almighty.' Melcombe puffed angrily, making sharp sounds. 'And if that was not bad enough, it was in a box that once held a pair of scales that can be traced right back to me. What were you thinking of? I'm done for.'

'I'd not heard they'd found her...' Ringham was smoking slowly, exhaling through the side of his mouth, eyes narrowed to slits, an elbow resting on the top of the car door, trying to exude an air of supreme confidence. He stared into the misty woods and contemplated this revelation.

'But in the garden? How could you be so bloody stupid? We agreed to take her off somewhere. I trusted you to do that, Barnaby.'

Ringham was silent for a moment, flicking ash onto the ground. He stopped the flashing indicator and the sounds within the car were replaced by the cawing of the wheeling birds, the panting of his dog and the slight burning sound of the two cigarettes as the men pulled hard making the tobacco flare and crackle.

'Sit, Hades!' Even Ringham was finding his beast annoying and the powerful dog reluctantly slunk back on the tiny rear bench seat. 'Let me explain. You'd taken the trunk to London, and seeing the taxi convey you to the station with that monstrous cargo was a relief. But I was tired, and starting to feel the strain, to be honest. Yes, I can feel it too. There was a lot still to do, all the evidence to burn and that horrible mess to clean up, all the blood to wash and bleach away. I knew we must have the bonfire and get the embers dampened down before nightfall or we'd have the ARP banging on the door.' He sucked on the fag. 'Time was running short.'

'It was a nightmare. But darn it, we did a decent job under the circumstances.' Melcombe was reflective, his energy spent. 'But the woods were so close. A few hundred yards away, no more. You said you'd bury it there...'

'I knew we should remove her from the garden, but the most important thing was nobody on your road should suspect a thing. If nobody saw her arrive or suspected she had been there, we could draw a veil across the whole affair. But if we put a foot wrong, we'd be finished. I'd parked the motor some distance away and walked to your house, making darned sure nobody saw me; but as soon as you'd gone to the station the blessed street became a hive of activity: first the baker's van, then the butcher's, although I'm damned if I know what they were selling. Whatever scrag-ends of meat he was peddling, it brought your neighbours out, and then, just as I thought it had quietened down, a bunch of boy scouts came around with a hand cart collecting junk for a Spitfire fund. I couldn't risk walking out of your house. It only took one person to see me carrying a large box and we could be in tight spot. So I thought it better to bury it in the garden, just heave that monstrous birdbath thing on top and get her belongings burnt.' He drew long and hard on his fag. 'I wanted all trace of her destroyed, everything put back in order by the time you returned. By not telling you, I thought it would make it easier for you to live there until you moved away.'

'I suppose I can see that... I just thought her boots and a few non-flammable things were under the birdbath. '

'No, the big stuff went to the boy scouts. I nipped out and left a bundle by the gate whilst they were occupied at another house. I hardly need point out that I was especially careful not to be observed. I don't believe they stopped to question why they were there, just gladly hauled the lot away. It was untraceable.'

'At least that makes us equal.' Melcombe's breathing was laboured.

'How so?'

'I concealed the existence of the Cobra's Eye and you lied about what was buried in the back garden.' Melcombe forced a weak smile of triumph. Privately, Melcombe felt an odd surge of relief.

He'd called Ringham almost immediately he'd realised that Betty Askew was dead. He was desperate for help. He knew he could never hope to conceal the death and remove all traces of her on his own, and so had called 'Mr Fix It,' as Barney Ringham was known to his friends and colleagues. He'd responded immediately and with a chilling coolness that was both a balm to the doctor's frazzled nerves, and yet had also frightened him. Ringham appeared quite unmoved by the situation and able to plan and plot the grisly distribution of her body parts as though planning nothing more taxing than a vicarage tea party. Melcombe had even wondered if this were a task he'd performed before. That thought was disturbing and set a little alarm bell ringing in his mind.

As they were completing the appalling task of butchering her body, Melcombe had felt the compulsion to do something he had never fully understood at the time, but which now seemed to make more sense. As Ringham left the cold washroom to find the rubberized gas cape they would use to wrap the torso within, the doctor had swiftly deployed a sharp scalpel and sliced off one of the monogrammed buttons from Ringham's blazer, which he had left carefully draped across a chair back, away from the blood and gore. He'd slipped this distinctive and specially-commissioned button into a neat slit cut with the same scalpel into the layers of varnished paper pasted on the inside of the trunk, having first smeared it with the blood of the mutilated hunk of meat that once had been a young woman. A little calling card, and one that he felt offered him some protection, although he knew it was dreadfully risky to leave any clue that could be traced to either of them. It was perhaps reckless, but it placed Ringham right there, incriminated, without a shadow of doubt. The button might well ensure that his friend would keep on protecting him, continue to keep him safe and do anything to maintain this deadly secret. It was just a case of deciding when he should play his ace and tell Ringham.

For his part, Ringham knew nothing of Melcombe's thoughts and nodded, almost imperceptibly. He might concede the point that they were equal, but was not ready to voice it aloud.

Hades suddenly sat upright, pressing his snout to the small rear window, the hackles rising down his back like a ridge of dark trees. A deep growl, throaty and anxious, filled the car with an ominous rumble. His front paws shifted in small, rapid movements on the smooth leather, and his big head swung from side to side as he tried to gain a better view.

'What the devil's got into you?' Ringham twisted in his seat to try and look at his dog, which was clearly upset about something outside. The growling was continuing, but now frequently interrupted by a thin, whining note that betrayed fear, accompanied by the flashing of the whites of his rolling eyes.

'Stop that!' Ringham thrashed an arm at the dog's haunches, but Hades just redoubled his efforts, pawing frantically at the window, claws scratching at the glass. At that moment the dog realised this was futile and tried to force his big head over the seat, between his master and the door frame, and so out of the opened window. 'What the hell's got into you? Get down!' Ringham looked flustered and angry.

'Look, there's someone in the woods,' Melcombe pointed, his hand trembling. 'It looks like a young woman in a white...' He was peering through his spectacles, his jaw now gaping. 'No... but that's impossible...' Melcombe wiped a drop of perspiration from his forehead and blinked.

The dog was now forcing his great bulk onto the shoulder of Ringham, the horrible growling and whimpering filling the tiny cockpit.

'Get off me!' Ringham opened the driver's door and both he and the dog spilled out. Ringham almost bundled over, such was the frantic urge for Hades to give chase, barking furiously as he powered through the long, damp grass at an alarming speed and leaped across a narrow drainage ditch filled with black, stagnant water and rotting leaves.

'Come back! Heel!'

Melcombe eased himself out of his seat and painfully waddled around to the driver's side of the Armstrong Siddeley. 'You should control him. He's dangerous. God, I never liked that that dog!'

Ringham look worried. 'Come back! Here, boy!' He narrowed his eyes as his dog ignored the command. 'He's never done this before...'

They now started walking in the tracks of the dog, trying to see both the beast and the pale figure slipping easily between the wet tree trunks. She was elusive and moved surprisingly quickly. Hades had to repeatedly change tack, as though this was a deliberate teasing game on her part, his great head lifted high and snout sniffing noisily, interspersed by furious machine-gun bursts of barking and painful whimpering. But the pale woman was able to avoid being mauled with consummate ease. First she was in one place, then she suddenly vanished between the many green and grey trunks, only to re-appear far away on the other, the dog's rippling back brushing noisily through the brown, orange and pale yellow bracken. His feet pounded on the leaf-mould whilst the black birds maintained their cackling high above. Apart from these sounds, the wood felt unnervingly empty of life.

'He might hurt her, for God's sake. Call your dog back!' Melcombe's face was florid and flushed, but despite his obvious discomfort he lumbered after Ringham in painful, lurching strides. Ringham for his part had sensed impending trouble and was now chasing after his dog, drawing away from the slower and obviously ailing doctor.

Melcombe stopped, leaning heavily upon a tree, his hat in one hand and head hung low as he gasped for air. Unable to carry on, he watched Ringham slip out of sight. He had no breath left to call after him. The trampling feet grew quieter and the wood fell still.

Not even a squirrel to set a high branch swaying or a nuthatch darting up a trunk. He suddenly felt very alone, an overwhelming sense of emptiness dousing him like a cold shower that made him feel sick at heart. He was shivering and utterly miserable.

How had he come to this? A once-respected doctor, a man with nearly £600 in the bank, a valuable cottage bought with cash. A retired gentleman with a raft of investments in his portfolio, now standing in a gloomy copse of trees, aching from head to toe, his heart painful in his chest. It was pathetic. And he was frightened.

There was something dangerous in this wood, something silent and elusive. He sensed that it meant him harm. All he could see were dank trees quietly dripping rainwater onto leaf and ground, but, whatever it was, it was close, and sending out darts of pure malice towards him. He could feel it drilling into him, and he was petrified.

What was it about that pale figure that had induced him to leave the warmth and security of the car? Why had he not locked himself in and just sat tight? Or driven away. For some reason, he'd imagined that woman walking in the woods was that poor, dead girl. It was verging on madness. And why were they chasing after her? Oh, why couldn't Barney just catch his dumb dog and come back? The dog had dragged them here, of course, and yet he sensed Barney was not immune to the spell and he'd been pulled deeper into this unattractive place as though lured here. Melcombe noticed with gloominess that his feet were wet and becoming cold, and the bottoms of his trousers were damp. The back of one hand had been scratched by a thorn and was releasing a thin dribble of blood. He watched as a drop of scarlet dripped onto the yellow leaves.

He pulled himself upright and looked about. He could just see the white of the car and heard Hades whimpering in the distance. Why was that ugly brute so distressed? The sound was almost painful, and Melcombe derived no comfort from knowing they had a powerful dog close to hand to offer protection. But from what? A phantom?

The likeness had been striking: the pale mackintosh, the brown hair and the same style of hat. All night he had sensed her presence, felt her stalking about the cottage hospital, waiting outside his bedroom door, standing near the park wall on the street below, pushing the wardrobe door ajar and peering at him from the inky depths inside, and now here she was, luring them into this wood and delaying their escape. Why had Barney pulled over, why here, of all places, to talk?

There she was, beside their car. He stumbled towards her, legs quivering like jelly and almost refusing to work. 'Hey! Hey, you!' His voice fell flat and dead as though he were shouting into a pile of surgical lint. 'Wait there!' He was afraid, almost sick with apprehension, but he was also angry and tired. Enough of this madness, he wanted to confront her, whoever, whatever she was.

She looked up as he drew closer. When her eyes met his it was as though he'd been plunged into a bath of ice. His vision was playing tricks on him, perhaps because he was in such a state, making her appear one moment bright and clear then dull and faint, as though clouds were swiftly crossing the sky and she was first kissed by sunlight then cloaked by deep shadow in rapid succession. He reached the edge of the trees, and the wide verge of grasses that lay between them was a distance of only five or so yards.

There could be no mistake now. He could never forget that slightly funny, freckly face and those pale eyes. He recalled them looking at him, imploring him, he could hear her begging him to let go of her hand, to just take her money.

Betty Askew raised her left hand, the fingers slightly splayed. He could see the pale skin stretched taught over the small bones, her ring finger bare. She twisted and turned her hand to make this all the more obvious.

'Go away! Leave me alone!'

She stared back, her bloodless lips parting.

'What do you want from me? Did you send that man into my house?'

Betty raised her other arm, both hands now stretched towards him, reaching out with fingers so thin and delicate, like twigs on a tree in winter. There was no passing traffic on the road. Where were those men in their racing cars and the usual grinding noise of the heavy lorries that thundered past with annoying frequency? Melcombe was transfixed, unable to pull his eyes away from her and yet praying for a passing car or bus that might break the spell between them. But there was no relief, just the constant cawing of those blasted birds.

He clasped his hands to his heart and let out a cry of pain, eyes bulging in their sockets as her hands slowly dissolved into dust, pouring soundlessly to the ground to leave two vicious, red-raw stumps pointing accusingly at Melcombe. She laughed soundlessly. He fell forward, his vision now red with a bloody mist, no longer sure what was real or imagined, but he thought her head appeared to fade into nothing; an appalling headless, handless body that was left standing in mute testimony beside the two-seater.

'What the hell's the matter with you? Stop that infernal noise, you idiot!'

Ringham was shaking the doctor, and none too gently, trying to pull him up off his knees to his feet. 'Shut up!' He slapped the doctor's face then clamped his mouth closed to stop the hideous wailing he was emitting like a pig being inexpertly stuck in a backyard killing.

Melcombe looked at Ringham in surprise, as though he were only just aware he was there. 'It was her. It was her!'

'I've no idea who she was. She ran off and Hades came back.' Ringham clicked his fingers and the dog, tail between his legs but hackles still ruffled, slunk quietly and obediently through the open door and into the rear of the car. 'Wait there!' He slammed the door shut.

'It was the girl. She's come for us...'

'What are you on about? She disappeared somewhere over the far side of the wood. Who was that beside the car?'

Melcombe started to cough, his hands pressed to his chest. 'Oh...oh...'

'What's wrong? Look, take it easy, deep breaths. There's no one here.' Ringham glanced up and down the eerily empty road, suddenly deeply worried about the state of his colleague. 'Don't do this to me. Pull yourself together, man!' But Melcombe keeled over, his legs collapsing and mouth and eyes open in a horrible rigor of pain and terror.

'Don't die on me... Not here!' Ringham stared at the crumpled form on the ground and knew it was too late. 'You bloody fool.' He wiped his brow and closed his eyes for a moment, trying to think. It was his turn to take deep breaths. He opened his eyes again, scanned the area to check that there was nothing approaching, and then set to work.

Melcombe was a slim man, and Ringham had kept himself in trim playing tennis as often as he could manage and enjoying the occasional fencing lesson, so he found the dead weight reasonably easy to drag backwards through the undergrowth and beneath the great stand of trees. The wetness of the long grasses and the slippery clay underfoot aided the dragging of the body, but long fingers of wild rose and bramble tore at Ringham's trouser legs. His expensive, hand-made brogues struggled for purchase and he had to dig them deep into the sticky earth in order to pull the body into deeper cover, releasing a smell of mushrooms and rotting leaves as he did so.

There was no time to properly hide the corpse, so he just scooped armfuls of dead leaves and piled them on top. It was not a good job but it might evade detection for a few hours, if he were lucky. He sprinted back to the car, calculating how quickly he could drive to the station. He could hear Hades barking furiously in a yelping, frantic noise that made his blood run cold. What had got into the animal?

He stopped dead, face blanching. 'Flats!' He spoke aloud, staring in disbelief at the Hurricane, which was now sitting low to one side, the tyres completely airless. 'But how? When... it's impossible. No, no!'

He ran forward and knelt near the front tyre, eyes working frantically, pupils dilated in shock, trying to ignore the slavering jaws and big paws of his dog, now pressed to the inside of the glass, constantly barking. He could see the valve had been pulled right out of the tyre and tossed away, ensuring a complete and rapid deflation. These were not punctures, but a deliberate attack. Like pancakes and only one spare. He beat his fist on the mudguard repeatedly, causing Hades to bark even more anxiously.

'Stop! No use flying off the handle and losing one's head.' He spoke aloud, as though to his dog, who was now quiet as though exhausted and sensing something was wrong. Ringham opened the car door. 'Come, boy,' he called Hades out, but held him firm by the collar and hitched a strong leather leash retrieved from the glove compartment to this. ' Keep quiet! Time to hitch a lift.'

He looked at his mud-splattered clothes, at the dirty wetness on the knees of his trousers where he had knelt down, at the pulls and small tears from the brambles and his dishevelled shirt and tie. He took a moment to smarten up, then opened the car boot, grabbed the long overcoat lying across their two suitcases and shrugged it on. Once buttoned and belted he looked more like his usual dapper self. Still a ruddy disgrace, but I might just pass muster.

He hefted his leather case out of the boot and stared unhappily at Melcombe's. Grabbed it he slammed the boot lid shut and started to walk, but after about twenty yards slung Melcombe's case over a dense blackberry bush and into a thicket of briars, sending the petals of a few last, late flowers falling and launching a group of startled sparrows into the air. After checking the case was not visible, he and his dog walked on towards the Green Man.

CHAPTER FORTY-TWO
Brackley Hatch
28th September 1950

The AA patrolman was dressed in a neat brown uniform with trousers that flared like jodhpurs tucked into tall, brown leather boots beneath a long, brown overcoat belted at the waist. He sported a peaked cap with a waterproof cover and was carrying a pair of huge gauntlets coloured bright white for the greater part. Trinder thought, rather uncharitably, that he looked a bit like a Fascist brown shirt, but kept this to himself. 'Run through how you found the body again, please.'

'Of course, sergeant. I saw the car in question beside the AA call box. I assumed the driver was inside and, as I had noticed our badge displayed on the radiator grille, I pulled over to offer assistance.' He waved, somewhat unnecessarily, at his splendidly shiny, yellow-and-black BSA M21 motorcycle complete with air-smoothed fairing, Cyclopean headlamp like a bold silver eye and a special sidecar that carried his tools and spare parts. This was shaped, rather ominously, like a coffin and was almost exactly the right size for an average sized human; the narrow, pointed end facing forwards and a long, hinged lid along the flat top. Trinder could imagine lifting this to reveal the missing driver, laid out with arms folded across his chest.

'There was, however, no sign of the driver. I checked inside the sentry box, of course, in case he was sheltering inside, but he was nowhere to be seen, so I looked at the car and saw immediately what the problem was. He had been unlucky enough to suffer two flat tyres...' The patrolman pointed towards the car and Vignoles and Trinder instinctively looked in the same direction. 'Dashed bad luck to lose two tyres in one go, but if he'd run over some broken glass, then it could happen. At first I supposed he'd walked away for help, although we do always advise our members to remain with their vehicle until assistance arrives. I decided to assess what shape his tyres were in and how best to resolve the problem, then motor after him, to advise the gentleman that help was to hand. However, I noticed something odd about the situation, and that was the fact that the tyre valves had been dismantled. Taken apart, in point of fact.'

'Could this be accidental?' asked Bainbridge. 'Is it possible they became dislodged?'

'No, sir. At least, I've not seen the like, and whilst I could perhaps imagine one valve failing like this, for two to do so is quite impossible. They had been taken out and the tyres let down deliberately.' They all nodded, his assessment appeared sound. 'I cannot find the missing parts of the valves.' The patrolman shrugged, 'I can only guess that he took them out and took them away, but for what reason I cannot imagine.'

'Or someone threw them away, to disable the car.' Vignoles was scanning the weeds and grass at the edge of the lay-by. 'We'll need a thorough search. I want to know what happened to them.'

Trinder frowned and bit his lower lip whilst making a note.

'They were trying to get away from Brackley, presumably from us, so why stop here, and why dismantle the tyre valves?'

'Maybe someone was trying to delay their escape.' Vignoles was staring at the two flat tyres, as if they might give him an answer.

Trinder turned back to the patrolman. 'Then what did you do?'

'Well, I was a bit puzzled to be honest, stood scratching my head, then noticed all the footprints and the trampling down of the grasses, over there.'

Whilst he was speaking Vignoles was walking gingerly to one side of the visible imprints in the mud at the verge, careful to not step on any of them, with DI Bainbridge close at hand and doing likewise. Vignoles was pointing with the stem of his pipe at a number of especially deep and clear impressions. Bainbridge was nodding acknowledgement.

'They looked fresh and led from the car into the woods. I noticed the paw prints and realised that he must have a dog, so thought maybe he'd taken it for a walk whilst waiting for one of our patrols. I went to look for him. The route was quite obvious, if you take care to observe.' The patrolman pointed at the crushed undergrowth and heel impressions. 'You are the experts, of course, but it seems to me that something was dragged along here that flattened the grass. It's made quite a trail.'

'You have good observation skills.' Trinder gave an approving nod.

'Thank you. It pays to keep your eyes open in my job, sir. Anyway, I had not gone far when I saw his feet sticking out of a pile of leaves.'

'Did you approach the body?' Trinder asked.

'I did, but carefully. I immediately got a bad feeling about the situation. Anyone would, under the circumstances, and so I was extra careful not to walk on any footprints around the vicinity. I'm no medical man, but he looked pretty dead to me. I mean, nobody alive lies on their back with their eyes wide open and with leaves piled over their face, do they?'

'You did well. We'll need to take a formal statement later.' Trinder closed his notebook and asked the patrolman to wait with his motorbike and sidecar combination in the company of one of Bainbridge's uniformed constables, then joined Vignoles and Bainbridge as they picked their way to one side of the trail and into the woods.

Dr Melcombe looked undeniably dead, dumped on his back with his legs stretched out from beneath an untidy and ineffectual pile of leaves, mud collected around the backs of his shoes and smeared over diamond-patterned socks with more mud and twigs and the odd leaf in the turn ups of his trousers, indicating that he had been dragged backwards whilst either unconscious or dead. His face was a distressing sight. Perhaps the gusty breeze that set the trees shivering from time to time had done the work, or maybe it was the hand of the inquisitive patrolman, but some of the soggy, autumnal leaves had fallen away to reveal his staring, bulging eyes behind spectacles that lay at a crooked angle across his nose, a speck of dirt and a few drops of rain from the canopy above spattering the lenses. His mouth was open, as though locked in an endless cry of pain. It was a compelling and unnerving sight, as though the doctor was soundlessly screaming at something in the trees above, and all three men at some point quickly glanced upwards to check there really was nobody there.

'I am loath to move anything until you can get a forensic photographer here and a doctor to pronounce life extinct.' Vignoles had his unlit pipe clenched between his teeth. 'But we need to make a rapid assessment, I cannot afford to delay.' He gestured at the corpse. 'This is a poor attempt at concealment. There are footprints, drag marks, a body hastily covered and a very distinctive car abandoned close by, all of which smacks of blind panic. There's nothing planned or pre-meditated about this.'

'Do you think he was killed, sir?' Trinder was peering at the body. 'No obvious sign of blood...May I?' He reached towards the leaves covering the dead doctor's chest.

'Go ahead. Collar is undisturbed; neck looks unmarked. Could be a heart attack? Or maybe poison, going by his expression, though he looks more like he was scared to death.' Vignoles was watching as Trinder gently cleared the body of leaves.

'There is no obvious sign of physical attack, from what I can see, sir.'

'No dog bites, either,' Bainbridge observed.

'Good point.' Vignoles was looking for paw prints in the vicinity as Trinder worked his way around the many pockets on Melcombe's suit.

'I can't see a wound or any blood. Got his wallet...with all the usual stuff inside... and there's a ration book, ID card.' He inspected it. 'Yep, he is indeed our Dr Percy Melcombe. His house keys I suppose?' He jingled them.

'No diamond ring?'

'No, sir. Though I would imagine that was taken.'

'Indeed, the diamond may well have precipitated whatever happened here,' Vignoles agreed. 'Though those flat tyres are bothering me.'

'Oh, but this is interesting.' Trinder stood up and Vignoles and Bainbridge stepped closer. 'A train ticket with a reservation. On the Mid-Day Scot from Rugby to Glasgow. For today!'

'Scotland? Can we assume the other man, this Ringham fellow, was also heading north?' Vignoles pointed at the ticket with his pipe. 'I think it possible; it would be a good place to avoid detection for a while.'

'Your hunch was they'd take the train, and by golly we've got him nailed if that's so!' Bainbridge grinned in triumph.

'It's no more than a hunch, but it will serve as a starting point. But what happened here? Two men on the run and one valuable diamond ring. Do they argue, perhaps the driver pulls over and they lay into each other? One dies. Is he killed or... maybe his heart stops during the struggle. Ringham is forced to hide the body, then discovers the car is immobilised. But who did that, and why?'

'A third party was here?' Bainbridge offered.

'I think so. Did he leave with Ringham?'

'Or kidnap him?' Trinder looked unconvinced by his own suggestion.

'Don't forget Ringham also has a dangerous dog as protection. This could have been an ambush, but perhaps they struck a deal and they've travelled on together.'

'Surely it's too obvious?' Trinder added a note of caution, indicating the train ticket. 'This is a giveaway.'

'Not if he was hoping his attempt at concealment would buy at least enough time to get up north and lose himself in the wilds. It's a strong lead, so we must follow it. Added to which, we've put word out to the neighbouring constabularies and the transport police are on high alert, so he won't be able to run far, not in this area, at least.'

Prior to the patrolman's arrival, the three policemen had spent a frantic half an hour, each hitting the telephones and telex machine, and Vignoles giving urgent instructions to the stationmaster and signalman at Brackley Central, ensuring that the telegraph system was kept hot sending a description of the car and its occupants across not only the three counties surrounding Brackley but far and wide across the railway. Word was spreading, and policemen were becoming familiar with widely-telexed descriptions of Melcombe, Ringham and a possibly dangerous Alsatian Wolf Dog, and no doubt these same policemen were also discussing the style and performance characteristics of the Armstrong Siddeley *Hurricane* compared with those of a Jaguar or an Alvis, or any number of other cars, their attention caught by this glamorous vehicle as much as by what crime might lie behind the manhunt. Slowly and surely, the net was spreading.

'It makes sense for him to get as far away as he can, and as quickly as possible. The Scottish express is his best chance. Bainbridge, I need you to take over this crime scene. You know the drill: doctor, photographer, a finger tip search of the site. And get your chaps to work more magic on these footprints. I think plaster casts of these might well match those you took at the church.'

'Wilco. Leave it to me. And we got two good paw prints from St Peter's, so if they match those near the car we're really getting somewhere.'

'Indeed. Now, if we could have the use of your driver and car, we need to catch this train. This ticket is a single from Rugby Midland to Glasgow. A crack express, with just eight coaches and no standing allowed. The guard will know if he was expecting to collect two gentlemen and a dog at Rugby.' Vignoles looked at this watch. 'It's 2.05, we can just make it, but Bainbridge, will you please call Rugby and have the express held until I arrive. They'll be furious, but use my name and position and don't take no for an answer!' He pulled a face, 'I'd rather not delay the Mid-day Scot, but we need this man, and trapping him on a train has its advantages.'

'Righty-o.'

'Ringham must have hitched a ride, or was in the mystery person's vehicle,' Trinder observed.

'Looks that way, sergeant. I'll get all our patrol cars and bikes on the roads around Rugby,' Bainbridge added. 'We might just apprehend him before he gets his train.'

'Do so. This is a desperate man in a tight spot. The more visible we can make our presence, the more likely he is to make another mistake. Now we must get going.'

Ringham had in his mind that one of the racers would pick him up in something sporty and fast. The driver would be a rich young man, or maybe an ex-fighter pilot. Someone daring: a rakish type who would not ask difficult questions and yet would be up for a mad dash to a station and relish the chance to put his foot down and do some proper road racing. Maybe the man would do it purely for the adrenaline rush; or maybe a crisp banknote slipped from one leather driving glove to another would buy his silence. The driver would wink and give him a knowing smile and as he roared away, imagining that the strange, well-bred and expensively-dressed hitchhiker was on his way to a thrilling, illicit rendezvous with a vampish dame.

But instead, Ringham got his worst nightmare.

The little Austin K8 van slowed without Ringham needing to stick a thumb out. Nor did it give him the option of waving it past. Painted pink and cream and branded loudly with the name of the paraffin company for which the driver was working, it was a cheerful-looking vehicle that looked as though it might have escaped from the pages of one of Enid Blyton's new Noddy books. The K8 had a flattened front with an elongated silver and black radiator grille, with no suggestion of a snout like bonnet; the split windscreen curved smoothly into the roofline to suggest speed and modernity. Speed would not be an option, however, with its noisy and smoky engine and heavy gear change. Ringham convinced himself it would suffice, and at least Hades could sit in the back with the suitcase.

The driver had a thick, grey moustache and wavy hair of the same colour. A cigarette was tucked above one ear, alongside an arm of the National Health glasses that balanced on the end of his nose, over which he peered at the road, and through which he read from the neatly-typed sheet of delivery addresses resting on the centre of the steering wheel and clenched in place beneath a thumb.

The driver's window was wound down and he called to Ringham. 'Hello chum, got a problem?' This was to be the first of a ceaseless string of questions, the man apparently unable to take 'no' or a cold, glowering silence for an answer. Ringham regretted accepting the lift the moment they were installed inside, finding himself forced into concocting an ever-deepening series of lies and evasive explanations. He was struggling to find a solution to his predicament, and really did not need this intrusive interrogation, which served merely to remind him of how bad things were becoming by the hour.

The driver was desperately eager not only to offer help, but to commiserate and to discover and fully comprehend Ringham's exact travel plans in order to offer his own advice and assistance.

'Puncture? No problem chum, we can get that fixed up in two shakes of a donkey's tail! I've got a jack in the van. What? Valves gone? Well I never, that's one in a million. Not heard the like of that before, rotten luck. But you know what that is? That's this bloomin' austerity for you. You just can't get the same quality any more, it's all shoddy goods nowadays. Hey, but that's a fine motor. What a little beauty! We'll swing over and have a look... What? Oy! Steady on mate, you nearly had us off the flippin' road!' He fought to bring the K8 back onto a straight line. 'You shouldn't go grabbing the wheel like that. Blummin' dangerous that is! All right, all right, keep yer hair on...'

They motored on a short while in silence, but it couldn't last. 'Still, you can't just leave that car there: someone'll nick it. Things are not like they used to be and there's plenty folk around here nowadays that will steal that in a flash. Oh, in a hurry are you, got no time? So what's the pressing rush? Got a train to catch... right, got it in one! Where you going from? The Mid-day Scot from Rugby? Phew wee... that's class, that is. I can see why you wouldn't want to blow a ticket on that in a hurry. Haha! I can get you there in time, no need to worry. Here, we should get to know each other. My name's Graham Rowlands... Pleased to meet you, Mr Jones. We should be a little less formal I think, everyone calls me Gray or Graham… So you're Sam? Sam Jones. I never forget a name or a face, Sam. Good to meet you, chum. But look, I've been thinking, if I were you, I'd get that motor fixed up somewhere and then go on a later train… To a wedding? Aha! Of course, Sam, and now I see why you're a bit preoccupied and tense. I don't blame you mate, I'm sure I'd be the same in your predicament. So what's your daughter's name? Nice… Where does she live? It's just I've got my Auntie Dollie up Glasgow way and I tootle up every so often and I might know the area. Just asking, Sam! All right…all right, but you need to calm down a bit. I can see how's you're anxious about not missing that wedding and all, but there's no need to lose your rag, we're well in time. No, I don't care what you say, but that car, well, it's way too nice to abandon for…how long did you say you're going away? A few days?' He sucked air between his teeth. 'No, listen, I've been thinking this through, I can call my friend Richard — lovely man, salt of the earth is Dicky Coulson — he's got a garage out Halse way, near Brackley. Actually, you must have just driven through it on the way. Well, he's a good mate and I can get him and his mechanic to come along, get the tyres fixed up and then park her up at Rugby station — ready for when you come back. He can leave the keys with the stationmaster. It's a big, busy station and they'll be able to keep a beady eye on it. Just the cost of the tyres and a drop of petrol, that's all, no problem. Eh? Just being helpful Sam! All right, please yerself.' He fell silent, rather hurt that his new friend did not seem to appreciate his help. The silence lasted only a few seconds, though.

'By heck, that police car is in a rush. Flippin' menace those patrol cars they use nowadays, rushing all over the place like nobody's business. I can remember when they just had bicycles! Haha. Eh? No, it can't go any faster, my foot is on the floor already. Look, I'll stop at this phone box and give Dicky Coulson a call. It won't take a minute and we're still well in time for your train. We've made good progress. No, listen Sam, we'll get this sorted out, and then we can get you on your train and you can relax.' The van pulled to a halt and the driver hopped out, leaving the engine running.

The K8 was pulled over beside a red telephone box close to a short bridge over a small culvert overhung by tall rosebay willow herb and enclosed by tall hedges of reddening berries and overarching trees, set between bends in the road in either direction. There was also a telegraph pole and a postbox on a short, metal post, and the rooftops and smoking chimneys that formed the edge of Rugby could be seen between the trees ahead, whilst the little river meandered its way towards a distant embankment, along which a long train of coal wagons pulled by a black locomotive rumbled, illustrating the proximity of the west coast main line.

'Just need to bob into the back, I've got a stack of coins in my jacket pocket in there.'

Ringham mumbled something about letting his dog out before the long train journey, but as he slipped out of the cab he picked up a heavy metal wrench that had been lying on the floor between his feet and felt its weight in his hand. There was no time to think this through. The van driver knew too much, despite his hasty lies and all that nonsense about a wedding in Glasgow. But it was the mention of the name Coulson that had tipped the balance. Could it be the same family? Brackley was a small town and it was plausible. He was starting to think Melcombe had been right when he'd claimed that the diamond was ill fated, that it was cursed. Nothing was going right, and he felt like he was spinning too many plates and they were starting to fall.

No, this Rowlands man would remember him as clear as day, and he'd even warned that he never forgot a face. If the van were stopped on the journey back from Rugby station by that patrol car, the driver would make the connection and the balloon would go up in an instant.

'Sam? What you doing with that?'

He lifted the wrench high and slammed it as hard as he could onto the man's head. It made a stomach-turning noise and Rowlands crumpled like a rag doll into a heap on the van floor, Hades growled in his ominous, deep rumble, sensing danger. Ringham tossed the wrench behind him and heard it splash into the water, then roughly hauled the man by his shoulders, taking care to avoid getting the bright scarlet blood on his coat. He huffed and puffed and dragged the body as quickly as he could to the side of the culvert, then made it topple over. He could hear traffic approaching and could not risk looking to see how the body had fallen, instead he dashed into the callbox and, with head bent over and hat brim low, he mimed talking. A couple of cars raced past without slowing. The danger was over. Moments later, he let out the clutch and the little van roared away, leaving a cloud of exhaust hanging in the air.

Princess Alice was at the head of the train, resplendent in a fresh and shining coat of express blue set off with black-and-white lining and 'British Railways' in cream, sans-serif letters on the tender sides. The livery evoked something of the magnificent locomotive's previous life, a time before wartime and austerity measures demanded she was stripped of her exotic, air-smoothed outer garments and the hidden 'crinolines' that held this in place — not unlike the whale-boned corsetry once worn by the real life princess. This covering once removed revealed a leaner, fitter and indeed very nicely-proportioned body beneath, and so Princess Alice, along with sundry duchesses, were unceremoniously disrobed, and the brief, heady days of streamlining along the west coast line were banished forever.

She had been one of the old London Midland and Scottish Railway's avant-garde streamliners, one of the 'Princess Coronation' class at the cutting edge of locomotive development in the mid thirties. Encased in a metal, air-smoothed layer of skilfully hand-curved and shaped panels with a bulbous nose that punched the air as she roared through the Westmoreland hills, powered down Shap and scythed her way through the splendid isolation of the Lune Gorge, Princess Alice had been dressed in a glorious pale blue with silver 'speed whiskers' and body stripes, hauling a string of special coaches that continued the livery along their sides in a strikingly beautiful expression of pre-war excitement and pride.

But now, with a great pair of smoke deflectors like elephant ears on either side of the thick boiler and a curiously flattened 'forehead' before the smoking chimney — a legacy from the streamlining — the engine champed and snorted impatiently at the platform end at Rugby Midland. The powerful locomotive communicated, in a manner no other machine could rival, the impatience of her crew. The two men were of the top link, selected from Camden shed's best, and they were not used to being kept waiting. Even in these difficult years, when the railway system was still buckling under years of overuse and insufficient maintenance, great efforts were always made to keep the named expresses moving — and to time. It was considered vital that the pride of the Midland Region was upheld and that the confidence of the wealthy and highly influential passengers that travelled on them was not shaken.

The driver was smartly attired in a white-collared shirt and carefully-knotted dark maroon tie beneath a clean set of 'blues' that still retained much of their colour, with a cap placed exactly level on his head in a manner that would have pleased a drill sergeant. He was leaning from his cab window, eyes fixed on the guard standing beside the stationmaster — resplendent in tails and a glossy top hat — both men deep inside the smoking, Stygian gloom of the train shed, and rendered as silhouettes by the brighter light from the far end.

There was a brief flash of gold as the stationmaster's pocket watch on its chain was inspected once again and compared with the grand station clock that everyone knew kept perfect time. The fireman — as equally well-presented as the driver — was fiddling with the injectors and trying to squeeze a little more cold water into the furiously hot boiler and so prevent the engine's safety valves from lifting. He was silent, but privately fuming that this unexplained delay might cause him to commit one of the sins of the top link: that of 'blowing off' whilst standing in a station. The sharp noise of the lifting valves would startle the travellers and, whilst the jets of steam would loft high into the air, this could dislodge the years of accumulated soot from the front of the filthy-black station roof that spanned the tracks and would create an unwelcome shower of dirty water. It was frowned upon, and if his driver gave him the benefit of the doubt, the guard would certainly not let the matter go unmentioned when they finally clocked off in Glasgow.

'Come along...you've checked your watch enough times.' The driver grumbled, his expression imploring the guard to blow his whistle.

'The board's still on. Must be a problem down the line.'

'Mebbe... but then why is the stationmaster and the guard looking like they's expecting someone?' The driver glanced at the signal that held them trapped, and along the wide expanse of criss-crossing silver rails that lay ahead. The main line looked clear and inviting. There was just a smoky 8F with a train of box-vans waiting to pass through the station to one side, though posing no impediment to their own departure, whilst the station's petite pilot engine was taking water against the opposite platform side. The driver of this little locomotive raised an eyebrow and shrugged sympathetically, but was equally puzzled by the delay.

'Oy! Look at that!' the fireman exclaimed. 'Latecomers!'

The driver turned back and shook his head in disbelief. 'That takes the biscuit. Just like they always say, it's not what you know but who you know. Probably pals with one of the directors. Proper winds me up it does, when you see that.'

'Makes me want to spit. They're too darned lazy to get here on time — but that's the gentry for you, mate. Bring on the revolution!' The fireman agreed, although his ire was ameliorated by the hope that they would now get underway a fraction before the fizzing valves blew their tops. His pride would be saved. 'Right away!' The fireman watched the signal lift, then immediately opened the fire doors and hefted his shovel.

The driver lifted a gloved hand in recognition of the urgently-waved flag and the overly-sharp toot of the whistle. The guard was clearly none too happy about the situation, either.

'2.44. I reckon we can make the time up by Crewe. Come on, old girl, let's get you going…'

A great cloud of grey-black smoke lofted into the air, pulsing in time with the roar of the pistons. Whump—shoo, whump—shoo, whump—shoo… With the sanders hissing and steam engulfing the massive driving wheels before shredding beneath the blood-and-custard coloured coaching stock, the relatively short and exclusive train was soon in motion, offering little resistance to the combination of a powerful engine and the skilful regulator work of its driver. Without a single slip on the greasy, dampened rails, the Mid-Day Scot was underway and soon roaring north towards Crewe, its final pick up before the long and unstinting race to Carlisle Citadel.

Vignoles and Trinder stood in the vestibule and took a few breaths to regain their composure, adjusting hats and straightening ties.

'Phew, that was a dash. Tractors and horseboxes are not conducive to rapid motoring.'

'They could have moved over,' agreed Trinder.

'So, gents, we followed the instructions to the letter and I am hoping there is a compelling reason for the delay?' The guard gave them both suspicious looks, his voice icily polite. 'No tickets, and holding us back seven minutes. I think you owe me an explanation.'

'Of course, and my sincere apologies for our late arrival.' Vignoles showed his warrant card and made the introductions. 'Could we step into your compartment? This is not for everyone's ears.'

The guard gave a curt nod, 'This way.'

He had what was little more than a cubicle with a bucket seat and a shelf supporting a pile of timetables and working instructions, a rule book, a set of red and green flags, and a handlamp. This was beside a long metal cage that occupied the majority of the brake coach, with just a corridor-width of free space to allow passage through to the far end. The cage held piles of parcels and packages, a great number of leather suitcases and trunks and what appeared to be a small forest of fishing rods and guns in canvas bags or smart leather cases, each branded with stencilled monograms, and a brand new Silver Cross pram with a luggage label tied to the handlebars, that rocked on its springs with the movement of the accelerating train.

Vignoles described the man they were looking for.

'Wanted for questioning, is he?' The guard's initial disapproval had been replaced by a sense of intrigue and a desire to assist this very important member of the Railway Detective Department. He'd heard tell of this Vignoles fellow and the stories were suitably impressive. He would do well to cooperate with the detective inspector.

'Yes, but you must treat the man exactly as you would the other passengers and I must warn you he has the potential to be dangerous. We must not provoke him. Do you believe he is onboard?'

'We were expecting eight on at Rugby, inspector, but I only counted seven, though that would be eight with the dog. Excluding yourselves, of course.'

'A dog?' Trinder asked.

'Correct. Quite normal at this time of year, though mostly people bring spaniels, retrievers and the odd hound. Hunting dogs you see? His was a hulking great black-and-tan thing. I had no time to speak with the owner as he was in a rush to get aboard. He just asked where he could find the dining car and took his dog with him.'

'Can you describe him?' asked Vignoles.

'The man or the dog?' The guard smiled.

The description left Vignoles and Trinder in no doubt that Barnaby Ringham was on board. 'Good. We shall take a walk to the dining car and assess the lay of the land.' Vignoles was lighting up his pipe. 'Do you have a newspaper or two that we could borrow? A quality broadsheet, something that might help make us look more like businessmen and less like coppers.'

'We always hold a stock of *The Times* and the *Daily Telegraph*.'

'Excellent. Now, is it usual for passengers to keep their dogs with them, especially in the dining car? I think it might be sensible to separate man from dog.'

'We do tether some in the cage here. It is kept locked, but I am usually on hand to give them water, if needed. If he is in the dining car I could respectfully suggest that his canine chum sits in here whilst he dines. I can be very persuasive.' The guard winked.

'Please do. But take care. Don't push your luck and back down if he rails against the idea.' Vignoles was warming to the man.

Ringham was seated at a small table for two next to the vestibule door, wedged at an angle into the comfy armchair beside the window. Hades lay on his side on the carpet, his outsized body taking up all the floor space underneath both seats and the table, feet extending into the aisle. He was panting almost in time with the rapid huffing of the roaring engine that was throwing clouds of steam past his window. The man had a double of cognac swilling around the balloon glass in his hand, a larger measure of which had already set his throat and stomach glowing. He was tired. Leaning back in the seat he closed his eyes. So much had happened that day already and still so much to sort out. He was in a tight spot. The trail of muddle and destruction he'd left in his wake was not only uncharacteristic, but potentially lethal.

Fastidious, cautious, careful and calculating — those were the strengths that had seen him make a successful career and swell his bank account, thanks to his secret life as the 'man who could' for the rich and well-connected. Got an awkward problem? A sticky legal matter that could do with 'smoothing away', with the help of some subtle, out-of-court influence? His methods were perhaps slightly less than strictly legal, but kept things out of the papers. Daughter got herself into trouble by an utter reprobate that would bring disgrace to the family name? Never mind, dear fellow, I know a man, he's very discreet and utterly reliable, who can sort everything. It will cost, of course, but then what price respectability and one's good name?

That wild fling on the Riviera has left longer-lasting consequences than planned? Of course, Barney Ringham completely understands the consequences if one's husband were to discover the cuckoo in his nest. Leave it to me. A short holiday at a discreet address and it can all be forgotten...

Yes, he had a pocketbook filled with the names and telephone numbers of some pretty dashed influential people who had good reason to help him out of this tricky situation. It was just a matter of trying to think how to best play this, who to call on first. The commissioner of the Metropolitan Police might not be too bad a place to start, after all, his daughter...

'Excuse me, sir.'

'Uh.. sorry.' Ringham blinked, already slightly befuddled by a mixture of cognac and drowsiness. He'd drifted off. The guard was standing beside him, leaning slight forwards and speaking in a suitably low and discreet voice. Ringham quickly gathered his wits about him. 'I beg your pardon?'

'Your dog, sir.'

'What's happened?' He looked startled.

'May I suggest we can accommodate him in the luggage compartment? He will have more space there, and we always keep a few blankets on hand for the very purpose, and a bowl of fresh water. He will be in good hands.' The guard smiled obsequiously.

'He's fine here.' He felt Hades lift a head then flop it back down on the floor, also tired after that curious incident in the woods that had precipitated the desperate mess in which his master had found himself.

The guard coughed apologetically. 'They will start to serve afternoon tea shortly and we always invite passengers to leave their hunting dogs, and the like, in the luggage compartment. Only in case a steward were to accidentally step on a paw or a tail whilst carrying hot tea, you understand?' He was smiling respectfully, in a manner that Ringham understood, and indeed often deployed, a look that implied, *I am demanding your compliance, but am offering you a polite and dignified way of acquiescing without losing face.*

Ringham took a deep breath and was about to bawl the man out and tell him to mind his own bloody business when he stopped and remembered that he would do well to not attract any more attention than necessary. And besides, had not Hades got him into this hole by running off like a thing possessed in the first place? He was fond of the dog, but right this moment he was exhausted, tired by it all. He could feel the energy leeching out of him at an alarming rate and perhaps it might be beneficial to let the guard look after Hades for a while. They were to be on this train for another seven hours, so why not let him stretch out and sleep in the van?

'Yes, yes, that is a good idea, thank you. His name is Hades. Here, take these biscuits.' He dug into the pocket of his jacket and extracted a paper bag. 'They usually keep him happy.' He heard a tail thump on the floor.

'Unusual name, sir.'

'Not when you get to know his character.' Ringham forced a laugh. He motioned his dog to stand and fastened a short leather lead onto his robust collar. Hades flipped his ears up and down and gave the guard an evil look, and yet his nose had detected a treat and so he licked his lips. 'Go along now! Good dog.' Ringham fussed the dog between its ears and indicated to the guard that now might be a good time to deploy a biscuit.

The guard left, with Hades tugging half-heartedly at the leash, but with sufficient strength to cause the guard to walk quickly. He wanted this dangerous looking beast locked in that cage as fast as possible. Ringham meanwhile leant back in the chair and told himself that he should try to resist sleep a while longer. He really ought to get the lay of the land.

Through half-closed eyelids he surveyed the other dining car passengers. To his immediate left were an older couple, both well dressed, she with pearls at her neck and a sparkling band to her tiny watch; he in a green-and-grey tartan suit with leather buttons and patches on the elbows, a cream shirt with a pattern of brown lines and a huge, handlebar moustache. He wore a monocle. Handy with a twelve-bore, no doubt. A deer stalker, or fly fisher? Ringham could certainly imagine him prowling the moors with a gun on his arm. Two businessmen, still in overcoats and hats, sidled in at that moment and settled diagonally opposite him, just a table away. They ordered coffee, then immediately opened newspapers without speaking another word. Was there a whiff of 'plain clothes' about them? No, they could not possibly be on to him this quickly. He must not let his imagination run away. After a lot of paper turning and folding, the two men settled on doing the crosswords, the older of the two smoking a pipe and resting the folded paper on a knee crossed over the other, his eyes occasionally flicking up and towards him. He was in the man's line of sight, so there was surely no reason to be suspicious.

Ringham jolted awake. Crewe. The train had stopped but he had only just awakened, and he observed as if in a trance the people on the platform. They stared back with looks of envy, taking in the white cloths and diminutive lamps on each table, the matching, bone china coffee pots and cups, the bottles of wine being uncorked by one white-jacketed steward, while another expertly handled a silver platter laden with trays of unrationed delicacies, including pots filled to overflowing with strawberry jam, piles of freshly-baked scones and stacks of neat, triangular sandwiches served, rather wastefully, without crusts.

As the train started to move, the covetous faces slid smoothly to one side, to be replaced by a gaggle of over-excited schoolboys in grey shorts and green blazers and caps, running in step with the accelerating train and waving at their top 'cop' of a blue-painted 'namer' steaming towards Scotland.

He had been undecided about changing trains at Crewe, but now it was too late. The option was taken away and it was non-stop into the dark of night and distant Carlisle, or Carstairs, Motherwell and Glasgow. He clicked his fingers and the steward appeared at his side. 'I'm ravenous, young man, so what can you offer me? No, come to think of it, don't bore me with the menu just bring me something hot. Anything, but it must be hot, and lashings of it.'

'Very well, sir. Perhaps some soup to start?'

'Yes, yes… whatever you and the chef can rustle up. Oh, and a bottle of burgundy.'

'As you wish, sir. We have a fine selection on board today, would you like to choose from the…'

'Just pick up the first bottle you find and bring it to me! I can pay, don't worry about the cost.'

'As you please, sir.'

So, those two men were still working on their crosswords, were they? He stole another apprehensive glance. Whilst he'd been sleeping, they'd stowed their coats on the racks above and looked slightly less like policemen, or was that just the restorative effect of a nap settling his jangling nerves?

Ringham took out his cigarette case and flipped it open, selected one of the Moritz from inside. He lit up. The wine arrived and tasted surprisingly good. He was feeling far more relaxed, now cocooned in a corner of a warm dining car, enveloped in the smell of food drifting in each time a steward passed through to the galley kitchen mingling with that of cigars — and even a trace of expensive perfume. It felt strangely secure, a world away from nosy van drivers lying in a foot or two of muddy water with their heads bashed in, and from the body beneath a pile of leaves. It was hard to comprehend all that had happened today, it felt like a bad dream, and nothing seemed real or urgent or pressing. Besides, he was starting to formulate a plan, and that always got him back onto a more even keel. He was thinking through a series of telephone calls to make, favours to call in, and overseas travel plans to organise. He had more than sufficient funds in his bank and had taken the precaution of packing his passport. And then of course, there was the ring.

Ah, yes, the Cobra's Eye. He glanced at the other passengers in the now almost-full car. They were all settling down to eating and drinking, including the two gents across the way. The light outside flared into life as the low-lying sun slipped beneath a thick shelf of cloud and spread a carpet of gold across the land, drenching the interior with its glorious Midas touch.

He slipped his hand into his jacket pocket and checked the little box was still there. It was ridiculous, but he felt a glow of triumph. This was something special. A haul of such value — all the more spicy for being unexpected — and so, despite the traumas and problems, he suddenly felt stupidly happy. He almost wanted to laugh out loud.

Catching the steward's attention, he informed him that he would return shortly for his soup, and asked which way to the toilet. Once in the vestibule he dropped the window on one of the doors and leant on the metal frame to allow cool air to brush his face. The swaying motion, together with the swish and rush and rapid dum-diddly-dum sound of the train, and the constant beat of the engine were soothing. He wedged a cigarette in his mouth and took the little box from his pocket, flipping it open with a thumbnail. He gasped in wonderment. The sun striking across the Cheshire plains set the stone alight and it burned with its strange fire, a beacon of brilliance that at times pierced his retinas with tiny jabs of light.

He was no romantic, but there really was something spectacular, even magical about this stone... it was so handsome and so compelling. No wonder Percy had kept it for himself. He couldn't really blame the silly old fool. Of course he'd killed her! Percy's story was so inane it was laughable. Come to think of it, he'd probably done more with her as well... But it was strange, surprising, as the old bugger had always been so reliable. Straight as a die and coldly efficient in his dealings with the women who visited his surgery. Perhaps the diamond had turned his head? It made Ringham wonder at its savage power. It had certainly brought a lot of bad luck and Ringham felt a tingle down his spine.

He changed position, to allow more sunlight onto the stone and less sooty smoke into his eyes, the vestibule at times filling with a swirl of pungent exhaust, but he could not shake off that uncomfortable sensation of dread that tingled all over like an itch.

'Do you mind telling me where you acquired that, Mr Ringham?' A hand gripped his shoulder.

'W—what?' He spun around, twisting about in the cramped space with some difficulty. The business gent with the hat and the silver-framed glasses was now standing very close to him, his tall friend not far behind, blocking the vestibule gangway.

Instantly realising this was trouble, Ringham tried to shrug the man's hand from his shoulder. He jabbed his free arm outward with great force, attempting to bat away the policeman and gain some space, but as he threw out this arm his body twisted and he caught his other elbow on the metal edge of the window frame. The ripple of searing pain caused his hand to jerk into the air. Though it took just an instant, he instantly comprehended the appalling consequences of this uncontrolled action. With face contorted in pain, and the plain-clothes policeman observing with a comical expression of surprise that seemed frozen like a snapshot in time, he watched in disbelief as the little ring lifted from off the velvet box lining and twisted and turned, flashing as each perfectly-formed facet reflected the intense sunlight, like a minute, spinning catherine wheel, until it was swept into the powerful current of air and vanished, sent flying to tumble between the tracks and lie lost and unseen to lodge between the stones, or perhaps it bounced and pinged away to land in the brackish water of the drainage ditch that edged the line.

'N—o—o—o—!' His voice wailed like a banshee as he elbowed Vignoles viciously with a force borne of desperation and leant dangerously far out of the window, his back buffeted by wind and a stream of dark smoke enveloping him as the fireman shovelled another round on the fire. He stared, stunned, aghast, down the whole length of the train, which was now curling around a gentle bend, desperately trying to identify the length of track it must have landed on.

'We must get it! We must find it!' he shouted as he reached outside for the door handle and turned it.

'We're going too fast! You'll kill yourself!'shouted Vignoles, horrified at the man's impulsive and utterly reckless action. The door swung open and the vestibule instantly turned cold as the sound of the thundering Stanier Pacific swelled and reverberated around the tiny space. The noise and the rush of air, the sulphurous smoke and the telegraph poles pulsing past the gaping doorway, created a terrifying mix. Ringham fell forward and, as Vignoles stepped backwards for fear of tumbling out after him, Trinder grabbed his boss swiftly around the waist with both his arms and leaned backwards, feet planted firmly on the floor.

'The cord! Stop the train!' Vignoles shouted, reaching up for the red-painted chain that applied the brakes. He yanked it with all his might and they both heard the brake shoes come into contact with the wheels. Ringham was swinging by his arms, fingers curled over the bottom of the window opening in a firm grip, face turned to one side and pressed hard against the lower panel of the door, legs bicycling uselessly in the air.

'Hold on! Don't let go!' shrieked Vignoles. It was hard to get his voice to carry and the sound was pushed back into his mouth by the air rushing through the open door. 'We'll haul you in!' Vignoles grasped the doorframe with one hand and braced a leg against the inside of the carriage. He attempted to reach forward and grab Ringham's jacket.

The train was complaining, juddering and creaking ominously in a truly horrible fashion, the wheels emitting a painful and unrelenting squeal like a thousand fingernails down a blackboard. They could hear wineglasses rattling furiously in the galley, something heavy hit the floor, a raised voice, a door slamming violently shut. The engine had changed its note, the driver frantically cutting off steam, but eight hundred or so tons of train travelling at 70mph just cannot stop at once, and must labour under terrible stress for quite some time before it can even begin to reverse the massive forward momentum.

Vignoles wobbled unsteadily on his feet; the carriage moving in an alarming manner, hunting and pitching dangerously and throwing him from side to side. His hand was struggling to maintain any grip on the smooth doorframe as his own body-mass tried to wrench him forward and pitch him headlong onto the sharp ballast stones flashing past the open door in a dizzying blur. He stretched his arm out once more, desperate to grab the man's collar or whatever came to hand. He made one final frantic effort and...

And then Ringham was gone. One moment he was there, the next nothing; just the door swinging even wider, leaving Vignoles clutching at air. Both he and Trinder heard a cry — an animal yelp of pain — but the train just continued its relentless forward movement as the acrid smell of burning brake blocks filled their nostrils, making them both suddenly sneeze. Vignoles felt his hat fly off his head, there was a breaking of glass, a shuddering and deep groaning of the wooden-bodied coach straining to hold together, a scream or two and calls of enquiry as curious faces appeared in the corridor. A man was shouting to someone to crouch on the floor. Vignoles thought he heard a woman's voice declare: 'Oh, we're going to crash, we're going to crash!'

The train finally came to a standstill and an eerie silence fell for a few moments as everyone took stock, patted themselves down in the realisation that they were indeed alive, now checking nothing was broken and appreciating that the Mid-Day Scot had not crashed or rolled over on to its side, and that, aside from a few bruised shins, banged foreheads and some broken glasses and spilt tea, the train was apparently undamaged.

And Ringham was a fighter, Vignoles had to give him that. Despite two broken ankles and some appalling cuts and bruising, with blood streaming from his shredded hands, elbows and knees, he gamely hauled himself along the track on his hands and knees, dragging his feet behind; a grotesque, twisted figure in a dark suit leaving a stain of scarlet along the line, scrabbling at the stones and searching frantically for the tiny diamond.

Vignoles stood at the opened door of the carriage and watched him for what felt like an age, such was his slow and excruciating progress. But Ringham was going nowhere, despite his manful efforts to the contrary, and Vignoles was shaken from his thoughts after what was probably only a second or two, by a sudden explosion of noise as the passengers all started talking at the same time, as doors and windows were opened, faces peered out to look along corridor onto the railway, questions were asked or shouted in strong voices. A dog was barking furiously. The guard quickly eased Vignoles away from the doorway and dropped down to the track.

'I must protect the rear of the train. Can you look after the injured party? Bring him back onto the train, if at all possible. You know where the first aid kit is in my brakevan, don't you?'

Vignoles nodded assent and commanded Trinder to mobilise the stewards to call the train back into some semblance of order. They must ensure that nobody left the train and to quieten everyone. 'Tell the head steward to give them all a free drink! Brandies all round! And see if there is a stretcher in the guard's compartment.'

It was now his turn to drop on the tracks. He stood there for a moment, assessing the situation. The train was stopped on a gentle curve, leaning slightly to one side due to the camber, the gleaming blue locomotive in the distance releasing little drifts of white steam like a racehorse might after a strenuous steeplechase, as a lazy curl of smoke rolled over the open country that surrounded them on all sides. He could see newly-ploughed fields with great drifts of lapwings wheeling around and starting to settle down after the disturbance, and there were hedges reddening with berries and trees tinged with gold and reds and the rooftops of the odd farm building. Very pretty, but an ambulance was going to find it hard to gain access.

The driver was now standing beside *Princess Alice*, peering into the motion with his gloved hands resting on one of the great connecting rods. There was every chance the engine was damaged as a result of the emergency stop. The huge connecting rods were of the finest forged steel and could handle incredible forces, but even these would twist or buckle after such a sudden, enforced stop. If that were so, they might be here a long time as they awaited assistance. The fireman was leaning out of the cab and looking anxiously towards Vignoles, who indicated with his arm towards the tiny figure on the track way behind the train. The fireman appeared to understand and quickly dropped to the ballast and started walking towards him.

The guard was steadily tramping away from the rear of the train at quite a pace and Vignoles caught a glimpse of signalbox roof in the far distance. The signalman was their sole connection to the outside world. He could inform control of the need for a relief engine, if necessary, protect the section of track, alert trains on the opposite line of their presence, call an ambulance, or call for uniformed officers to accompany Ringham to hospital.

Vignoles looked at Ringham. He had rolled against the outer rail and slumped into a semi-recumbent position. They needed a stretcher to lift him back into the safety of the train. His dog was barking furiously from the luggage van and Vignoles hoped the beast was securely locked up.

And what of the Cobra's Eye? Vignoles decided it could wait. It had brought enough misery already. Perhaps it would be better to never recover it and just let it lie wherever it had fallen; to sink slowly into the ground and be swallowed by the lank grass on the railway verge or work its way between the continually-shaken ballast, never to be seen again. Well, there was time to think about that later, as it would be a devil of a job to find it. Right now, the Mid-Day Scot was being held up by a badly injured man on the track and whatever awful crimes he may have committed or been involved in, they could also wait for another time. Barnaby Ringham needed urgent medical help.

CHAPTER FORTY-THREE
28th September 1950
Leicester Central

The trunk was an ugly beast painted an oily, viscous black on the outside, the colour applied liberally and without particular care over the wooden panels and metal strengthening straps, over the sturdy corner braces and even the carrying handles, yet another coat on top of what looked like many previous such finishes over its long and hard life. In places the paint was cracked, blown and mottled as though about to lift away, and the whole trunk was liberally covered in years of grime and what looked like ash and fine brick dust. It also stank rotten as though recently lifted from a sewer.

'Oh! What is that smell?' WPC Lucy Lansdowne held her nose and gave PC Blencowe an admonishing look the moment she stepped into the Detective Department office. 'Ugh! Did something die in here?'

'In a manner of speaking, yes.' Blencowe looked grim-faced and did not look up in reaction to her outburst, but instead continued to adjust the fit of the heavy rubber gloves he had just pulled on whilst looking down at the reeking chest, eyeing with trepidation the dreadfully ominous staining on the paper lining that told a silent but not less unappealing tale about the liquefaction of human remains.

PC467, Simon Howerth, had backed away once the lid had been lifted and was frantically wafting a sheet of cardboard to try and dissipate the foul stink that had accumulated inside during the years it had been in police storage. 'It is grim.' He coughed. 'Could you open the window, please?' He looked a bit green around the gills.

'Gladly!' Lansdowne rushed across the office and hauled the sash window down, allowing the noise of the station to enter the room on a draught of cooler air scented with the familiar coal smoke of the busy station. 'What is that thing?' She stood by the window and gave the trunk a suspicious look, immediately aware there was something ominous, almost sinister about it. It was an ugly object and it seemed to cast a dark and depressing spell.

Blencowe, having prepared himself for action, looked at the WPC. 'I had it brought here because of something young Howerth here was reading a while back. Wasting his time as usual reading scandal and gossip in a trashy crime magazine,' he gave the lad a wink, 'but for once it actually proved useful as he got me thinking about a cold case, or should that be a cold trunk?' He gave a lame twist to his mouth. 'It was a magazine with a feature about unsolved crimes, including one about the unidentified corpse in a trunk left at Broad Street station. No head, no hands and naked. They couldn't get an identification from the bones and the rotted flesh....'

'Oh don't! Was it in there?' Lansdowne pointed at the ugly black trunk.

Simon nodded and put the cardboard down and started pulling on a pair of gloves that had been lying at his feet. 'That's right. I can't believe Blencowe really sent for the evidence so we can have a closer look. It's awfully exciting! Even if it does pong to high heaven.' He still looked queasy but was fighting it, determined to play his part in what was his first official act of detective work.

'It played on my mind.' Blencowe continued. 'What piqued me was that I'd not heard of the incident at the time. It was back in '45 they made the discovery, though they had no idea how much earlier it had been sitting there. Could have been there weeks or even years, I suppose that was half the problem.' He dropped to his haunches at one end of the trunk and started to run his fingers along the edges, guiding his eye over every inch, occasionally stopping and looking intently at an imperfection or blemish, of which there were many. 'Then there was this business with Miss Askew. You know, with her head and what are probably the bones of her hands discovered but her body still missing and it set me wondering.'

Lansdowne was still eyeing the trunk with distaste, but she too was managing to replace her natural instinct of revulsion for curiosity. 'So you think the corpse that was found in there could be her?'

'A distinct possibility. The sarge reckoned it had to be worth looking at.' Blencowe stopped and looked up at the young detective constable. 'At the risk of this going to your head, I suppose one must thank you for suggesting we trawl the Great Ouse for the bones of the other hand.'

'Yes, why did you think of that?' Lansdowne also looked at the constable. 'It was inspired.'

'I...I just guessed. If one hand was on the steep embankment, perhaps the other had rolled down or was thrown into the river.' He had no intention of confessing his night-time ghost-hunting activities. 'I am sure any of you would have thought just the same.'

'I'm sure we would.' Blencowe was eager to rein any sense of over-confidence in the young man and turned back to the trunk. 'The body could have been put in here about the same time. Thinking along those lines, the sergeant arranged for the bones that were recovered from inside this trunk in 1945 sent to the lab, where the head and hands are already. If it all fits together like a jigsaw as we suspect, then we've at least reunited her, poor lamb.' Blencowe was peering at something on the outside of the lid, but then let it drop down again and shifted his position so he could look right inside.

'Her parents can lay her to rest, at least. All of her.' Lansdowne observed. 'That would be something.'

'What are we looking for, exactly?' Simon was concentrating on the outside of the trunk, not yet quite ready to plunge his nose into the stench of decay and mould rising like mist from a swamp.

'I don't know. Most probably there will be nothing. The Met found nothing back then, so why should we now? But I just wondered if they looked hard enough, or if there is some detail that makes more sense now that we suspect Melcombe and Ringham were involved.' Blencowe gave a shrug and started prodding with his finger at the stained brown paper stretched taught across the wooden ribs of the interior. Some of the paper was glossy and smooth, as though lacquered at some point, long before the body had been placed inside. 'This finish would have helped stop the liquid running out. Some of this is as tight as a drum skin.'

Lansdowne approached and stood to one side leaning forward, her hands on the top of her thighs. She watched them work. 'People always used to line this kind of trunk, it sealed them. More to keep the dust out, rather than to stop anything putrefying from leaking out, of course. Ugh, but it is a vile mess down there.'

'I can't find anything on the outside.' Simon looked disappointed. 'I think some of the paper they used beneath the top layer of brown were newspapers and all covered in this shellac stuff, or whatever it is. Do you think if we could date the newspapers they would give us a clue?'

'Apart from telling us what paper the owner liked to read, I can't see that would be much help...' Blencowe was running his gloved hand around one of the bottom corners, feeling each crease and curve. 'Ah, now what's that? A very slight bump underneath the paper. Could be a raised nail.' He looked up at Lansdowne, concentration etched on his face as he used his fingers to feel their way inside a tiny, cleanly-made slit. It was a cut in the paper so perfectly formed it was all but invisible. 'I'm not sure, but there might be something wedged down there.' He removed his hand, dug into his jacket pocket and pulled out a sturdy penknife. Lansdowne quickly opened this for him, unlike him she was not wearing thick gloves, and he set to work with the knife blade, stripping away the paper, that was brittle and dry or rotten and soft in turns.

'Should you be doing that to a piece of evidence?' Lansdowne was frowning.

'Ordinarily, no, but to date it's yielded absolutely nothing and serving no useful purpose except taking up space. If there really is something in there and it can lead us to the killer, I reckon it has got to be worth a look. You are my witnesses.' He peeled away another strip of paper and all three took an intake of breath.

'Is that a button?' asked Lansdowne.

Simon picked it up, holding it between his gloved fingers for all to see, turning it slowly in different directions in a movement reminiscent of Betty Askew showing the Cobra's Eye to the Dirty Girls Brigade in Woodford loco. 'Silver, I reckon, though awfully tarnished. And some letters on the front...'

'A monogram.' Blencowe looked pleased. 'That looks interesting.'

'B and R. That's British Railways. Can that be right?' Simon was puzzled.

'That's no railway button. Far too elegant and refined.' Blencowe replied.

Lansdowne moved closer to get a better look, careful to not touch it with her ungloved fingers. 'It might have a fingerprint if we're lucky, so handle it carefully, constable. I think I can see a hallmark on the back, and perhaps a maker's name. This could prove handy.'

She nodded approvingly, her revulsion at the noxious box silently fumigating the room now forgiven. 'I agree, the style and design are way too fancy for British Railways.' She took a sharp intake of breath. 'B and R? I think we know the man who commissioned this and, better still, we have him in custody. That's *Barnaby Ringham!*'

'Got him!' Simon cracked a smile.

'We're a step closer to doing so. If we can prove this is from a piece of his clothing, then that puts him right there when her body was sealed inside, he won't wriggle out of that too easily!' Blencowe looked chuffed.

CHAPTER FORTY-FOUR
3rd October 1950
Brackley Central

'I think I heard voices!' Anna motioned to her husband, her hand a blurred, pale shape moving through the darkness that enveloped them like a thick blanket. They both fell silent and listened, but distant nightbirds somewhere far off, a motorbike engine kicked into life in the valley, and the sough of wind in the trees was all they could hear.

'It came from the far side of the railway.' Anna was tilting her head to one side straining to catch any sound.

Vignoles, who had tucked his spectacles into his breast pocket, lifted the heavy, ex-army night vision binoculars and surveyed the opposite side of the main line. The image was a washed out version of reality rendered in shades of black and white and making anything pale, such as a human face, little more than a pale smudge, but despite these he could not see anything that suggested there was someone there.

The strange, faraway honking, like the barking of oddly asthmatic dogs, was now mounting in a steady crescendo, with first one calling and others answering in a rapid, modulating succession that was almost hypnotic with its complex rhythms that never quite resolved into a repeatable sequence. They both looked up and watched a loose 'v' of great birds etched black against an overarching sky of slightly paler cloud backlit by the dregs of light from an invisible moon.

'The Seven Whistlers...' Anna's voice was hushed.

'Whooper swans.'

'But are they?' There was a flash of her white teeth as she smiled. 'Even you have to admit that there's something in all this. Why sit here otherwise?' Anna was talking softly, in short, breathy bursts. 'And the signalman was quite adamant about her having been here most nights.'

'True. And some parts of that odd case only made sense if—' Vignoles concentrated on studying an unrelieved mass of black shapelessness to their right. '—if somehow, a long-dead woman managed to take a piece of evidence and move it from one place to another, to our advantage.

'Exactly. Though I agree with the signalman in that we are too late to see her walk abroad now. And in way I'm glad.' Vignoles lowered the glasses and gave her a look.

'No, really Charles, he was right. Since you reunited her bones and with the promise of a proper burial once the trial of Ringham is over, they've seen nothing of her at the station. She's just vanished. It's because she's at rest now.'

Vignoles grunted and went back to searching the bank. After a short while he felt Anna's hand touch his sleeve, her voice an urgent whisper. 'A light! Over there!'

'Got it.' It showed like a white disc flashing three times in rapid succession, then doused moments after. 'There's someone on the far side, part way up the cutting towards the Buckingham Road, he's signalling...' Vignoles was speaking softly as he tried to make sense of the thick, dark mass of bushes, trees and night sky.

'To his compatriots across the way from us.'

'I've got him in my sights now...' Vignoles shifted position, resting one elbow on a knee as he knelt down partially concealed by a sturdy fence post. 'Moving down the bank, probably coming to join them.' He could just make out a moving blob of black bobbing and ducking; just a murky, moving mass that was too grainy to reveal any detail like an over-enlarged section of a photographic print. However, he thought it was a man in black wearing a cap.

'Who are they? Why are they here?' Anna was straining to see anything, but was now convinced they were in the presence of others acting suspiciously beside the railway.

'They might well say the same about us.' Vignoles lowered the bins for a moment and darted her a glance. 'I'm not even sure myself why I'm here...'

'I can see him now!'

'Aha,' Vignoles was tracking the man's progress again. 'Youngish, slim build...'

'No, opposite. He's standing up.' She guided Vignoles's arm in the direction and he swung the two barrels of the night vision binoculars onto the standing figure Anna had spotted. After a moment of adjusting the focus he obtained a clear image, aided by the traces of light spilled from the signal lamps.

'Earnshaw? Edward-blinkin'-Earnshaw!' Vignoles stood up and let the heavy binoculars drop to his chest on their leather strap, whilst ducking through the fence and quickly checking the line was clear, though he could tell by the red lights that the signals were set at danger. He was not seeking cover now, but boldly striding across the twin running tracks, his booted feet striking the stones with a strong, confident sound. 'Hoy there! Stay where you are and don't even think of running!'

'Cripes, we've been rumbled!'

'You have at that, Earnshaw.' Vignoles was soon close enough to see the startled face of the young fireman. 'And what exactly are you doing lurking about... Oh? Two of you?' Vignoles stopped dead in his tracks on the grassy verge of the permanent way. It was now his turn to be taken aback, as the figure of Laura Green rose out of the grass dressed in what looked like Land Army jodhpurs and a thick, ribbed green sweater.

'Er, good evening, detective inspector.' She tried her best to sound as though this were the most normal place and time to meet.

'It's not quite what you think, sir,' Eddie hurriedly blurted out, however he anxiously looked towards the Buckingham Road bridge and Vignoles, catching the movement, did the same. A short distance away a figure was standing and observing the meeting.

'Come on! I can see you.' Vignoles beckoned with his arm and the figure reluctantly moved towards them, his steps slow and unwilling. Vignoles ducked under the fence and stood close to Eddie and Laura. 'And what explanation can you give me? No, wait until your friend drags himself here, and then tell me.'

PC Simon Howerth could hardly bear to lift his head, hoping the brim of his cap and the dark of night would somehow protect him from the inevitable carpeting now coming his way. Vignoles, however, had apparently lost the ability to speak, just looking at each person in turn; one could almost hear the sound of cogs whirring and mental machinery clunking into place, though that may have been the signal wires and pulleys being activated.

'I think I had better explain, sir.' It was the voice of sergeant Trinder.

'Sergeant?' Vignoles looked stunned. 'How many more of you are hiding here?'

'It really is nothing untoward, it's all quite above board. We...well, that is to say; I—I thought it best we got a result from this line of enquiry before I briefed you on the operational details. Didn't want to waste your time. And we are all working for free, not on overtime, I hasten to add.' Trinder tried his best not to look anxious.

'Operation? You four are...doing...what, exactly?'

'Working undercover, I suppose you might call it a stake out...'

'Surveillance would be more accurate. But under strict instructions to just observe...'

'Making notes! We did so once before and...'

'You will recall the considerable success from dragging the river bed for more bones, well that idea was a result of a similar ghost-watching operation, and it has to be low-key because we would only frighten the ghost off if I brought uniformed officers along and posted them beside the line. You see, it has to be this way, sir.'

'Stop! Not all at once.' Vignoles waved his hands. 'Just one at a time! Now, sergeant, did I hear mention of ghost watching?'

'Er...yes. I thought...that is, I wanted to see for myself.' Trinder mumbled the words. The others looked shamefaced, rather like guilty schoolchildren each staring at their feet and shuffling uncomfortably.

'I see.' Vignoles paused. 'So you came here tonight to observe the so-called "woman in white"?'

'Yes.'

'And this is not the first such operation?'

'For myself, it is, but the others have been once before, and with surprising results. They actually saw the woman and she led them to the river. It had to be a sign, a clue...and so it proved. PC Howerth gave us the lead to look in the river as a direct consequence.'

'I see.' Vignoles bit his lower lip.

'May I ask why you have field glasses with you sir?'

'You may not. And have you seen her, sergeant?'

'No. Not yet. It is still early, I suppose. Ah, what brings you here, sir? We did not expect to see you.' Trinder looked apprehensive.

'I—I got wind of something unusual going on. A tip off, and thought I would take a look.' It was Vignoles who now appeared uncomfortable. 'Kitted myself out with suitable gear,' he touched the binoculars by way of example, 'and I've been watching your antics with these for quite a while and with some puzzlement...'

'Oh, don't play games with them, Charles!' Anna was crossing the railway. 'We came here for exactly the same reason. We also wanted to get a glimpse of this celebrated "woman in white" at Brackley station!' Anna was laughing. 'Why not?' She threw her arms wide and shrugged her shoulders. 'Though we've seen precious little so far and I don't think we will now.' Anna was now part of the group gathered at the side of the line.

'So you did believe me about seeing the ghost going into river, telling us to search there?' Simon piped up.

'It made complete sense to search the river below the viaduct.' Vignoles darted the young man a mildly rebuking look, not wishing to concede too much ground. 'There was sound logic to the idea.'

'Why do you think we won't see her again, Mrs Vignoles?' asked Laura.

'Because she will soon be given a proper, Christian burial. You've reunited her once-scattered remains at last, and the awful man who took her life paid the ultimate price for his crime, with his life. The other felon involved will get his just desserts in due course, with a bit of luck. A wrong has been not exactly righted, but ameliorated. So she is at peace, and no longer needs to walk the land like a restless, haunted soul.'

'Or fly across the sky...' added Eddie, glancing upwards.

Trinder gave Vignoles a look that silently voiced the question, *and do you agree with this hypothesis?*

'Perhaps we will never fully understand what happened here. There was someone hanging about the line, that much is certain, and maybe it was just a local girl with a reckless desire to play dangerous games, but now perhaps she's seen the error of her ways and given up. Or you really did see the ghost of poor Miss Askew?' Vignoles sounded conciliatory. 'But everything seems quite in order now, and there have been no new sightings reported. Certainly each train that passed since we arrived here did so without being forced to stop, and the station staff and the signalman confirmed that this has been the case for some days now.'

'And I'm chilled to the bone, hungry and desperate for a cup of tea!' Anna spoke up. 'It is high time we all decamped to the station and pressed one of the porters there to get the kettle on. I have a bag with just enough sandwiches and biscuits inside to go around.'

'Same here!' Laura laughed, patting her own black leather railwayman's shoulder bag.

'Right, that's agreed then. Back to the station!' Vignoles was glad to change the subject. 'PC467, it will take us approximately six minutes to reach the station and in that time you will formulate a wholly convincing reason why the greater part of the Detective Department are tramping along the side of the London mainline in the dead of night. The explanation must not involve ghost hunting. And it had better be good,' he added, *sotto voce.*

CHAPTER FORTY-FIVE
7ᵗʰ October 1950
Ashby Magna

It had been a glorious October day; warm yet with the scent and taste of autumn on the air; that almost palpable feeling the land was winding down in preparation for winter. The sun had just dipped below the line of undulating trees on the horizon, leaving a cloudless sky washed pale yellow mellowing through lilac into deep indigo. The platform of Ashby Magna station was now dyed with the tints of this glorious sky, rendering the windows of the little station as rectangles of solid colour.

Charles and Anna were seated on a wooden bench with the station nameboard forming both the back and tall divider from the twin bench on the opposite side and offering shelter from a light breeze gathering as dusk drew down.

'I hear Private Coulson's remains will be brought back to England.'

'Yes, the War Graves Commission is working with the family to try and achieve this. And I hope they do. There is a considerable cost involved, but the sale of that dratted ring will ease the burden on the family.' He made a wry face. 'I suppose it is the least that cursed diamond can do for both families; to see the two lovers lie together in that grave at St Peter's. It's going to cost a pretty penny to get the monument cleaned up on top, as it was badly stained by that young man's blood. But even so, I find it heartening that the Askews and Coulsons have agreed the split the money from the sale of the ring between them so something good will come of that unhappiest of diamonds.'

'It will raise a quite a sum when it goes to auction, I should think.'

'It will, Anna. And good riddance! Even if I had the money, I would seriously think twice about buying the Cobra's Eye.'

Anna looked at the tiny diamond on her own engagement ring, letting the deepening violet of approaching night and the flare of the gas lamps illuminate its tiny heart. 'I agree. It is an incredible stone, and one's first instinct is to desire it. It seems to appeal and encourage the baser aspects of one's nature. Think how it turned that doctor's head. He could never have even worn it, but he still wanted it so badly, desired it so much that Betty lost her life. What a horrible waste of a life.' She gently circled the stone with a fingertip. 'No, it has not brought happiness to anyone, and if anything has just brought sadness, violence, even death and ruined so many lives.' Anna looked along the straight tracks that vanished to a point a long way distant.

'You are right. The British Museum has done a lot of research on the Cobra's Eye, because as with all really special gems, it has a documented history, if you know where to look, and it appears that it's left quite a trail of sadness in its wake. The Indian prince who first had it set on the gold band as a ring died of fever, together with his young princess, then at one point — sometime towards the end of the last century — it was owned by an antiquities trader in Alexandria. But he was killed — by a British naval shell of all things — leaving his young bride widowed and with the ring, travelling in the desert. One supposes she lost it whilst there and Coulson had the misfortune to stumble upon it when serving under Monty.' He gave a mirthless snort of derision. 'It is a perverse fact that the notoriety of the diamond and its chilling link to death, murder and even to a ghost, have done nothing to reduce its value — the complete opposite in fact. It is now being trumpeted as a 'cursed' ring and the value has skyrocketed. Though I supposed this is just our human nature enjoying making connections between completely random events, imagining there is an external force at play when really each stroke of bad luck is unconnected.'

'Are you sure? I wonder...'

Vignoles fell silent, and instead of replying he opened the small, hard-backed book with the green cover in his hands and flicked through the pages, clearly enjoying the feel of the smooth paper, the smell of printing ink released from pages still fresh and newly bound, approving of the way the book opened perfectly to allow the pages to lie flat. This was a detail he appreciated in his own copy of the same book; his, however, was now showing signs of frequent use and bearing a considerable number of neat red underlinings. He looked at the columns of black printed numbers and curious names on the page, reading them as he might read the Apostle's Creed from his Book of Common Prayer; a book almost exactly the same size and weight to that now in his hand, and he smiled as he read part of the curious, indeed puzzling, litany of sonorous names.

Colorado
Flamingo
Papyrus
Humorist
Spion Kop
Call Boyn
Spearmint
Sir Frederick Banbury
Flying Scotsman
Solario...

The neat underlining of Sir Frederick Banbury in red Biro that he had discovered was perfect for the job stood out boldly on the page; a solitary intervention on an otherwise pristine and untouched spread. He now turned to the title page and taking his fountain pen from his jacket pocket, he carefully inscribed a dedication.

> *To Sunny Jim,*
> *I knew you would want this one in your book.*
> *It looked splendid!*
> *Always in our thoughts,*
> *Charles and Anna.*

He put his pen away and held the book open to allow the ink to dry. 'It makes no logical sense of course. A bit foolish I suppose.' His voice was oddly gruff. 'Perhaps I should have given the 5/6d to the hospital instead, but...' Vignoles tailed off.

Anna put a gloved hand on his leg and gave it a squeeze. 'It makes perfect sense. And he will thoroughly approve. It is quite the right thing to do. After all, he never came to the station without his loco spotter's book. Not once...'

They looked at each other, and stood up. 'Of course, some lucky little lad will no doubt pounce on this first thing tomorrow, but if he gets hours of enjoyment from it, Jim won't mind.' Vignoles weighed the little book in his hand as he spoke.

They walked towards the far end of the island platform, the only people on the station platform. The large, dark, blue-and-cream running-in board at the far end was planted on two sturdy supports in a small rectangle formed by a low wall holding a little flowerbed. The roses were still blooming and big fat bushes of lavender around the edges released their perfume as they brushed against the outreaching fronds. Anna lit a candle inside a small, rectangular lantern that she was carrying and now stood this on the corner of the wall, its light illuminating the purple flower heads. Vignoles then placed the 1950 combined edition of the ABC of British Locomotives beside it. They stood a moment together and then turned smartly about. Anna slipped her gloved hand through her husband's arm and walked towards the covered steps that led up to the road bridge.

'Of course, he won't really know anything at all about this. But it's still nice to pay our own little tribute.' Anna gave her husband a sad smile, eyes glassy.

'Indeed. All common sense says so. However...' He squeezed her arm that bit closer to his. 'Don't stop walking and don't turn around, just listen...'

As they walked along the empty platform, behind the sound of their own feet there was the slightly uneven tread of another following behind. A softer, lighter, single footstep followed by the sound that just might be that made by two rubber pads like one would expect to find on the end of a pair of National Health Service issue crutches... step, tock, step, tock...

Anna looked at Charles, hardly daring to breathe, and they hesitated for moment, the steps pausing exactly in unison. All was silent. He kissed her and they moved on, and the little sounds once again kept time offering a suggestion of someone following them.

Step, tock, step, tock...

But neither felt in the least disturbed or unnerved, not a shiver of fear or anxiety. Far from it, they were smiling.

THE END

Inspector Vignoles will return for another adventure in
New Brighton Rock
Spring 2013

Other Inspector Vignoles mysteries

SMOKE GETS IN YOUR EYES

(published 2007)
ISBN 978-1-904109-1-74

THE MURDER OF CROWS

(published 2008)
ISBN 978-1-904109-1-98

THE TORN CURTAIN

(published 2009)
ISBN 978-1-904109-20-4

THE MARYLEBONE MURDERS

(published 2011)
ISBN 978-1-904109-21-1

NEW BRIGHTON ROCK

(forthcoming, 2013)
ISBN 978-1-904109-24-2

Available on 24-hour order from all UK bookshops
from Amazon.co.uk and online bookstores
and direct from the publisher via our website
www.hastingspress.co.uk